DRY BONE MEMORIES

Dry Bone Memories

Cecil Foster

KEY PORTER BOOKS

National Library of Canada Cataloguing in Publication Data

Foster, Cecil, 1954-
    Dry bone memories

ISBN 1-55263-311-X

    I. Title

PS8561.O7727D79 2001   C'813'.54   C2001-901689-1
PR9199.3.F572D79 2001

The publisher gratefully acknowledges the support of the Canada
Council for the Arts and the Ontario Arts Council for its publishing program.

We acknowledge the financial support of the Government of
Canada through the Book Publishing Industry Development
Program (BPIDP) for our publishing activities.

Key Porter Books Limited
70 The Esplanade
Toronto, Ontario
Canada M5E 1R2

www.keyporter.com

Design: Peter Maher
Electronic Formatting: Heidi Palfrey

Printed and bound in Canada

01 02 03 04 05 06 6 5 4 3 2 1

To and for
Sharon Morgan Lewis

Your young men shall see visions, and your old men shall dream dreams....Blood, and fire, and vapour of smoke.

— THE ACTS 2: 17; 19

I once referred to story-tellers as Death's Secretaries. This was because all stories, before they are narrated, begin with the end. Walter Benjamin said: "Death is the sanction of everything that the story-teller can tell. He has borrowed his authority from death."

— JOHN BERGER IN *A STORY FOR AESOP*

A house on a hill.

Avoid the manchineel tree which bears a fruit that resembles as small green apple. The fruit and leaves of this tree will blister your skin.

— BARBADOS HOLIDAY TIPS:
TOURISM DEVELOPMENT CORPORATION OF BARBADOS.

MAIN ENTRY: man·chi·neel
PRONUNCIATION: "man-ch&-'nE(&)l
FUNCTION: noun
ETYMOLOGY: French mancenille, from Spanish manzanilla, from diminutive of manzana apple
DATE: 1630: a poisonous tropical American tree (Hippomane mancinella) of the spurge family having a blistering milky juice and apple-shaped fruit

— MERRIAM-WEBSTER DICTIONARY

You will have to live again and again, times without number; and there will be nothing new in it, but every pain and every joy and every thought and sigh and all the unspeakably small and great in your life must return to you.... The eternal hour-glass of existence will be turned again and again — and you with it, you dust of dust — Would you not throw yourself down and gnash your teeth and curse the demon that thus spoke?

— NIETZSCHE IN *THE GAY SCIENCE:*
THE HEAVIEST BURDEN

It was the one time with no music, certainly not on the inside. A time of new beginning, when I was merely the son of the preacher man, no more a singer. No sound yet. Still, no word. No light, neither, and no darkness. Not in the temple. Not from my lips. Not my voice. Stillness. And without form. Just, remarkably, a hollow dissonance in the serenade. An ending, too. A restless precursor denoted by a soothing harmony, when all was good and, also, when everything was bad. Before it all and even now. Such silence. Indeterminacy. Such is what we heard in the hallways and corridors. Spaces. Music in the depths of this quiet. In the inner sanctum and on the outer portals, even after the tragic rending, before the squealing propulsion from nativity's canal into merely darkness. No sound. Time only. And, yet, no peace, either. No joy. Not in the bedrooms and the kitchen; upstairs nor in the basement, for the tomb is the womb, too. Truly, as God is my judge, nothing, from which we must explain everything. For what else could we call that to which we held so firmly, which always seemed to escape the grasp, but which we could never lose, that even now stares me in the face? Still. What is it? Really, nothing that we always called music. Not this disruptive silence. And me as lost as anybody else. Truly. Not even a preacher and far less a singer: for the conquered and subdued mountaintops of our homeland are too far apart, the gulf too wide, the valley too low, with nothing between them, not a being. Now, look at us. On different *heights. Stranded and marooned so near the pinnacles. Broken and fragmented. And, after such a long and arduous journey: to arrive at separate and distinct destinations. Variations and versions, but no voice. Not the singularly final goal. Still, caught in the same void born with the choices and dreams, and a future, perhaps. Perhaps. Paralyzed and voiceless. Unable to come forward, or to command. A choice for a future; a future for choices. Voice and vision, vision without voice.*

Back then I did not speak because I would not. For a voice presupposes a future, a face that will come, and possibly a name. A name for onus and accountability. And, perhaps, even an answer. A voice not only giving a command, but receiving also, of encountering what you do not want to have, or to hold, or to touch, or even to know. Ultimately, the voice that calls and to a name that is already named. Giving form to a moment, and a body too, in anticipation of the next. I had been conscious of another time when there was a word more awesome and resolute in its truth. So sublime and so beautiful too. I was not sure in any way that mine, clothed in squeaks and a stammer or two, would not only call forth just the bad and ugly, as the earlier pronunciation did, but that it also would not produce much, much more. So, I did not speak. No bad. My bad. No command from me. Now, look at what good we have become. Now, I, too, resigned to finally answering the same calling I had always rejected, to acknowledge a strident command to explain my choice, why I must speak and why now. Why answer to the call from the future? And without the accompaniment of music. For, still, there is none.

We had heard other things. Instead of the sweet symphony we had come to expect, we were listening to, what at best could be described as merely a wandering aria. A sound of a different tribe and a different time, perhaps. Perchance,

8

even the sweet enticing melody of a false prophet, an ugly genius. A rhapsody in blues for a blue lady. For let me tell you, this was a solo performance to the accompaniment and even connivance of the angry and misguided. If memory serves me right, something was loose and jangling. Wrong notes. Syncopated. Something sounding like drunken instrumentalists letting loose jarring riffs at the start of an old standard and, once started on a specific course, never recovering, never even getting the chance to correct an error. Never, in a preacher's word like mine, receiving redemption and atonement, neither pity nor mercy. They could start the music, but once started, it could never end. The song, shaped by its beginning, must travel the course, stick to the tracks on which it is started, if it is to be a specific song. So, is the command, the inescapable ordering in the presence of the flailing baton. Musician and magician: maestro each, conductors both. Geniuses. Even back then, we knew the story well. Or was it the versions of the same story? Or could it even be the unique, true and authentic version of different stories? The beginning identified the ending. In the essence. One chord; one lick; one cry. A word. The very first. One more trick; another song. Repetitions and cycles. They had repeated themselves and, to remain faithful to themselves, they must again. For what use is a baton or a wand without the power of command, and to do it all over again and again and tiresomely again, the wand as baton, a baton for a wand. Encore! Bravo! One more time! *Even if they don't restart, there is always the promise of a beginning, the potential in resumption.* One last time. Then the curtain. Let it fall, man, let it fall. *The voices rising from the pit. A new version, the same trick, the same thing.* One more pigeon, or a rabbit, or an egg. Another tune. Just one more, please.

For we were like those players, lost in their madness and misdirection. Driven and compelled. We were the players forgetting their knowledge and learning. Driving blindly. They do not know who they are and from where they came. Wrong direction; wrong incantation; wrong chant. As my father would say, they do not know which God they're serving. For they had lost their way among the lines and scores, among the very directions pointing the way out. Thrashing. That was what they produced. A distinctive sound. Thrashing. *A frightened bird, flapping and fluttering; a rabbit but caged in a hat.* Voila! Yes, another one. *But the unintended result, nonetheless. That something vainly produced as accompaniment to some misplaced and lonesome aria. In the end, just a haunting ballad, perhaps, or maybe even, an elegy. Blues, my dear, fo' Mr. Charlie. Blues in yuh arse. Music: always the same thing.*

Something, it was; but what I did not know. For I knew it only as what it was not. No distinctive form. No familiar tune. I could not rightly discern and I could not choose for I did not have a guarantee that I was not not right. I did not have any certainty about the truth. All I knew that something moved in my guts, something that spoke to me when I heard such a tempo distinctive in the nothingness, a beat, mark you, modified by this time and this place. By an authentic time, a specific place. But, alas, this time without memory; this place without form. Without unity. Without our knowing. And nobody to bring the word. Father, not I. Don't send me, nuh man.

Such was not music. Or at least, not what we expected. Not this finite of death. Not this forgetting and this attempt to erase; this battling with and drowning out, these sliding boundaries. For how could that be good? Why should I risk speaking? All those absent sounds, so powerful in their silence and in our rejection. And me rejecting a father's call. How good could it be, with such strong presence, such silence that only served to remind me of what I missed? Still,

10

then again, how could it not be bad? With me hearing other voices, sweeter and more resolute. Biding time. Particularly, when they dredge up memories of those times, when the returning motif of old rose up again and came back to life in the hands of a master, those dry bones, dry bones, dry bones *re-invigorated and reclaimed in individual performances, of that voice that caused them to hear the word of God; this virtuoso producing a special interpretation of a music that cannot be frozen in time, but is recreated with every breath and every groan, a new man, coming out of the future, commanding the present to perform and produce.* Dry bones, get up! Get on up, dry bones, dry bones, dry-as-dust-bones. Breathe! *Music liberated fully in dance, in swing, stomp, snapping the fingers, tapping the fret, in just swirling giddily. In giggling. In waving the kerchief, in unplugging the ear. Another nickel, and another. Such riches. In all the many interpretations and the potentials that were and are to come. In a new woman, too. Oh, my goddess. For you must be born again. A music that has to be renewed, constantly, so that we may live, not merely survive. Transformed. Brought out of nothing. With merely a wave and perhaps a tap-tap-tap. No more* dead bones, dead bones, dead bones. *For the shinbone is connected to the knee bone is connected to the thighbone is connected. Is connected to and is connected from and is connected. So dance, dance, dance.*

This music of understanding and loving; those vibes of praising and loving the risk of risking, all coming together in such understandable syncopation. Another trick. Another track, too. Bounded in a unique structure of calling and recalling, of improvising. Command and compliance, order and chaos, so spontaneous but so directed too. Of life itself, I tell yuh, my brothers. Oh, yes, those were the days. The very best days. The very worst days, my sisters. And me without the word: let chaos reign. Me holding it in; refusing to let it out. With a tongue and a mouth, with a heart and a voice, but not a word. No music. No natural order or ordering. Just the skeleton and the body, the inner and the outer, just connected, but with no connection. Alone in the crowd. Limited and limitless. Sometimes, so tenuously. Some times something. The beginning, the ending. Connected by the in-between. By the missing when there is nothing. Between the first word and the clash of the symbols, the appearance of the called forth, and the first raindrop or the scratch of a match. The wholesomeness of the unity of the in between and in the call and response. All connected in their separations. In the indeterminable. The love of these contradictions in music. The unguided and misguided, too. Of life, itself. Of nothing like it. And. Just, chaos. Magician or conductor as conjunction.

And yes, dearly beloved, maybe, it is no longer your music, but it is mine. And come to think of it, even though we may now hate and despise him, reject and cast him off, it was his too. The spectre. This was the gift of our mothers and fathers; our legacy too to the unborn, or so we thought. For who among us is truly noble? Not me, true, and perhaps, not him, either. But who? And what is honourable, if not noble? The spectre? Tell me. And say it with a truthful voice. Guaranteed, if you can. Certified. Justify why you speak. We were at home in its serenity; bathed in its power; protected by its renewing spirit. Such music. We thought we knew with our eyes shut, our ears plugged, we knew how the melody went: each leap and digression, each bridge and chorus, each vamp inevitably merging seamlessly into something new and whole, randomly, something unidentified and even unintended, something hinting further at that thing so ill-defined but yet still frustratingly familiar, still always beyond our grasp, something with a beginning predating each one of us but never ending, too. Yet something that tickles in our

bones, that is written on our heart, that is ours for just one
specific moment, but coming out of nowhere and heading
beyond us somewhere, coming to meet us. Something, my
brothers and sisters, so ethereal and yet so apocalyptic. So
harmonic and so contradictory. A celebration of the love of
life and living and of their vagaries. Like we, such sweet joy
should have been at home in the house, sweeter sweetness
anticipated in the next arrival. In the next moment: the
mother of all the potentials and possibilities. Instead, we had
it not, not on that night. No joy. No hope. Not in us and not
in the house. No mother's milk. The one time no music.
Nada. Zilch. Nothing. *This is the word of a preacher. My*
word. And finally. A command without a future.

But on the outside, beyond our reach, for all we could
tell, harmonious music: The sound of drums, or so I remem-
ber hearing distinctly, drums: all types and sizes, talking
and barking. Oh, such spectres that could not die, that
would not perish. Promising and prophesying. A rhythm
and a bass. An oracle. So distinctive; so discerning, so anar-
chic. All of them in conversations, separate and still collec-
tive. So portentous, so unfixable, so sweet. On the lower
frequency my dear Eshu. The promise of the next moment,
the next time, the next one coming. Of all the potential that
awaits. So unrefined and natural. So ambivalent. Nothing
civil, processed or determinable. The music that is always
beyond our control; always the sweetest. Balls too big, shaft
too long. The music we try to control, to capture. To place in
a hat. For good or bad. That music: one time a requiem, then
a jubilate, but always a ballad of some sort. Always a story.
Oh Omeros, reminding me so much of the cankers on
Philoctete's shin, the kind of life sore that we laughed so
much at, from underneath the tree on the beach, Achilles and
Hector fighting with their cutlasses on the white sand beach,
beaches that were now, themselves, reduced too to sores, to a

stinking foot on which to walk, and for the flies to boo, too.
A story, always the first one.

Like the music on the wind, the call in the distance, the
same song but changing with the intensity and speed, and in
the cries of the darkest skies and the brightest morn. But in
unison, with itself and with us, too. All shaped by a moment
and its actors. A diapason accompanied by strange but sooth-
ing voices warning and lashing, but from a distance, from
beyond the soul, in some cavity somewhere out there, *out of*
our history, before we were what we are, but something still
near enough, within our very being, in our tomorrow, beyond
us. Within our grasp, at least possibly this time. Memories.
Knocking, knocking, knocking, but the damned door done
slammed shut against the rising tide long, long time ago. The
chains and leg iron firmly locked in place. The water already
rising, so we can't get over. Scars on the legs. For life. The
voices rising as high as the mountaintop; dropping as low as
the valley, drowning nothing. Too broken and fragmented,
now. Cooing and fretting, scatting and humming, crooning
and chanting, occasionally yodelling and preaching, con-
stantly singing, improvising, digressing. Ululation, too. So
spontaneously. Like in those dreadful ships of old with their
cargo of humans. And of many voices, mixing and paining,
fusing, trying to survive this passage, yearning and praying
for this too to pass, this moment, Lord. The one, the day thou
gave us, Lord. Life. Learning to live in the middle. As creole
and standard. Mongrel and bastard, too. Neither one nor the
other, but a unity in itself, dead and alive. The new music in
the old voices and experiences floating up from down in the
hole, below the decks. Oh, the spectres, sisters, as you know
them. Indigenous yet imported. Oh, yes, my brothers: the
spectres, as we try to control them. Inscribed in our beings.
The old music in the new voices. Surviving to the next
moment, for that is all that matters. For we must listen to

those voices. To when it comes in the storm, in the rain, in the wind, in the hurricane, and in the meanest of Tempest. To those now on the outside. Shut out. Rejected once again, even by their very own. Sold. Bondage. Imprisoned. Sometimes singing together, sometimes talking alone, sometimes testifying, signifying, crying hallelujah, hallelujah, halle-lu-jah. Jah! Rastafari! *Sometimes chanting to those in the silence, pleading with them to return and rewrite the song, or to write in important versions that have been left out, so that those in the noise may learn and without pain. A rejoinder. A reminder. A refrain. Everything building, as we thought, tantalizingly to an anticipated crescendo, as we anticipated, but instead, the moment of arrival put off one more time, returning to the recognizable melody at the base, every time to a new beginning on the lower frequency, those root chords, bold as bass, swinging so low, a haunting reminder and warning, the old tune, perhaps now a new song, a battaglia refusing to end, never reaching that expected dénouement, the genuine one, the preferred dissolution. For, obviously, the lesson was still unlearned and, because of that, the contradictions had, as punishment, to be repeated and confronted over and over and over again, the expectations and promises remaining unfulfilled and forever empty. Just like the Dream. When we can't move on. Feet tied, wrists cuffed, ankles chained, legs ironed. No next page; no next moment. But stuck and pinned to the same spot, unchangeable and unchanging, like the butterfly on the wall. Captured. Controlled. Ordered and placed. Like the most horrible dream, my brother; the most inspirational dream, my sister. Just like the riskiest of them all. Like the most unpredictable. The most constrained. Just like this living. And chaos.*

That night, such was the discord to the already plugged ears. Dissonance measuring the gulf between the expected and received, between the destination and the point of depar-

ture. Between what, according to the wisdom of our day, should be accepted as given, as having been won, the price for the blood that was shed, the beach front, the frontier between what still has to be attempted and what has been negotiated and even captured. Limits. Between the voice and the vision. A path made smooth: a way to the light. And all in such an orderly and predetermined fashion. The common goal that is still the paradise beyond the horizon, of which stories can only be told. Seen only by the voice. Articulated by the vision. The same goal, as was in the beginning and shall be at the end. For how can that be? Does not time itself, dear ones, and the experience of trying to change the goal, ever modify the journey itself? When they entered into this land, did they leave to those of us who came later the simple choice: to pitch our tent forever, the arrival of the arrived, or to rest only for the night and to keep moving at the arrival of the first light? The eternal wanderer or the newcomer? Limited or limitless? Perhaps, merely a blind man in a blind country. Do we build houses as trophies to the final victory, where we must dance in celebration and unity, where we must hang the unstrung bow? Or do we seek only shelter from the sun by day and the dew at night, acknowledging in the very construction that the battle is long and the victory still unsure, and that that is why we sing, that the only surety is the struggle and the music that keeps us going, the distinctive sound that is the twang of the strung bow, for life is such a low-down dirty shame, a crying shame I tell yuh? The assurance that music, its digressions, its riffs, the very lyrics and phrasing, is the only true history of this life. The only future, too, because it dares to promise. That only swinging to the music, rocking to the rhythms, just letting your body groove, that is the only cure for the pain, and it can only be fleeting. Until the next one. Hope, until the next time. For how can there be a legacy without a death, even if there is no mourning?

*They made choices, our fathers and mothers did, for them-
selves, and they made for us too. Then they bound us with
their word, cuffed us with their dreams, shackled us with their
hopes. With a promise. How good can that be? Is it just bad?
Where is the boundary in between? They offered us what they
chose, what they knew to be good. They did bind us. Yes, they
did. But, as they swear, for our own good. Tethered and prostrated to this rock, their livers plucked by the birds so that we
may know how to cook and how to eat, to know about the fire
and the water, and about the next time. And some of us did
eat and found that it was, indeed, good that these older folks
did not know of what they spoke. For which they are bound.
For when we take the prescribed pill, the one handed by the
nurse, or placed in the milk of the first moment, is it the drug
to make us sleep and to even forget, or is it the antidote, an
aphrodisiac promising a quick burst of strength, a sudden
powerful jolt so we can end our journeying in greener pastures? Do we rest and sleep, then, merely to regain strength
for the journey, and not to claim and possess? For some of us
and, brothers and sisters, please understand, this man of
whom we speak was one of us, and as one of us he found that
what they offered was too bitter and yet like the silence, too
sweet. No clear boundary. Not at first. Tell me, now, who is
rightly equipped to choose? Or to draw a line? Is it me? You?*

*We saw, then, the broken connection: nothing in between,
no bridges. No unity instead of choices and decisions, on that
night we lived the resigned confusion, really, on that night of
silent music. Of death on the inside. No dancing, not even
wiggling the fingers and thumbs. Yet we knew someone must
have danced. Absence. That's what it was. Listening, on the
inside, it was impossible to hum and keep a tune. So striking
was the disharmony between the age-old melody in the heart
and the vaguely familiar sounds bombarding the ear from the
distance. So distracting and lost. So alienating. Suspended.*

17

Petrifying and yet alluring, still. Stuck in a groove, unending. Truly, a different song. Something inviting us, even then, to venture out into the storm, to where as the man says the sky was crying, and to just live. To forsake the safety, to take the chance, to boogie and rap, but out there. To step out. To be washed clean in the pelting rain, to be tossed like the leaves from the trees, to defy the lightning, to roar back at the thunder. Slipping the surly bounds. To dance. To stand alone. Uncuffed, unshackled, unironed, unbound, and unpinned. Then to return renewed, having started on a new path, even if by choice, to the same ends. Hoping to find that when we return inside a different passage, the transfiguration so clear, this time with our own imprimatur, but, hopefully, circling back into the same melody struck at the beginning, into the same ending. The reconciliation that was our music was apparent only on the outside. In that beyond into which we had once again to go forth to capture, to tame and to domesticate. Tethered to a rope, fastened so tightly in a previous moment, by our fathers' hands. A line and a boundary that for us must now be elongated and pliable if we are to even have the choice of picking the fruit of the tree. To make our own choice. To begin our own time and history.

But inside — as I said, my brothers and sisters, with the thought and the unspoken word — just strange, frightening silence, and remarkably in a dwelling where, as I said, we had always had music and laughter. Purgatory. Inside where there was always togetherness and harmony. Where even I, Preacher Man or Brother Man, as this one of whom we now speak, in whose words, Preacher Man, he liked to call me, in this place where I sang silently and openly from time to time and where I dreamt big. Inside. Purgatory. Where he was a master and I a mere — and please, because of history, I pray that you take no offence at the use of this word, for I choose it with purpose, a word — slave. The master and the slave, master and even bondsman. Purgatory. Perhaps, Cain and Abel. Instead, as the old blues man sings, now, we ain't got nothing no more, 'cause once it's gone, we ain't got nothing no more, for it's gone, gone, gone. Not even a good memory. You can try to remake yourself. You just can't reconstruct the past. Not with bad memories. Not with evil memories. Sometimes you can't even bring yourself to sing a wonderful song, not with bad memories, oh the evil memories, for it might be too good for bad occasions or it might just be too bad. Not with bloody-well bad, bad, bad memories. Not with evil, the evil memories. You can't eulogize appropriately. For it's gone, and what do you have left to judge, but a thought, a memory, a fleeting moment? Both the history and its makers – all gone. All the missing parts destroyed, gone, gone, gone, buried so you can't even dig them up, just gone, gone, gone, far less reassemble them, far less put them on display pinned to the wall, far less mount them on a dais, under a glass, far less anything, far less the far less. Bones, bones, bones. Dry Bones. Not from the nothingness. Changed radically, not just modified. Even the song, too. Gone. So that you can wail and bawl all you want. It's gone. Wail if you want; bawl if you can, cry, cry, cry. Gone, gone, gone. Try your very best to come to terms, to bring it inside, to join them, and realizing that despite the singing, clapping and shouting, in spite of the singing and mourning, things do not always work out for the best. Still, we must keep on keeping on. Board the moving train, hop that moving boat, seat belt we arse to that moving plane. Gone. Walk if required. Run if we must. You have to keep moving, and if lucky, dancing. Gone. Gone. Sing the blues, if you must, gone, gone, gone, bang out an old-time calypso or just give a rap, jazz it up too, a hip and a hop to the hippity, for without the song, you ain't got nothing. Gone. Gone. Gone. Not even good memories. Nothing mama. Nothing papa. Nothing but

nothin'. On the inside. No identity. No music; then no danc-
ing. Gone. Gone. Gone. Nothing. Swallowed by the darkness
of time, hunted by tempo, lashed by the storms, haunted by
this crying shame. Gone. Gone. Shaped inescapably by a
past, mapped for an inescapable future. Buffeted and
reshaped. Boundaries, rigid and hard, fixed positions. Gone.
Only decisions to make and make and, once again, in contra-
diction, to freely make the same decisions some more. But, I
tell yuh, momma, I tell yuh, poppa, choices within the con-
fines of knowing that escape is only to another prison. Gone.
Such is, believe it or not, the real selections, the limits them-
selves, the inheritance. And is that good? The same old tune,
but with the newest variation. Isn't that good? A tradition
as old as our music. Good, ain't it good. Each of us speaking
our own truth, giving the homage in song, at the beginning
and at the ending, for, like the music, this eulogy that you
are assembled here to hear me give, it is ours too. We must
all struggle and compete to get it right. On the outside. In
our voices, separately and together as one, occasionally
accompanied, often without music. On the outside. We must
speak in our voices, recall the sounds and silences of our
utterances, behold the timbre and the excitement too, for
through the voice we can try to claim victory over the con-
tradictions, we can link the inside and outside, we can write
and say what we want. And is that bad? To tell for the first
time our stories and myths, and in our own voices, to our
music. Is that really bad? To sing defiantly about hope.
Now, ain't that motherfucking bad. Or to sound that way, as
we were in control when we know we are not, as if we knew
when to sing, when to dance, and when to do neither by
respecting the silence. If we knew how to speak.

Now, we too must bury without praising. We, who are
the music makers and the dancers, too, the friends and the
citizens. We the living and the dead: insiders and the out-

siders. For life's such a bitch. No wonder we always risk death, trying to capture and to still both the silence and the music. On the outside. To dominate and liberate. Both, before and after that night. Otherwise, how then can we dance? How can we talk without remembering? How can we claim when it is gone? And why would we?

Looking back, as I must, while straining to look forward, too, I must confess: yes, it's not easy to sing praises from on high. Especially, as is this case, from a flight of mercy way above the clouds. From outside of outside. How can I when I am the only one to escape? I, who is left with the memories, who is not just a memory. How good can that be? Still, a more daring gamble, I suppose, is to even make the attempt knowing full well the commendation is not only unexpected but, in this case, in all probability, unappreciated by the people below. By those still straining to slip the bounds. How bad can it be to be left behind? Perhaps, not too bad. Little as it is, I have learned that much. The evidence is now irrefutable. We need only to look at the desolation below and the billowing dark clouds over yonder. The past and the future: the memory and the moment. After such big bangs come these whimpering words, and from me the least of the apostles. No, I am not clever or crafty. Neither do I know all the truth, for I am not like some angel of history tossed by relentless winds from paradise. No man, not me. For, I, too, am just as guilty, just as mortal. For to speak would have been to condemn me too, and so, I chose silence. I did not utter a word. And then, just like that, in the twinkling of a moment, too late.

And, oh yes, I knew there are always risks. Ugly hazards that confront us in the beginning and in the ending, too. Jeffrey Spencer knew. And he chose to take the chance, the same way that I sense he always knew the beginning was also the ending, so that the ending was always there. A wand or a baton? And whose choice? That was how we were *alike, the unity between us. Both of us the product of the same teaching at the same feet. The same dream. For is it not true that in the reverie death was the beginning of life, just as life is the beginning of death, and that the only challenge for any of us is to know the difference?*

Yes, my brothers and sisters, I am now what I have always rejected. Now I preach; but now I also have no father. Me, a fatherless child. I feel that way. But aren't we all like that. Always rejecting, instinctually. We are all dreamers. Innately. From the first flickering on the wall, inside some cave, to the cracking of the mirror. How does anyone, far less someone as complicit as me, find adequate words to explain a gamble that failed, to explain away an allure that was so enticing? I know only that I grope towards the light. And that I must remember to remember, too. Forgetting is something quite different. And as I look out on you, in this hour of darkness, I must remember what someone once said: that when it is difficult to make an oration, when the eloquence and talents are lacking, when nothing good can be said of the man and the times, when there is even a fear of speaking, it is appropriate to begin a public funeral eulogy by celebrating the city. The embodiment of the man and the times. The city. The occupied space and place. For there has to be something good. A meaning to life. We too can talk about the city on the hill, the one that even now still beckons each of us, I suppose. The fulfilment of the next moment, the promise attained. What in this temporal place we think is still possible. Then, we can move on to talking about such niceties as probity and virtue. When our hopes and dreams rise up. By that time even death would be weeping for the dead and might even be forgiving enough to punish those who irrationally sacrifice themselves for a dream with a sentence of peaceful rest.

In our solemn reflections, my brothers and sisters, as we leave this place for the next, in our transformation into our-

selves, as we commit the dreamer to the nothing from which it comes, I want the thoughts of that sage to be our guide. For we are contending here equally with a time and a place, the embodiment of them in one man, and separately with traditions handed down by forefathers as incarnated in all of us. And for me, wherever I might now be condemned to roam, any explanation, inadequate as it is, must always return to that night. Always a spectre spooked by spectres. That was when we noticed the deep silence while hearing the distant music. Outside. When inside we tried not to kill ourselves to get the blood for the sacrifice that was supposed to have saved us all. When we wanted to be good, once again. But when I didn't speak. For I too was scared of the life outside, and of all the electrifying chaos. For in the end, in all her creation, we know the prologue is an epilogue that is also a prologue at the epilogue's beginning. So let me now speak. For this, oh my friends, is true, that there is now no friend. Not in the end, nor in the beginning neither. No connections. Not in-between. So let me speak, and not just because you command.

arpeggio

remember, or think I do: once upon a time, another beginning.

Suddenly, I was sitting bolt upright, aware for the very first time, conscious particularly of the soaked bed and the wet clothes clinging to my belly. My diaper must have leaked through the side. Aware of the darkness that I always hated so much; realizing that I must have entered this isolation when a reassuring lullaby deceptively enticed me into sleeping; now, mindful of the voice crying out into the night. Such were my first impressions. I knew and owned that voice, or must have thought I did, for to whom else could it belong? Instinctively, I knew that such sounds always brought me what I wanted, and as far as I could tell they always would. My trick; my incantation, too. My command. What I wished, I got when there was such disharmony, when that voice uttered forth. Creation of dissonance always worked. Out of the darkness, first the light, and then she would appear. Always. My genie. Called forth by me; conjured up by me. These were the noises that always reunited me with what I missed most, taking me back to the very beginning when everything was together, unfragmented, and I was happily lost, when in such an infinity I had no separate form. Honey as milk. Especially, when it was so dark. A voice that was the one sure way to announce my presence. My method for being heard even, as I had learned, when I could not be seen in a world beyond full of darkness and without form.

Now, the voice in this empty space was calling out again. Perhaps, once again afraid of the darkness of the night, of being shut into a room alone, of being cut off. A voice that knew its powers, that could now act on its own. Commanding. I remember the rest of me sitting in my gloom, comforted by the voice crying out, rebellious, bawling loudly and even uncontrollably. So frightened I must have been then that I remembered finding it hard to recall exactly what it was that terrified me so, why I would be screaming so loudly. I tried to remember what else I could have discovered that I had lost in the fragmentation. But I could not. All I knew was that I was alone, enough to frighten me, and in such darkness. Only the voice understood that the fear must have been so strong that it preceded my consciousness of anything, came before I realized what I was actually doing, before I could make sense of such a fright, whatever it was, before I must have even had the presence of mind to scream. My instinct must have taken over, awakening me, alerting to the danger and why it had to cry out for me, cry to make me whole again. All I heard were the screams, loud and long, enveloping me, indistinguishable. The longest moment ever. This was not some still, sweet voice. And I understood, because of all that I knew, better had to come.

And true enough, the door opened, just as I expected. The light came: a broad beam, out of the darkness, broken by a long shadow entering the room. Silent and strong, a figure, that, I noticed once again, but now for the first time in a strange and different way, was triumphantly reclaiming some of the room for the light. But I was happy. Happy to know the darkness was bound to be fleeing now that she, the maker and provider of all things, had entered. I could see the shadow, and the footsteps were eminently recognizable. In walked Mama, just as I expected. Dressed in her white nightgown, her hair in rollers, and the usual evening powder on her neck and chest. An announced arrival. But there was something unfamiliar, as well.

Usually, I would stand at the end of the bed, in full view, and with the knowledge that any sound I made, sometimes even my silence, but usually a cry or a laugh, would guide her to the right spot on the bed. From there, I could reach out for her to take me. For me to cling to her as she tested my diaper for wetness, kissed my cheeks, my belly, my back as she turned me over, or even squeezed my tummy as a precaution against hunger. Then she would take me into the other room, with the light and the soft music, to join whatever was already evolving, always some kind of music in progress, and holding me against her breast, humming along, she would rock me until I drifted away again, into this soft unity and sweet reconciliation, into a silence filled only with the imprint of her voice. This time, however, still listening to the screaming voice, knowing that its loudness alone would bring her to me, I remained sitting in the shadows, among the wet and cold clothes and bedding.

And then it happened. I swear: for the very first time, and that is what left me numb. She rushed past me into the shadows. The next thing I saw was my mother reaching into what must have been another bed on the far side of the room. Someone, so much like the image she always showed me in the mirrors, someone maybe a bit more elongated than I was reaching out to my mother and she was muttering those cooing sounds that I had heard so often, but now so unfamiliarly distant. *Come to Mama.* My words. *Come to Mama. Don't cry now.* Our special words. *Don't cry.* It was almost as if I was in the other bed and another part of me was in the wet and cold just watching. For I could not feel her touching me or lifting me, even as I saw and discerned what she was doing, could not smell the sweet, warm breath blowing into my face yet again, near my nostrils. *Come to Mama. Don't cry. Don't cry.*

The crying stopped. I could hear the music, soft and low, from the outer room. Through the door, I saw the light that she had left behind, a room fully reclaimed from the shadows. A new gift promised. And I saw myself clinging to her and she kissing me and walking away from me but with me. But at the same time, I realized I could not be seeing what I was seeing. Not really. For it was so unreal: I was still sitting in the shadows as she swept by my bed, holding whoever it was so close to her, hurrying as if she felt too much noise might awaken someone else in the room. Momentarily, she stood in the doorway, listening. And then, she was gone. The door closed, the light disappeared. I could hear the music no more. All I could remember was the silence now that the crying was gone. Now, as I discovered, that I was separated, perhaps forever. And I could remember the smell of my mother, the powder on her neck, breast and arms, as first she passed by my bed, those intimate smells of closeness and unity, and then, as quickly as that, she was gone, leaving only the trace, a mere lingering whiff.

I sat alone in the cold and silence. I wondered: if I was with her how come I was still sitting on a wet bed, smelling what could only be traces of her, when, from what I had noticed, I had seen someone like myself clinging to her, wrapping his arms around her neck, just as I always did, resting his head on her shoulder, and most likely smelling the powder of the evening, just as I was at that moment. The mirror was real after all, did not depend on my waving, as she had shown me, as I had come to believe. And perhaps, if I didn't know then, at that moment I must have realized there is a difference, that things are not always as they appear. That, maybe, me and another part of me could be in different places at different times, that only a part of me at any given time could be with Mama. That the deliverer does not always come, that it might never come for me. That in the other room what was already in progress would, so unimaginably, continue without me.

But this could not be happening; it could not be real, not the reality that I had come to know. And even back then, I must have realized the power of a dream. I had come to understand the control and the hold of a dream: how it can prevent you from shouting, from speaking out, how it can split you. I learned how hard it is to be awake in a dream. For when I tried to cry out, I had no voice. When I tried to move, I couldn't. When I tried to stand, I was unable. Something was stolen from me. I had lost the object and the reason to make me move and cry, but not the one thing that still made me cry and miss what was missing. Now, I was unable to cry, far less able to speak. I remember continuing to sit in the darkness and in the cold. Immobile. And in this paralysis, I felt the warm tears running down my face, voiceless, for I had come to a startling realization of permanent loneliness at that very moment.

Somehow, and in this confusion, I must have fallen asleep. The next thing I remembered, it was bright morning. My father was putting on his working clothes. I remember a black collar at the beginning of a day always to remember. Black: the distinctive colour of the band he placed around his neck. Then, he, too, was gone. And then I must have realized, even at such an age, that, no matter how much I may wish, desire or will, it is impossible to awaken from some dreams. Colours, I now knew, matter. Complexions do, too.

In the doorway, in the early rays of a fresh morning, was Mama, watching Poppa departing. Standing by her side, holding her hand, was someone who obviously wasn't me, as I had come to accept, but someone attached to her nonetheless. I would never forget that sight, or the feeling. More deadening than the numbness a few hours earlier, than that weird feeling that had protectively ushered me into sleep. There was simply no feeling. And this time the pee did not leak through the side, even if the results were the same. Then she confirmed everything. She spoke.

"Good morning, honey," Mama said as she and this attachment, sucking on his two fingers, came to my bed. "Good morning. Honey, I want you to meet someone special. This is Jeffrey. Jeffrey, say hi to Edmund. Go on, Jeffrey! Say hi! Go on. Edmund can't talk yet, but you're bigger than he is, you can talk. Say hello to him."

I don't remember if he spoke. In fact, I am most certain that he didn't, for he didn't remove his fingers from his mouth. He just stood there, holding on to my mother. Why wouldn't he: he had won her. And, indeed, and it is not just because Mama said so, but he was bigger than I was. Something else I remember: I was really starving before my mother returned and offered me the nipple for my first milk of the day. Even then he was there looking on. I remember the robbery.

∾

"A bad dream, man," Jeffrey Spencer kidded me many years later. "In any case, I'm older than you and I don't remember nothing so. I don't understand how you can remember all them details, man. You sure you ain't making them up, that it's not a dream or something? That you ain't just making a leap so as to get things started in your own mind, man? For a justification?"

"No, Jeffrey, I remember what I remember," I said. "I know. I know."

"Man, that's great, I tell yuh, all them details and from so early," Jeffrey said. "You are good at those things. Not like me. In any case, I don't have the time to stuff my brain with all them things from the past, all them slights and things. They don't matter to me. I'm all about the future. That how you and me are different."

"Perhaps," I said.

"Different," he emphasized. "You the Preacher, man, needed by the people to bury the dead and to keep them from coming back. The past, history, that's you. Me, I guess, I'm more for the living. For the present."

As he said, some things, and slights too, must be forgotten. At least until the appropriate time, until the future, of all things, coming as she does, decides. Until she chooses and exonerates with life. Until she confers the blessing. Otherwise, there can be no forgiving: neither in the beginning nor in the ending. Yes, Jeffrey always forgot. I was always forced to remember. That is why that night, and its spectres, haunts me still.

ତ୦

We were marooned in, of all places, the Great House. That's when it started for me. Facing the decisions. The choices in the dark. All the people who really mattered to us — those still among the living, and the spirits of the recent dead — all of us inside this fortress; every one of us seeking shelter from the horror and unseen terror dancing in the darkness outside. Presumably, we were bonding like old times: our extended family, a remarkable fraternity forged iron strong through these generations, our ultimate refuge. A time-tested ensemble, our social compact, if you will. All of us entering two by two. But for this gig, all of us feeling only the hollowness from the luxuries around us, each of us tasting that queasy dread from the emptiness of unfulfilled lives and times, every one of us adrift, still drowning. No music, and for me, no video, either. Harmony, if that's what it was, only in silence. All of us recognizing even then, conceding quietly perhaps, that with newness and rebirth something important and vital was lost forever. Gone but not forgotten. But, at the same time, something new was happening — but only in the rain and thunder of creation. In the greenness to come. For once we have sinned, there is simply no going back. Creation happens only once. And that unless we act now, we could lose what little we still had, even time and the few sanitised memories. For as my father had drummed relentlessly into my head, ours is a jealous God; time so unforgiving; memories so unforgettable. This time none among us might be worthy of salvation, none worthy of petitioning for the turning away of this face of evil. Without redemption, we could lose it all. Drowned like rats even as we cling together in pretend safety.

Even the music in the silence, like the rainbow placed in the sky when it looked like the sun wasn't gonna shine no more, our tradition promises as much. If only we could wipe our journal clean.

൭

It must have been at that point that I first realized how thoroughly disillusioned I had become. When, as you might say, I began, my brothers and sisters, but only so tentatively, to toss in the towel. I can never tell for sure. For as I found out, as I am here to testify, things just have a way of happening, like Nature's symphonies, like anything new and evolving by fading one melody into another and another, a new creation in its own time and pacing. For in the end, there are really no safe places. No pure time. No final resting place. No comforting music, either. No promises to keep, no mother's lullaby. Not for people like us. For even if we felt we were products of our times, we knew that we were no longer the sons of our fathers. We had consciously chosen to be different. And who knows at what point bad arrives? For is there a specific moment, an obvious action, and doesn't, at least sometimes, good just stink? We rejected the proffered legacy, refused the gift. Changed the old music, not just the lyrics. On that night of burial and the chance of a new beginning, we could hear the cattle lowing, and even a baby crying but we knew nothing beside the nothingness of knowing that in this darkness all cows were black. No angels were visible. How could we know the way if there was no revelation? And, no, I am not making excuses. Perhaps, in the end, I didn't leave just then because I had no morality. Or maybe it was because I had too much.

Still, it must have been around the same time that I finally asked what's the use? That night in the big house, battered by the storms and the winds, I seriously questioned for the first time if this turmoil was worth the price. In my mind, I would eventually have to testify, no other signal moment or event was as auspicious. But again, who really knows, it might not have been then. For after that epiphany of sorts, the dénouement I anticipated was teasingly put off for another time. It should have taken only a small nudge here and there, reminders of what was so near that night, to encourage me to act. I know I was not an unreasoning animal. Yet, it took more — too much more. Too much time. Too much silence in between the realization and real action. Too long without a voice, a stifled song imprisoned in the head. Too long doing *nuthin'*. Why? Perhaps the music, started in an earlier era and in another place not quite here, had to be played out and in its own time. It could not end before its time. We can never run away from our natural finish. Perhaps it is even a bad thing to try.

Only now, as I sit in this plane thousands of feet above the Atlantic Ocean, heading for what I don't know, do I realize how pivotal that night was, that I saw it as a last chance to choose another way, but that I did nothing. Not a peep, really. *Shudda done somethin', man. Anything.* But not a whisper. Not one note, and all the while me thinking I'm some damn-well singer. Truly. I, perhaps vainly, thought that we, too, would have emerged in absolution to a new day, to the light refracted into a brand new rainbow, with the pot, the milk and the honey awaiting us in the forgiving greenery that comes after every storm. It should have been a time to be contrite and to atone. To reflect and come to terms. To cry, Father, my Father, oh Father, never again. To fall on our knees and to lament how much we, the young inheritors of such great legacies and traditions, had smashed them all and, in building our palaces and counting houses, ended up constructing replacements that were neither lasting nor wholesome. How in our rush to embrace the new, we had virtually wiped out our collective memory, leaving us with nothing on which to build afresh. We had no ancestors. And we wanted none. We refused to fall on our knees. We accepted no gift, no legacy, because we had no time for mourning. We preferred the collective amnesia my generation was so keen to induce. To rattle the bars of our cages, perhaps, thinking that the sound was victory itself. There'll be no limits, we screamed. No boundaries. And because of these choices, after all these years, what do we have? No music. No, none at all. Not for our eulogies, not even for dancing at our wakes. For the music of silence was broken when we spoke, for to speak is to choose. For even the limitless must be limited and the outer edge of what is without boundary must be a boundary. So it is spoken and formed.

Only now, I feel compelled to give this eulogy, this testimony, really—an assertion that I should have given elsewhere—only now do I know the true cost of hesitating, the true price of so much more: the true value of everything. For in falling, did we trip over the very obstacles left in our paths by our fathers? Yes, did they tangle up our feet by building fences at the very edge of the land they promised and the crags of the abyss? Or did we willingly throw ourselves, purposely running to gather speed from the safety of their land and then taking a leap, consciously, just for the exhilaration, only to realize in mid-flight, the desperation of the moment, of an untethered rope? Of no boundaries. Only to grasp much too late, that we cannot go back, cannot stop ourselves from falling, that any action, once started, must come to its natural ending? Must come to its very own conclusion. And if we did miscalculate, were we wrong to even think of gambling? How can we not want to taste the fruit, even if it is forbidden, even if we suspect that it might even be bitter? So that you may understand my aporia. For suppose, just supposing, we did find that one apple that was sweet and liberating among all the others on the tree. An apple that was also good. And even if it was indeed bad, should we be denied such pleasure, such adventure, prevented from trying? I don't know. Not even now.

Eventually, they all must come together. All the memories and dreams must. All the versions, all the tellings and retellings. Just like streams flowing into an ocean like this one, at this very moment, down below us. Only then can the music assume full form and move on to its natural ending. But not before the many sources and beginnings are counted and accounted for. Like those trains on different tracks heading to somewhere, that one place out there, all coming to a common junction. Each with its separate beginning; each choosing its own route; all supposedly moving in their own time, each to its own rhythm, all to their beat. Yet, they must come to that place when they all become as one. We all must. So was it with all that happened and of which, in a different time, I am now compelled to recall in testimony before accounting for an ending. I must set myself apart and bear witness. When I feel called upon, as the only one capable, of giving a virtuous eulogy, of speaking honestly about a friend

among friends. To speak honestly and of the only person I can ever know; to testify about me, too.

This is where the moment slips from the present into the future, when we must choose and in making a decision come to realize that nothing from the past can determine what is to be and, at the same time, that every thing of the future will forever carry those traces of the past. In that instant, we are free yet imprisoned, just like the flies caught in the spider's web: some seemingly of their choosing; some trapped and ensnared; some simply caught in moments of indecision; others just serving a specific purpose. Each committed to the future that it does not know and cannot even try to shape. A future that it can only hope will be kind and have a smiling face, and an understanding and forgiving heart. So, it is now with me, me the eulogist and witness: I decided for a future that I do not and cannot know and in so doing, yes, I betrayed a shared past. I am now in a new time dependent on a new beginning, and recognize that nothing is new and yet nothing is old, either. The ways of those old dry bones testifying to once upon a time when they lived, to another time of their death, and to a time of hope for a rebirth. Of an understanding and knowing mother arriving with the light. I must hope for the future and that someone, a soul mate perhaps, someone in an uncertain future, will smile on me, will love me and give me a chance to live again. Someone would command me, like a spectre. I can only hope and I can only plead my case to the future. I can only pray that, you, whoever you are, you to whom I must speak, coming out of the future to meet me: I need you and I need you to choose and redeem me, knowing that I am forever touched and soiled by memories. Memories, to which I must always return, that will forever interrupt and disrupt other times and discourses. That will perhaps even mar a future with you. That is the risk. For what is a man that you should even bother with him? As a woman you would know, as only you can. As the giver of life you always did and always will.

Indeed, sometimes, I wonder about these things, much as Jeffrey did, when in mid-air he must have looked down, down, down, looked all the way down, looked into his horror, and no matter how he stared, no matter how he wished and even prayed, still he could see no bottom. Worse, he could not stop; certainly could not reverse. This was not a pit from which he could easily crawl, for first he would have had to hit bottom. Even then in free fall he must have realized that if there were a messiah she had come and gone, gone, gone, and at his hands. There could be no arrival. That's the story of that night. The lament and the requiem. The celebration, too, that unforgivingly sticks like a leech in the mind, like a scar. But our hope is always for a second coming: that is the story of my father and of his, too. And of his mother.

Even now as I go through this intense interrogation, even of myself, as I try to tell it all, starting each by each, with every narrative and angle, with its own beginning and ending, separate as they are, heading for a beginning of my own I know not where, I fear. And I hope: You out there will help me to smile again. You whoever you are. You are without this history and these doubts. You who will come untouched and virginal in a new moment. You who are so free of these memories and of these voices, except perhaps mine calling out to you, conjuring something out of nothing as yet. I cry out to the one who would make me live again. Come forth! *My voice is calling because I need to live and to be free.* Now, free me! Break these chains I've been dragging all this time, these chains I've made linkbylinkbylinkbylink. Unconnect me: differentiated, indeterminate, make me. Connect.

And, until you come, I will try to push on: to fly away, even though I, too, do not have wings of a dove. I try to tell the truth even as I know it, as I make it and as it makes me.

In these moments in-between and connected to what has happened and what I want. I know. In agreeing to an earlier cost, I must now pay the price: I must explain everything as readily and precisely as I can, for I must by law to my inter-rogators. They command; I must obey. I must be a witness: a betrayer and turncoat to some, and I must be moral. By law, I am obligated to cooperate fully with them, the penalty too for a future, ironically not of my own making, but which only they can give me. In some place that I don't even know. Reborn, like before, in a place not of my choosing, in tradi-tions and values not of my consent, not of my agreement, joining a game long underway. That is why I need you. That is why at this new beginning I must make sure to cry in my own voice in the hope that you will pick me, for it's me, it's me, it's me, oh, Lord, standing in the need of prayer. It's me. It's me, it's me, Oh Lord.

So I'll speak into a tape recorder for them; for you, and so you may know me better, I'll unburden myself in a letter, perhaps not in a formal manner, but something, maybe noth-ing more than a note or a postcard, that if I could, I would place in a bottle, cork it, and throw it into the ocean below, so that it can drift carrying the message of another time, going wherever the tides take it, buffeted and bruised, but carrying deep within the memories, and the dreams. But even then, I am not free to write. There is no bottle. Perhaps, no cork either. Perhaps, not even a good dream. Proscribed, constructed and constricted by a time and a place. By a moment and what it offers. I can only compose in my head and try to prepare myself for your questions. And, if you could, how do you capture voices and bottle them? I will be faithful as I can. I'll try my best. For I want you, I want them, I want everyone, to hear the voices I heard, that I am still hearing. All the voices: as they spoke to me, as they told me their story, as they, too, eulogized in confession. As they sang and wept. Lamented and castigated. Maybe you'll hear as well a requiem not for a people, but for a time, a monody not only for the dream, but also for the dreaming. For in beginning this eulogy how can I not start with the lament that, my friend, there are no friends. I want you, them, I want even me, to understand. All spectres needing death so they can live, even if spectres need bodies so they can die. That is why there have to be so many beginnings, so many stories, just like the song.

So, please, don't tell me how long the train's been gone. It doesn't matter now. For it's gone, gone, gone. Talk to me only of the next arrival and of the next one that has already left the station and is acoming *to meet me. Hallelujah! And, yes, don't bother shouting from the mountain top. Hallelujah, Hallelujah. Whisper the good news in my ear. Hallelujah! Hallelujah! Halle-lu-*Jah, Rastafari.

As I stared through the window into the darkness, and as I heard the lashing of the waves against the shore a short distance away, I knew the emptiness in that house was no different from the calm before foreday morning. That is when in the moment's stillness all you can do is sit and think, reflect on what could be and what should have been. On goodness and evil and the sliding scales between them. And at every point, to pray for some residue of good. And think about missed omens. When you have to confront yourself and all that is in you. When you find yourself, brothers, looking into the eyes of an animal, searching the heart of a beast, sisters, testing the natural strength against which we always fight. Tasting. And, in my case, wondering if I could escape this imprisonment of mind and soul.

Our customs tell us it takes a storm to cleanse and baptize. But we know a heart and common sense are also necessary for a commitment. The inner truth must match the outward show. No use emerging from under the water without first confessing. Otherwise what is buried in the water? Where is the resurrected man? So on that night, even as my mind told me we could all be headed for perpetual darkness, even as I looked around me at the long mourning faces of all those who should have felt specially chosen to be sheltering from the worst storm of our lives, sheltering in one of the biggest and most pretentious houses ever built in this land, yes, sitting pretty in the abiding assurance that the winds could howl and the rains could drum on the ceiling and windows, and the elements could trumpet their worst, rumble and jive, scat and grumble, that they could not touch us. Couldn't come in. Yet we knew the dread of fragility. For our guilty consciences realized that after the storm, just as the old folks taught us, must come the future. They believed it would be a time for a renewal when all is created as if for the first time, and so we hoped. All except the memories, but they were plastic and erasable, or so we felt. We would emerge like the baby clothed in the nakedness of hope and surety. A certainty created and tested by experiences. What would we have if we had no confidence any more, what would we be if we could no longer forgive? For even if forgiveness springs eternal like hope, it is not the same when you cannot forget. Forgetting is the liberty, not the forgiving. And so I chose to forget. I took the liberty. Time, my dear friends, did not.

For on that night, amidst all the turbulence, there was still a voice deep within pushing me — offering perhaps the same enticing promises so many people of my age were hearing — demanding of me not to give up, at least not just yet. Now, it had pleaded, was definitely not the time to surrender. We were born to be ambitious, an inheritance that we simply did not have the choice of rejecting. We were made to be strong, building on the legacy that had withstood storms and hurricanes and fires and even ourselves. In each of us was the promise. Each of us was moulded and shaped to continue the quests born in another time. For we had come out of the bowl into which all things good were mixed. We had been touched and shaped and breathed on. We were the keepers and the fulfillers. We were damn good.

The voice was telling me I was young and invincible, made of tougher metal, hardened by fire, cooled by the purest streams. I was special, a chosen son of a young nation, it reasoned. I was lucky, even. I could escape what might appear to be inevitable for others, even the owner of the Great House or the young woman we had buried only a few hours earlier. All it would take is erasure, the forgiving that upholds the forgetting and the recognition that life, even as lived in the religion of our fathers, has always demanded sacrificial lambs. Nobody likes to be sacrificed, but sometimes there is no choice. It is for the good. The food of time and change, of growth and progress. It is against this, I told myself, that we must look to hope and to forgiveness just in case it becomes our turn and we were to dare to say we were not lambs. This, the voice explained, was the risk. This, too, is life.

In this way, the voice was telling me that I should stay and gamble just a bit longer, if only because I, too, was lucky and magic. For perhaps, just perhaps, it challenged, after this storm would come a new beginning, a very different beginning, not what the old folks predicted, for they were stuck in another time, their boundaries made of iron. There would be new opportunities for me to exploit, possibilities unthinkable just one generation ago. I wanted to believe that I knew what I wanted and that I had a choice. Jeffrey Spencer felt that way too, the voice had whispered. He had heard the same sweet voice. He had glimpsed the shadow before his eyes. And like him, I felt trapped in the pull towards this destiny, as if I was merely an actor

44

plunked into a play that was already written. Each time one of us misspoke or made the wrong move, each time we improvised just to be fresh, we heard the voice off stage calling forth for an ending and a new beginning. The voice shouting: cut, cut, cut. No, no, *no*. Everything that we did, every experiment, had to be erased. It had to be eradicated. Until we could no longer think. Were no longer free; no longer at liberty to create and invent. Could only follow the voice. Young gods reduced to robots. Until we accepted the specified role entrusted to us. We wanted changes.

But I did believe that all that I wished for would be bestowed on me as long as I remained faithful, worked diligently as my mentor's assistant, refrained from challenging him, learned from him, carried his bags, acted as his ears and eyes in a very dangerous business. I was the repository of his trust. We believed that Jeffrey had found a way to slip beyond reach. I did not always approve of how he did it, but he escaped nonetheless. And while I accepted that this escape might only be temporary, and that eventually, he could be netted, we knew the joy that came from believing we were free. Free to have neither a legacy nor an ordained plan other than our own, not to have anything that wasn't of our own making. Deliverance could not come through the voice of a preacher no matter how much I was pushed in that direction. Aunt Thelma understood that much. That would be merely a rebirth of the old.

But there was something else. Secretly, I believed that I could shatter the bond that tied Jeffrey and me so fast. He was the pioneer. I would follow, but I always believed that I would eventually branch off onto my own course. For it had been going on a long time now, this battle between us. We both knew he had won the struggle between us over direction and timing and, to save myself, ironically, to protect that very important part of me so few people knew, for my own deliverance, I had given in unreservedly to him. Sometimes, it is better to find a lesser sacrifice. At least that was what I thought.

That was our compromise. He knew that so clear and unambiguous was this victory over my doubts and fears that he could go forth, concentrate on more pressing matters, secure in the knowledge that as the master he never had to give a second thought, knowing I could never betray him. For me it was a matter of waiting — the very essence of having hope.

Sitting in that crowded room on that menacing night of storms, I tried to block everything from my mind, everything but concentrating on how to survive the tempest. I knew it would not be easy. For I, also, had to survive other less welcoming voices. Most irritating of all was a single harsh voice, the unrelenting admonitions of that tireless preacher and prophet, the real one, my own father. Indeed, if Jeffrey had his trials, so did I. And they were both of the same kind. Symbols, alike. And so it was on that night.

I remember. Particularly, my father sitting by a window that night. He looked calm and peaceful in his silence. Not happy, but at peace. Resigned. Even from his vantage point, I don't think he looked outside, not once. Not even when the lightning lit up the sky and allowed us a glimpse of the world beyond the protective cocoon of the Great House. I tried to imagine what my father was thinking, what he would say to

anyone asking him about the significance of such a night. I knew that he could not help thinking about the people of his island, the people among whom he had spent every day of his life. The common people, he called them, the salt of the earth, people like his best friend, the grave digger. For my dad had never left the island, not like his best friend in very youthful exuberance had departed once, only to hurry back home, to fight for liberation, for and among his own people. After hearing his friend's stories, my dad refused to leave, not even as a young man when so many people flocked to so-called greener pastures in colder lands. Where they found themselves fighting the same battles but in someone else's guise.

He stayed at home, among his people, the same ones God called him to minister to, he would say, to teach and to guide, a people from whom he said he would never run away. Neither, he promised, would he stop telling them the truth. For these were his people, he would tell me. He knew them and they knew him. They shared the same traditions, liked the same music, responded to the right calls; they nurtured the same hopes for the future. They worshipped the same god that gives and confirms the truth. He knew their politicians, their nurses and their gangsters, too. They shared the same loyalty. All the hopes and dreams of these people were my father's, and by extension, indeed because of him, were mine, too. Patterns repeat themselves; a call, as the saying goes, begets a response, which begets a call. Some predictable, others disruptive and destructive when they resist or deviate. The cycle must continue to its natural ending and then resume all over again, point after point. That was the consistent message of my father, to the people and to me. Unwavering in reconciliation: one message; one call and the appropriate answer. Undeviating.

I too had not gone overseas to study, for every legacy has it price. Some things, I admit, are the way they are. They

47

have their own pattern and tempo. Their own rhythm and pacing that defy explanation. But then I remember the beauty of our music, what has always made it great, how it must digress, how it must be contemporaneous but spontaneous. Why? Simply because it is. I wanted to disrupt one narrative, just to continue it differently. To give my own colouring. I did not like how in their response, the unending refrain was always the same. The people were always calling for me to pick up my father's mantle. I wanted my talents to rest elsewhere. Not only was I a good listener, but I was a singer too. Aunt Thelma had come among us and had spoken her truth. The stranger had become one of us, lived with and produced for us, transformed us, and, becoming one of us, she had now moved on, leaving only her words. Her commands, too. Shaping us in her image. I knew I could make it beyond the shores of this island, like so many had, and honing their skills and talents in response to her challenge. Just as the oracle predicted. Mine would flourish if released.

But no, I stayed behind. In return, I dodged. In my soul I resisted. I had to keep myself pure and faithful. I would be a part while remaining apart. I would not be boxed in and moulded, but at the same time I would not appear unmindful of my father's wishes. I would know them to spurn them, to reject that foisted upon me. Oh yeah, I rejected one calling for another.

As a true prophet, my father knew when to praise and when to chastise. He said he always prided himself on asking the big question, and at the right time. He and his best friend knew how to read a time, he said, and perhaps it was that confidence that lulled me into thinking there was always a natural barrier beyond which it was not possible to go: someone would eventually raise a hand, cry halt and ask the right question. The stray sheep would be brought back to the fold, caught just at the edge of the abyss, the chicken snatched away from the closing jaws of the mongoose. I wanted that kind of choice. To take from what was offered the useful and to replace all that I rejected with my own. For if, in good taste, a gift cannot be refused in whole or part, do we then have the right to use it for whatever purpose we see fit?

As a historian who must make note of specific moments and turnings points, my father knew instinctively when to boast and to congratulate; when to reprimand and correct these people, his very own, and, specifically, me. He would save us from ourselves. We could rely on him. In the fullness of time, I would understand how these things work, what it took to be a guardian, but by then it would be too late for the people I loved.

On such a night of such fury, my father, the preacher, would be thinking of the people, many of them huddled in shacks that would be tossed away in the hurricane, some of them probably dying in this fury, all of them needing redemption. Even for such rugged people, hardened by centuries of natural adversities, he knew this was the worst night in memory.

My father had always preached that nights of hurricanes were special: a time for everyone to confront dark and ugly personal recollections. A time for atonement. In silent negotiations, on these nights of storms, the people would memorize the words for the next memorial plaque to be placed in the parish church. This would become the reminder of death exacted and of sacrifice given, but also, and at their insistence, a certificate of the rebirth contained in a contract. A rainbow. A reminder and a promise, too. For they too want to remember, while holding their God accountable to the promise secured by their blood.

People like my father were always interceding to ensure the price of their people was adequate, and if possible fair, and that all sides kept their part of the bargain. And, since he knew that it was people like me who tended to forget, who let the plaque lose it glitter, who refused to polish and shine it, whose memories dim, we got specific and detailed instructions. Turning points should be acknowledged and remembered, even the missed opportunities. My father knows the Other Side always keeps its promise. Its word was the Word. And when we deviated, punishment was assured, often swift and spiteful. It was back to the original covenant. Non-compliance carried a heavy price. Aubrey Spencer, the grave digger, always knew when the Other Side was angry and had suspended the agreement. When it turned away the side of its face that was good. This was when he was busiest. The biggest fear was that one singular and misguided action could result in the voiding of the contract, in the erasure of every one of them that went before, the turning away of the benevolent and beneficent face forever.

My father had to be thinking such thoughts, as the billows raged. Secured as best we could, in the strongest house any of us had ever built, we, too, heard the sounds of hungry lions roaring on the outside. Who would dare to look outside for confirmation? Who would not seek the safety of inward looking? Who wanted to look on the side of the face that was not good? Most of us didn't, especially the elders. Times like these were a chance for them to pray that the punishment being exacted was a temporary redeeming exercise, a national catharsis, soon finished but not quickly forgotten and hence never needing to be repeated. A time to promise, to make no demands. Yet some of us did look out. The more defiant ones, those of us crying out that every agreement must have at least two sides, and probably a third for the ambiguities: that one does not just give and the other just receive, the stronger imposing its way; the weaker accepting. The words for the plaque must be negotiated. Even from a position of weakness. And, yes, that intentions, not only outcomes, must matter.

I remember other things, too. This time how, methodically and purposefully, the elements were going about their business of destruction, their teaching of the lessons of humility. Sometimes, it is not only the pain, but the method, too. And for all we know, perhaps, there are times lessons should not be learned. Not that my father and Mr. Spencer would agree.

Flooding and destroying were made easy to explain this way. Everything precious had to be wrecked, returned to its primordial formless forms. Nothing was to be spared, it seemed, except this mammoth house in Lodge Road that would survive because it was big and strong, more resolute than even these strong winds, than even the driving force behind the torrents, a sign of how far we had come. It was big and bad and ostentatious. Unreproachable and impervious. Defiant, unyielding, just like those who loved and cherished it, those who would dare to look instead of averting their eyes, those straining to see beyond the limits of the light. Unbending and unbowed. Just like how all the young people like me wanted to be; just like what Jeffrey had shown us we could become. Arrogant not weak; modern not old; daring not cowardly. On this night, nothing weak appeared worthy of salvation to us. Not even the dreams of the old men and women, who had lost their powers, but who still said they knew better. The same people who wished there were ways to stop every generation from repeating the same mistakes.

I knew my father was right to think this way. He did not need to look for the proof. At least, not through a window, not at that very moment. He carried the memories of past transgressions, the price to be paid every time. It was painful and fresh in his mind on this night; the punishment necessary because in the brightness of the day the lessons were so easily forgotten. And because of faulty memories, or hardened backs and blocked ears, we now had to endure it all over again. He did not have to look outside the big house. The raging tempest was within.

ᘓ

Like any effective preacher, my father is an exceptional storyteller. Over the years, he told me many tales. Parables, he called them. Deceptively simple stories to which I should always look for greater meaning. Stories his father had imparted to him; some of the same myths and legends told for generations, from the beginning of our time; stories, some like the ones I am now relating to you, brothers and sisters. So that in the midst of the hurricane, just as I am now sitting in this plane, I couldn't help thinking of what conclusion my father expected me to draw from this experience. And looking back, now, more importantly, to the lessons I had missed. For there must have been some story, some analogy, some part of our glorious past, that could fortify us and help us through that night and this. The bigger lesson. Or is it the small story? The missed and the overlooked!

Unfortunately, back then, I could find nothing in my anaesthetized memory. Looking around the house, and daring to peek beyond, I saw little that was old, but much that was new. Not just simply a rebirth but a new creation, a severing of the past. The only thing remotely comparable to the all-night drubbing—and now, so many months later, I still don't know why this story forces itself to the surface, why it resonates so — was the time generations earlier when the southern half of the country was razed by a terrible fire. I remember when my father first told me that story, how his voice dropped and sounded sinister. I was afraid. The terrible incident started, he said, when three lions, two tigers and a leopard escaped from the African Circus visiting the island, invited by those celebrating Discoverers' Day.

These exotic animals had appeared enticing and attractive. The islanders felt secure in the knowledge that a simple flirtation would do no harm. After all, they were still in control. When they got tired, they would simply ask the animals and their foreign keepers to leave. No problem there, they reasoned. They could end any flirtation when the passion cooled. And they could do it suddenly, in the nick of time. But, as I too would find out, things don't always work out as expected. The animals escaped and took refuge in the cane fields around Lodge Road. Scared by the thought of entering a jungle of razor-sharp cane blades to confront these hungry beasts, the islanders didn't know what to do until someone suggested fire as a solution. Suddenly, everything had changed. Once started, how can it be ended, how can the continuous and never-ending unfurling be stopped? Does it take a word, or is silence the fuel and not the cure? All the poor people knew was that nothing was happening the way it should. The world was unfolding but not according to the agreed script. And without a working script the people had forgotten how to act. So had the no-longer tamed animals. Spirits that had long satiated their taste for flesh, slaked their thirst for saltiness, blocked their nostrils from the odour of burnt offerings, these were revived and restored. And they roamed freely. And once they had bolted from the cages, they were no longer at a distance or controllable, no longer harmless playthings, no longer domesticated.

These hungry animals now were capable of coming into a house, or attacking helpless children as they walked the streets. They slaughtered sheep, goats and cows. Many a man told stories of travelling late at night and seeing the haunting eyes of one, or maybe two, of the animals waylaying some prey. Frightened little children dreamt of getting mauled. The people didn't know what to do. They no longer held the power. They smelled only the rancid odour of fear. They learned once again a jilted lover could exact a painful price. Domesticated can always become wild again. Betrayers, like the naïve, had to be punished. A price for the rebottling of whatever had escaped.

That was when the government decided to torch the cane fields to flush out the animals. But the direction of the wind changed and instead of razing the fields, the fire turned ferociously on homes and buildings, leaving charred desolation in its path. No one knew what happened to the animals. It was the heavy rains that saved the people that time.

They buried the dead with little fanfare. I don't recall my father ever mentioning a plaque. Maybe the people were just happy for the chance to rebuild. So grateful that they sought no concessions, knowing full well that not even the suggestion would have been entertained. It would have been unusual for my father to leave out so important a point as a plaque. But, then again, maybe, it was me, how I understood what I heard, how I imagined what I had not experienced, and what I chose to forget. Maybe I had not listened as carefully as I should. Or maybe, purposely, my father did not mention a plaque. Perhaps, even he, the keeper and explainer of the rules, did not know if the horror that had escaped had been captured, or if it were just asleep out there, somewhere, beyond some boundary, just waiting to be awakened by hunger pangs or by the smell of someone inadvertently stumbling its way. Someone bold enough to go to those areas that are unrestricted but from common sense never used, areas marked by primary brush and trees, with vines and apple trees. And once the horror was awake: well, there was no plaque, for there was no agreement. No limits on the horror. Just a lull, and at the menace's own bidding. No protection and no cause for decorum. The older folks knew that. Maybe.

It was fire that time for the purging. This time, in my mind, my father was like the lawyer awaiting the worst, the client now on his own. The pleading ended. Resignation. In my mind, I keep hearing his voice, at times soft, at times harsh, saying, on this the night of the great hurricane: water and wind. Next, who knows? I heard him. The deep voice in the silence calling forth the word, squeezing out a promise, for at least with a pledge we might know the ultimate price. On that night, we simply dreaded the thought of a next time, and that it might be fire. For if we, his very own people, were to repeat the order faithfully, it had to be fire again. For like the client in the dock, we too knew that it was out of fire and out of water that all things

55

come. That is what we believed and what we knew: the cause and the effect. Fire and water. These two founding elements. We, who are the meshing of the two, the mixing in the bowl, but only good if in moderate proportion. Too much of one drowns us so that we would have to be made all over again; too much of the other would incinerate us, so that we would have to be remade all over again. Either one reduces us to our purest form, to what we were before, before we were poured into the bowl, before water was made a limit for fire and fire for water, and we the conjunction and compromise. One essence good, one bad. Both, as we know, bad, except in the right proportion. Or, as I repeat, so we had learned. Now, we were having water, too much of it. So that the future that was nothing was now predictable. The only question, according to tradition, was what type of fire—for even an inferno would have to change with the times.

Legend said fire followed water, but a fire whose intensity was always beyond the expectations of the times. A fire that would do more than just burn. And I knew my father was not alone in this thinking. In his fear that it might be better to keep the cycle going, rather than to try for a break, a gamble that could, indeed, result in an ending much worse. Collectively, the older people across this nation dreaded paying the price for our casual flirtation with the Beast. On that night I also thought about the next time and I weighed the odds. With my silence I gambled. I was as pragmatic as I could be, I thought, without becoming foolish or unwise. I tried to console myself that if there was a next time, it could be different, or indeed it might even be avoided. I knew how times had changed and had released us from some legacies, for we had escaped the bounds and the bonds. Certainly, in a practical sense, there could be no fire starting in the same cane fields. For the land that grew the canes was now fallow. So times *do* change. This was the land around the biggest house on the island, land laid bare and barren so the size and importance of the Great House — with a large satellite dish on the roof — would be even more noticeable. Except for one field behind the house, a field, my brothers and sisters, that was to be part of a bigger and wider design. I never thought of a future fire coming from the sky, from another land, but burning, burning, burning nonetheless.

On that night of atonement, Aubrey Spencer, my father's best friend, knew most of the people had long forgotten the previous devastation by fire. As part of his warning, before entering anything into the books of good and evil, of life and death, he would say, sometimes a single story can only go so far. So far, yes, so far and no farther. People's memories are short and growing shorter. This time it would take more than the head of a politician for atonement, to pay for rupturing the promise to the past. He would say this if he too were to break his silence and engage my father in one of their all-night arguments. Everybody, not just an old grave digger like him, should know that much by now, he would say, so why waste time repeating or even accepting ignorance. That's why on such a bleak night, in his loneliness, he felt compelled to hum the only redemptive song that gives him solace, peace of mind and hope for the future — even if his own son, just like me, absolutely detested this hymn.

In the distance, over the howling winds, he too heard the angry seas roaring and bashing themselves against the jagged rocks. Only the high outcrop of rock prevented the seas from washing everything off the face of the island, into oblivion. Of providing more than enough work for this old man.

The waves pounded so heavily against the shore, they eroded the miles of pure white sand beaches, as if they were maliciously intent on ridding the land of the last of its natural beauty and inheritance. As if caught in a battle to the end between the sublime and the beautiful, and they had sided with one against the other. As if, knowing they could not reach the cowering residents, the waves had resorted to hurting the people in their pockets, leaving in place of the smooth sandy beaches gaping holes, rough dents, pitiful scars and stark ugliness. Just like the dead mysteriously washing up on the shore so frequently these days. And it was the trees, especially the mature and sturdy ones, some with plaques nailed to their barks attesting they were national treasures, that became unwitting allies of the wind and the rain. As if in this rebellion, Nature had enlisted all its allies. The trees volunteered quickly. Like brainwashed people bent on suicide, they willingly uprooted themselves. And in a deathly frenzy, they unselfishly paid the ultimate price by sticking to what they are good at doing, by virtuously crashing down on the miles of electric wires strung across the land, plunging homes into sudden darkness and threatening to execute with the sparkling wires anyone foolish enough to venture outside.

Only the big house in Lodge Road, the one that so easily reminded us of the great houses of another era, when our fathers' fathers were not free, houses weakened by time and human agitation, stood its ground. And with the house's survival came a deep foreboding message for all the people of Lodge Road, for the friends and enemies alike of Aubrey Spencer, the old respected gentleman grave digger, by tradition the final arbiter for all of us, and his son, Jeffrey

Nathaniel Spencer, the rising power on the island and throughout the Caribbean.

ೲ

Only hours earlier, we had buried the latest victim: Brenda Gabriel Watts. Twenty-seven years old, and as angelic as her middle name suggested. The angel sacrificed, her death a message, an unmistakable warning from the new lords of the land. Just like the landowners of old, they were absentee owners of ostentatious plantation houses. They were the very people who, according to rumours, were behind the building of this great house in Lodge Road, and of several smaller ones dotted around the island. The foreigners provided homes and the money for many of the emerging affluent middle class who, like harlots, joined them in the treacherous lucrative business. The drug lords had managed to ensnare all but a few of the elected. A few good men and women had triumphed on their own, and had built larges houses from honest labour. But they were the exceptions. These foreigners were the same people providing the work for Aubrey Spencer and my father. This death should have been a singularly sobering message. "Remember, you might not know the full price of your desire." Instead, we accepted the final push over the precipice.

Brenda Watts was now resting in a soggy grave two miles away from the big house. Some events require personal mourning and private expiation. This truth must be factored into any understanding of the thinking and behaviour of the one man who really matters in my story — Jeffrey Spencer — the man who brought us to this moment in his house. Knowing what we do now, what shall we do with him? What can we say of him? And is it true that gods do die? For if they do, if they disappear, if they do not come back to speak to us, can there be a future?

For as the sages have instructed, now that we have talked about the city and times, now that I have told you as little as possible about me and some of the other minor players, for we were not the hero or villain of this piece, for we did not act, now knowing all that: if we still cannot speak glowingly about the triumphs of life and about dreams, perhaps we can now find strength to talk about a man and his times.

From where Jeffrey was sitting in the bedroom listening to the rain, he told me several months later, he heard his father muttering to himself in the darkness. The old man's voice was rising and falling, indecipherably, breaking the monotony of the ceaseless drumming on the roof. Jeffrey knew that talking helped his father to think. The more his father thought, the more he wanted to talk, to express frustrations trapped in his chest. In his simple way, the old man, who had seen countless hurricanes in his life, was trying to digest what was happening, what had befallen the little girl he had admired so much, had felt so proud calling his daughter. He had kidded her about giving him a grandson or a granddaughter, with long hair like the mother's, before the good Lord called him home. Brenda had said, with her voice full of laughter, her dark eyes twinkling: "Allright, Mr. Spencer. I'll do it. Just for you. Just for you, man. But not for that good-for-nothing son of yours, though. Not for him. He won't know how to handle children. Just for you. I'll get one. Just for you. Then we can bring him up the right way."

Only a few days earlier, they had sat in the kitchen, in the friendly darkness, and chatted about everything and anything. About her plans for the schools, plans for a new gymnasium with weights and training equipment. It was to have an asphalt running track, and proper running shoes would be available, so the boys and girls would have some place to go after school, to get rid of their excess energy and keep their minds and hands employed. So they could develop their talents and join the long list of international champions emerging from this region. So they would not be tempted by the evil abroad in the land. She would do anything for the children, her children, as she called them. For if she and Jeffrey Spencer had one thing in common, it was a belief in the education of the children. That, eventually, is what kept them together, even after the embers had long burnt out and they knew that only the need to perform for the happiness of other remained.

But the price of a gym was too high for the government. She had confided in Old Man Spencer how difficult it was thinking of ways to get around a price running into millions of dollars. "People like your son don't understand," she had said to him. "He thinks there is always an easy solution. He thinks different from me."

"From me, too," the Old Man said. "He's his own man."

"Yes, and he has his own way of doing things," she said. Moments, like this, I remember, always caused her to place an elbow on the table, and to cradle her head. "His *own* way."

"His mother's child," he added.

"Try telling him it's not that easy," she said. "That everything has its own price."

Although Brenda never mentioned it to him, Aubrey Spencer must have understood that the drug barons had approached her about providing the funds. He couldn't avoid having heard whispers that ran throughout the area. And more importantly, he would have heard she had spurned and rejected them, just as everyone expected she would. Such rebuff the lords could not live down, especially not after they had unmasked themselves. They decided she could no longer live, no matter who her protector or consort was. Obviously, from his actions, Aubrey, even in this hour, could still convince himself he, in fact, didn't know for sure. And I would think that just to be safe, he didn't ask.

As far as I could tell, Brenda didn't tell him, either. Never mentioned to him anything about their approach and her rejection. The same way that she never let on to him that her relationship with Jeffrey had cooled some time ago, although she still continued to visit the house. Everyone, I guess, is a deceiver, with the best of intentions. A hypocrite even, when it is appropriate. Maybe she didn't want to worry this old man with something over which he had no control. When they talked, she was her usual happy self, joking with him and making him smile again. He would not have had the nerve to ask directly who had acted as the go-between for the barons, if what he heard across the land was true. She had promised him the grandchild, a bridge to the future. She would become maternal for their good. And with such a precious gift and legacy, he would be content to leave this world when his God called him and not ask too many questions beforehand. He would join his wife in the cemetery, knowing their sole offspring had chosen a kind, wise and feisty woman, just like his mother, Thelma, to help him carry on the family line. Aubrey knew it was more than a tradition that a man should at least be buried by his son; that no man genuinely blessed should ever have to live out his last days in the knowledge that his line is ended when they put him in a pine box. And because of a hard-ears son. Especially, a son that denies his father the choice of handing on to the future what the father's father had gifted in trust to him, so they could all live on. A son unwilling to learn the lessons of his forebears. "I'll do it," this heavenly spirit had pledged. "Just for you, Pappie." She had promised him a grandson, someone for him to shape into the kind of son of his choosing. An insurance policy shaped in a little bundle. She had promised. He had believed. And, now, on that night, sitting and muttering in the darkness, he too had remembered.

Earlier that evening, Jeffrey was on the phone again on another of those frequent overseas calls, his father thought, maybe from Toronto, New York, London, Berlin, Brazil or Colombia, for he was talking very loud to be heard.

The poor quality of the line, causing him to have to shout, could have been the first effect of the hurricane. If he didn't know better, the old man had once confided to me, he would think his son was giving daily reports to someone overseas. "I've never did know anybody to spend so much time on the overseas phone. Must be quite a bill to pay." Perhaps he was fishing for information from me, for even he must have known that money was no longer his son's primary concern. Pointedly, I made no comment. "Anywhere, tell him that I had to leave, that I can't wait for him and his phone calls and that he knows where to find me if he wants me. He can come and see me before he goes or after he comes back. He knows where I live." Old Man Spencer had noticed how Jeffrey would always leave the island after a long call. In most cases, he claimed to be on business, a trip to Boston, Vancouver or Paris to invest in the stock markets of the world. Other times the trips, he suggested, were to keep him current with international lifestyles, to prevent him from falling into a rut now he was back home permanently. He had to keep the memories and knowledge of living abroad sharp in his mind. His mother, were she still alive, would want it that way, he would disarm his father by saying. And his father knew that wherever Jeffrey went, I trailed behind.

"But I don't know," I had heard the old man grumble almost inaudibly, as if he himself reprovingly felt it was traitorous even to question. "I just don't know."

Aubrey had seen his son's broker's licence and it was still current. That licence gave him the right to buy and sell as much stocks and bonds as he liked in North America and Europe and to transport as much money as he wanted or the international bankers would accept. With this licence, he didn't have to worry about the Americans and their expanding dragnet, to keep their backyard and playground free of any scourges and illicit activities. He had no shortage of prospects, of wealthy people wanting to open plants and businesses on the island, providing badly needed jobs for the young people, and raising Jeffrey's stature as a man who had gone overseas and done well not only for himself but for others, too. A man who talked of such things as high finance and of doing business in the world's major cities, of making this island a safe place for business and development. A man of vision, some people were now saying of him. A leader in waiting. The same accolades his mother had argued could come to any of us but only as a result of living abroad. He had received the final polish and finishing elsewhere and it showed on him. There could be no doubt that he was building a base in his present position. He knew how to get new business for the island and none among us, as his father knew, felt as indebted as Prime Minister Watkins did. Aubrey Spencer recognized that his son had become inseparable from the prime minister, making him one of the most powerful and most influential people in the land. Some believed he had provided the prime minister with insurance for the present and received from him training and positioning for a future job.

But Aubrey also noticed something else: how his son often turned defensive and different after those calls, becoming more withdrawn and unable to look him in his face.

Now, during the hurricane he remembered how Brenda had made him feel young. This young woman with long fingers, big brown eyes and sparkling teeth, who would make sure an old man ate everything on his plate, even when he protested he wasn't too hungry; who kept him in conversation at the table while Jeffrey was called away to the phone, for another urgent call from somewhere in the world. "Come on, Pappie. Is that all you can eat today?" she had asked, so authoritatively, just so, how else could he put it, but so *caringly*. "No, man. You can do better than that. Eat some more. I don't know why you keep upsetting yourself so much so. Eat, man. Just for me. Take your mind off whatever is worrying you and think of your poor stomach, man. Eat some more. Just for me." And he did. He always did when she commanded.

Now, this diamond was gone forever. During his long life he had heard those final words so frequently: Man born of woman hath but a short time to live, rises up in the morning, but in the evening is cut down like a flower. Like one of the strong tamarind trees that, only a few moments earlier, had come crashing down on the pasture in front of the house, falling just as the lightning was cutting the darkness.

Usually, the words and images associated with a routine funeral would be gone from his memory by the time he rode the old one-speed bicycle home. He had become accustomed and immune to the effects of those words. They held no particular significance for him, except for the day he came home after his beloved Thelma was gone. Grave diggers are not supposed to cry at funerals, for what would be the message to the mourners? Traditions set limits, he knew that, so that poorly understood customs were perilous, like misplaced magic. Maybe, that was why the rains started. In his moment, help had come.

It was the wind, he knew for sure, that took down the big tamarind tree in the pasture. But it was something more powerful, beyond his imagining, more than he was willing to accept, that had cut down his pretty flower. Something that forced her to sacrifice herself to make sure the children would not be tempted. He would always miss her and, because he too was human, a father and collector of the debts and sacrifices, he would also cry and pray for the forgiveness of those who had done this terrible and ugly thing to her. And in his heart, he told me, with his penetrating eyes burning into my core, he wondered if his son, from a generation that finds relationships so disposable, missed Brenda Gabriel Watts half as much as he did. Perhaps, I said. Indeed, what more could I have said, me reduced to the role of guardian and listener. A role even my father had rejected, choosing such an auspicious time to go dumb. Thankfully, even on that night, nobody expected or really wanted me to speak. Words would not always do the trick. A night when it was good for a grave digger to cry freely. To lay down his burden.

"It didn't have to end this way," I found Jeffrey Spencer saying deep in the night of hurricane. The voice seeped out through the door and I quickly rushed into his bedroom on the pretence of wanting to discuss some matter with him. It was late and most of us, certainly those who could, were finally sleeping. I found him on the last of a bottle of rum. Haitian Barbancourt Five Stars, one of the priciest and smoothest in his collection. Which surprised me: rum, of all things. On such a night. Jeffrey was a man who, to this point, had drunk only socially.

He was holding the framed picture Brenda had placed on his nightstand. In the other was an empty glass. On the bed was the big imposing picture of Thelma, his mother, that usually hung in the kitchen. The glass in the frame was shattered, the sharp shards in the very place he would lie down. He was talking to the wind and the lightning. Or to his mother. Perhaps, even to Brenda. In the reflection of the window, he looked suddenly old.

"It didn't have to end this way. But you had to have things your way." He was sitting on the edge of the bed. At first, I thought he was praying. "You had to. Now, look at what had to happen. Look what happened. And I brought this about. Me." So this, I thought on reflection, is what really happens when we feed blood to the shadows to make them talk. When the gods don't respond. How then do we shut the conjured up, how do we stop them from talking? Do we have to wait until the taste of the sacrifice is gone from their tongues, the last of the blood licked from their lips? Can even the water in a hurricane, the drenching in a flood, wash away the blood and slake the thirst? "But I promise. Now I understand and I agree. I promise. I'll be different. I promise," he said. "I really promise this time."

I don't think he heard the door opening as I entered and stood in the doorway, or shutting as I slipped out. For the rest of the night, I was careful to sit outside the door, prepared to stop anyone from entering. Or to stop Jeffrey from coming out. Not in such a state. No matter what, I had to guard and protect him. We were brothers and I loved him. I heard his promise and his plans that night. For one last time, I told myself, I would stay with him. I was committed to an ending that was now his, too. Remember, sisters, I did bar the door. For if I did not let anyone in, my brothers, I also did not let anyone out. I withstood the night secured by a promise not specifically to me but to a higher authority. A promise that I took nonetheless as offered personally and irrevocably to me.

Deprived of sleep and frightened, as I was, still, I was not so far gone that I did not ask myself at what price this duplicity? Who is the master, Jeffrey or me?

This is the moment, I know, when I should have called out, and not only to the wind or a departed spirit. But, I still believed in the contradictions and that they could be brought together. I wanted, despite the mounting evidence, to continue believing that Jeffrey would eventually deliver for me, helping me to achieve my dream, and freeing me. That he would not betray me. That he would know when enough was enough, when we should say halt. So I stuck by him that night. I was a believer. Stuck in the faith. Other people, I remind myself, have sold their souls for less than hope. We, even Brenda Watts, to the very last, still believed in the dream of change and the transformation that would come with its attainment.

"When you have some time, we should sit down and talk about some of the things happening on the island," the prime minister was saying. "Maybe we can start putting things back under control, before they get any further out of hand."

The morning after the hurricane, the frightened people crawled out of their homes to survey the destruction. It was extensive. And to see the conditions agreed to for them. A calm and freshness hung over the island, as if the chance for a new beginning was just waiting to be embraced. The sky was of its deepest blue and cloudless with a watery haze in the distance. It was as if Nature, ashamed of being induced into such rage, was trying to turn a blind eye to its own doings. To the northwest, banks of heavy cottony-white clouds were drifting away. The sun smiled on everyone. It was just like the calm after my father gave me a good dressing down, when neither of us would want to talk about what happened, both hoping that the causes for the reproof would have gone away. Looking forward to that moment when we could hug again.

It was a new day, born of a night of storms. We were free again and in that liberty we would choose to forget. We could put the promises we made to one side, and re-negotiate conditions that we might have agreed to too hastily or under duress. So, in the light of such a gorgeous day, with all its possibilities and promises, we could see ways to improve on what we had promised; we could stretch the limits and extend the boundaries. I looked at the caution in the old man's eyes as he spoke to Jeffrey, and I knew what both were thinking. One of them had not forgotten what had happened just yesterday. One of them was already thinking of reconsidering, maybe of changing the tone, if not the terms, of the concession. So soon. Without remorse and without mourning. So very soon. And looking on, I knew that Jeffrey's father was neither ready to forget nor to forgive. Not so soon.

For most of the morning, the roads into Lodge Road were not passable. Big heavy trees blocked them. The water had dug deep trenches in the roadbed, excavating the asphalt, leaving puddles in the holes. Yet from the first morning light people made their way to Jeffrey Spencer's big house. And he met with these people inside the mansion, on the veranda or sometimes in front of the garage at the side of the house. Muttering and talking, seldom laughing or joking, searching for some star. They reasoned. Each brought a different tale and a different gift. Each asked for a blessing in return, a blessing that they must have known to be as useful and temporal as the dispenser. Yesterday's events confirmed Jeffrey's ascendancy in some subtle way, and they were not only arriving to pay their respects at a delayed wake. They were a strange collection of people making this pilgrimage: powerful men and women — the poor and the rich. This time not bothering to inquire about the health of a mother, now dead and gone, not congratulating a father, now placed on the sidelines and reduced to looking on.

Jeffrey treated them with equal indifference, as if his mind was elsewhere; as if, I wanted to think, after the

71

hurricane and the destruction, he was finally feeling the full impact of Brenda's death. As if he needed distance, the chance to make his own internal journey, to restore, rebuild and fortify his own constitution. Now to mourn. Until then everyone had whispered about how well he had held up under the strain. On how well he wore his mask, the makings of a good politician. That morning if they felt that way, they chose to speak of other things. They wanted the past buried.

One by one the powerful and rich came to his door. These were the people who intrigued me most, so much so that I wrote down their names. They behaved as if by visiting him they were fulfilling an expected duty, not simply offering him condolences. As if what they were doing was the proper thing to ensure some future remembrance or reward. As if they were answering to some spirit gone out through the land summoning them. Sometimes they stood around in silence and occasionally some of them talked: about the hurricane and about Brenda, but usually with more sadness about the damage done to their properties. Why I made a note of these observations back then, I don't know. The poorer people simply came to see what they could get. They always do, as we would find out again. And who can blame them? I made no list of their names. I didn't want anything that was found missing traced back to them.. I know it is unlikely they would thank me for thinking they needed such help. They seldom do.

Jeffrey hardly talked. His eyes, red from the drinking, flashed and darted about. The rich and the powerful had to force their cars through water to come. Their very expensive and fashionable vehicles stalled helplessly by the side of the road, as often as not, so that the rest of the journey had to be made by foot, the ending nothing like they had imagined or would have wanted. All of them almost naked, barefoot, pants legs rolled, mud between their toes. All of them at their most vulnerable with their clothes making them indistinguishable from the poorest and the lowliest, so different from the times they came to fete the night away in their splendour and glory. I was amazed at the power of this man who had chosen me to be his accomplice. For even in depths of such great loss, he was still treated as a conqueror, transfigured like the awaited Lion of Judea. But still, I made that list of names and in so doing, no doubt, I fixed them permanently in their action. Specific thought and actions were embodied in them at a specific moment and I wanted a lasting impression. Somebody has to be a witness: we must start a new history with a new beginning. A written record, even. Then, we can move on. I named them because the fear was still fresh in my heart, and I wanted to hide my face from the exacting countenance of evil. An evil that was now identified and recognizable if it were to come again in similar human guises. I was determined to keep a word, even when offered in silence. For it was offered for me and negotiated in my name. Some blood was shed for me. So, even if still not speaking, I wrote.

The list I eventually gave to the Americans was extensive. Commander Ignatius Primm, head of the Defence Force; Eric Thornton, the police chief; Sir Anthony Wiggins, the chief justice of the supreme court. Commander Primm even brought along a platoon of soldiers and put them to work clearing the roads leading to Jeffrey Spencer's home. This was their first task before they did anything else, Commander Primm had pointed out, even before taking the prime minister on a tour of the island. And I told the Americans other stories, and about who else were the midwives and the godparents, who were the magi, and who, if he could, would have drawn his sword and smite this first-born, this anointed. How Jimmy Ashton, the leader of the opposition, dropped by. This was the man who went around the island promising to clean up the drug business if he became the next prime minister, the man on whom the Americans were pinning their hopes, funding his campaign behind the scene.

Another story I told them was this. Later in the day when the roads were cleared, even Prime Minister John Watkins, a shortish man in his early sixties, dropped in. Unusually, he was alone in the car, without his usual security men. He sat behind the steering wheel talking to Jeffrey Spencer. And he talked too about Brenda Watts. Watkins had complimented Jeffrey before for making such a wise and beautiful choice for his wife. A strong and tough woman, he had described her. For choosing a woman, he said, capable of wearing the title as mother of the nation with honour when Jeffrey's time came, as surely it must. And he had promised that he would kill one of his prized Holstein calves for the meat at the wedding feast. Now, there was nothing to say, really. Jeffrey Spencer and Brenda Watts would never be married. The calf was spared.

"The governor general knows about what happened," the prime minister continued. He appeared to be whispering even though no one was near them. "He would have dropped by himself, but you know how it would look. He said he hopes you understand."

Jeffrey said little in response. He was dressed in a beige Carib suit and had a small briefcase resting at his feet, next to a puddle. He kept looking down the road as if expecting an arrival any minute.

"It's really too bad, awful, what happened to Brenda." He was echoing Jeffrey's words of the previous night. "Such a brilliant and dedicated teacher. I can still see her running and training the youngsters that she loved so much, you know challenging them to go farther, to be the best. A damn pity. And she was so young. So young." Suddenly, I made the connection. I realized that the prime minister and Jeffrey either reasoned the same way or took orders from the same people. I don't know why I hadn't made this connection before. "It didn't have to be that way. But you know how she was. Always gave it her all. We got to try and make this a safer place. That's the least we can do for her memory."

Again, Jeffrey said nothing. Then as if to change the subject, as if bored with thinking or hearing others talk only about this matter, or as if he had finally grown impatient waiting for whomever was to come down the road, he tensed his jaws and asked: "Can you give me a ride?"

"Where to?"

"The airport."

"But isn't it closed? I though we had suspended all flights."

"This is a charter, and we ain't carrying no paying passengers, so we can re-open it for just one flight out," Jeffrey explained. "The airport administrator approves of this exception. I told him it was okay for this one flight: a charter, remember. And in any case, he will have to let any planes bringing relief to take off and land."

"Oh." The prime minister's jaw sagged. He waited and when there was no further response, he clumsily asked, "Where to? I mean, where you're going?"

"Colombia. Bogotá."

"Oh," the prime minister said. His face tightened. "Going there pretty often, eh?"

"I have to nip over there for a quick trip."

"What kind of business this time?"

"I ain't too sure yet. Just that they called me over. God, you can't depend on anybody these days." Jeffrey glanced nervously once more down the road, opened the car door and sucked his teeth loudly in disgust for having been kept waiting. I could see in his eyes the anger ready to explode, the disappointment that the car he had summoned for the trip to the airport had not shown up. "I'm getting tired of this set-up. I gotta move on. We gotta change some things from now on."

"Be careful," the prime minister said after further thought. "Don't get caught up in anything over there. Watch how you travel and who you mixing up with, for you never know. The ambassador says the Americans are really serious about cracking down these days. Using the army, he tells me. Confiscating airplanes and boats. They got Bolivia eating out of their hand."

"I'll be okay, man," Jeffrey said. "I know how to take care of myself."

"Just be careful," Watkins pleaded. "They are very anxious to take back people to the States for trials for the slightest offence. Even misunderstandings. We can't afford any trouble. We're a small nation, you know. Too small to tackle with the big boys."

Jeffrey didn't answer. He settled comfortably into the front seat of the Mercedes-Benz.

"Aren't you coming?" he said to me.

"Sure. Sure," I said, trying to hide the surprise.

"Run inside and get your things, man," Jeffrey said. "We'll wait for you, but come with me, man."

I still don't know why I went. My heart was telling me to run and I didn't listen. Sitting in the back, I smelled the new leather of this car and remembered that the car had been brought into the island two months earlier — the newspapers explained — it was a gift to Jeffrey from a grateful German investor who had made a killing on the markets. Jeffrey had donated the car to the government for the use of the prime minister. Jeffrey never told me if this story was correct but I had my doubts. He was not always that generous. Nothing is the way it seems. When the opposition leader suggested that a man like Jeffrey might also want to make a similar gift to the office of the opposition leader, Jeffrey was curt and dismissive.

The prime minister started the engine. The soldiers, their boots muddied from digging the drains for the water, the bottoms of their green khaki pants soaked, and their hands soiled and dirty, moved out of the way. The Mercedes took off heavily, its shocks groaning with the encounter of each pothole.

As we were leaving, Jeffrey glanced over his shoulder at his father sitting at the back of the house. He was rocking in the old mahogany chair he had brought over from the house in the graveyard. He had spent the day watching us all through the same window he and my father had turned their faces away from during the hurricane. I know that Jeffrey was wondering how much the old man knew, whether in her final days Brenda had said anything incriminating to his father, anything at all that would make Aubrey so reclusive and pensive. Anything that could haunt us.

"How's he doing?" the prime minister asked as if reading Jeffrey's mind. Jeffrey hunched his shoulders noncommittally.

"I hope, after all he has done for me, he doesn't feel that I have given up on him," the politician said, looking steadfastly down the road, as if afraid to look at the house lest his eyes make contact with those of the old man. "The two o' we go back a long time together. He was always a solid soldier to the cause. Fought hard to help us bring forth this new nation. A hero of our Independence. And in all my election campaigns. Always fought hard. Just that I'm so busy these days, I can't find the time like before to stop by, to talk to your old man. But I'll drop by soon. Just too busy right now, you know."

Jeffrey did not answer. He had heard the same words, the same excuse, before. He had not told his father. There was no use, or need, to tell his father that, like him, Prime Minister Watkins could no longer, in clear conscience, look the old man in the face. For how can you look in the face of good when your heart might be evil?

Jeffrey never really got along with his father. The two Spencers, cut from the same genetic cloth, were shaped by experiences, beliefs and temperament into totally different garments. One was the idealist; the other the pragmatist. Each obstinate in his own way, whether virtuous, just or even practical. Obviously, the difference was in the cut, too, not solely in the cloth itself. An important distinction.

The way Jeffrey saw it, his father's outlook on life was too simple and conservative. It was too much of the simple garment, if you will, nothing more than an aged cultural artefact. These were characteristics Jeffrey told me that he rejected utterly and unreservedly. He wanted to be a free spirit, aware of where he had come from, confident of himself, but released from having to drag countless chains behind him, clanking irons stacked on his back by someone else. He would have to validate for himself any contract made in his name, any promise entered for him. He accepted that the old man thought him too flashy, too boastful and full of pride. But again, in Jeffrey's mind, that was not too bad a criticism. Not in these modern times, he explained. In this light, as I listened to him, all I could think was so much for that like-father-like-son stupidness we have always heard. So much for a father's pride; a son's respect. And so much for a restful conscience, a heart at ease secure in the knowledge of knowing and loving. Of handing off the baton and of careful stewardship and respected legacies.

"Aren't we all more than the names our fathers and mothers gave us, than the land from which they too sprung, and can we not aspire to change even the name they gave us?" Those are the kinds of questions Jeffrey asked often, words shot at me, but the sentiment aimed elsewhere. "You tell me, am I wrong? Are we not our own men and women, free to do as we please, just as long as we are respectful? Tell me, Preacher Man, 'cause maybe I have a thing or two wrong, wrong, wrong."

I did not always agree with Jeffrey, but neither did I always accept his father's point of view. So that unable to reconcile these two positions, I also refused to conciliate. Not like Brenda, who went so far as to take sides. She, too, she had argued, had freedom of choice. She too could discern right and wrong. She too recognized that past debts must be paid before newer ones are accumulated, and that if the past is not an absolute predictor of the future, for the present that was all that was available. And like Old Man Spencer she felt it should not be discarded with abandon. "I'll always make my choice and I'll always speak me mind on certain things," she had said. "'Cause we have to learn, and what is there to learn from?" But such directness and lucidity was not me. I am always trying to find the middle ground, to put off offending until I can find a compromise, or the issue solves itself. Always hoping, and never speaking.

Yes, my brothers and sisters, truly, there was no denying the differences were profound between these men. The variations touched every aspect of their lives, thoughts, aspirations and, of course, their relationships. And let me tell you, as far as Jeffrey could tell, his father believed life was just a meaningless expenditure of time between captivity in a woman's womb and an unspectacular, unruffled sojourn on this earth. A planned journey, the details mapped out, with all the crags and gullies colourfully marked off, all the worthy scenic sights underlined; a journey assiduously designed that must be followed. It was a pilgrimage with only the occasional pause. A brief time-out here and there to admire a flower, perhaps, but never to change the landscape once it has been tamed and cultivated. No rebellious veering off onto a side road. No chance of travelling an unknown path chosen by some unknown force, a whimsical power to whom the traveller must submit. What young man could tolerate a life so neatly packaged and predetermined? So lacking in spontaneity, in risks. This was another question the younger Spencer was always asking. Jeffrey wanted the essence of living; he demanded more than just to be handed life and an accompanying roadmap. Otherwise, why not the gift of a stillbirth, he argued, where the certainty of the route to arrival is never in doubt, is just experienced in truncation. Why not just fix him at birth, pinned to the wall: absolute in death. And from the beginning, unable to become anything more or less. No becoming. Didn't his mother give him a life, a receptacle to fill? For wasn't his father's approach the confines of a prison? Or even the grave itself? This was not in keeping with the aspirations of a man who knew he was on the verge of greatness as long as he was willing to gamble everything for a big chance, as long as he knew and accepted the odds. No, no, no. Not him. And a thousand times he told me so. That is why I know.

To put it another way, for we must view and remember all approaches, his father's way wasn't dramatic enough for Jeffrey. It wasn't good enough to sit back and protect the gains of previous generations, hunkering down on what was handed us by those who fought for independence and political representation, for making our island a better place than it once was, and to be contented that times were not now so bad. Yes, times were better since our parents' youth, when they were subservient to foreigners and had no control over their futures. But they had fought against the restrictions of their time and they had won. That did not mean the battle was over forever, or that the current fight was only to safeguard what they had achieved. We still had mountains to climb and rivers to cross. I, for one, had big dreams of international acclaim as a singer. Who among us does not secretly thirst for fame and success? So I agreed that we could not be contented and laid back. Life requires taking chances, putting what we already have in play, in the hope, if not dream, of improving. Of moving to another and higher stage. If our fathers gave us liberty, it must be the freedom to push the boundaries and to gamble, to reach higher ground without having to drop to our knees and strain at the neck because of a restraint. There must always be other and greater levels for the next generation.

Jeffrey knew his old man hoped this much for his only son: a long, fruitful life. Nothing pretentious; nothing harmful; a careful recognition that there is always an accounting in the end, an end that could appear in the next moment. A safe house and home. This wasn't what Jeffrey wanted. Give him any day a short enjoyable life rather than a slow withering one, he reasoned. And if he must worry about the sudden appearance of the end, let him have the safety of strong walls and a sturdy roof—the strongest of them all that have ever been built—as an intermediary so that he could keep the raging torrent at bay, until there was a negotiated agreement on the ending. That was his approach, one for which I had full sympathy. If he entered the history books it would be on his own terms, for blazing a new path, not by conforming to the wishes of an aged generation now content to set themselves boundaries, not by fitting uneasily into a confining mould. And when the end came, he would rather be cremated anyway and his ashes tossed to the trade winds.

Yes, even as a boy, Jeffrey had disagreed with his father. He had signed a pact with himself that he too would make the most of his allotted time on this planet. But, unlike his father, there would be one major difference. In his old age, he had to be better off financially than his father could ever dream of being. That was how he planned to count his blessings. In terms of wealth and spending power. In the ability to buy a house or a car, and decidedly not measured in the way people looked at him as, content but poor, he walked the road. They would admire him for the cars he drove along the narrow streets, for the big houses and for the control he had over their lives. It was a pact he had signed with himself, renewed every so often, and which of late, he had taken to asking me to witness. "I'm more practical," Jeffrey always explained, "more like her and less like him, I guess."

If there was another signature, it was his mother's. From early she had understood how debilitating the confinement of living in a graveyard would be for someone like her son. She had made her own pact, making the most of what had been offered, and she had been happy. But that was she. If she were in another time, free as she made him, his mother would have gambled, risking it all, savouring the enjoyment of chancing and living. But she was a woman in different times, and even though she was strong and determined, she was not completely free. Her time had not yet come. She could only gamble on him, signing that contract, and giving her time to him.

Jeffrey had every intention of fulfilling his dream, even if it meant flirting with danger. He would prove risky gamblers can also win. He would prove he was right to strike out on a new path.

And in the end, what happened to Brenda certainly proved his point. She should still have been accumulating chips at the table of life in reward for her good clean living and sacrifices. Obviously, his father's assumption didn't take into account someone appearing at the table with a loaded gun or with a butcher's knife. So much for his father's hypothesis. And for Brenda, who had a choice.

And yet despite this, Jeffrey had attempted valiantly to reach out to the old man. For what can you say, when you cannot change to suit the world and you try to transform the world to fit you? He wanted to have some sort of relationship that would resemble that of a father and son: the type of relationship he would like to have with any son he should ever get. But no matter how hard he tried, he didn't have the knack for a simple, pleasant conversation with his father. The stilted talk would inevitably lapse into a deadening silence until one of them gave up and mercifully left the room. Only his father could fight and conquer him and Jeffrey hated anyone having this kind of control over him.

When he was overseas, particularly when he lived in Toronto and New York, it was different, as there he didn't have to look his father in the face. All he had to do was to send the old man a regular card or a letter, filled with the constant recitation of how successful he had become. Parents, particularly mothers, always like to hear such stories, even if they suspect they might not be totally true. He would write the letters his father expected, taking care to choose the words that showed he was proud of his own achievement but not too swell-headed. Or he would write to his mother. It was easier and less pretentious that way. She was always good at interceding with the old man. And she would get his father to take the money Jeffrey sent in the letters, the surest sign of success abroad. Or he asked friends in the business, some of the women he was seeing, to visit his parents and sing his praises when they vacationed on the island. They played the part, telling his father what a great guy he was, how he was continuing to acquire the finer things of life, perhaps in the mistaken belief that by impressing his father they would receive a favourable recommendation. And Aubrey always seemed to like Jeffrey's women. And the music he sent with them, records of all the classics that his father listened to on the gramophone. At least in this regard, they seemed to have the same taste.

But then his mother died and Jeffrey returned home. Opportunities were now more plentiful on the island and he had learned much abroad. And then, he found Brenda and used her as a bridge to the old man. As if he was so scared of dealing with his own father, or felt his father found him so untrustworthy and shameful, he needed someone as a go-between. For a while it worked well. Until Jeffrey and Brenda started seeing things differently. He didn't know what Brenda had told his father. But whatever it was, he didn't put it beyond his father not to remain suspicious of his own son.

෨෨

But even Jeffrey would admit he had contributed to this suspicion and distrust. There was the time he approached the old man about using a plot in the cemetery for business. He had thought about it for a long time before getting up the courage to talk to his father. He had rehearsed the opening of the conversation a million times in his mind. There was no reason for his father to turn down the proposal.

Yet it was with a trembling voice that he raised the matter. Would his father allow him to pay some of the boys of the district to help keep the area clean, he had asked timorously, as if he wasn't a grown man. It would keep them out of trouble and it would severely lessen the old man's workload. The boys would keep the area clean, grow a few crops, and Jeffrey would get the government to pay the cost of hiring them. With his ties to Prime Minister Watkins, all details would be worked out without any fuss. If the young men worked hard enough, the money could contribute to buying something for the gymnasium, their very own contribution to the track and field program. Teach them responsibility, too, he said. The only stipulation was the old man could not breathe a word to anyone. Jeffrey said he didn't want anyone to know of his unselfish generosity and he didn't want the opposition and the loudmouth Jimmy Ashton to find out what the government was spending the taxpayers' money on. This was only because he was still not ready for active politics, and not because he or the government couldn't defend the work program on its merits against any opponent. Jeffrey would select the boys. He didn't even want Brenda to be involved, he had explained. He wanted to surprise her.

His father gave his approval unquestioningly and the project started well. The response was so enthusiastic and immediate Jeffrey did not have the heart to impose the condition that his father should stay away from that section of the cemetery.

All was going well, until the old man came to the big house one day and angrily announced the boys were a bunch of vagabonds. He didn't want them hanging around the graves any more, desecrating the hallowed ground, and that he had pulled up all their infernal plants and burned them in a giant bonfire. He was seething with rage. It took some time to explain he had gone into the area to find out what it was keeping fifteen boys so busy and what could be in the bales they loaded on the trucks every Friday evening. He didn't directly confront Jeffrey, as his son had expected. Instead, he kept angrily talking to himself until he finally retired to bed. "Damn desecration. Not even respecting the dead."

Brenda was different that night. She was cold and wouldn't speak to Jeffrey for a long while. She simply sat in the front of the house staring out the window towards the main road, her face contorted with anger, her eyes watery. The relationship would get worse from that point on. Even though Jeffrey believed she accepted the initial explanation that he didn't know what the boys were doing in the graveyard, that he was conceding he was not as good or reliable a super-visor as she, that he didn't and wouldn't have approved of such gross deception, that for punishment he had banished them to neighbouring islands, the relationship was mortally wounded. Brenda ques-tioned him constantly, as if setting mental traps expect-ing him to let something slip under pressure, to contradict an earlier denial. Fortunately, he told me, she didn't really know who she was dealing with, how careful and smart he was; that he could not be tricked or surprised so easily. That he made sure he was always in command. Always in control.

And, as if I could possibly forget, he reminded me that, as a young boy, he had mastered the arts of becoming the trickster. It was obvious Brenda sus-pected him of other more damaging things from that day. But she never had proof, or he, in a bold counter-attack, would dismiss protestations of pain and disappointment as small-mindedness, as he was wont to do even as a boy. With a wave of his hand, he would dismiss it all: everything, every concern. The relationships — with Brenda and with his father, too — only got worse, for I guess magic can only do so much. But still he kept on. This, as he confided, was a gamble he had to take. Knowing Jeffrey as I did, I felt it wise to keep my own counsel and to bide my time. For as he had taken to reminding me, I had my own memories. I knew what he could do. Perhaps, in the end his father really did know his son, too, and like me waited too long trying to know and adjust himself.

Aubrey Spencer, my brothers and sisters, as I was saying, was a simple man. We must remember that. We must treasure this perspective for a keener understanding of everything else. Seventy-eight years old and slightly stooped, he was still the head grave digger at Christ Church Anglican Church, the final resting home for just about anyone who lived and died in the parish of Christ Church. For fifty-three tough years, he had been a grave digger, finally graduating to the chief of the staff fifteen years earlier. The appointment and experience confirmed his status in the district, for little boys knew he wasn't afraid of the dead. Parents could use him to instill discipline by threatening to ask him to unleash the restless spirits of the wicked on wayward youths.

The job also came with a small two-bedroom house from the church — not much, but he was never a man of extravagance, maybe because he knew ultimately everyone came to the same end—and the right to choose which funerals to preside over. That was why he wouldn't let any of the younger men near Brenda Watts's final resting-place. His *daughter* deserved the best. So that after the funeral all the older people, who like him understood and treasured traditions and the meanings of the little things in life, could look at her parents and relatives, and without uttering one single word, communicate with their weepy eyes a message spanning generations. They could truthfully say he had given their beloved Brenda a decent and tender burial, had held her up in unblemished honour in the eyes of the community, even beyond the reach of the drug barons. And family and friends, contented with such treatment, just like him, could leave the grave-yard sad and grieving at the deep loss, but knowing the decent people of the community wanted to share the hurt with them. Realizing in the very defeat of death, they, as a strong community, had banded together to claim some fleeting victory. That this spirit was free to rest.

This was why we forged extended families on the island. Why some of my fondest memories are of evenings in that house in the graveyard, of my father and the grave digger talking, arguing and singing. I remember particularly Old Man Spencer strumming his guitar and improvising those sweet songs and melodies, and our mothers joining in and we all just singing. Sometimes I got to give a good lick or two, solo or in a duet with Mr. Spencer, the real singer. Only once can I recall Thelma taking centre stage, belting out those fiery, throaty ballads, scatting just like everyone said she could, and that was on a very special night.

It was a night of triumph for Thelma, even if her husband did not realize it. It was the genesis of what made Jeffrey the man he became. Even if he was not happy being his father's son there was no denying he was his mother's child. Although he seldom talked about those times, I know Jeffrey must have remembered them, too, even if they were memories he chose not to cherish. For as he explained to me, he had moved on. If I wanted to be like him, and I could by following his example, I must move on. He promised to show me the way to success. And, oh my brothers and sisters, I wanted that success.

The younger grave diggers, even his assistant Othneil, who was all but ready to take over from Aubrey, didn't fully understand this tradition of honouring a lived life. Nor would they act to suit. Othneil was ready and capable physically but not mentally or intuitively. Like the people of this younger generation—Aubrey would tell my father, who was of the same mind—a generation that could think only about making an extra dollar, or of putting another bath in the house, or of building a great big house. They could not understand the symbolism of these things, not when they were so adrift from their moorings.

The same way they didn't fully realize there was a message in everything: in living and in dying; in the way to throw dirt on a grave; in the songs to sing. There is a special way of burying the beloved. That difference was marked by the way he would dump the dirt over the box of a known villain, someone the people were proud to be rid of finally, and by the way he would soothingly and lovingly caress the body and casket of someone whose passing made them all grieve.

When Aubrey Spencer was in one of his moods, he would sit talking to himself, unmindful of whoever listened. Talking as if interceding or explaining to his god or ancestors, those to whom he felt ultimately accountable. Mumbling as if in open debate over what should be written in judgement and with how much severity. Invariably, the conversation with himself would come around, frustrating for him, to the inevitability, and not necessarily the futility, of it all. Of life. A passing phase. As full of contradictions as promises. A blink of the eyes. He could be morose, or he could be lighthearted, but in either case he understood death and the need for peace and rest. Maybe that was why his friend the prime minister sometimes talked about leaving a mark in life. A signal of the passages among the living and acceptance amid the chosen, elevation to the status of elder specially garlanded and acknowledged, the statement on his tombstone more of a testimony of an inheritance, of his social value, a kind of bank book testifying to all that he had saved, invested and left for another generation. So his living was not in vain.

Brenda would listen and tease him and ultimately decide his mood, lovingly manipulating his spirits. Aubrey Spencer never expected she would fall into his hands. She was so full of life; of laughter, hope and inspiration. She was the future and he dealt only with the past, and the two should never be the same. Each should have its own time and tradition, as was traditional. And he loved her so much. When she did come his way, he did the only thing a simple grave digger could do: send her off with the best burial while hoping some historian made a note. And he cried, even before the heavens started, and wished it were different and that the past did not have to rain on the future.

O n the outside, as I am compelled to recall, Jeffrey Spencer was defiantly proud. Oh how I remember him for most of that night. His house was holding strong, this house that was so much like him: big, strong and portentous. From inside these solid walls, he should have felt safe and secure. But that night there were also the doubts, and spirits that disturbed him in his bedroom.

Listening, I heard his accounting, as he roamed the room, banged on the bureau, shouted at the wind and challenged the night. For some things, he pleaded, he could not be held responsible, or, at least, not fully. "Let me explain," cried the voice muffled in the wind. "You have to hear me. Mitigation. Mitigation. Time. Time. Time." With these excuses, only Jeffrey knew if, indeed, he had tried his best.

Only he would know why he offered this pact for a new beginning. Brenda's dreams must live on, he promised the winds. And, if the dead should be honoured, only the living can be saved. Her sacrifice must be worth something, more than the giving up of herself in place of so many others. Decisions outside his realm and influence were not his to make, neither was he always aware of the thinking or the specific reason for any action. Sometimes, he was simply told, and this time no one had said anything to him. Not one solitary word. And, besides, he would never have hurt Brenda, or allowed anyone to do so. He was absolutely confi-

dent of that. For why would anyone think him such a beast? A woman in whose arms he slept so peacefully, even the night before she disappeared.

Although Jeffrey had not made any admission to her, he was now willing to concede that he must get out as soon as possible. But it must be the right moment to walk away, to say enough, time to stop gambling. He just needed time to adjust to the world, to learn to listen to his father again, without appearing to be too old, a conservative in young men's clothes, a traitor to the dreams of the youth. Brenda and the youths: were they not now joined as one? he asked. And if he worked with them, for that was all the material now left him, wasn't he also keeping her alive, nourishing her dreamers, nurturing her dreamers and, in them, claiming the same future as her? Wasn't he? he asked. Wasn't he? Weren't we? Why I still believed what I heard, I don't know. Maybe I still wanted him to make the right decisions not only for himself, but for me too. I told myself that he would not have known; he would not have agreed; he wouldn't have. No, no, no, not him. For he was my man, Jeffrey Spencer. From a little boy, he would always proudly find the way out, and I inevitably would trail him to the exit. Still, in the end, when all is counted and tallied, when allowances and discounts are factored in, he would always, yes always, find a way out. And in the nick of time, yes he always did. That was how he stayed. Timing was everything, his very essence. And I believed.

First came the knock. Startled, I looked at Jeffrey and before either of us could answer, the bedroom door flew open. In walked my father and Mr. Spencer. We were caught in the act.

"Edmund," my father said sternly. "I thought we told you that there would be no more *sweeties* for you. Not until you have served out your punishment."

"Yes, Dad," I answered.

"And you know what happens to little boys who misbehave and do not listen?"

"Yes, Dad."

"And I thought your mother and I told you that if you broke this promise that we would not let Jeffrey come over to play with you. Not until your punishment is past. Didn't we agree to that?"

"Yes, Dad."

"And, Edmund, didn't we tell you that you have to learn a lesson about breaking rules? A lesson about wanting to *obey* rules, for it is better in the end to obey than to break the rules and have to be punished. Didn't we, Son?"

"Yes, Dad."

"So why are you breaking the rules about the sweeties?"

"He didn't, sir." I heard that voice. I couldn't believe it.

"Jeffrey," Mr. Spencer said. "You be careful now. Watch what you're saying. Otherwise, you too could find yourself in trouble."

"But it's the truth, Dad. Edmund is telling the truth. These sweeties are my own. I got them from Auntie Esmay."

"Oh, really," my father said.

"She gave me a packet. You can ask her."

"Now. Now. Now," Mr. Spencer said. "*Jeffrey…*"

"Look, I have the box right here. She gave it to me. I was just showing Edmund, and we were *counting* to see if what they say on the outside of the box is right.

If there are forty pieces in every box. I swear, sir, we didn't even eat any."

"Obviously, you couldn't have," my father said. "Not to have so many left."

My heart sank. It was true that my mother had given him a box of candy, the very box he was holding up as evidence. She had taken it from the plate where she kept all the candy she offered to the children visiting our home when their parents came to talk to my father. And she would also take from the plate the boxes of candy for children attending confirmation classes, especially those she felt deserving of a reward. She had rewarded Jeffrey for being a good friend, for helping me to learn my lesson by coming to spend time with me, for sharing in a punishment that was not his. Jeffrey had taken the box from her and put it in his pocket, and with my mother turning to talk to Jeffrey, I had quickly slid a packet into my pocket. And it was also true that we had not eaten any of the candy, for we were playing first, intending to eat later, or at least for one of us to eat the contents of all the packets, later when one of us would be celebrating. We had emptied our packets on the desk in front of us and were competing to see who would win the combined bundles, who would eat the whole pile, unifying his and mine while the other looked on. Hardly had we tossed the coin a dozen times when the door opened and in walked our fathers.

"So, were they forty in the box?" Mr. Spencer asked.

"We don't know, Dad. We were going to count them just now."

"Jeffrey, anybody can see that there are more than enough sweeties on that desk to full up more than that box you're showing me," his dad said. "So come on.

What are you telling the two of us? You can't get all of those inside that little box."

"But it's true," Jeffrey maintained. I could now see even greater trouble coming. I wanted to speak up, to be spared an extended punishment. But I also didn't want to put Jeffrey in trouble. I didn't want to give his father a chance to say that he was growing tired of telling Jeffrey that he should become more like me, that he should always tell the truth, that he must be willing to learn his lessons by taking his punishment instead of avoiding it, instead of talking his way out, that he could not expect to grow up thinking that there was always a way to avoid paying the full penalty. Jeffrey glanced at me, and I saw the warning in his eyes. But I wanted to speak so badly.

"Edmund and Jeffrey," my father said, "it seems like both of you are now in trouble. Edmund, your mother and I specifically said no sweets for you. Yet it appears as if you had a box of sweets yourself. From where you got it I don't want to guess, but I sincerely hope it was not from the candy tray. That would be stealing, and the eighth commandment says: Thou shall not steal. But more than that, you were gambling. Not very good decisions to limit your chances, to bet on just one outcome in the face of so many combinations and permutations that are the fullness of life. Remember, we, Mr. Spencer and I, too were young. Every schoolboy in our times used to play the same game. It's not new. I only have to take one look at the two piles in front of both of you and at the one in the centre, the pot for the winnings. The signs are there for everyone to see."

"Yes, Dad," I stammered. "I mean, no, Dad. No, Dad."

"It doesn't have to be that way," Jeffrey interceded. "It could be different."

"And Jeffrey," my father said, "you know what we think about lying. Don't you?"

"Yes, sir."

"So do you still claim that all those pieces might have been in one box?"

"Yes, sir."

"Okay," my father said. "Let's prove it: trying putting them back into the box, if indeed, they did come from the box."

By then I was ready to confess. We had gambled and lost. I could hear him reaching over and drawing to his side of the table the pieces in front of me, and the pieces in the pool, adding them to his, the final step before judgement would be announced on both of us. And it was Jeffrey's fault. I could feel the tears welling up in my eyes as I squeezed them tighter. It would have been so much easier and, perhaps, less costly to have told the truth upfront. For how could the container hold more than the true contents? It's not natural. Now, I thought, it would only be worse for me, naturally. And then he would laugh at me for crying.

"See," Jeffrey declared, triumphantly. It was the sound of victory in his voice that caused me to risk opening my eyes. The desk was empty. The stuffed, bulging box was in the centre, where the pool would have been. Our fathers looked at each other.

"I see," my father said.

"I see, too," Mr. Spencer said. I was sure I even detected a new pride in his tone. "Anyway, you two try and be careful now."

"And, Edmund," my father said. "You are still not allowed to eat any of those sweets, you hear me?"

"Yes, Dad."

Then they were gone. It was in that moment that I really started believing in magic and in Jeffrey. I had learned that I should not doubt him, no matter the odds. And to think I almost ruined everything by speaking out of turn. I remember: that candy was the sweetest ever. And I remember, too, that try as I could, I could never recall what happened to the second box. How could that piece of evidence just disappeared? Maybe the magician took care of that too.

He had built the house since his mother's death and his return from North America. As one version goes, it was built like the homes he wished for but couldn't own at the better addresses of Toronto, New York, Miami or Beverly Hills. It had three levels, a fully furnished basement and a large indoor Olympic-size swimming pool. It had wet bars on each floor and near the pool, rooms crammed full of African art and sculptures, exotic European paintings and trendy Asian artefacts, and the most expensive electronic and audio system he could import. He had it all. Even the latest security devices attached to every window and door, monitoring systems that chime *bing-bing-bing-bing* so ominously at the cracking open of a window, the opening of door. This was not natural to houses in this land. All this security, the monitoring and the ominous wrought iron bars — prison bars even on your bedroom windows! A camp, and fortified, too. Such unnatural foreignness! His father detested the strange feeling of always being watched, of not being in control of his own space and movements. In the middle of the night, he could not even risk going to the bathroom without setting off some stupid alarm. He could not feel free and at home, but an intruder, even a thief. This constant reminder that, like the sheep tied out in the pasture, the pigs in the sty, he could roam only as far as the end of the rope around his neck, or within the boundaries of a pen. Perhaps that was the way other people lived, but Old Man Spencer was adamant he couldn't, that his skin would never stop crawling at the very thought of such imprisonment.

"I don't know how you can live so," the old man had said. "Your mother and me didn't raise you to live like this. A man shouldn't be a prisoner in his own house. That's why I like my little old shack."

Then there was the radio, perhaps only fractionally less intrusive than the security system. It could monitor just about anything broadcast in the area, even coded aircraft and military communications. Jeffrey spent hours fiddling with the dials and the knobs and then making his long-distance telephone calls. The big house was his home and his office, the place where he received people on business and where he entertained them. From here he ran the affairs of the nation's airline and his lucrative offshore brokerage business.

On a night like the one that haunts us, the house offered his father the safety that couldn't be found in the old wooden shack the church had built decades ago. The same way his foreign connections gave him political clout and financial protection, the like of which Jeffrey could never have dreamt before he got into the business, and which his father would never ever be able to understand. It was the biggest house in Lodge Road, built on land that until Jeffrey's return was an old sugar cane field. Those unproductive fields, the embodiment of servitude and proscribed dreams, were to be put to better use. Yes, Jeffrey had big ideas and plans for that part of the island—dreams with which he wanted to dazzle his father and prove his way the right one.

Nobody could miss this house nor overlook the rows of cars usually parked in the driveway for his parties. The house was pink, just like the great Spanish haciendas he had visited in Florida, right down to the iron bars and the satellite dish on the roof. The colour stood out against the greenery of the background vegetation. Last Christmas, he and Brenda had decorated the plum and cherry trees that grew near the front door, and even the large ackee trees on the edge of the property. They had strung them with rows of colourful lights Jeffrey had brought from Canada. Then they had invited the children from the neighbourhood to join them at the lighting.

Brenda had asked Jeffrey to play Santa Claus. After all, he had lived in Canada, she joked, lived as close as anyone she knew to the North Pole. The children from the vicinity had stood transfixed, their eyes wide open and mouths gaping, watching the lights. For they had never seen anything like this before that was not on TV or in the cinema. And Brenda was happy because the children were happy. And his father was pleased and contented—at least for the one day—because Brenda was happy. They had all stood in the road, sipping the rum-spiked sorrel and singing Christmas carols. This was their best Christmas in a long time and Brenda and his father said so repeatedly.

From the way his father was sitting in the darkness and talking, Jeffrey could tell the old man was also thinking about

100

Thelma, his mother, and how even in her death she had returned to him a son.

The old man had told my father that he knew that people thought he should be glad to have such a caring son, someone with such esteem and social standing. For didn't their holy book say blessed is the child who honours his father and mother. But he could not be happy, not with a son who rejected everything that he and my father had struggled to achieve, who now expected him to worship not only false but foreign idols. Why should his son behave like a historian from a foreign country coming among the people and discovering there was nothing worthy to record, nothing to write about, all because the barbarian did not have the essence in his blood, did not understand?

Whenever he allowed such thoughts, Aubrey got angry – for permitting himself dreams, as if he were a boy again and not seasoned by experience and tragedies. For still searching for ways of bringing the frayed ends together, and for visiting his son and his great house. He knew that he was all too human and that he saw the approaching day of no return. But he could not bring himself to lift a hand, and in so doing to bring down his only son.

I remember, too, brothers and sisters, that we always travelled a lot, Jeffrey and I. Lonely trips, with just the two of us alone in the first class sections or even on the entire plane. These times always seemed to make him feel despondent, suspended, causing him to want to talk and confide. And since I was usually the only one around, he confided in me, even the most intimate matters, and as usual, I was a good listener, seldom even speaking back, just letting his thoughts ramble

101

and bounce off me. Such passivity was second nature to me, brothers and sisters.

So I knew from him that Brenda was one of the few women he felt he had really loved, the way his father loved his mother, the way a strong man always gives in to a woman who somehow has his code. This was an astonishing admission. In the three years he had been home, ostensibly to be the director of Prime Minister Watkins's ministry of tourism, and during the ten years he had spent travelling the world, he had had no shortage of women. He had prestige as the chairman of the island's airline, he had power and the handsome broad-nose looks that complemented authority, something in his mind like a legendary Toussaint. Around the time of the hurricane, he was finally beginning to enjoy himself and to demand more from the power and influence he was accumulating. He boasted that he was the only person on the island that could pick up the phone any hour of the day or night and call the prime minister and expect, in fact demand, an answer. And he now had money, enough to keep any woman happy or to give her whatever she wanted. And he had picked Brenda—or was it the good in her that had picked him—only to find that she didn't want any of it.

In the stream of words that were typical of these moods, my brothers, Jeffrey told me his achievements were also mine and that of all other dreamers like us— the poor boy who made good up North and actually returned to live among his people and to show them the way. To teach us, but this time to show us what can be done without having to go abroad, without having to choose between a father who wanted his son to stay on the island and a mother who had demanded, insisted and even fought her husband, for him to go abroad.

He could have remained overseas until he was old, decrepit and washed out, dreaming of coming back to die, forever chasing an elusive dream in a strange land, never having to make a real choice. Instead, he came back. And when he could have gone to any island in the Caribbean, he chose to make a point by returning to the same village in which we were born. He came back home. To the father he had left. To himself, really. For, indeed, this king is not without honour, not even in his village. He wanted to make up with his father. Not to find succour or balm for his wounds, but to make a difference. To show by example and, still forced to walk in his mother's footsteps, to bring back home all he had dreamt and achieved up North. To please his father and, at the same time, to respect his mother's memory in a final reconciliation. And, he boasted, he came back as a young man, to boot. Strong, healthy and secure, and unlike so many others, without a criminal record, without first having been rejected and thrown back, like all those unsuitable immigrants. But in his relationship with Brenda he ended up perpetuating the struggle of his mother and father, as if condemned to be his father all over again, and Brenda, his triumphant mother. Torn by the conflicts of seeking a victory and of securing a peace. Vindicating one side while loving the other, all at the same time. That was why he joined Brenda in the quest to bring the best to the schools, to have that special academy that would unify the dreams of a father and a mother like his. He would reconcile the actors and the characters, and he would produce a new ending. For this reason, he and I hardly ever went to a foreign land without making inquiries or returning with boxes of books and supplies for the school they were planning.

It was the heaviest of ironies, but he never saw it. And that is why, I believe, that especially on trips abroad he had resumed his search for the right woman, ironically, so much like his father and so different from what he was now telling me, for what he could not find at home. Perhaps, Brenda knew this too, she knew he had resumed looking, but as the mother of dreams she said nothing publicly. For, she must have believe, the time was not yet right.

In the time following his return, as with any rebirth, I guess, Jeffrey found out that just about everybody trusted him. And that included me, his executive assistant. I was fascinated, intoxicated really, as he peeled away more of the layers around him, promising he would show me how to be successful like him, how not to be poor or powerless. He encouraged me to pursue gospel music, a compromise between preaching and my urge to sing. There was pure music in my voice, he said, especially when I used the full range, when I dropped low as in whisper, when I bellowed rough and sublime as if reaching for the skies. There was that range. I had it, he said. A painful, hurting but sweet music that reminded him of gospel music, a commingling of jazz and blues and calypso and reggae. Even rap and hip hop. The gospel that the good news has already arrived. The time had come. The young and the old; the classics and the emerging. I could speak to them all, and like them all. Gospel would provide my own reconciliation. And he would guide me to this peace. He knew some of the world's top promoters and producers and would gladly introduce me to them, would tell them I was like a brother to him. He even knew the investors, too. Stick with him, he said, and he would hook me up good. I trusted him. Everyone did, except in the end Brenda and, perhaps, his own father, the two people he so badly wanted to impress, but somehow just couldn't reach. The main characters in his play would not agree to his changes.

The relationship with his father was understandable, I had told him, the same as that of my father and me. But such differences were perfectly natural. We shouldn't fret up our heads over such things, I joked. I was sure our fathers before us had similar disagreements with their fathers, as our children should have with us. That is how a people grow, by challenging the previous generation's achievements and viewing them as stepping stones on the way to greater successes, not by tilling the same old ground over and over, reaching for goals set by another generation. Jeffrey believed this, and I, too, to appease him offered it back to him.

Brenda was different. Somehow, she always managed to appear aloof and unconquerable. Too strong, especially to him, and I think he secretly feared her. He could never account for why Brenda challenged him but acquiesced so easily to his father. Who had changed: the women of the modern generation, his father, or just he who had gone abroad and seen things differently? He would not solve this puzzle until too late, and the search for answers had ensnared us all.

Still, this subterranean conflict with Brenda was what drew him to her, especially when he saw her with groups of barefoot school children playing in the school yard, all of them seemingly under her control. His mother too had cared for the barefoot youths, dreaming big things for the one that always clung to her dress. Fifteen or twenty years earlier, he could have been any

105

of the boys, barefoot and with only a dream that had been placed in his mind. He liked the way Brenda treated the children. How she helped create dreams and placed them in their minds. And speaking as man-to-man, whether to boast or simply to acknowledge limits that only men can know, he told me that definitely no other women had ever appealed to him the way Brenda did. Certainly not in bed. None of them could get his body to shudder, or his entire guts to turn to jelly, to cause big goose pimples to rise on his back and on his arms, and for the hair on his head to feel as if they were singularly and individually rising on ends. This is what she could get out of him, almost at will, when she ran the tips of her slender fingernails along his lean body. Or when she licked his ears with her tongue and rubbed the tip of his penis on the soft inner parts of her thighs. By the time he entered her, he would be mourning and breathing so loudly, he would uncontrollably spoil this battle of wills by climaxing too quickly. Frustratingly, that was the way it was the first several times, before both of them learned how to control him and to extend their mutual pleasure.

This feeling of helplessness made him so angry and impotent. Like he had learned nothing from all the previous women, from mastering life in other places and cultures, as if he were a mere puppet in her hands. Not a man like his father, for he had to concede that his father had controlled his mother. He had been in charge, even if she had won the odd battle. Jeffrey saw this as another factor that showed him to be less than his father. For his father had set boundaries, even for his mother, and then for him. So he continuously fought with Brenda, rejecting her while clinging to her. All the while cussing himself for being so helpless and so easily manipulated. Of seeing himself perpetually as just a barefoot boy in her eyes, no matter how much others venerated him.

It wasn't because making love with her was so great, it was that she had such unacceptable control over his body. The same kind of mystical control she had over the children and, of course, his father. Eventually, she would make a grab for absolute control of his mind. And she would lose: for she had to lose, failing badly as he awakened and broke free just in time. For there was no way she could win, could be allowed to win this battle, and yet for him to be strong. In the end how he saw himself, not how others saw him, was what really mattered. And he did not like his reflection in her eyes but he was not prepared to change. And perhaps that was what did her in. In a moment when he was not vigilant and she was, perhaps, too aloof to condescend, to ask his help and even shelter. When he looked the other way, he allowed the evil he thought he controlled to clip its bonds, enter his island and take his woman. It was the moment Jeffrey Spencer lost control of events.

Hear my testimony, my friends. Yes, I must witness. How they quarrelled so frequently. Nothing too serious at first, but Jeffrey complained that with time she started to push, to speak about the horror of her discovery, and about willingly inviting a blight on the future. Brenda kept saying that he, as the director of tourism, as a government official, and as role model, as a man who supposedly knows different, who said he had come back to show the way, that he should do something, that he was obligated to do something, that he be a positive example to the youth. Yes, brothers and sisters, that is what he told me that she told him.

How he should be helping the children to dream. Even when he protested angrily, she would not relent, saying that to accept things his way would compromise her principles. She would continue to fight to change him, the one area in which she would not adjust or accept defeat, the same way she would fight tenaciously to keep the deadly drugs out of her school and to build the gymnasium for the children. There could be no reconciliation.

Then she was gone. Snuffed out just a few yards from the same school she tried so hard to protect, her life extinguished like a roach. We had searched high and low without finding a trace of her. Only when her body started to smell did we find her in the cane fields. A group of her students on their way to school one morning had smelled something they described as *funny* and had seen what looked like a blue dress in the brown dried trash from the canes. When they investigated, they got the fright of their lives.

The police were quick to the scene, as if they were anticipating the call. They covered the body haphazardly with a white sheet, piled white lime disinfectant on the spot, and brought it out of the field on a canvas stretcher. The autopsy was held the same day. Even before the results were official, everyone knew how Brenda had died, how she had suffered. In keeping with the now familiar tradition, her throat was cut — from ear to ear, her tongue pulled through the opening — the surest message of what happens to informers. The price for not cooperating. The cost for messing with the drug barons.

This time the police didn't even bother to issue the usual statement of how hard they were investigating, of how concerned they were with the escalating violence visiting the island. In any case, nobody would have believed them.

❧

"That's mine," I had shouted at the first sight of the big red Chevrolet driving by.

"Mine," Jeffrey claimed, pointing to the hotel.

"And mine," I said, touching the big tree. It was tall with many branches, the leaves broad and sensuous to the touch. But what I remember most were the red flowers at the end of the branches, some nestling in the leaves, some on the ground and on the road that ran underneath the branches to the entrance of the building. And I remember the seeds on the ground. Hard and black, strong, just like the bark of the tree. Like some of the long roots that ran above the ground and then buried themselves deep within. Looking up, I saw all that I owned: the branches and the leaves through which I could see the cloudless blue sky so far away, but all mine, the green leaves, spread like a blanket to offer enticing shade, the flowers, some buds breaking free, some in full bloom, others withered on top of a whitish bulb, the pod that contained the seeds that would fall to the ground. It was all mine.

"That's a good one," Jeffrey conceded. And I smiled. It was a rare occasion that I won. "Come here. Give me your hand and let's cross the road."

Joined as one against the dangers of the traffic, we walked from the playing field and the majesty of my tree onto the road and crossed over to the beach, where our mothers were already in the water.

"That's a good one," he repeated uncharacteristically. "The cordea tree. Very strong. And pretty too. The flowers. Always a good sign, the flowers."

109

But by then, I had also learned not to be lulled into a sense of security with my bigger buddy, Jeffrey. He was not only older, but he was smarter and could run faster. It was always hard for me to catch up. Already, he knew so much. As soon as we had crossed over the road, I resumed staking my claims.

"That's mine," I shouted, pointing to the spreading almond tree. I knew it had to be my lucky day. First the cordea and now the almond tree with all the yellow almonds so easily in reach. We loved the almonds. We loved to stuff our pockets with them, all the big fleshy ones, and we would take them into the water. We would dip them into the salt water and eat the flesh, dipping them before each bite, revelling in the salt and sweet all at once, the hot sun beaming down on us, the right feeling of cool water and heat. If we felt generous enough we would offer one or two almonds, but no more, to our mothers. Then, with the almonds reduced to their hard inner casing, we would pile them on the beach, beside a slab of concrete, with two handy stones, and we would bathe in the surf, riding the waves, ducking each other and creating such a commotion that our mothers would have to call to us.

"You boys don't swim too far out there!" my mother would call.

"Jeffrey, you is the *biggest* one," his mother would shout. "You be careful now. Be the example."

And after a swim, we would come to the slab of concrete and we would crack open the almonds, along with all the dried ones we had collected from under the trees. We would eat as many of the nuts as we could. Nuts that were long and thin and wet, not like those ugly hard and dried-up ones my father brought home occasionally in a tin. Nuts that my mother used only when she was grinding them for the Christmas great cake with all the various fruits and nuts that she soaked in rum. These almonds, directly from the trees, picked by our own hands, were important and these were mine because of my uncontested claim.

But I had exhausted my choice in that round and I knew there were still many more prized options. Such as the sea grapes. On another day, I might have gone this route, but today I had a different inclination. Already the sea grapes were bunching on the trees, big purple bunches, looking just like the real grapes we saw in pictures and in the fancy supermarkets with the green apples from beyond our shores. In fact, these were the favourites of our mothers. While they might take an almond or two, they would pick bunches of the grapes from the trees, eat the thin skin encasing the sweet juice and spit the seeds that were as big as small stones into the water. Eventually, there would be a flotilla of seeds drifting on the water between our mothers. The grapes would have been my next choice. But I just knew it would be Jeffrey's pick.

"That's mine," he shouted, pointing towards the sea and away from the sea grape trees. "That tree is mine."

"What tree?" I asked. "I don't see no tree that you can eat from."

"That one over there. The big, tall one." He pointed. "Can't you see? The tallest tree over there, over by the chairs. You can't miss it. With all the leaves and them little green things on it."

"But I never see nobody eating them yet," I said.

"Sure they can. Let me show you. Look at all them things that look like little apples. When you pick them they give you milk. Look!"

Jeffrey ran to the tree and started to collect the green fruits on the ground. I tried to be one better than him. I picked all the fruits that were in reach, with no concern for the milk. And I am sure I saw Jeffrey pick up the fruits, put them in his mouth, bite into them, chew and swallow. So as not to be outdone, and so he could not eventually claim to have eaten more from my tree than I did from his, I ate as many as I could, desperately ignoring the increasing sting and the itch and the burning.

"What you two doing there?" his mother shouted. "Come away from that tree this very minute. Don't you know you shouldn't play with manchineels. Stay away from that manchineel tree, you hear me."

We walked away and went into the water some distance from our mothers. But the stinging, itching and burning were too much. I had to tell my mother. By the time we got home, the blisters were severe. On my hands, my back and chest, my legs and feet and on my palms. But most painful were the blisters on my mouth, particularly my lips and on the inside.

"You should know that the manchineel tree is poisonous," my father told me that night. "Not all trees are good; not all trees are evil. You have to know which is which when you choose. Stay away from the manchineels. Remember, it is big and beautiful, all right, but I don't think it ever gives a flower."

To this day, I don't recall ever seeing one blister on Jeffrey. Many years later, as we sat in the plane travelling back home, I recalled the incident for him and he laughed. And at least, this time, he didn't accuse me of making up any of my memory. Curious, and now able to ask him, I said: "How come you didn't get any blisters?"

112

"Maybe," he said after a long pause, "maybe, because I am different. Or maybe because I did something that you didn't do."

I wanted to ask him directly if the difference was that he had not *eaten* of the tree or had not actually *picked* the fruits, if the difference was merely in the doing and not so much in the thinking or even naming, if the difference was that things were not always as they appeared, that we can never be absolutely certain about anything, but I didn't. Instead, I asked more generally, what did you do?

"I claimed the tree, remember," he said. "I took mastery over it. I made it mine. I took the right to control it and to give it up and walk away whenever I wanted."

I remember, I said.

◎◎

And then it all came crumbling down, and at so great a price. Not only on the two of us, but on the very people Jeffrey himself had tried to protect. Caused by the very thing that we all refused to name, refused to question, refused to let slip from our mouth. The nameless phenomenon whose presence we felt but whose existence we could not identify lest we gave it life and substance. Without a name, perhaps, we hoped it would go away. Our fears would not be confirmed. We would not give it life and form. Not one word. For collectively and individually, we all knew what it was like when you look at the broken body under the shroud only to see that it is yours and that you cannot awake for the body could no longer breathe and talk, and sing. And that the dream is unending.

For despite all the many versions, all the beginnings, all the various sources, the indisputable fact remained: Brenda Watts had kept an untimely date with Aubrey Spencer. As predicted by the music; as foretold by the first bars, the first chords, the first screams. The same ending, the same accounting. Time had arrived and had also stopped, the future ended and collapsed into the present, time that robbed us of innocence and demanded responsibility, that cared nothing about our wishes and intentions, and which, for a healing and exoneration, could only be mended by time and the threads of traditions long established and verified. We could turn only to the ways of the old, for they are the parents of this time. And that is why we always have to linger on this event, why we must always return, to name it in the hope of fixing it and making it powerless. To let it rest. Why we must constantly repeat ourselves, trying all the different methods and approaches for a true accounting, looking for what might have been overlooked, erased or left out, but eventually, all coming inevitably to a recognition of what really happened. So that our narrative can move on. Conjoined. When all voices become one. Just one story. One version. One voice. With the connected and the in between shaded in, accounted for, and uplifted. The music once started, the course now set must play out inevitably to its own ending. One song.

Perhaps, only Aubrey Spencer understood. For this was one of the times the old grave digger wished his calling was not to administer the last rites to the people around him, to see the wooden casket lowered gently into the ugly, insatiable hole he had finished digging only hours earlier. Then, as his best friend, the priest, my father, intoned his final prayers, and the scores of mourners lifted their quavering voices in final song, even higher than the tall, slim casaurina trees with the fidgeting birds in them – when the male members of this extended family had finished lowering the box into the rich earth and released the brown leather canvas straps from their trembling hands – he had unobtrusively stepped forward. He named himself. He took the responsibility, or indeed, he let it claim him, gave it a body and a specific time and place.

Old Man Spencer removed the four flat slabs of board around the gaping hole and gently threw them to a side, making sure the boards did not drop one on the other. Such indiscriminately clanking sounds, like the tolling bell in the church steeple, would further remind the mourners of their own inevitability. It would moreover disrupt the natural rhythm of life and death. Debauch the timing and transition. For there would have been no interim, no pause to reflect, no silence when the lingering music is still fresh in the mind.

On special occasions, Aubrey took handfuls of grass. Earlier they had been all wet from the rains that preceded the hurricane. But the rain had stopped long enough for us to gather and for him to drop the grass onto the box in the hole. In this way, he could muffle the sounds of the big boulders, of heavy and unbroken clumps of earth, crashing down and banging on the casket. No, there could be no big bang, just a calming and pleasant whimper. For we are human only. Nothing like that for a crescendo, an attempt at which would be so ill-timed and anarchical. Just a soft recommittal to that from which Brenda had come forth once, and with such violence. Kicking, screaming and bawling. She might have been abused and defiled in life; she would not, like some adulterer of old, be stoned in death.

He knew these things and their powerful meanings, and without speaking, he acted. So that no one could say he – a blasted grave digger of only God knew how many years, who should know how to put down the dead peacefully and

115

decently — was being disrespectful to the departed and to the weeping family left behind. That he was sitting in sullen judgement. Being violent. Or that he was biased, unfit for the job because of something he didn't know for sure and which, for his preservation, nobody would voluntarily confirm nor deny. Or above all, that his judging, so violent and disproportionate, was doing everything possible to exonerate his son, if indeed, exculpation was needed. Or that he was antagonistically hurrying along the mourners. So that he won't have to face up to anything, would not have them around to linger and to remind. Showing him there could be no forgiveness. No forgetting, either. Holding him in judgement. Condemning in sentence and in silence. So that in passing judgement he won't also be judging himself.

This would not be Aubrey's choice, so he painstakingly made the only decisions possible, to show how he felt, even as he knew there was no way he could ever change the outcome. With speed that belied his bent back and heavy age, he hacked away at the mound of freshly dug dirt around the mouth of the grave. Using the hoe, with a wooden handle no more than three feet long, and working from a crouch, he meticulously filled the hole with the black, clogged dirt, carefully and as slowly as he could while still hurrying, just for Brenda. That was all he could do, given the circumstances, given his role and limitations, given his doubts. And given his sentence.

Then the full ramifications dawned on him, the grave digger. How in naming himself, he might have decided who should accept the cup of the bitterest gall. And his hands trembled; his heart fluttered. For the first time since he had buried his wife, Thelma, three years almost to the day, he knew in the depths of his heart that this job rightfully belonged to someone else, to one of those who simply saw the workings differently, as just a money-making occupation, of just understanding machines that dig holes and then dispose

116

of bodies, with the press of a button causing all to descend and disappear. Maybe it was thinking of what had happened before the funeral that slowed him right down, made him feel his age, an old man, feeling resigned. Or, maybe, it was the unspeakable fear in the pit of his guts that there was at least one person in the entire world with whom he absolutely and utterly did not want to keep such a date. Never. Ever. Not me, Lord God.

Whatever it was, this realization caused him to take almost fifteen torturous minutes to close the hole, a job that usually took him about ten minutes (Thelma's lasted thirteen) and on a good day a mere seven or eight. He felt cursed, as if the entire land was damned, now he, an aged man, was burying with such repetition children, mere children. Repetition. For what else could he call people like Brenda, but children, the future, who could very well be his own offspring or the mothers of his grandchildren? Wasn't it said blessed is the man that sees his grandchildren and is buried by his offspring? Of knowing he had kept the only real promise demanded of any of us by our humanity, that he had helped and contributed to saving us all from returning all together, and for the very last time, to that from which we came, from the very beginning, from the fire and the water, erased, to the nothingness this last time, and forever. That for at least one more generation there would be the good from the merging of these elements. For at least one more generation, his, and all the promises he had inherited, had been kept, insured and handed on for a legacy. The very reason for which he was born, for which there was ever a beginning. A promise to part the water and the fire by binding them together in the right proportions. So that he can go to sleep knowing all was well, at least for this time. As he confided in my dad, there is no joy in burying anyone's children, most of all your own.

And if he needed a signal he was right to think this way, it came as soon as he had taken from Mother Enid Watts the special bunch of flowers. They were red and pink roses, carnations and green ferns neatly intertwined in a wreath. He laid them carefully at the head of the grave. Just like so. He laid them out, sweet and pretty. Tender as the night. With this final act, Mrs. Watts was once again overcome by heavy grief from losing an only child. Had it not been for the presence of the men, she would have swooned onto the grave, onto the fresh flowers mourners were heaping on the distended mound. She knew she could not sleep peaceably, not now. Neither could any of them, for it was their child too.

And no sooner had the gravedigger placed the mother's wreath and tenderly adjusted some of the others to form a symbol of the cross, than the heavens opened. A strong chilling wind blew off the ocean. Cold and haunting; vengeful and vexed; hungry. There was salt on its breath, heavy and seemingly unslakeable. On the wind, with the first rains, with the waving of the treetops, judgement was being confirmed and exacted, the sentence executed, finally, the promise of the rainbow banished until another time, the plaques sent hurtling. Until a people had learned a lesson, until old men did not feel the need to cry and despair for the future. Until then the angels with flaming swords would guard the resting-place of the dead, banishing the sinful from the garden, refusing an entire people entry. I like to think the sword of one angel was my father's words. Jeffrey must have felt the same way about his father, and about his haunting, penetrating eyes.

By the time most of the mourners got home from Brenda Watts's funeral, they were thoroughly soaked. The rains had intensified, the winds were up, just as the radio bulletins had promised all day. Defiantly, Enid Watts had refused to put off the burial, not even when threatened by hurricane.

So, while Nature sat in judgement, the people had no choice but to put aside worldly things that otherwise would keep them occupied. Two by two, we went to the nearest ark. We took only the smells of the day's sacrifice with us, that peculiar mixing of soil and water lingering poignantly in our nostrils. And when we had all entered, even as I heard the howling voices jeering, even threatening to enter and to deal with us, I slammed the door shut. I bolted it. Who says anything about fairness, of why we should be inside so strong a fort while the innocent were on the outside? Who understands justice of this kind?

In the gloom, each by each, together, we had no choice but to sit in the darkness of the night and hear the words of judgement: the hurricane destroying everything around us. We knew we had to keep our arses quiet, lest the judgement be prolonged. And for contrition, to think of the devastation in all its forms that had befallen the little island, which had to be cleansed away. This was true even for Jeffrey. That night he could not avoid the talking shadows, far less silence them. Still, it was we who were safest in the strongest house ever built on the island and, as Jeffrey might have said, proving that any ending can be changed. What delusion! We would learn that it might be easy to begin an action but it is not always possible to influence what we have created or to end what we have started.

Perhaps now you understand why Jeffrey would make a promise on that night of the hurricane and why I would be tempted to believe him. It was not only for our sakes, but also for that of his father. And for the love of the dearly departed. It was a promise made in blood.

Then again, maybe this is true: without a plaque what is worth remembering? And aren't one-sided agreements usually negated at the first indication of changing fortunes, when all reminders of weakness can be forgotten? That a name named and surrendered under duress must ultimately be rescued and reprieved. The signature of defeat and capitulation must be erased at the first opportunity. Jeffrey, my brothers, believed so. No name; no word. And without a word, there can be no name. Yes, my sisters, he really did believe. Oh, yes, he did. His promise just melted away in the warmth of the next day's sun, for the danger was past now and strength had returned. He believed we were free to wrestle with the future without the handicaps of a forced commitment. How could I not have named what I feared and whose presence I suspected?

Now having seen this arrival from so many different angles, now perhaps you know why I have to keep seeking to purge myself before I can go on. These repetitions and reflections are necessary before we can arrive at a new beginning. Before the music can start all over again. Yes, in a life that's short, we have to press on: let the dead bury the dead, they say. And the ghosts and spectres, too. Name them, perhaps even in stone. Indeed. But in so doing, we also need to pause to honour the memory, too. My question, now, is how long should we have paused? How long do you tarry, oh Lord? Jeffrey didn't. And in the end, neither could I.

adagio

She was waiting for us in the bright late-afternoon sun as we made our way out of the immigration section of Aeropuerto Internacional El Dorado. Through an alcoholic haze, the result of the now empty twenty-six-ounce bottle of Old Brigand resting in the aisle of the plane, Jeffrey smiled at the slim woman. She was in faded blue jeans and a jacket, her straightened hair reaching down below her shoulders, big brown eyes sparkling in her face. She was walking briskly towards us out of the waiting crowd. Her eyes, he later told me, were what did it to him. I could only wonder if he saw the same thing that I did, or if we saw only what she wanted. For even then, I suspected the messages the two of us received were very different. We would recognize and relate to this stranger in our different ways.

"How was the flight, Mr. Spencer?" she asked in a perfect North American accent. This surprised us. And it was the voice that did it for me. Soft but bold and strong, and the intoxicating way she stressed some words, the inflexion and emphasis, as if she was chanting. A soft voice with a hint of laughter and a tantalizing sense of worldliness. A promise. So lyrical, as if floating on air. But for Jeffrey, it was the eyes. Always the eyes. He gave in to her perception of him. And she placed him. This and more he would concede when we

122

compared notes much later, but that first meeting was crucial, the sight of her coming towards us, as if materializing out of some different time and place, coming to meet us. And she won right away. No contest: for she knew with whom she was dealing; he did not. Over his shoulder I watched, making up my own mind, searching for a meaning, keeping my counsel, but listening to the voice. For me there was something strong and confrontational hanging in the hot, dry air, something disguised by the soft cool voice, and the eyes.

"Er... Fine, I guess," Jeffrey finally answered, staring at the long-legged woman, looking her over from head to the flat leather Spanish sandals on her feet. He allowed his eyes to linger longingly on the firm hips and thighs in the skin-tight jeans. He figured she was probably no more than twenty-five years old, but I sensed she was older. The same eyes that captured him were what alerted me to her true age. So brown and deep and haunting. Perhaps a testimony of experience; superior knowledge; of so many and different worlds; the same as a camera whose shutter has seen too many pictures. But, I would concede, still very mysterious, still so alluring.

As if indifferent to our reactions, she reached for the briefcase being held by the chief flight attendant, who had carried it from the plane. I watched the body language and listened. I knew I was not wrong with what I thought I was reading.

"What's your name, *Senorita?*" Jeffrey asked. "Seems like the boys really know how to make me feel welcome, eh?" They were standing face to face in front of the Avis Rent-A-Car counter, where some Americans were haggling noisily in snatches of English and Spanish. He could see the line of fine black hair above her mouth. When she returned his smile, her lips parted slowly, revealing teeth that were white and uniformly even. Her face was beautiful, the skin smooth and moist, without the slightest trace of makeup.

In some way, she reminded him of a revolutionary, too. For beneath the smile, even he could tell there was a hard edge, what he expected of a guerrilla fighting up in the hills. These were the people he never hoped to encounter. Modern-day savages: beyond the pale of any measurement of civility. Reading about them was enough. It was enough for him to fly into Bogotá and to fly back out as quickly as possible, never to linger in a land of such political savagery. He never felt comfortable. Underneath her beauty and the smile, he sensed toughness, as if she could just as easily be at home slipping into the jungle or underbrush with a rocket launcher over her shoulder as she was mingling with the airport crowd and holding his brown leather briefcase. When she moved, every muscle, every limb was in sync.

There was something loveable about her and something utterly frightening and threatening, like the land itself. The promise of a war held in check, of a truce, but not a stalemate for her sensuousness was obviously uncontainable. Not even in peace, or in the semblance of it. The body was the power and the glory, the temple holy and united, and she did not have to flaunt it: we just smelled it. And, yes, I can tell, even now brothers and sisters, what some of you are saying: so soon. I can hear the incredulity and disbelief. How could he forget; how could *they* not remember just two days earlier. Indeed, so soon. Jeffrey had to be aware of the appearance. But then let me, brothers and sisters, ask a few questions: how soon is too soon, especially if

124

you were already on the lookout? Tell me that, and truthfully. How do you know when your future will come forward to meet you, and should you simply say to it, brothers and sisters, no, no, no, not now. Go away, come again another day, because we don't want to play. Should we sing that song, because we are not allowed to play, not right now? Speak up and tell me, and in words that are true for all cases, for all times and seasons. So should we have waited, even if we knew that to wait and to remorsefully deny ourselves was to miss an opportunity? And for what: merely to keep up pretence, a disguise for the sake of a father? How free can you be, then? And how much is this kind of waiting just convention, tradition and ritual? Really, should we bind the future by waiting, by dead rituals, or should we celebrate life and the newest opportunities? Oh, tell me. And is this why our Messiah may never come, because we are always in mourning? Indeed, tell me, how long is too long if waiting it is the mere continuance of pretence and if even the dead knew the search had resumed. Who of us will not reach out and grab the future if he or she recognizes it? Otherwise, what use is hope and the promise of a new beginning? Tell me. For after all Jeffrey too was human. I know I was.

The ambivalence Jeffrey felt in her was the opposite of the immediate certainty and desire she produced in him. Like the spring we bathed in when we visited the volcanic Mount Soufriere, where streams of the water could be hot and cold at the same time. Maybe because of these apparent contradictions, he found her deliciously sexy and planned to tell her so at the very first opportunity. I, too, read that much in the contradictions. But perhaps for different reasons.

"Margarita Lopez," she answered. "But most people call me Maggie. Come with me." She beckoned with her free hand and took a couple of steps away from him, giving him the first chance to admire her tight behind. The Americans were still haggling with the exasperated man behind the counter. He seemed irritated as if he just wanted to be rid of them. Maybe because of the confusion, the Colombian was shouting at them in Spanish, and jiggling a pair of keys on a ring in front their noses. The Americans were screaming in English and waving fists of U.S. dollars in the air while making vain snatches at the elusive keys. Margarita passed by the counter without as much as a glance, as if she lived daily with such chaos and understood that it would sort itself out. But I did look back. I saw the American grabbing the other man by the throat.

"My car's over there." She pointed with her index finger. "The grey and silver one. I'll take you to your hotel. You'll meet the others later tonight."

We walked to the car, Margarita leading him, and, as usual, me following. Because I liked to walk behind, I was able to discern what people said and did behind Jeffrey's back. They never seemed to care what I thought of these surreptitious actions, a clear signal that, more than likely, nobody considered me important. I was invisible, always standing in his shadow. And that was why I saw what he never did — the way she had to force herself to walk close to him. That was why, even from the days I hung on to my mother's skirt tail, I saw and heard much more than people thought. Jeffrey could never know all that I knew, not unless I told him.

"You will be meeting with Alberto Gomez," she said, checking over her shoulder as she drove the car out of the roundabout and merged with the traffic zipping by. "I understand you met him before" It was as much a statement as a question.

"Alberto Gomez." He puzzled over the name, suggesting that he remembered someone with that name only faintly.

"Yup. He's taken over from Manuel."

Manuel was more familiar to him. He was the man who had actually recruited him: first as a mule to carry some of the stuff into Toronto and ship it in courier envelopes across the border into New York and Boston. Later, when they suspected the Canadian and U.S. authorities were catching on to their scheme, Manuel suggested that Jeffrey might want to return to his native Barbados and set up a business there. It worked out even more fortuitously for them when the government also made him chairman of Caribbean International Airlines.

"Where's Manuel?" Jeffrey asked. "I always liked dealing with him."

"In the United States. The Yankees grabbed him. Just came in here, as if we were some little two-bit country and grabbed him. Can you believe that! Took him back to the United States." She was angry and the quick change of her mood was startling.

"What about Jose, *numero dos*?"

"That bastard," she swore. Her brown hands tightened around the steering. At the same time she sank her foot into the floor, causing a sudden surge from the engine. The speedometer needle rushed up to 120 kilometres an hour and kept on going. "He got what he deserved. The fucking pig, Yankee lover."

I glanced through the side window, adjusted my headrest and primed myself for the smooth ride, to listen to the music on the radio and in the voice. At other times Jeffrey would have been ecstatic to be in such top-of-the-line luxury, with all the toys and bells, with all that power under the hood. Now, he was not in control. There was nobody he knew or could name. I decided to leave him on his own by appearing to slip into the music playing on the radio.

"Jose's the canary that sang on Manuel. Really set us back. Just proves you can't trust anyone. He laid the trap and led the American army to Manuel. Turned out he was an FBI plant all along. He was even planning to testify at the trial against Manuel in Miami. But we got to him first." She didn't need to explain further.

"A lot has happened, eh?" Jeffrey stammered. "Are things still the same as before?"

"New leadership; new plans. Now, only professionals. People are all the way in or all the way out, no more amateurs. No more toying around," she said. "No more dead wood. That's why Alberto is meeting with all the top people in the business."

Over the music I could hear Jeffrey breathe harder and deeper.

Margarita willingly agreed to come back to Jeffrey's hotel room after the meeting, which as we found out, had now been rescheduled for later that night. By the time he was ready to broach the subject with her, he had recovered from the alcohol, and had showered and changed into a conservative suit he had bought from the store in the basement of the Fairfax Hotel. Forewarned by Margarita about the new regime, he thought a more traditional look was preferrable — he had brought only casual clothes with him, none of which he now felt created the right first impression. Then he had joined her in the lobby of the hotel where they could sit and talk before he left for the meeting.

"Are you inviting me for a drink?" she asked, without a moment's hesitation. The response pleasantly surprised him.

"Maybe I am. Would you come?"

"Maybe," she answered teasingly, "if you asked me. Maybe after I've gone home and changed out of these clothes."

"What time could I expect you?"

"Oh," she studied her watch, "the drive home is an hour and ten minutes each way. Your meeting begins at seven and should take... oh... three hours."

His heart dropped. Three hours? What could be so important that the meeting would take that long? What did she know that he didn't? And didn't they want only professionals, no more amateurs, no more room for people like him?

"I could be back here 10:30 to 11-ish. How about that? Around eleven."

"Fine with me." He hoped he was not betraying how badly she had rattled him — but he was still thinking: three hours, and with people he wasn't even sure about! "I'll meet you at the bar."

"No. I'll come up to your room. I'll park in the back and take the elevator up. Easier that way."

"Don't want your boyfriend to see you with me, eh?"

She walked tantalizingly away without answering. He remembered the broad smile on her face, so full of promise, enticingly assuring him she would definitely be back and, just maybe, as the walk suggested, they might actually enjoy their time together.

129

A few minutes later, he heard the heavy revs of the car's engine, a burst of energy and then she was streaking by on the road in front of the hotel. Jeffrey could feel his manhood rise, a burning in his guts, just below his navel. There was no way he wanted this meeting to run beyond 10 o'clock. Certainly, not beyond 10:30, he thought, for what could they want with a player as minor as him and in a region so far on the periphery?

☉☉

When Alberto spoke, he kept his hands propped on the table, the fingers knitted together, the wrists pointed upwards as if in prayer. From the moment he walked into the room, there was no doubt that, despite his quiet and unassuming demeanour, he was in charge, no doubt of who was the most powerful. Despite Alberto's smaller size, Jeffrey found him intimidating. Something powerful, that really didn't take size or height into consideration, that made him stand out from the others in his inner circle.

"We feel you're a good man, a committed man." He spoke softly and slowly, wringing his hands, as if washing them with invisible soap and water. Jeffrey could not help thinking of antiseptic, because of the hand washing, but also because of the smell of the room. So deep in a basement, behind such fortification, the sounds so hollow as if disappearing into a vacuum. But it was the smell of emptiness and sterilization that stayed with him. "We need your ideas for the Caribbean and beyond. From your base, you're perhaps the only real link we have into North America. Both for getting the goods into the market and laundering the money for us."

The exercise was beginning to have a familiar ring for Jeffrey, reminding him of the time they hired him, if such a word could be used for the loose arrangement. It had happened through the intercession of a brokerage colleague then, the interview over coffee in the downstairs food court of the brokerage, in the marble-terraced underground world of downtown Toronto, where everything was so clean and sanitary. The second time, they had come to see him in his new home three years ago once he had relocated. Then, his main contact spoke just as softly, explaining just loudly enough to be heard over the raging music and the nearby surf: yes, they were looking for new challenges. Just like him, they had turned their back on up North; they too were tired of exploiting the traditional markets; tired of the falsity and duplicity; tired of boredom and order. And they had the sophistication that was far ahead of the intended new markets, so there was virtually no chance of getting caught. The system was in place, but it needed people. They needed someone with just the right awareness, an involvement that wasn't even nearly as deep as in Toronto or New York. Just to be the eyes for them. No messy hands, no open associations. They would do all the work and he would collect the money: merely for keeping them in the know. Whatever he did with the money was his business. If he started a drug rehabilitation program, that was his affair — it might even be encouraged and supported, because such endeavours would help to deflect the gaze. And they operated with one primary rule and it was that he or anyone like him was to be free to do what he wished — he would owe them nothing, and they wouldn't control him. He could do what he wanted: build a house or even a gymnasium; to buy books or to spend it all in rum shops buying votes. Feed the children, or teach them thrift by paying them to cut the grass beside the streets or in government parks. They could even grow flowers. Joint ventures with the government, if he wished. It was all up to him. He would be on the border; inside and outside, his choice. Just as long as he knew that anyone carrying on their line of business in this part of the world was not one of them. In turn, they made a commitment: they would never hurt the children. That was their promise: following a stringent moral code, not to sell directly, but to use the island merely for transshipments. But to *deal* on the island, they would never descend that low. Workers, not consumers: that was what they wanted. In any case, they had enough buyers in other countries with foreign cultures. People intent, anyway, on destroying themselves with or without any help. Why waste time selling to such a poor market, when there was an unlimited, wealthy one just ready for the tapping? And that was another reason they knew he would like a loose association: they knew how much he loved the people of his island, how angry he would be at those selling directly to his people; this way he could provide protection by making sure he kept the bad dealers out by helping the good ones. Of course, that was not to guarantee that the bad guys would not have some temporary successes, for they were dangerous, and if they really felt threatened, they might even strike as close to home as possible without harming him personally. For they knew to harm the hair on any of our people would bring a quick and swift response, and they won't want to meddle with us directly. Not at all. And, he should never forget: that what he was entering was not a life sentence. He was free to leave anytime. Just keep the money. Just keep his mouth shut.

Sitting with Alberto Gomez now, he remembered that discussion in the second meeting outside the rum shop, on a Friday night, as the people of the area played and celebrated late into the night. At one end was the music of yesterday, under the sign on Lexie's Bar, with offerings on a black background of breakfast, tea, coffee, ham and eggs, fish and cheese cutters, or, in red paint, fish, chicken and drinks, but on that night specifically promising *the best of the oldies but goldies*, with the older men and women dancing and whirling and dipping so smoothly and adeptly to the music out of the towering speakers, out of an earlier time, even before the creation of a new nation. Dances that you had to graduate to; steps that could not be learned overnight. Waltzes for the men and the women standing on the outside, catching a fresh breeze off the sea, letting their dripping shirts dry, or those plying between the concrete dance floor, sparsely decked with one or two buntings and streamers, and the bar next door, with its own promise of bar-be-q, chicken, grilled fish, fried fish, burgers, wings and seacat, what the locals called the young octopus. No boundaries; no barriers. And at the other end was the booming sound of the ubiquitous bass and the drums, of the younger people jumping and prancing and winding their waists, music that is useful only to the young, to those whose waists are still flexible and supple, who like to sweat and get hot, who didn't even mind rolling on the ground in play, man an' woman in a gyrating struggle, in the heat of the evening and of their sweat and blood, right there, in that moment, right before your eyes, on the ground. To the pounding music. No airy sounds,

133

but pounding-pounding, banging-banging, jamming-jamming, and then pounding, banging, jamming some more. Right, there on the ground, or standing with *one foot 'pon de shoulder, anudder 'round de waist*, pounding, banging jamming. Of the young, so many in vests or sleeveless shirts, cut-off pants, or shorts of the latest New York style, putting their empty beer bottles in a pile and *wukkin'-up, wukking-up, wurking and just doing bad, bad, bad* around them, the pile getting higher by the minute, the smoke in the air already acrid. This was a music given them at birth, a rhythm that would remain in their bones, even when their waists became too old and arthritic, when they sought out the slower, older and more golden ballads of lost love, misplaced hope, regrets and miseries, when they waltz and now just spin and dip and reduce themselves to merely fancy footwork, for the waist has been tamed and even disappointed. And it can see the approaching end, of even the night. A dance and a music that traverses an ocean that with the ease of travel was now a mere pond; music and dance handed to them too through their navel strings by their parents.

He remembered: an interview that was, at that moment and in that time, taking place in front of Crystal's, with the sign over his head offering fish, chicken, rice and stew, salad. Next to the Lazy Eddie's, its sign partly hidden by the tall almond tree and its copious green leaves, but offering, at least, Frutees and other local drinks along with the imported Coke and Pepsi. Sitting with the smells of fried fish in the air, the laughter and giggling of men and women drinking beer and sugar cane brandy, arguing, teasing and dancing. Boats bobbing in the water, the twelve lights in pairs along the sides of the pier that runs into the

134

sea, into one big red light at the end. Gentle remembrances: of ghost-like fishing boats off in the shadows awaiting rebirth through repairs and repainting, in anticipation of the new day. A shop that was the venue for an interviewer to ask him merely to dabble. Nothing too deep, it promised. Dabble. A shop on that very cusp, where he could hear the music of the old and the young, where he could see the young and old dance, frenzy and sedentary, where he could be part of both groups without being in either. Or a shop where he could have just declined and continued to eat the slab of fried fish on the white paper plate, with the hot yellow pepper sauce to the side, and drink his beers, all of them beers with the names Banks, Carib and Red Stripe. All his, and by name. Just like he liked to do every Friday and Saturday night. To talk a little politics in the rum shops. And to go home and sleep peacefully. To be free to come back to dance and to watch the dancers and players without first having to put his conscience to sleep. Memories: of living in the open, fully; of knowing that from where his father slept that he could hear everything that happened so close to the water every Friday and Saturday night.

"As you know, we have problems of our own here in Latin America and in the U.S.," Alberto continued. This time there were no sounds trying to drown him out, no simple pleasure to vie with the business of the moment. Just civility and the cold. And only Alberto Gomez talking this time. But inside him, so empty: not even the smells of frying fish. "Solving these problems will keep us occupied for some time. On top of that, there are a couple of new initiatives, expansion plans really, that we are contemplating. We will also need your help in that area. We have to rebuild."

This was the first official reference to the problems of Manuel's arrest and extradition to Miami. The U.S. military was no longer playing games; it had become ruthless, intent on getting to the very source of the trafficking. And the attorney general in Washington had made it quite clear that he intended capturing high-profile people in the Organization and of making public examples of them. As a result of these threats, Alberto Gomez made clear, his first job was to secure the business's operational base. He planned to build a strong edifice to repel any aggressor, be it another business or a state. This meant doing whatever was possible to deflect attention, while rebuilding the business at home. This required having the right people.

"We don't know the islands of the Caribbean or the culture of the people as well as you do, Jeffrey," Gomez said across the table. Three lieutenants flanked him on each side. Throughout the meeting they were silent, just as Alberto used to be when Manuel was in charge.

Standing behind him on both sides of the door were four burly men in black suits and black berets with Uzi guns barely concealed under their jackets. Not once did they smile. Such outward signs of friendliness were not the traits of the ruthless Los Niños, *the boys,* in their late teens and early twenties and in the military arm of the business. They were so frightening, so unfamiliar and incongruous to anything Jeffrey knew, to the images in his head. Each boy that in his mind was better suited to finding himself in a ring dance, *for there is a brown boy in the ring, tra-la-la-la, a brown boy in the ring, for he likes sugar and she like plumbing and plumbing and being plumbed,* and of some young and healthy girl grabbing him, maybe even the Dance Hall Queen, the very goddess herself, in her finery, her elaborate costume of so many colours and her delicately coiffured hair, manhandling him and throwing him on the ground, showing him her motion, and teaching him the facts of life, not making fun, motions and *movementations, think she mekking fun,* stories about the birds and bees that his mother would never have told him, that only he could learn himself, right there on the ground, right there with foot 'pon shoulder, another 'round the waist, and pounding, banging and jamming him, until he learned his lesson, until she civilized him. Until he learned how to really live, and about life. But instead, like hollow men, bereft of life and emotion, denying the vinegar and piss flowing through their veins and into their waists and balls, these young boys spent their time on guard, with big heavy guns, suppressing the bulges in their pants. Jeffrey shuddered at the thought of ever seeing anything like Los Niños on his island. These were definitely not the boys who would be dancing and prancing back at home, the same boys, to clinch the deal promised in dance, stealing into the dark with one of the young girls, perhaps, intent on doing more than just strolling along the water's edge on such a night, frisking, if they must, for anything but weapons. The same way, how could he ever forget, Brenda had taken him strolling, into the dark, on a warm evening, how she pulled him closer than her perfume and sweat, and had set him flowing. The same way she made him remember, always, even then, the same way something in him would always make him reject the lifestyles associated with the untamed Los Niños. He was sure their arrival on his island would never happen, could never happen. They would be out of sorts. They would simply run away before they drowned in such steamy torrents. Such a show of force would be as unnatural on the island as it was natural in this bunker. So he quickly dismissed the troublesome thought from his mind. Or he tried, as much as the music and the images would release him into this wilting sanity. And the memory of what happened when she first walked him into the darkness, accompanied only by the competing rhythms and the presence left behind.

"The Americans have no right to kidnap—for that is what it is, kidnap—a Colombian in his country, in his own house, defiling the sanctity of our homes and the sovereignty of our country. This is the land our fathers fought for. We have given the government another fourteen days to return our brother Manuel to the people of Colombia. I mean, this is not Bolivia or Chile where the Americans have a history of doing what they like. We constantly have to be reminding all sorts of people that we have been an independent sovereign nation since 1819. After all this time, we shouldn't have to remind anybody."

There was an air of resignation, but also practicality, in his voice. The principle was what matters and the principle was bigger than the man, bigger than a Manuel or anyone else. The principle that the business must always survive, that ultimately anyone could be sacrificed for the greater good. To Jeffrey the salient message, when all the expected bravado was stripped away, was quite clear: the choice had been made. Jeffrey Spencer, now officially one of their ranking people, the elevation thrust on him whether he wanted it or not, should know the terms and conditions of the job and the perks which came with such elevation. The insurance too. "Meanwhile, Manuel's family will never want for anything. We know how to look after our people." Eventually, even the family of this top man would have to get on with their life and it would be a better one if the organization was not only around but thriving.

Implicit also was something equally profound: an understanding and expectation that the Organization, with its tentacles reaching out almost everywhere around the globe, knows how to look after those betraying it. If it must sacrifice to thrive, it will make sure others pay the price for this imposition, for this disruption of normal life and patterns. Jose and family had found that out. Jose and his closest family members and friends were dead—their bodies scattered across Bogotá and in the cities of Medellin, Cali and Barranquilla on the Caribbean coast, in the very places where they had run in a fruitless attempt to escape the deadly vengeance. The homes of those who didn't die were burned flat, a fate worse than death, particularly for their children, who would remain homeless for the rest of their lives. For their destiny was now fixed irrevocably. They were now living in the slums of Bogotá, a long way from the high life to which they had become accustomed. And even when it seemed the Organization had exacted its harshest punishment, two of Jose's brothers living in Miami were found floating in the ocean with the Organization's trademark on their throats. Their homes in Miami were looted in daylight and their cars bombed and burned on the streets in front of their houses. There would be no forgiveness for Jose's family. No forgetting, either. They would never escape this poverty. They would wake every morning to Jose's legacy; every night they would seek in sleep refuge and shelter from this bequest.

"We have declared war on the United States in self-defence. The executive has decided to set up a defence fund into which we will place thirty per cent of all our revenues. This fund will be used to buy the weapons and communications equipment needed for victory, and to pay off officials everywhere."

Jeffrey would recall for me how he shook his head in agreement and how, because he did not know what to say, he smiled.

"We don't plan a long drawn-out war. We plan to deal swiftly with El Presidente Futado and his Yankee friends. They won't forget easily; they won't touch one of us again. Ever. That's my commitment. But the success of this war and keeping money in the defence fund will depend on your good work at home and in keeping the channels open — that's why we are counting so heavily on you, Jeffrey. You know the islands, you know the politicians and influential people. You know the ship captains and pilots. You've done good work in the past and we know we can trust you to develop the area. To exploit the full potential; to launch the new businesses to make us respectable. We will do whatever is necessary, give you all the resources and the support you need to pull this off. We know our intentions are honourable. They are based in our history. That battle will be the priority; it will keep us busy for the next while. That is why we will have to rely on you, Jeffrey. The work in the Caribbean, into Europe and the normal channels into North America and the Middle East, is vital and will be our main source of income until we

140

have straightened out matters here and in the U.S. I guess what I am saying is that our people here and you and your people in the Caribbean are now joined in one struggle. As we say, a fraternal struggle. For if we are the scourges of this region, as those American officials so condescendingly call us, then you are too. After all, this is our—yours and mine—region, too. Welcome!"

"Thank you," Jeffrey had found himself saying softly, as if in crooning whisper. In his nervousness an uncontrollable smile broke on his face.

෨

The meeting went much faster than he had expected. What was he to make of it: all the decisions had been made for him and before he even entered the room. How then could I turn my back on him? For by trapping him, they had trapped me too. Still, for good reason, he did not come to see me when he returned to the hotel. He simply went to his room to think and to start preparing. Even then the deal was not fully completed for his night was not yet over.

෨

Jeffrey saw the flashing red light on the phone as soon as he entered the room. Picking up the receiver, he pressed the preset button, expecting the usual voice-mail, but instead he heard a voice at the front desk.

"Message for me?" His voice sounded authoritative to him. The way he felt it should be, should have been when he answered Alberto Gomez. When he should have said no. The way he would ensure it would be from now on.

141

"Yes, senor," the male voice said. "From damsel. She come eleven."

Jeffrey Spencer looked at the clock radio on the lamp table. It was 10:32. "Thank you," he said and hung up the receiver. He sighed. Maybe he shouldn't have worried about her either, he scolded himself, the same way he shouldn't have bothered so much about the trip. But it was everything that had happened at home — Brenda Watts's death and funeral, his father's reclusiveness and the damage of the hurricane — that rested with such burden on him and made him so nervous and unsure of himself. Then to be surprised by Alberto Gomez. So that he had to mumble and shake his head, but to say yes. The previous contract torn up and he didn't even know he was coming to renegotiate, otherwise he would have prepared himself, he would have even found an excuse, any excuse really, to, for the first time, decline their invitation. Oh, how he hated feeling trapped!

From damsel. She come eleven. The sound of the broken English with the Spanish nuances was repeating in his head. Lyrically. He liked it. Particularly the word damsel. It was such deliciously old, quaint English. Something with a past, a good history, but still valuable. It was such a perfect name. This time the damsel coming to release, at least for a few hours, the hero, the knight feeling so trapped and frustrated, so unable to think straight because his mind was so muddled. He decided he would call her that from then on: Damsel.

He picked up the phone again. The same voice answered. "I'd like to make a call to Barbados." He gave the number and waited a few seconds for the connection.

"James Court, the prime minister's residence," a familiar voice said in his ear.

"Ginny?" he said, trying to be even more authoritative. "Jeffrey here. Jeffrey Spencer. The big boy's in?" However, even at that late hour, the prime minister was out inspecting the damage from the hurricane, so Jeffrey left a message that he wanted the airport re-opened again in the morning and, after joking with Ginny, hung up the phone. This was the last bit of business on this trip. The message to the prime minister also served another purpose: confirmed he was safe and had been as careful as he had been warned to be. Now, he was free for the rest of the night. If only he had known of this new agreement he would not have agreed to anything else before leaving home. For he knew he still had commitments back home: the promises he had made. Would there be a conflict? Could he handle both and could he still get out? He wanted to think, but time was getting away. He had a new commitment and there was still much to do, to plan, and to just think. No, he did not like not having choices of his own making. But right now he needed a bath, so he could feel clean and even refreshed.

He had left at least twenty minutes to prepare for the Damsel, he thought, walking into the bathroom, stripping as he went and mindlessly letting the parts of the three-piece suit fall to the floor. His father would have called him sloppy; even as a boy he did this. His mother would have asked him to be careful, asked if he knew what he was doing, but she would not have asked disapprovingly, not like his father. She would have appreciated his need to take risk. But for this moment, for this night, he didn't care one damn what his father thought. Or what his mother would have, either. At least, he would try not to care about anything. He would be his own man. Just as long as the

Damsel was on time and took him where they could chill. He would enjoy the music, so he could relax from thinking and wondering. Later, he might even dance. And find a way to reconcile the two commitments — the one he had agreed to the night of the hurricane and this new one that was forced on him only an hour earlier in a place of such orderly calmness. But whatever he did would be *his* choice, and without contradictions.

When the first soft knock on the door came, he was still in the shower, so he missed it. Only after he had turned off the water and was standing before the misty mirror, almost the length of the washroom, did he hear the faint tapping, like a bird pecking against the outside. He grabbed the pants that were draped over the door. The big heavy and fluffy white towel, tucked around his torso, fell to the floor. He hastily stepped over it on his way out. Pulling up the zipper, he threw a quick glance at the clock radio. If it was Damsel, she was ten minutes early. When he poked his head out into the hall, she was already a couple of steps closer to the elevators.

Something — perhaps a subliminal warning — caused him to take special note of her early arrival. Or perhaps it was quite simply that, by being early, this woman had made the first rip in his well-thumbed manual on what to expect from women, negating particularly his staunch notion that any female would always be late for the first couple of dates. With this seemingly insignificant action, she had taken control, disrupting his timing and pacing for the evening and beyond. So Jeffrey had no time to listen, not even to his own early warning sentries.

"I was about to go down and phone up," she said softly, almost disappointedly, when he closed the door behind them. As she walked ahead of him, he took the opportunity to size her up again. She was wearing a calf-length floral dress with a split running up the side almost to the top of the thigh, and she looked quite different—a lot more feminine than when he had last seen her. The dress was sleeveless and simply cut. The preponderance of white accentuated the curves in her body. Now, he could see her arms were muscular, but not bulky, somewhat like what he expected of a physical fitness fanatic. Jeffrey couldn't make up his mind which he liked better: The tom-boyish girl in the tight-fitting jeans, with the suggestive hint of intoxicating femininity, or the feminine look with a mere suggestion of ruggedness.

"In this hotel, people seeing me standing in front of the door on a luxury floor like this might think funny of me," she said. "You know what the security is like in a place like this."

"What?" He laughed loudly.

"You know what I mean." She was smiling, her eyes bright in the light, the long strands of hair bouncy on her shoulders. "A young woman, standing in front of the door of an obviously powerful man. Knocking and nobody answering. You know what they'd think I am."

"A prostitute?"

"Really?" she asked.

He had put on the T-shirt with the islands of the Caribbean forming a semicircle on his chest and was sitting on the edge of the bed pulling on his socks. When she had come into the room, he had apologized for not being ready and had kicked to a side the discarded clothes on the floor. Now he wondered if he had also misspoken by so clearly betraying the sexual thoughts on his mind, being so forthright with the answer, for speaking the first unchecked thing that came to mind. She had dismissed the apology with a wave of the hand. He needn't have bothered about offending her.

"Well, you know there is no shortage of supply around here."

"I wouldn't have no need to think that," Jeffrey said. He was trying to make amends for the earlier intemperate remark, even if she appeared not to be offended. Some people are good at hiding things, his father had always warned him, especially if talking to someone who might have some influence over them. He would not like to lose any chance at her merely because of a stupid statement.

He finished dressing and was now giving her his full attention. "Still, I guess I got a lot to learn about that line of business," Jeffrey said. Quickly he added, "Especially now I have been asked to look into its possibilities in the Caribbean." The words in the last sentence rushed out, all lumped together, the way they do when someone is making a surprise announcement, or when the aim is to impress, but knowing the high chances of failure.

The words did have the intended effect, he noticed. She was looking at him through the reflection in the mirror. For a fleeting moment the smile disappeared from the face he saw in the reflection. Her eyes seemed to turn cold, steely and focused. But the change was so fast, Jeffrey paid no special attention. Instead, he looked through the window. Down below were the bright lights reaching out from the heart of the city. Many of the nearby ones were the small fires in the slums, maybe, for cooking the evening's family meal. Some of the fires were parts of the refining process, the cottage industry for the poor and homeless, that provided the money for the late-night cooking. He wondered if any of the fires belonged to members of Jose's family.

"You know, we can sell them damn tourists anything. Particularly the ones who see the Caribbean as nothing more than a playground," he continued. "We only got to organize that aspect of the business, and as you know — " he was now standing in front of her — "that's now my job. My mandate, I suppose."

"Is that what Alberto told you?" she asked. Her voice was calm and silky. Her face, as it was earlier in the day, was still without makeup although she had painted her nails red and was wearing perfume. In her youthfulness, looking so natural, she was simply beautiful. And he wanted her, if only for the night.

"Yup," Jeffrey said. "That's part of my new mandate." He felt like bragging to her, trying to overwhelm her, hoping she was smart enough to read between the lines and not to resist him later in the night. She should at least know he was a rising star in their organization and that he should not be slighted. He could very well have some say about her future. He should put this promotion to some benefit.

But most of all, he was making such comments because he liked her. Just looking at her, smelling the warmth of the perfume, he could feel the urge and heat coming back into his groin. The intensity was even stronger than when he'd first met her. The combination of her sexuality and the knowledge of his new powers produced such strong and overpowering thoughts, emotional surges, he couldn't keep them bottled up. He felt sweetly intoxicated, but not drunk.

147

"Just like a new line of clothes... or shoes. That's how I see it. A diversification of business is what I told Alberto." Even as he lied, he glanced at the rug and noticed she had slipped her stockinged feet out of the white leather shoes. They were at the sides of the chair, not neatly placed together, toes to toes, heel to heel the way fussy people did—like Brenda Watts had and his father still did. She looked at ease, at home, as if she had no intention of leaving. "Can I get you something?"

"Some Coke?"

Jeffrey was standing near the cabinet containing the bar. He spun around, almost bumping his head on the protruding half of the cabinet door. She looked normal as if it were a usual request.

"Really?" he asked half-questioningly, as if expecting her to reconsider, to ask for something less exotic. Something found in any legal bar and something that would help him to maintain confidence in her. Wasn't it an unspoken rule in the company: while they sold the stuff, they'd never use it themselves, even though he knew some people did not strictly adhere to the corporate policy? If he didn't know better, if memories of the meeting were still not fresh in his mind, he would have thought she was putting him to the test, perhaps anxious to report to Alberto Gomez whether he was as clean as they expected.

"Oh," she groaned on realizing what had happened. "You didn't think that... *ha, ha, ha*... Holy Mary you didn't think...*ha, ha, ha*... That's funny."

Laughing loudly, her voice sounded so pure and sweet. Innocent. Tantalizing. The laughter was contagious. He started to smile too, and then to laugh as freely. He breathed a sigh of relief. He had always promised himself that he would sell as much as people would buy, to anyone who could afford the high prices, but he would never use the stuff himself. He had been able to look at Brenda Watts and say without a quiver in his voice he had never used the hard stuff, a toke or two maybe, but never ever anything harder.

Replaying the encounter in his head made him feel as if he just had another close scrape with his conscience. He wondered how long that would keep happening. And would these thoughts — Brenda Watts, his father, and how their view of life was so different to his — keep popping into his head at inopportune times?

"Pepsi would do?" he called, still bending before the refrigerator.

"Oh, dear," she groaned. She had crept up on him. Because of her stockinged feet and the heavy pile of the carpet, he had not heard her approaching. Her movements made absolutely no sound, like those of a cat. She held his face in her hands and pulled it purposefully towards her. "You seemed to have had quite a shock back there. Let me soothe your poor heart. With this."

She kissed him, slowly, passionately, assuredly, letting her slim tongue dart into his mouth and engage his in some kind of cat-and-mouse game, but always making sure he never won. At that moment, the music he heard was absolute. From then on it would always be the same serenade, a monophony with the same motif and movement. "I should prepare you for what to expect," she whispered. "When you open the new line of business. I've helped with that sort of business here. I can show you some of the fringe benefits."

She kissed him again. This time more firmly and as passionately. Suddenly, he knew for certain that he was no longer in control. It felt funny. From the time he was a little boy and had his first sexual experience in the grass behind the cemetery, he had always been told a man should be in charge of the woman. Should be the one to make the first advances, to be the conqueror. Any woman who came on too strong was no good. Not worth the effort. In Toronto and New York, even as an adult, this philosophy governed his dealings with women. He had struggled so hard with Brenda Watts, and in keeping with the strength of her principles had expected to, before bedding her. That was why Jeffrey's father always liked her. She wasn't loose, he had said, and she didn't knock herself about. In his eyes, Damsel was different, more accommodating, more willing to please. And he was enjoying it.

"Every woman can be a whore," she was saying as if reading his mind. "I'm yours tonight."

She kissed him again and in the embrace they fell back on the big double bed. The refrigerator door was still open. Under her dress, he could feel the smoothness of her firm muscular body that matched the strength in her hands and fingers. She seemed stronger, physically and mentally, than any woman he had ever gone with. And by the time they fell off to sleep, their clothes in piles around the bed, he had been totally drained. At the end he was so exhausted he didn't notice — just as he wasn't aware of anything else she did in the room — when she got out of the bed to close the fridge door and stop the coldness from taking over.

In the morning, she was no longer in the bed. The bright sun was seeping through the glass door, under the heavy curtains and he could hear the sound of the shower. Jeffrey rubbed his eyes and for a moment a smile broke out on his face as he remembered the ecstasy of the night before. He could smell a lingering mixture of perfume and their combined sweat on the pillows and the covers. Almost as quickly, the smile was gone. A momentary panic that he might have overslept and caused the aircraft to be delayed replaced the smile. But Jeffrey wanted Damsel too much for him to dress and head for the airport without tasting of her again.

There was no doubt the next time he returned to Bogotá he would be looking for her. But that could be several weeks or several months. Nobody knew for sure. And even if it were only two or three days, he would have found the wait too long.

They made love once more. This time more aggressively, as if battling each other for dominance. And when it was over, she remained on top of him, head lifted, the mane flowing backwards, her eyes closed, breathing rhythmically. He felt happy and relaxed and thoroughly spent. And he drifted off into a quiet relaxing sleeping. She must have dozed off too, for when she woke him, he had only seven minutes to get to the airport.

"You gotta get up," she said, although making no effort to get up herself.

"I could stay like this, with you, forever." He hugged her tighter and she wriggled against him, her firm nipples rubbing his chest.

"You gotta go. Maybe the next time." There was a painful harshness in her voice, as if contrived, as if she was preparing for a return to the distance between them. "Maybe some day I'll come over to your lovely island, I'd love that."

But he didn't want to let go of her. He held her for another five minutes. They said nothing. All he wanted

151

was this fantastic woman. The memory of Brenda was already dimming. Then the idea struck him. And he liked it instantly. Except, he wondered why he hadn't thought of it before.

"Why don't you come with me, now?" he asked. He had no idea what commitments, whether business or family, she had in Bogotá, but he was willing to risk rejection.

"Me?" she asked, raising her upper body up once again, the locks falling back, to look him in the face. "Me come with you? Where to?"

"Barbados."

"I don't have a visa or anything."

"Visa? No problem. I can arrange that for you. Just that you gotta want to go. And you must let me call you Damsel."

She shook her head and kissed him passionately again. So much so he was tempted to try again, and would have if she hadn't controlled him by firmly pushing him away and keeping him down.

"I might even be able to help you set up the new business," she volunteered haltingly. "When I'm with a man, I like to do everything with him."

He hadn't thought of that. And she was right. She had the right experience for recruiting the women for the new line of business. The Organization would be further impressed. He would get all the praise. He would rise another notch in their esteem and he would survive. After that it was just a matter of calling the airport and delaying the departure. This was the moment Jeffrey remembered me.

"*What* do you think I am," Jeffrey Spencer was shouting. I was too. It must have been a good thing that nobody could hear us in my hotel room, otherwise someone might have called security. Morning had found me by the window watching the sun coming up, the lights stirring down below, the calm giving way to an early bustle, and the anger and anxiety in my chest intensifying. Waiting for him. Now I could not put off until we returned home what was on my mind. He had to know that I simply could not be part of his plans. So when he came to tell me about the delay, I lashed out.

"What foolishness are you asking me?" I shot back. "How do you mean, what do I think you are? You are the same Jeffrey Spencer that I grew up with. That's why I can't understand what you are telling me."

"What, Edmund," he said. "What. Not who. The question is *what*. *What* do you think I am?"

"I don't know what you mean. You're just confusing me. All I know is that we had agreed that we don't want anything more to do with this business. Now you are telling me something else."

"Come back to the bloody question I just asked, Edmund," he said, slapping his hands together. "That's where you have to start. At the beginning. *What* do you think I am? What kinda person do you think I am? All you can tell me is who I am but that says nothing about what you see as the real me, my intentions, my wants, and desires; what makes me tick, angry, what makes me laugh, what are my dreams. What am I? You can tell me about the things I've done and the things I might do. But you can't tell what I am, what I am at heart, what you know I would want and what I would do. Then you can name me, you can fix me. So, do you think I am some kind of a monster? A

153

monster taking the shape of a human being? Do you think that I don't have feelings, just like you, just because I am not crying? And do you think that I, too, don't want the best for everybody? What do you think I *am*, man?"

"Jeffrey, all I know is that only two nights ago, I heard you making a promise. Just two nights ago, yuh know, man. A solemn agreement. I heard you with my own ears. It was almost as if she was in the room body and soul, not in some grave. And you were saying that we would change, that this thing is already getting too deep, that there might be other people moving in on us, getting out of control. For this is a very lucrative, a very dangerous business that we are dabbling in, and we are amateurs. We are just amateurs getting into water that is getting above *we* heads now. A promise we made to Brenda, a promise for Brenda, you know, man. I remember that quite clearly. And I agreed that I could live with that agreement. That is *who* I thought I was dealing with: that is *what* I thought mattered to the real Jeffrey Spencer. The one that was revealed to me by the light of the hurricane, the voice I heard over the wind, not the Jeffrey Spencer standing here in front of me in some hotel in Bogotá, telling me to wait just a bit longer, tarry just a while longer. I came over here with you, thinking that you would be getting out. That was what I thought was the reason for your coming over here. That's why I was glad to come with you at such short notice, thinking that you were so anxious to cut these goddamn ties. I saw the look on the prime minister's face. You saw it too. You must have heard it in his voice. And we all know what it means. I'm sure he would like the same thing too, for us to cut out now. This thing's getting too serious. I just wanted to cut a

154

few records. Not for you to be getting me and you in so much deeper. I can't take that, man."

"Edmund, remember what Mama used to tell us." He was talking softer now and reassuringly. "Remember. You gotta remember, man. You's the one with the memories. Sure I know how you feel, but there has to be some trust, you have to step back and ask yourself why would Jeffrey Spencer do this, and the only way you can answer that question is to understand what, not just who, but what is this man you call Jeffrey Spencer. I am the same as you: the same boy that listened to our mothers and fathers. In my heart, I am the same as you. I might be a bit older, but still no different from you, really. Remember Mama said that we are complementary; we need each other, one the preacher and one the singer. That's how I see it."

"I know," I was controlling my anger now, too. "I know, Jeffrey. But I keep remembering the promise. The contract that *we*, you and me, made only two nights ago, man. Only two flipping nights ago, Jeffrey. It ain't that long, man. You remember it, don't you?"

"Yes, little brother," he said, putting an arm around my shoulder. "Yes, Preacher Man. Always the preacher, always the conscience. And that is why I need you. Who else can I trust? Who else would understand? Who else would bail out, and without hesitating one second to question, when I say it is time to go? Who else has a conscience so pure, pure enough, if I may say so, for two people? For the preacher and the politician. Who else would be able to hold my ass to accountability, and could do that without me getting vex or cussing them out? Just like you are doing right now: requiring me to explain. Is there anybody else who could be standing here and having this conversation with me? And I taking it, knowing that you are doing it for my good, for our good, that even having this conversation is hurting you, and that *you's* somebody that I can trust. Somebody who'd always be on my side and won't set me wrong. Somebody I'd trust, man. Nobody else would understand what I am saying; nobody else because they don't understand what is the bond between us. For that is what we are like, big guy. Tell me, who else but you, big man?"

Jeffrey walked over to the window. Below were the streets of a foreign land. We had come to a strange place. Only I was wailing, crying a river, lamentations. I watched his shoulders hunch as he stood gazing out. And when he spoke, it was softly, his words bouncing off the strong window pane and rushing back to me with staggering force. Words to which I had no answer. Words that once again, coming from his mouth, must have become mine. For, once again, I could not speak.

"You know, Edmund, I've been thinking a lot about this recently. Even before the hurricane. Look at your father and my father. They are always talking about some agreement. Some contract. Just like you and me right this minute. Take your father, for example, always talking about heaven. Do the right thing, he says. Live a righteous life. Do no evil. Do only good. Keep your side of the bargain. And my father agreeing, saying don't disturb this, no angering that, no gambling. But suppose, just suppose, Edmund, that there is really a heaven and there is a God, just as they tell us, and that there is a contract that if you and I live a certain way when we die we would go to heaven. The agreement says that live according to these ten rules and you go to heaven, no questions asked. But suppose you and me, suppose we lived according to our side of

156

the contract and live according to rules, always strict and on the straight and narrow path. And suppose we turn up at the Pearly Gates and St. Peter says, wrong place: you must go down there to Hell, to all that fire and brimstone. And we say, but we did what you told us to do, we lived according to the agreement, check the contract. And St. Peter looks at us and says, with one of those mean Old Testament looks on his face, a look that you know right away he just don't like you, that says, *I know, but I change my mind. No fault of yours, I just change my mind. It's just that I don't like you. Just don't like the two of you, so I change my mind.* Tell me, Edmund, what can either of us do then? That's why we have to trust that whoever it is that can help or hurt us is on our side. That they will do the right thing. So that if you have to rely on trust, there's no real need for a contract. As I see it, it's a fact of life: you have to know what, not just who, you have on your side. That's why I need you. And that's why, in return, I ask you what, not who, do you think I am. Is there trust?"

೧౨

An hour later, we were at Damsel's apartment, on the way to the airport. She grabbed a travelling bag and hastily stuffed some clothes, jewellery and perfume into it.

"You can get anything you want in Barbados," Jeffrey chided her.

She reached under a multicoloured collection of panties, pantyhose and bras and pulled out a stack of bills, in all sorts of currencies, but mostly American dollars.

"For an emergency," she said, waving the money in the air. "Guess this is one."

157

nside the wide-bodied DC-10, Jeffrey tried relaxing to the reassuringly smooth and musical purring of the engine. I sat in another section, lashed to my seat, and trying my darnedest to block everything out of my mind, to plug my ears from the siren's calls. The captain had reached the cruising level and, the aircraft was floating gently, with only the sound and push of the powerful engines to remind us that we were suspended 35,000 feet above the mountains of South America.

We were heading north, flying parallel to the Pacific coast on the west, across the rugged cordilleras with the compact Serrania de Baudo range miles below. The aircraft seemed to be following the country's most important river, the Magdalena, historically the so-called lifeline of Colombia, snaking between the eastern and central ranges into the Caribbean, now one of the chief arteries for the flow of the main business of the Company to the outside world.

In another ninety minutes or so we would be well over the Caribbean Basin, clearing the continent at a point between Cartagena and Barranquilla and heading east over the blue water and the dots for islands off the Gulf of Paria. Those islands would be part of Jeffrey's territory, his seat of power. As we flew across the region, he planned to point out the islands to

Damsel — the big ones and the small, the French, the Spanish, the Dutch, the English and the American islands — particularly those with American naval bases poised to create problems for him and the Organization. And to show his expertise, I knew he would want to identify the smattering of land by name — Aruba, Curacao, Margarita Island, Martinique, St. Vincent, St. Lucia, Dominica, Trinidad — for they were now his, all of them, names he would automatically assume Damsel had never heard. He would identify and fix them in her mind by size, population and, of course, by marketing potential. Surely, such knowledge would further impress her: she would understand that he was a man who definitely knew his onions. To him, even with different names, at that moment, imbued with a new authority from looking down on them, all in one gaze and from on high, they were now all the same, transformed into a whole that they had not been on the outward trip. The same way that in those olden days ships full of another cargo didn't care which island they called upon first, just as long as the navigators got the business safely to port before an eruption, revolt or plague destroyed the payload, ruining the chances of some foreign entrepreneur. A time when one port was as good as the other.

Jeffrey confessed later that on this trip my father appeared before him like an apparition, although maybe it was merely a stern voice in his head. My father told us that for every Scylla there was a Charybdis, the many-headed monster in the whirlpool, the snake that can strike out quickly and swiftly with fangs that are gunboats and short-takeoff planes; the Scylla that is the cave that was like that very airplane in which we were travelling. All those sweetly sounding voices and their dreams were songs lulling the conscience into a very, very deep slumber. "Sometimes, it is just a matter of choosing the lesser of two evils, of knowing which one will be the most temporary," he believed my father was telling us at that moment. "Make the best of what you've got. Then make your choices. At the right time." He believed that my father would understand that not all choices are between good and evil. For sometimes there is simply no good to be found, and then what do you do? My father, he argued, had never hesitated to tell us that sometimes the answer comes in lashing one of us to the mast, allowing the visionary to look for a way out, to navigate the shoals on either side, to ignore the screaming voice, so as to lead those with hardened and plugged ears, those too weakened and fearful to overcome dangers that are also challenges. Truly my father would have been appalled but Jeffrey believed he had been chosen to lead. He believed he knew the limits, when he must step off before tipping and hurtling beyond hope. That point had not yet come after all: he still had enough leeway. He could keep away from the whirlpool and skirt the enticement in the cave, and he might even be allowed to listen to the sweet allurements and to pick any good out of the bad, all the while searching for that safe passage. And with this, he and I embarked on the next, and fateful, stage of our journey.

☉☉

Jeffrey glanced through the window at the rolling waves below. A ship was steaming in the opposite direction to the plane, the sole moving thing. How lonely and frightening it must have been back then for all those pioneers. How tough it must have been for his mother, he found himself thinking, when she set out on her journey, swimming against the stream. Heading in the opposite direction to all those earlier migrants. That was good for her, back then; it was what was required for her to get life under control, to start anew. Yet, he recalled, she never blinded herself to the reality that the solution for one person was not applicable to all others. She didn't believe everyone had to take the same path home. Maybe that was the jazz singer in her, he thought. The individuality. Just like in a good song, we can all begin from the same position, then as we go along, we start meandering, everyone soloing in his or her own time, but keeping an eye and ear for the central tune and melody, everyone eventually arriving at the ending in harmony and unison. His mother recognized that the success of her son, her only pickaninny, lay in his ability to join the natural flow, to head in the same direction as everyone else, but always making sure he was different. He would decide when he had had enough of this music, or when he needed a variation. He would decide, turn his back and walk way, choose another life. No regrets. That was what he liked about his mother, her faith in him and the choices he made. Maybe she didn't have the words to express her thoughts and ideas as he would. But he understood and appreciated what was driving her, what was behind her thinking.

Jeffrey pulled his mind back to the problem at hand, how without getting too involved or overexposed he was to make a difference in the Organization and by extension his island, his region. But he could not sit back and expect matters to take care of themselves; he had to force them. He had to devise a plan to make each informant totally reliant on him, from the children at school to the old fishermen knitting nets on the beaches keeping an eye on movements on the horizon. He had to seize the moment. Timing: that's what is important. He had to build a special relationship with each one of them. His money had to be their sole source of income. He had to encourage them to start to lead lofty, exaggerated lives — to be hooked on a standard of living. They could escape the poverty trap inherited from their ancestors. That would be their new freedom. They would no longer be tied to a lifestyle set long ago. Instead, they too would travel and build big houses. In return, they only had to ensure that they always supplied him with useful information. He would teach them to dream. He would show them how to beat the Organization at its own game, and how to become totally free one day. This way some good would come out of the situation in which he found himself. But in the meantime, they had to work. He would rise to the moment. With that decision made, he felt ready to convey it to me. So he called me over, and as Damsel slept, we chatted in back.

The bottle of expensive rum was half-empty and his glass was full. He was in a reflective mood. There was a sense of calm around him but, as he later explained, it was because of me that he had been visited by an unexplainable feeling of dread that was making him jumpy, insecure and even doubtful of his ability. Could he really pull off this job?

This position would bring unexpected and new dangers. But he had to push on. He had to remain as if he were just what I had called him earlier, an amateur. He had to be professional while appearing to those who matter as an amateur, so that the professionals would not think him worthy of attention, would think of him as a foot soldier, would not send any of the many-headed monsters to get him, would not think he was deserving of such attention. He would have to be a professional at appearing amateurish, so that his father would never suspect, and by the time he might, Jeffrey would be out of the business. But with enough cash in his pocket, enough money to help him fund any campaign, to ease his entry into a higher calling when Prime Minister Watkins moved on.

Jeffrey sipped the rum. He had drunk so much his mouth had lost the ability to appreciate the taste. When he told me this, I had the image of the very rich man compelled to overindulge, only to find that, while the first spoonfuls are delicious, the more he eats, the less satisfying is the food. Growing up he always dreamt of sitting down to a table of 32-ounce steaks and bottles of the best alcohol. That was his idea of success and achievement. When he could sit at such a table every day, any time of the day, he would have arrived. So that at his pinnacle, he would gorge on steaks and expensive drink, even though he knew that such gratification would be bad for him. Would make him vulnerable. He knew that all the steaks and trimmings could never taste and look like the ones in his dreams, no matter how hard he looked or wanted them to be, no matter how many he bought, no matter how he cooked them.

Jeffrey put the glass on the table in front of him. He needed someone to switch off the vivid voices in his head. The same voices were buried deep in his conscience and they forced him to listen, as if he were a hapless guard obliged to listen to repentant prisoners who felt compelled to tell their stories in most lurid details.

Undoubtedly, one of the voices was his mother's. Sometimes I wonder if he would have lived his life the same way if one of these voices meant to him what it did to me, if I had shared with him the image that I always carried around in my head—the picture of Auntie Thelma sitting in my mother's kitchen, and just talking, but obviously aware of the presence of a little boy within earshot. And then my mother's second opinion, countering and clarifying Auntie Thelma's confusing word. In the end, I guess, each of us needed our own mothers. But I needed his more than mine.

"My dear, nobody, not even you, coulda really understand why I stopped singing, why I would never sing again." They were in the shade, legs spread apart and skirts dropping down between them, seated on stools, one on either side of the kitchen door. This way they could still see who was passing by outside while keeping an eye on the two of us inside the house. It was a breezy day, with the trees in the backyard singing, the tops bending in the wind. Occasionally, the roofing crackled loudly from the heat that caused the women to fan themselves vigorously. In their hands were glasses with the same ice and lemonade as mine. Although our drinks came out of the same pitcher, theirs was different. I knew that. I had learned that much from my own experience and from my mother's constant admonition that there could always be more in the mortar than the pestle. Some things merely *looked* the same. "But all I can say is that you would have to understand how I grew up, what it was like for us in those projects. Momma and Poppa had done just like everyone else from down south. They had jumped on that old train heading up north. Folks from all over were headed north, to the land of paradise. There was food and work and the Negro was people too. Up north they were. Even people from down this way in the islands were joining that rush up north. All them *seamens,* them *travellingmens,* that from the beginning of time always carry-go-bring news throughout the region, as if it is just one big neigh-bourhood, with just different streets and enclaves. So my momma and my poppa went along like everyone else, my poppa going first and then sending for my momma and the three kids, me being the littlest one. Now, you gottuh know something else about my poppa: he was one mean guitar player. Could sing too, good, good, good, but not as sweet as my momma, for there was always something rough, a bit o' pain, in her voice when she sing. She used to be in the church choir, momma was. Folks say I got my voice from my momma. I liked it when we sang in the choir, with Poppa and the other mens, down on the low frequency, singing that low old bass, just swinging on through, like a train moving on down the tracks, and me and the rest o' womens singing on the higher notes, just following, them leading, always the bass leading and guiding, from the chest, right beside the heart, we used to say. Just the bass, something no woman can ever do, that is what I remember about Poppa and the other mens, holding their ears shut, closing their eyes, the deep dark voice, so rich, from down in the stomach, and so low. One time I find myself swaying to the music, just swerving, as the bass hit the really low notes, then it would come on back to lead us through the night, through the darkness, through the valley and through forest, through the mountains and the desert, we was a-moving, and little me, not knowing any better, but just feeling the rhythm in my bones, just feeling the spirit lifting me on up above the bass, floating, and I started to move my feet and to clap my hands and then I saw how everybody was looking at me and then I see the pastor, with one big frown on his face. When we did finish and was leaving, I hear him tell my father: worship is serious business, in my church it is. We do not go for no devil music in this place of worship; we don't want no dancing, just sanctifying. The next time something like that happens, I will intervene. I will stop it right that moment, *bram so*, down comes the curtain, at the very first instance. Rebuke the devil. And while he talking to my poppa, I see all the young women and girls, and a few boys too, giggling to themselves, but pretending to be real serious when the pastor look at them. So that was it for me and singing in the church. Plus we was moving any way. On the same tracks, the train clanking and clanking like the bass-man himself. I got to learn to hang out with all them musicians, got to understand how the business worked, or didn't work, how it was like life itself, but I learned all that from my poppa. Well, the three o' we children growing up in this small, piddlin' place, freezing in the winter, too hot in the summer. Chicago don't mean that much to me, I tell yuh. Don't mean nothing, except for the music. The house I remember most was right beside these *big-able* tracks. It used to shake every time one o' them great big trains, Northfolk, Suffolk, Pennfolk, always some kinda name with some kinda folk in it, always carrying and bringing

166

folks, used to rumble by, shaking up the house, making the cupboards, empty as they was, dance and rattle like we had something in them. And it used to be every fifteen minutes, them trains went by. Lord, now I wonder if we used to have any sleep, how anybody could sleep in a place like that. So all shook up. But tiredness would make yuh do anything. Still, it couldn't be any peace; couldn't be any quiet. And when it wasn't the train, it was the people cussing and swearing, somebody fighting, mens and womens drinking and carrying on, somebody preaching 'bout the wages of sin and how we'll burn in hell, the little biddy boys and girls playing and screaming, and the music. There was always music. Sweet music, or sad. That's what I remember best. The mens and womens meeting in front a little house somewhere and the guitar groaning, the piano through the open door going, somebody on a horn, a banjo, a drum, and somebody wailing, belting out a soulful song. With time, I was the one wailing. People say I was the best to come out of the region. Put me in all kinda competitions. Won a few, too, I did. But I always enjoyed singing in the neighbourhood. That was how I met Charlie. He was this boss guitar player, could do a number on them scales, all them riffs and thing. Always finding extra notes, so that this great blues singer *ooman* wi' she big-big-big black bottom once say to him to cut out trying to show she up, playing all them extra notes. I tell yuh, people used to love them solos of his, said they didn't know one guitar had so many notes in it. Said he was a fool on a guitar, if you ask them. Could sing too, Lord, he could, but I had the more better voice. Just like my momma and poppa. People used to come from all over just to hear me put down a scat or two. I would take a word like, well something like, love and I would find all of these different and funny ways to emphasize that one word, like *lu-lu lul-lu-lu –uv-uv, looove-uv-uv*, just emphasizing you know, just holding and extending one part, then the 'nother, or that was what I thought I was doing, having so much fun, forgetting the pain, and then I would make up some words and phrases that weren't in the original song, adding *a shuba, shuba, shuba, taka, takaaa, ta,ta,ka,ta,ka,ka* and I would be composing as we going along, telling a story here and there 'bout something that happened around us, or was on the news, somebody born a baby or celebrating a birthday, or getting married, or the mens going off to a war somewhere. Mens travelling on the land and on the seas. A travelling man, have no hope, have no home. Just a travelling. Or the rent man coming and nobody ain't got a red cent. Still, more travelling, arunning, one step ahead. A different man, The Man, that. Or this man ahurting them womens, real bad. People feeling low; sometimes high. Used to sing about them things, too. Because I was lonely in them days and I didn't like how my momma used to treat my poppa and I didn't like how he used to allow himself to get treat. I believe a man gotta be strong to be a man. A woman may test him, but a man gotta stand up and be strong. Yes! That was how I used to think about things, before I had a child of my own and now I have to think over some things, maybe put my foot down. 'Cause yuh does change, girlie. But I used to think that way. Still do sometimes. So, when Charlie comes to me and say he got this gig in a band on this boat that does carry all them rich people throughout the islands and them places so, down through the Panama Canal and the islands, sailing out of St. Louis or Miami, and that the band is looking for a good, good singer and he tell them about me. So I should come with him. So, it was a morning after my momma and poppa did fight like cats and dogs all night. I picked up my few little things, my little tacklings, one was a pretty dress Poppa did give me, and I up and run off with Charlie. We took the train back down south, way into the night, a long trip. When we arrived, Charlie, he come back home to me with a long, long sour face. Like some hang dog. Hear 'im tell me: them say they don't want no singer no more. Just like that. Him say, them say they hire this little French girl just two days ago. That they like the way she does pronounce some words, kinda different, kinda nice to them. So I says to him, okay, but what I'm agonna do now. You want me to head back up home, 'cause yuh better know I ain't going back up there, and if yuh ain't know I telling yuh now, or yuh just want to go on about your own bidness by yuhown self and left me be, for I can fend fuh meself. He says, no, no, no. You coming wid me. We-ah getting married. Them got a rule on the boat that wives of the band people can work, serve at the tables, wash dishes, them kinda things. So me and Charlie get married. It is true that I did *like* him, that we did have we fun together from time to time, after all we did be young and healthy, and he might even kinda dida like me, for he didn't have tuh marry me, nobody was holding no gun at him head, me neither, but I don't think either he or me would say that we were in love wid one another, not the kinda love we did sing about in them songs. We just wanted to be free, and if that was what it took to be free, we just took it. Just like so. So, I got on the boat. Worked in the kitchen. Kept Charlie looking clean and smooth in his clothes and the uniform they did give the band to wear. Him did look sharp nuh razor blade in his clothes when I did done wid him. Tell him words to say in them songs he always did writing, for he would come to me and say, Thelma, you good, good wid words. This is a song about this or that, say about potatoes, and I would start rhyming off all sorta words, some that make sense and some that didn't make no sense at all, but just sound good, and the next thing we know the band got a new song, the people dancing and all them white folks so happy. In my mind, I could actually see certain things happening when we're making up a song. Vision, Charlie called it. But I wanted more outta life and then at one port, in Martinique or some island, the band had this big problem when the little girl singer didn't come back on the boat. She ran off, maybe with some man, used the boat to get a passage down there. So them left in a pickle and Charlie says to me, you know all the songs, hey you even help me write dem, go on and sing. So I belted out a few and then nobody didn't even miss the missing girl. I was the singer. I sang in all sorts o' ports, on all types of seas: the smooth and the rough, even the rough, rough, rough, when I thought the ship would sink, when we had to say, Captain, this ship is bending low, nobody dancing, but I had to keep singing.

"Then Charlie started getting mean to me. Drank, me and he too much, both o' we did, 'cause the booze was cheap on the boat, and at the various ports. Said he didn't want to be married no more, didn't like the stupid job on the ship, wanted his own band and that he just wanted to be free. A different freeness, he did want. And, to tell the truth, me too. I did feel that way, too. So, he was always telling me he's divorcing me and me telling he I don't care what he do. One night he even flashed some papers in front of me. I was becoming like my poppa and momma, except it was Charlie beating

170

me up. Once he busted muh lip, so bad I had real problems singing. Once, he almost broke all the fingers in
both of my hands, so I couldn't hold the microphone.
Had was to sing with the microphone in a stand a few
nights, well made me feel like an animal in a cage, for
when I sings I like to move around and move all over,
not stand in one place, fixed and rigid. Another time, he
gambled away all my money when we got back to St.
Louis. Turmoil, I was in turmoil, life a living hell. I had
no place that I wanted to be: I could not go back home
up north, 'cause I hated the place and everything up
there. Still beats me why anybody goes up there, except
for the education and to learn the ways of the world. At
the same time, I didn't like being down south. It's too
nasty, leaves a bad taste in my mouth. It wasn't safe
there neither, and I didn't like it on the ship. It seemed
that I could not have peace and quiet and also music. I
had always to give up one if I wanted the other. And I
didn't like singing no more. 'Cause I started thinking
about how things always seem to turn out bad between
the men and women I know all my life. And I knew
back then that it was always a problem when a woman
is strong, 'cause in the end Charlie just didn't like how
the mens and womens would come onto me, didn't like
the way they say I could sing so sweet, that I should be
making records and big money. He didn't like neither
that he had was to come to me for them special words
for his songs, 'cause how he could then say that it was
his songs when the words belongs to somebody else. I
know them things. Charlie, he and me was too strong
with we one another. Too mouthy me was for him. Him
saying I betray him, when I don't know how I could do
that, when I was only looking after my own interest.
When I only claiming what is mine. Not in competition

171

with nobody. And I know this wasn't a problem with Charlie alone. It would be the said same thing with any man I was going to be with. I know back then that I had to make things right in my life. I remember a sister in the church once telling my momma to have a cup of water in her hand whenever she quarrelling with Poppa. And that for she to take a big mouthful o' the water, but she wasn't to drink it. Just hold the water in her mouth, don't drink any, don't let none fall out. Do this for the love of peace and quiet. But don't talk. I know I had was to keep my mouth shut, constrict my throat. I knew it was my singing, always was, that caused bad things to happen. I decide that I would have to think again about this singing business, for life might be better for me with any man I'm with if I didn't lead the singing, even if there was no music.

"So one day we put into this port here, on this island, and I come ashore on my free time, all by myself, so I could think. Get some peace and quiet. And I saw these mens singing and playing. One man say to me, why you looking so sad and he started to sing a song that he was making up right there on the spot. About me, about this pretty looking women, about pouting, about looking sad and about pretty women pouting and looking so sad. That I should let the sunshine in, let the sun, sun, sun in, let the sun shine in. And it reminded me of all the good things I wanted to remember. So I joined in and them mens were so surprised that I could match them, them say them thought I was a Yankee and that they didn't know that I would know calypso music and I say I ain't singing no calypso, I's singing jazz and blues and them laughing at my accent, saying I have a funny-sounding twang. Then, they invited me to come and eat with them 'cause they were roasting fish on the beach, roasting

172

corn and breadfruit in a fire between some rocks, using the salt water of the sea to boil things in, cooking in an old kerosene oil tin can, and the food tasting so good. Then, one of the mens say, you ever did see a Bajan funeral? Now, of all things to ask a girl to, *a funeral – Bajan or otherwise!* I mean it ain't like being invited to a play or a dance. So I say no. He says you want to see one, `cause I working at one this evening. I'm the junior grave digger and I want you to come with me, 'cause I want you to spend more time wid me. And he looked so cute, especially when he laughed and I saw the big-able split in his front teeth, the dimples in his jaws. You know who that was. So, I went to the funeral. The time come and gone for the boat to leave the island, so it lef' widd-out me. I don't care 'cause I like the island and the peo-ple. The music. So I stay and me and this grave digger man living together, saying we'll try to make a life of we own. I find out something else: that I can't let anybody know that I already married to Charlie, otherwise they would say how I can't stay on the island, because I need Aubrey for immigration purposes; and I can't leave and go back up north because I don't want anybody to accuse me of bigamy and throwing me in no jail, 'cause Aubrey and me did hold a real church wedding with all the glamour and the expense, all the coconut water, the roast pork, beef stew and pork chops, green peas and rice, macaroni cheese and two towering black cakes with all the icing on them, you gotta remember that day, Esmay, you gotta 'cause you own Frederick did do the marrying, so I stay put on the island. Which I didn't mind because it was the peace and quiet that I wanted most. Me and Aubrey man and wife. And I hope nobody never recognize it is me Charlie's wife, the singer. So, I never sing no more. Then, the voice got old, not as good as it used to be. So, now I *don't* sing in public any more. I try to live righteous, to live my music, rather than sing it, rather than just drawing attention to it. It's too spiritual for that. For as the good book says live your life so that men may see the good in you. So that if you hear me singing, you know it gotta be for a damn-good reason. I keep my music within, in a special place, and I only bring it out and show it off on special occasions. For all them reason, but because I don't want no trouble, I just stay here on this island. Every now and then, even now, somebody or the other will still ask me: don't you miss home, and I would ask them back, what you mean by *home*. In fact, I would tell them that what they does call home, I does call a neighbourhood, just part of the *hood* as them young people on the streets out there or on the TV would say. Home has music, the music. That is home for me, not just some place, or a place. But most people still don't understand how I does think on this matter, sometimes not even the man I does live with. And when I talk to them two boys of ours, I does see the confusion in their eyes too. All I can say is that some day they will understand. They will grow up and they will understand. This is my home now. Aubrey is a good man. He does do the singing in my family, I does enjoy listening, enjoy knowing he has something to sing, that he always have a song and not just a melody. I don't feel an outsider, never did from day one, not like how I did feel in that church or even in Chicago, with Momma and Poppa always fighting. But in my heart I always feel something hollow. I feel that I betray him by never telling him the full story right up front, by never telling him that I don't know for true if Charlie did divorce me, so that I don't know what is really what between he and me. But then, who hasn't betrayed

174

someone or another at some time in their life? So, I just live, knowing that some day even the music will betray me. For, some day it must end, too. At least, for me."

She paused for a moment and I heard her gulping the drink. My mother cleared her throat and offered to refill the glass of lemonade and whatever was in it.

"Thank yuh, girlie," Aunt Thelma said. "Music and preaching. Them two always go together. Everybody done know that a people like we, the way that we are; we will always need singers and preachers. That is what I keep telling them two boys me and you got. One a preacher; one a singer."

"But why a singer and a preacher, Thelma? What's the difference between them?"

"Vision for one thing. For the one a *remindering* of all we have come through. Like a travelling man. One to look to the future. The other to keep the past alive. One to lead; one to dream. That's how I see it."

"But which one to do what?" my mother asked.

"Well, if *you* don't know for yourself that's a problem for you," Aunt Thelma said. "A real big problem. I know that I know which is which. They have to figure it out."

I looked at Jeffrey. He looked at me. We each thought we saw the same thing, one preacher, one singer. But, in truth, we both wanted to be the singer. And again there was no preacher. For we knew who we were, the same as what we thought Aunt Thelma meant for us. And if we didn't know, we were sure she would tell us, but in her own inimitable way. Or as, she suggested, that experience would.

Something else I remember. It was not many days later that Jeffrey showed up with the coconuts and some other tackling in a big paper bag. For some time, we had been begging his mother to make us the sugar cakes that she made so well. We simply loved the sugar cakes, as did our friends at school. Somehow Auntie Thelma had taken the local recipe and mastered it, not so much by adding new ingredients, but by also varying the proportions. The result was the treat that like any blessings she showered on us sparingly, which in shape and content was a sugar cake like any that we could buy in village shops or from the hawkers with their trays on their heads, or from the vendors of fruits and condiments sitting on a rock or on a stool in the shade of a large tree. At the same time, the sugar cakes were special, so different to taste. But, even as our pleading grew more frantic, she seemed increasingly decided not to make us the treat. Instead, she suggested that we should make our own. "At least you won't have anybody to blame if they turn out any different from what you expect," she said, "and you can take all the praise if they turn out just right, you see what I mean." When we argued we didn't know how, she laughed and then painstakingly spelled out the recipe as Jeffrey wrote the ingredients, measurements and methods into a notebook. And now he had all the ingredients in the paper bag.

That afternoon, we took the coconuts into the backyard, and just as we saw Thelma do it, we bore holes into the mask-like face of the coconuts and let the water drain through them into a cup. When the coconuts were empty, we blew into the holes, so hard that our cheeks puffed, the way we had seen the adults do, secure in the knowledge and the tradition that this blowing would make it easier for us to separate the meat from the shell. Then, holding the coconuts that special way, in the palms of our hands with our fingers spread, we smashed the coconuts on a large rock, causing the shell and the white meat to shatter in so many pieces, but in our hands. A whole now divided into many pieces; none scattered, as they would have if we had simply hurled the coconut against a rock or placed it on the ground and just struck it forcefully with a hammer. All the pieces were still in our hands. With knives, we easily scooped out the meat and grated the pieces into a big bowl.

As our mothers talked, we boiled the water from the bucket in a pot, added the oily water drained from the coconuts and, reverentially, we measured exactly all the ingredients from Jeffrey's notebook. We added the sugar and the essences and we stirred the sticky syrupy paste, taking care that it did not burn, but that the sugar, coconuts and grated ginger formed a thick paste. When we thought it was ready — just as Auntie Thelma would, we had taken a bit of the mixture off the wooden stir spoon and had tested some of it between our thumb and fourth finger for granules — after we wiped off the kitchen table, just as Auntie Thelma would, and then we took steaming dollops from the pot. They cooled on the tabletop into the brown sugar cakes that we knew everyone would just love. The smell they gave off, as they hardened into the precious cakes, would have fooled any of our friends dropping by and noticing Auntie Thelma in the vicinity.

But Auntie Thelma was not impressed when Jeffrey and I presented our mothers with a plate of our very first attempt at doing something meaningful for ourselves, these sugar cakes. My mother, however, was the opposite. She broke one, bit into it and turned it over to look at it from as many angles as possible, as if she could not believe her eyes and taste buds. The smile on her face made my heart warm. Auntie Thelma bit the sugar cake without breaking it and held up the remainder in front of her eyes.

"Who you two say make these sugar cakes here?" she asked.

"We did," Jeffrey said, as baffled as me.

"We used the recipe that you gave us, remember," I said.

"I remember," Auntie Thelma said. "I remember. And that's the problem I'm having with these here sugar cakes. They could just as well did be make by me. I want the two o' you to make *your own-own* sugar cakes. Not mine. Not what you can go down the road and buy from anybody else, but your own. Make something of your own. That is why when I make my sugar cakes they does be different from anybody else. Because they're mine."

We were baffled. We had expected praise and hugs and pats on the back. We expected her to tease that we could now go into business making and selling sugar cakes, that we would put the hawkers and shopkeepers and fruit vendors out of business, if only because we were capable of making the best sugar cakes around, sugar cakes even as good as hers.

"No man, people got to be distinct. Yuh can't keep copying and copying all the time," Auntie Thelma said. "Otherwise, you'll just be like a parrot. That is why I keep telling you two that you got to go out and experience the world for yourself and when you do, you got to make things your own way. Yes, man, I believe everybody gotta experience all the whole world, both the good and the bad, the high and the low, take your chances, change an ingredient here and there, make a bad sugar cake the first time but keep improving until you make it the best sugar cake anybody ever did taste. 'Cause the best thing would be, no matter how it taste, good or bad, it is your own. It belongs to you and nobody else. And if it turn out to be the best, well, what more can anybody ask for. But I can only talk. I can only beat up my gums talking. The choice belong to you two, the young generation."

She bit into the sugar cake again. This time, she shook her head, glanced at my mother, and shot us the look of approval that we wanted so badly. At the same time, we knew that while she was acknowledging that the sugar cakes were good, that they were even up to her own exacting standards, at the same time something was missing. We had not pushed on beyond where she had left off, beyond the point to which she had taken us. We had not even made a tentative step in the direction she had pointed us. We were still the babies, holding on, afraid to let go, frightened to forget. "You know what, you can take them sugar cakes and give them to your fathers, particularly you, Jeffrey," she said as we were leaving the room. This time, there was a ring of laughter, of possibly resignation, in her voice. "Your father will love them, 'cause all the men I know are like that. Your father'll say that they taste just as if I did make them. He's that way: once he finds out something's nice, he don't ever mess with it. You can't improve on anything that is already the best, not for him, you can only keep on copying and mimicking. He don't change things for changing sake. Just the same old thing. Sometimes I gotta remind him that the old people like to say that variety is the spice of life. But not for him." She was laughing louder, indicating also that she was perhaps growing tired with this episode and wanted to move on to discussing something else with my mother. "God knows, that is who he is. You two, my own two children that I love more better than anything else in the world, that I want to see become the best they can ever dream of, you two got to know if you want just to be copiers."

೧೯

And this was why, for the first time since the meeting with Alberto Gomez, Jeffrey had descended from the emotional high to the reality of the enormity of the risk and increased personal danger that came with this job. He was only now understanding how inextricably and unexpectedly he had been drawn into this vortex. Jeffrey was like a straw floating in the ocean, feeling the sudden upward draught of the warm air sucking it into the eye of one of these devastating hurricanes still roaming the Atlantic. He was now part of a power structure that the people who mattered to him would call the seat of corruption. Even now his father would dismiss it as nothing more than a den of thieves, a scourge on the islands akin to the visitation of death itself. Or of the most destructive tempests.

He had accepted the elevation. In fact, now he was inclined to celebrate it, to look for the more optimistic aspects of the situation, and this acceptance, more than anything else, was the symbol of how much he had changed, so that even his mother might not recognize him. It was also the clearest indication of the growing chasm between him and his old man. Perhaps this was the price he had to pay for his independence; for making sure in his old age, and unlike his father, he would not have to rely on others. He would never end up like his father. He was too daring, too smart to allow this to happen, to allow his mind to be caged by all those traditions that had enslaved and trapped his father. In a way, too, the acceptance was the clearest sign that Jeffrey was too like his father and he now would not change.

Jeffrey's memories were different, but just as haunted.

"Sure, your father is a big fellow in the church, but that doesn't mean one damn. Don't you know it is my father that supports the church?" The voice of his high school friend, Mark Toppin, came back like a boomerang he had angrily thrown away in frustration years ago, with such force and such distance, it took all this time for the mocking remark to come back. This assertion had been the genesis of everything he wished and hoped for, and everything he later rebelled against. The pain was the same as when Mark Toppin had thrown out this challenge some twenty years earlier. Even the fact that Mark's father was eventually jailed for embezzlement did not lessen the hurt, for by then Mark and his father were wealthy enough that he spent less than a year in prison, and at the end of the sentence the family simply immigrated to New York with all their money. Mark's father was not even as well respected as the grave digger, but he gave his family a better life, and took personal risks to do so. Only a few people would have considered the Toppins traitors for putting all their money in a business in New Jersey. People like Mark Toppin were the demons that drove Jeffrey on. For what was a year, or even two or three, compared to a lifetime? Why not accept a small deviation, a digression, a riff so as to return to the original motif, intention and destination in a stronger position than before the detour? Indeed, why not grab the moment and shape it, before time, as it always does, snatches the instant back and makes it conform?

∞

"We must use every means available to us," Prime Minister Watkins was saying, "every means possible to improve our lot." With his eyes shut, Jeffrey saw the fiery politician flailing away at the air. It was an image permanently engraved on his mind, the picture of this animated man speaking to the throng of people in the national square. People and their voices like waves, like the waves he saw from the plane crossing the water, the waves that brought all these memories back. And he laughed. He told me he did: at the idea of how he had risen to walk with prime ministers, at how he could even achieve so much more. For he too could become the puppet for his own puppeteer, as well.

"We must re-examine," the voice continued, "we must re-evaluate all the things we have rejected out of hand because other people told us we should. We must be a nation of new thinkers and we must create the wealth we need for our improvement, by our own selves. What might be bad for countries like the United States and Britain might not necessarily be bad for us; and what is good for us might not be good for them." Jeffrey had written the words; the passion behind the delivery had been bought by the money promised for supporting the illegal business.

Watkins had come to power promising the islanders much and he had tried just about every legal means to achieve these dreams — that he would gener- ate enough wealth through exports and industry at

182

home to guarantee happy retirements for the elderly, that for all of them there would be self-sufficiency. Nobody could doubt that he genuinely wanted to deliver such things as education, health care and a profound improvement in the standard of living for the next generation. Nobody doubted that he wanted these things to spring organically from among the people, to be theirs, to be a gift to themselves and their future. Such would be his legacy to this island. But with limited financial resources, realistically he could only do so much. And that, Jeffrey thought, has always been the traditional ending to this particular story: dreams that die in the light of reality, dreams smashed against the rocks of the island, not cradled in a palm that could recollect them and rearrange them, but scattered into the very sea, each to its own ordination. Good intentions that remain unborn or just drown or drift away like misspent flotsam. All because of a people content to remain within boundaries. All because a gift, once received, had to be used according to the rules that came with it. Maybe that was why so many people stop dreaming, and why, because they are unable to say no, thank you, they simply accept the gift and wait for the water to cover their heads. This is the part of the story that his father always neglected to tell. Good enough is definitely not well enough, as his father would say. A promise has to be kept. The intention behind the gift is more important than what is in the package, or even the package itself.

Until Jeffrey had returned home three years before to advise the prime minister how to turn the island into a financial paradise of offshore banks, trading houses and a brokerage firm, nothing had worked to improve economic prospects. Conditions on the island were in fact still slipping, deteriorating as the international market for sugar slid, the small hotels went out of business, unable to compete with less expensive vacation spots elsewhere, and the paltry foreign aid dried up even further. The government continued to be under relentless pressure from a liberated and youthful generation to produce for them.

When Prime Minister Watkins could deliver nothing more, his popularity plummeted, forcing him to hurriedly think of a new strategy, or to accept what was offered, strings and all. Reluctantly, he saw the political wisdom of giving Jeffrey a free hand, receiving the gifts offered and passing on the offerings and burnt sacrifices to the others. Jeffrey's was the only good short-term offer to come his way. And times were brown, very brown, the colour of the sun-drenched grass. It did not take much persuading to co-opt the prime minister, for the bulldozers to move in and remove the shanty homes replacing them with five-star hotels, a convention centre, a technology school and high-rise buildings. The fields, many already fallow because sugar was not profitable, would be used for other things. Where there were once fields of sugar cane and of yams, potatoes, okra and eddoes, there were now big square buildings of uniform height and size, parking lots with recently painted lines for parking expensive and imported cars. Young men and women filed into the buildings in the morning, when the sun is gleaming off them and everything is so bright and wonderful, and they filed out again in the evening, when the sun is waning and the softer, spent hue hangs lazily from the glass, the shadows merging in the parking lots. The young women, particularly, were dressed in tidy uniforms as if they were still at school, as if afraid to let go of a part of their life now past. Unable to forget. So they hold on to whatever is given them.

It was easy in the good days before the novelty wore off. Before the prime minister too needed a quick fix even if he did not know the reasons for our trips to Bogotá. He, too, had become just as trapped, even earlier than the two of us. But for a while the magician produced. Jeffrey merely had to point out how, in two years, the Americans and British intended to reduce cane sugar imports from the island to almost zero and bananas would no longer get preferential treatment in Europe. He only had to mention Jimmy Ashton, tired of life in opposition. "You know Jimmy. He won't hesitate to accept my offer," Jeffrey had said. "If you don't want it, we will offer it to him. It's as simple as that." Even as a dabbler, an amateur, he had power, a strong hand in any negotiations. From then, the prime minister was putty in his hands. He became even more malleable when, for good measure, Jeffrey pointed out the possibility that the burgeoning tourist industry would be destroyed if the Organization and the Americans turned the island into a battlefield, for this was, perhaps, the most frightening thought: any hint of danger would be enough to scare the hundreds of thousands of tourists away and leave the economy in ruin. Jeffrey would use his international contacts to gain an agreement that they would stay away from the island, that they would leave the island free to follow its own dictates.

Jeffrey smiled. All fortunes were not provided by fate. Not for him, any way. He remembered his father saying to him as a little boy how impossible it was to

take a glass of rum from the bottle without first breaking the seal on the bottle.

"You have to take off the cover," the old man had
said. "The longer you wait, the thirstier you'd get. It's
as simple as that." Prime Minister Watkins was facing
the same dilemma. It was obvious he could not maintain his pristine goodness and attain his goals. Neither
could Aubrey Spencer's son. The same way he had
first rationalized, he did again. He could not afford the
luxury of worrying too much; he must be pragmatic,
must have a good plan, with escape valves and paths
built into it, with time for pleasures and enjoying the
good life. He must bury the ghost of memories, he told
himself. From then on, he had to be concerned only
about the future, about demonstrating his worth to his
father, and my father, and to Prime Minister Watkins.
And to a doubting Thomas like me, he must show the
way. He also accepted that if he was so wrong somebody was bound to let him know. Such trust would be
the check telling him when he had tarried too long.

There was another Jeffrey I knew. I will always
remember.

In a moment of defiance, I had decided that I would
not go to Sunday school. I was tired of hearing my
father's voice, at home, at school when he came to
assembly to take prayers with us Monday mornings
and Friday evenings, at morning service on Sundays
and once more later in the day at Sunday school. I had
noticed how some boys did not have this burden. They
just played. They went to the sea and played bat and
ball on the sand, diving into the water, over the waves,

to recover the ball one of them had struck into the water, shouting and laughing, their bodies drenched with the water, their white teeth gleaming in the fresh afternoon sun, just bowling and batting and having fun. No girls present. And me passing by and heading once more into the presence of my father's voice. Long before me, Jeffrey had decided there was an alternative. He had told me about the boys playing on the beach and how it was so much fun just to watch them rather than to put up with boring Sunday school. When he did not show up at Sunday school I covered as best I could for him. I met him afterwards and filled him in on the discussion, just in case his parents were to ask.

I decided to change this routine one afternoon. I got dressed as usual, took down my best pants from the hanger, put on the white sleeveless vest and then the white shirt my mother had just finished ironing. I put on my socks, reaching up almost to my knees, and my pants which reached down to my knees. I fixed my tie with a knot, the type Jeffrey had shown me, the style that I now used in place of the old-man fashion my father had taught me. Taking the collection quarter from my mother, I kissed her and stepped out into the sun.

"Remember to come right back home after Sunday school, you hear me, Edmund," my mother called from the shadows in the house. "Don't stop around to play. For you know how much you like to play. And if you play, you will only get your clothes nasty, and you will have to wear back dirty clothes to church tonight. You hear me?"

"Yes, mum," I said. "Bye, mum."

But I did not go to church. Instead, I made a turn that took me along the beach, where the boys were already playing. I stopped underneath a tree and shouted to them. I lingered and I threw the ball back to them when it was hit in the direction of the tree, and even though I was not part of the game, I, too, was playing. Five more minutes, I told myself. Then I will definitely leave. Another five minutes went by and then another and just as I was leaving, one of the boys came over to talk to me and I promised myself that I would leave in another five minutes, even though I knew by then I was already late for Sunday school. But I could not get away. The balls kept coming my way. Then it was too late. I would have no explanation for arriving so late. The collection plate would have passed by. So, seeing the hawker come by with her bags of nuts and candies, I put the collection money to another use and I fed the boys playing on the beach. Then they were gone, except for those at the far end of the beach. All of them heading home for one reason or another: some to eat, some to do homework, some to bring in the sheep, goats and cows from the pastures. But it was too early for me to return home without suspicion and, besides, the water looked so inviting, the waves rising and falling and I could hear, could even see, the young boys further on still at play, how they were laughing in the water, how they were diving and returning to the surface to wipe the water away from their faces, to reveal white teeth, peals of sweet laughter, and I wanted to be like them.

Fortunately, nobody was on the beach. I took off my clothes, all except my underwear. I folded my socks and put them in my shoes. I put my tie in my pants pocket. I folded the shirt, pants and vest too. I placed them on top of the shoes, in one pile, underneath the tree, where I could see them from the water. And I ran into the water, thinking that I would bathe for just a while, and that I would come out, slip out of my underwear and into my pants and shirt, into my socks, and I would go home and sneak into the house, so my mother would not see how my hair was. And then I must have died and found myself in another world. When I returned to the tree, my clothes were missing. I could not believe my eyes. I stared at the spot—there was not even an indentation in the sand, not even an impression from the shoe or footprint. Just vanished. Perhaps I had not returned to the right tree; to the right part of the beach; to the right beach for that matter. So I started running frantically from one tree to another. It was like I was going from one world to another to another and then back again, with someone playing a trick on me, with me knowing that I just had to find the right tree. But I could not. I should have been home by now. The underwear was getting cold against my skin; the breeze was not as warm, and I didn't want to bathe any more. I wanted to go home. But I could not risk walking the streets virtually naked. I knew some-body was bound to see me and to report me to my father or to the school master the next morning. And, underneath the tree, the very one from which I had thrown the balls, bought the nuts and sweets, where I had placed my clothes in a pile, I crouched down, afraid to sit any more on the sand that was now getting too cool and gritty for my arse and legs, and I shivered. I cried softly. For I was a big boy and could not afford the indignity of crying too loud. But I cried. I watched the sun retreating, making a slow dive below the sea, sinking out of reach, but promising at least some cover for my nakedness.

"Hey, big boy, what you're doing there? You hiding or something, man?"

189

I was so happy to hear that familiar voice.

"Why you didn't come to Sunday school? I was looking for you. Something wrong with you?"

"Jeffrey," I said. "My clothes. I don't have any."

"What happened to you?"

"Somebody like they steal my clothes or something. I was bathing."

"Shit, man."

"All I have is my underwear, and now it's full o' sand, and cold too."

"Okay, give it to me!"

"What?"

"The underwear, so I can go and wash it out for you. I might have to go home and get some clothes for you."

I handed him the underwear, thinking he would wash out the sand and promptly return it to me, that I would now stand underneath this tree until he came back with some clothes, that I would think of an excuse for my mother, that I would stiffen my back and heart for the inevitable lashing from my father. But Jeffrey did not return. Not right away. I was under the tree, stark naked. It must have been an hour, perhaps two or three for all I know, before he showed up. I was at the point where I had stepped from underneath the tree, thinking in my folly, to risk the worse, that maybe under the cover of darkness, with a burst of strength, I could just run all the way home, even though people might laugh, I would just keep running, even though my lungs would feel like bursting and that I should stop and catch my breath, I would just keep running, with the palms of my hands covering my balls, just running.

In Jeffrey's hands were not only my underwear but my shirt, pants, socks and shoes. They were all dripping wet, soaked.

190

"I find some boys over there playing with your clothes," he said. "I went up to them and said, hey what you doing with them clothes. And they laugh and run away. I pick them up. I don't know what they did with your vest and tie. I'm sorry, man."

I put on the wet pants and shirt and I walked home barefoot with the socks in my pocket. By the time we got home, my mother and father had already left for church. I put the clothes in a basin of water and crawled into my bed, waiting for the judgement that was now inevitable.

"Tell me something," Jeffrey said before leaving. "Why do you like them trees so much?"

"What trees?" I asked.

"The one you were under from this afternoon into the evening. Why you like them so?"

"What you mean?"

"The cordea trees, the one I saw you spending the whole afternoon under. Why you like them so much?"

"Oh," I said. "I didn't notice."

"Okay, Preacher Man," he said. "I'll see you tomorrow."

"Thanks, Jeffrey. I don't know what I would have done without you."

"No sweat, man."

"Jeffrey," I said. "Just in case they ask: what was the golden text at Sunday school?"

"I don't know, man," he shot back. "I don't know."

And he disappeared into the darkness.

SEVEN

In the calmness of the first class section, with wisps of white clouds drifting by outside the window, Jeffrey could reflect and rationalize why he had chosen to go this route, why in the end he had no choice but to stray from the approved path. So far he had done quite well for himself. But he could not explain away all his fears of the feeling that he'd turned bad, that he'd sold out, like a Judas giving it all up for a few pieces of silver. He had not grown into the law-abiding, God-fearing man his mother and father had hoped. He had already betrayed the trust of a few very special people and would most likely have to betray many more to remain at the top of the heap.

"Mr. Spencer, you're too hard on Jeffrey." He could see the headmaster sitting at a table talking to his father. It must have been after some funeral, for that was the only time the elitist headmaster passed by the house. "He's going to grow into a fine young man. You don't have to worry about him. And he's doing quite well with his studies too. I am very hopeful for him. So don't be so hard on your son."

"I hope what you say is true," his father had replied calmly, as if he wasn't too convinced or swayed by the headmaster's views. "As you know, Mr. James, Thelma and me, as parents, are instructed by God with certain duties. We have to bend the tree while it is still young and we have to make sure we keep pointing him on the straight and narrow path. Jeffrey must not only open up his head to take in the learning you're teaching him at school and reach all the potential you and others say he has; he must also learn respect and how to walk around this island with his head high, his conscience clean and his hands strong and unstained. Not only book knowledge."

"He can do it all, papie Spencer," the headmaster assured him. "He can do it."

☙❧

The first time Jeffrey had such knots in his stomach was when he was twenty years old and on an aircraft headed for Toronto. For him, this was the memory associated with the party held the eve of his departure, when his mother found a special way to send him off to fulfil the potential headmaster James and others had spotted in him. But I remember the occasions for other things, too. For me, this night was the time Auntie Thelma sang. She was front and centre, in her long white dress, sleeveless, her scatting lasting into the morning, her voice strong and powerful even without an amplifier, the session ending only with the arrival of the first rays of sun, when Aubrey Spencer, his bass on the low frequency, put down his guitar for the last time and mopped his brows. When Auntie Thelma hugged my mother. I remember the music, the sweet songs and even a mother's lament. Jeffrey remembered those times, too, but for other reasons. Because he had never been in a plane, and because none of his family had ever had that privilege, although they could relate with great vividness the horrible experiences of others who had entered the steel birds, he was afraid, sitting bolt upright in the plane, expecting to hear at any moment some tell-tale noise indicating the plane was out of control, hurling to certain destruction in the Atlantic Ocean down below.

But fliers have to take the risk, the same way the early European seamen in sail boats risked everything in the hope of finding another route to India and ended up in the Caribbean, in the Americas, the home of the drugs that were now as precious as the shiploads of spices and gold the European adventurers had hoped to bring back from Asia centuries ago. The same way the cargo out of Africa sang, sweet and low, about their betrayal. About their wretchedness. When you couldn't even trust your own, not your mother, not your father, not a brother, sister nor friend. No one. All of them were on the take, and you were the sacrificial lamb. Singing about their redemption, too, not by their hands, but by some amazing grace. Of reconciling them all in song as they slipped into the unknown that was the future. With only a song.

But the initial fear of flying didn't last long. After an hour, he was actually enjoying the flight. Just like almost everything else in life; and as you know, brothers and sisters, there is always greater trepidation at the thought of doing a thing than actually doing it. Once the action begins, or when it's been done once or twice, the sense of danger, the fears, the wounded conscience receded, sometimes disappear totally, leaving the person, as he explained, to wonder what was the big concern in the first place. Leaving the person to enjoy the ecstasy of conquest, of the new creation. A new music, transformed and pushed beyond a state boundary, the silence forced to recede some more.

194

So it was taking possession of the first drug ship-
ment off-loaded at the Toronto airport holding his
breath while watching the men from a reputable shipping company deliver the containers to his office. And
so it was on the very first flight out of Barbados just
over fifteen years ago.

Everything was a journey into the unknown. He felt
as he had when he was a little boy, spending the afternoons at the beach playing with the other boys who
didn't have to waste hot afternoons in church. The first
time he skipped the weekly drudgery, he had left
home as if he were going to the church, had taken the
ten cents his mother had given him for the collection,
but he didn't turn up at the church. With the collection
money, he and his friends bought a pack of cigarettes
and twenty mints to kill the smell of smoke on their
breath. As he shared the illicit gains, he knew he was
buying their commitment not to inform on him. This
was his first lesson of how money could demand such
friendship and loyalty.

Still, for the next couple of weeks he had lived in
dire trepidation of being found out. When nothing
happened, he tried it more often, arriving at the beach
with the mints and the cigarettes, sitting under the
trees and taking off his shoes and socks so he would
not take back home sand in them for his parents to discover. As far as he knew, he had been resourceful. His
father had certainly never hinted that he knew of
Jeffrey's illicit afternoons.

Sometimes his father could be like that. Secretive.
Or talking in parables: "You can buy land under the
darkness of night, but you can't hide and work it.
Eventually, everything must come to light, even things
done under the darkness of night."

That was why, even now, Jeffrey didn't know whether to believe his father was ignorant of his doings.

∞

But Toronto did not give him the kind of challenge he wanted. Enrolling in the fancy Osgoode Law Faculty at York University wasn't easy. They didn't accept his qualifications from back home, despite what the catalogue from the Canadian Consulate had suggested. Neither did they claim to see any evidence of the innate academic prowess observed by people like headmaster James. With little regard for his feelings, they bluntly told him he would have to spend two years upgrading his education before he could be reconsidered. He took this on as a challenge, but lost. Osgoode was unattainable, even if he did eventually get into the university's business faculty and excelled. Still, Jeffrey had the first harsh lesson of life, the first dashed dream, the shattered hopes of returning home in glory like a conqueror from foreign exploits, all bedecked in his long flowing black robe and lawyer's wig to prepare him for the springboard of politics.

Even then the Immigration Department gave him student visas for only three months. Four times a year, in humiliation, he had to trot down to the main immigration centre to join hundreds like him. Although the government offices didn't open until 7:30 in the morning, by 5 o'clock a line would already be formed, snaking around the building. He soon learned to present himself at the centre the night before to secure a favourable position in the line. And once there he had to stand in the same spot all the time, in snow, or rain, chilly winds or warm nights. When the sun came up, his feet and toes would already be numb and his bladder bursting so that sometimes he simply took out his penis and fired away up against the wall, all the time hoping the cops wouldn't pass by. He couldn't afford to lose his place in the line. And he would be so hungry. But he hated coffee, and doughnuts, too. Then he would finally see an immigration officer and be made to feel humble and humiliated all over again, answering the same questions every time: "Are you working, you know it is illegal to work? Do you have enough money to exist on for another three months? Let me see your bank book" — as if every time he was begging and beseeching them to let him have the privilege of staying in the country, as if they didn't believe that he was a student.

"No, sir, I'm not working," he heard himself responding. So often it was at the tip of his tongue to retort how could he find the opportunity to look for work when he spent so much time standing in lines and begging for the right to be in the country. He didn't and he never forgave himself for being such a coward. "The money is from my father in Barbados; he sends it every two weeks. The supporting letter is from the Anglican Church in Barbados. He works for them."

"I see," the officer said, reading the letter, refolding it and placing it in the passport. "That's quite a nice letter, eh. We got to be very careful who we allow to stay and study in this country."

"I know."

"And did I read that letter right?" the officer asked, breaking into laughter. "Did it say that your father is a *soil technician*? That's not some fancy agricultural position, eh?"

"No."

"I didn't think so," he said, stamping the passport, not even bothering to look up as he asked the question. "So, what is a *soil technician* in your country?"

"A grave digger."

"Oh," the officer said, startled enough to look at him. It was one of the times he was so proud of his father and his ability to shock strangers. For his father's job always proved one thing: that no matter who we are, we would someday, in some country, in some moment, meet someone like his dad. In that way, we are all equal, and he saw and heard that equality on the faces and in the voices of those who normally liked to forget.

But the effect never lasted. It was just as quickly forgotten again. They returned to the earlier moment, as if nothing more than a twinkling of the eye had occurred. Sometimes, he felt the officers wanted him to pledge eternal gratefulness for being saved from being sent back home, to the moment before reminded of their mortality. They would want to eradicate that one human bond by restoring, reconfiguring and refashioning the inequities and inequalities. From early on, he knew that because of the colour of his skin he would always be made to feel he was an outsider, less than an immigrant who came from somewhere in Europe. Later, Jeffrey's father's eyes glazed over when his son explained how this experience had changed him. How it would change anyone. "Small things have big impacts on small minds," his father had responded, banishing in a carefree manner any importance associated with this treatment. "Everybody just got to know who he or she is, what they are. Nobody can take that from you, once you know who you are." Small or not, Jeffrey's mind had changed. The gulf got wider.

198

It was even worse the few times he crossed over the border into the United States. "You said you were born in Barbados," the stern-faced immigration officer said as he thumbed through the passport, looking at the document as if he thought it was fake or from one of those pretentious two-bit islands that actually believed they were a sovereign nation. "And you're a student. Which university?"

Four times out of six they took him off the Greyhound bus and sent him back across the Buffalo Peace Bridge by taxi, at the U.S. government's expense. And they did not even give him an explanation. Just the indignity of being bundled into a car and having his passport handed over, not to him, but to the scruffy taxi driver for safe keeping until he was safely off precious U.S. soil.

๑๑

"You know how to deal with these... er... people," the broker was saying. To Jeffrey's surprise, he had been called by someone at Canadian Insurance Ltd. looking to recruit salesmen to let them loose on unsuspecting immigrants. He would always tell himself if he turned out bad, ended up on the wrong side, it could be dated back to this interview.

Canadian Insurance crystallized everything for him, made him see he could achieve his goals of power and financial security only by stepping off the track on which his father had put him. Maybe, he had told himself, his mother had been too optimistic. Obviously, there was no future in legal studies, no room for a black man to make money quickly, even if he could break into the hierarchy of this monolithic profession.

"You're one of them. You know who has and wants insurance," the bespectacled interviewer said nonchalantly. "The trick is always to get a list of references from each person you talk to. That's how you make money. Always make sure you leave with two things: a signed contract of some kind and, of course, the list of names. Names, that's what matters."

Jeffrey would seek out the new immigrants and sell them any type of insurance policy and, most importantly, get the referrals. But there was no money in ripping off poor people like himself. So he moved to selling bonds, mutual funds and shares of companies with dubious listings on obscure exchanges. The commissions paid right off the top were good, and his friend Vincent Smith, another Bajan he had met in the immigration line, showed him short cuts to making money. It was well known in the business that Vincent was the top black man in this investment business, that he was unscrupulous, too, just as long as there was a steady stream of commissions. He also showed Jeffrey how to keep one step ahead of the security regulators and jail.

"This is where the money is," Vincent Smith had said. "Selling bonds and mutual funds to rich people who have other expensive habits. Not selling fucking insurance and ripping off people like yourself. You need people who can get into leverage. You need a banker who'll back you, just as long as there is something in it for him. Leverage, man."

Soon they were buying and selling much more than commercial papers. Six months in the job, Vincent's volume was so high he was employing Jeffrey as a full-time assistant, using his own brokerage licence to buy millions of dollars worth of government savings bonds, treasury bills and just about any stock he could get his hands on.

Jeffrey would buy the stock for hundreds of people he didn't know and had never met. Vincent supplied him with a list of names every week. The money was always in cash. And every week he provided the same stern warning that whatever Jeffrey did, he was never to buy securities or deposit large sums in the United States.

This struck Jeffrey as strange: many of Vincent's clients were American and, when they cashed in the short-term portfolios, they all demanded payment in American dollars. Every Friday, Vincent gave him another list of names and bank accounts into which to deposit the proceeds from the sale of the securities he had bought a short while earlier. The volume became so great that soon he was working exclusively for Vincent and making the highest commission in his brokerage house. Every summer, they took some of the top clients to golf tournaments or on special trips. Vincent always wore his white shoes, with his Rolex watches and his fancy cars. Talking quietly, always deferential, his eyes sharp and flashing, the smile quick to his face. The handshake always at the ready. And his big house on the side of a hill—such a long way from the days when he sold chunks of pork for his father back home, or when he started out selling used cars in Toronto.

Only once did Jeffrey make a mistake. He issued a cheque through the Bank of America. Vincent almost hit the roof, and calmed down only when assured the financial instrument was drawn at the Toronto branch of the bank.

"I should have known better," Vincent said later by way of a reprimand. "I should know you can't do anything in the fucking United States without they asking for a social security number. That's what makes doing business in Canada so easy. There is nothing to trace."

Eventually, it got too hot. There were too many complaints, and the regulators started asking questions that could land them in front of a judge. They abandoned trading in bonds and stocks and mutual funds.

Vincent started a travel company. Jeffrey accepted the offer to be a partner at Executive Wholesale Tours. His job was to seek out new destinations and make deals with hoteliers and restaurateurs. Vincent took particular interest in chartering planes and flying them empty to exotic Latin American countries, or filling them with people looking for last-minute sell-offs. They would go to any destination if the price were right. Such people were his best cover, as long as they understood that the weight limits on their luggage would be strictly controlled. One Friday night, Vincent turned up at Jeffrey's apartment with two first-class tickets to Bogotá. "Let's go and see the sights," he said. "Maybe we'll find a few people down there to do a bit of business."

That was the first of several trips to Colombia. Each time they left from a different city in Canada or the United States. They never flew the same airline and they paid for the tickets in ruffled dollar bills. Jeffrey had no idea he was being recruited.

On one trip to Bogotá, Vincent abruptly decided he wasn't going back to Toronto. He looked scared and worried. It was the first time Jeffrey had seen him like that. Instead Vincent said he was going home, back to Barbados, a place he had not visited in thirteen years. He was prepared to abandon everything in Toronto and to start afresh in the land of his birth. Until he sent the all clear, he got Jeffrey to promise not to tell even his friends where he was.

Jeffrey took over running the travel agency, telling people he had bought Vincent out. Three weeks later, the

202

documents saying he had paid $500,000 for the agency turned up in the mail. Even a cancelled cheque with his signature was included. They were posted in Miami and all looked legit. The Canadian government accepted the documents and turned over the business licence to him.

Much later he found out what had happened but by then he was in too deep. His friend had left the country one step ahead of the RCMP and the FBI, who were working on an international drug cartel case in Miami. The Canadian government impounded all of Vincent's property, except for the travel agency, which, of course, was no longer his. Jeffrey read in the newspapers of the arrest and trials of several people in the United States and Asia — some of whom he recalled doing business with — and about how the governments of several countries had deemed this the most successful sting operation involving banks.

But business went on despite the setback. Some procedures changed. Jeffrey became the main contact for the special supplies to Toronto and Vancouver and Montreal, especially after a chat in the food court downstairs from the brokerage at which he worked. He learned the usefulness of chartering planes and not cramming the cargo hold with passenger luggage. Without missing a step, he filled the void once his friend was gone.

And like Vincent, he learned how to skip the country ahead of the RCMP and the FBI who were trying to cut the pipeline leading into New York and Detroit, Buffalo and Seattle. By then he had a much wider network, but the territory was too big and he didn't know all the people. It was not surprising he would make a slip, a forgivable one because of his enthusiasm. His bosses simply told him to abandon everything and flee. He should return home and cool his heels, while his trail ran cold and the RCMP and FBI become concerned with more active suppliers and distributors.

By then Jeffrey's mother had died. And, as he once told me, it wasn't true that the fatal heart attack came from finding out what had become of her son. It wasn't true, he insisted. The death made it easy for him to argue he was returning to take care of his father. After all, he had made enough money overseas and, in an age of computers and telecommunications satellites, a businessman didn't need to be in North America to close deals there. Nobody questioned his intentions, particularly after he built the mammoth house in Lodge Road and his father moved in. Everybody accepted the house had been built with proceeds from real estate and from the sale of Executive Wholesale Tours.

ꔷꔷ

What Jeffrey also learned from Vincent was not to even try the stuff. Not once. One morning, Vincent's body was found floating in the water off the island's south coast. Nobody needed to explain why and how he had died. As his dependence grew, Vincent had started to talk too much, and he was not producing, causing shipments to go missing. Vincent had never readjusted to living back at home. He could not fit back in, remaining a stranger in the land of his birth. He was too international in his outlook; too constrained and imprisoned on the island. In the end, despite his talents, he was of no help: not to the people, not to the bosses and not to himself. He had to go.

More to the point, he had made the unforgivable mistake of collaborating with an informant from the

United States, someone who had come to the island as a tourist and befriended him. Someone in the U.S. Embassy tipped off the Organization before too much damage was done. One night, his bosses rented one of the cruise ships that took tourists on sightseeing trips off the island. It was supposed to be a private party for the men and women in the local branch of the Organization. Vincent was allowed to snort as much as he liked, to drink as much as he wanted and to consume all the food he could handle. Below, a calypso band was blaring away and the guests were dancing and singing at the top of their lungs. Jeffrey saw the nod of the head summoning him from the hold of the ship. At the same time, two burly men stood guard at the stairs, just in case they had to stop any of the revellers from going up for a breath of fresh air — for the inconvenience was to be only momentary. A mere pause.

Few people heard the iron anchor with the body attached splash or see it sink into the water. Until the very last moment, Vincent probably didn't understand what was going on. If he didn't, it was his own fault: he should have been wise to the ways of the business. And he would have been if he still had a brain. Jeffrey recalled feeling a sour lump in his throat and wanting to vomit as he heard the pitiful sobs and pleading of his friend. Just as suddenly, it dawned on him this exercise was as much a message to him as it was the ultimate punishment for Vincent.

Later, when the dancing and the party finished and the guests were too drunk to realize what was happening, they pulled up the anchor and cut the body loose. It fell heavily into the water again and promptly disappeared. For nights in his dreams he would see images of the face, the bulging eyes, the contortion of terror on the cheeks and in the opened mouth. The informer was found in her hotel room the next day. The telephone wires were ripped from the wall and a red contact book was on the floor with the leaves torn out. Apparently, they got her before she could pass on any damaging information. The maids found her in a pool of blood, her tongue hanging through the gash that used to be her throat. The message was clear. Nobody had to tell him he was in charge and he better not fuck up.

Of course, every storyteller has an agenda, and it is not always the truth. Somewhere in this mix of things, Jeffrey would have had his interview outside the water-front restaurant. Sometime along the way, I assumed, these things could only have happened this way.

☯

Aubrey Spencer refused to bury Vincent. "He got what he deserved," the old man said. "Many of the people around here benefiting from his wickedness will get the same treatment too. At least, they will from me. They better not look to me to bury them."

One of the lesser grave diggers did a haphazard job in a signal to the community that was as powerful as the slashing of the throat by the barons. The informer's body was sent back home for burial.

☯

I closed my eyes, squeezing them tight, hoping for numbness and diversion. But the voice was relentless. Hurting as usual. And spiteful to me, her son.

"Never mind," she was saying. "You did try your best. And if you did your best that is the most anybody can ask

206

you to do." And she was hugging me, so tightly that I smelled the mixture of perfume, sweat and talcum powder. But even then that wasn't enough. No consolation prize ever is adequate, my brothers and sisters, especially when you know the pain of deception and betrayal. It is always present in my mind, just as it was that day in the aircraft so many thousands of feet above the Americas, just as it is now in another plane so high above the Caribbean, and as it will be when I come back to ground. I was looking – for perhaps the millionth time – over my mother's shoulder at the plate with the sugar cakes, so meticulously arranged, all almost equal in size and shape. The perfect sugar cakes. A part of me, now beyond my reach.

We had taken Auntie Thelma's advice, but on this occasion we had decided to work alone. I took my own coconut, sugar, essences, water and spices and boiled them in my mother's kitchen, knowing that Jeffrey was working on a similar concoction in his mother's home. We had agreed to take the sugar cakes over to Auntie Thelma when they – our best work, with our special ingredients – were cooled and fully formed. In a blind test, she would judge which batch was the better. The timing and the surprise were to be the key. Only one of us would get her blessing. Jeffrey had suggested that too. But at the last moment, Jeffrey changed plans. As I was laying out the last of my treats, he grabbed the plates, and with me following unsuspectingly behind, he marched into the room where his mother was sitting.

"Mama, look what we've done," he announced. "We decided to take your advice. But we decided that only one of us could be the champion. Here, take one of mine."

"What you boys are up to, now?" she asked. "I don't know why boys always have to be so competitive."

He pushed the plate with my offering in front of her. She took one and bit into it, a smile breaking on her face. She took *another bite, as if fascinated. She looked at her fingers as if to confirm the sugar had dried perfectly and that no syrup was on her hand. Then she took another bite.*

"Now, try one that Edmund made," Jeffrey said, pushing the other plate at her. I almost died. She bit into one of the ill-formed and still sticky sugar cakes, but, try as she might, she could not hide her preference.

"Well, Jeffrey, I must hand it to you. If I must be honest, I must say I like yours the best. They might even be better than mine."

"Yes," Jeffrey said in elation. He spun on his heels and took the rejected plate and its contents back into the kitchen, leaving me, speechless in all my frustration, to deal with his mother. For how could I explain that he had stolen my blessing, that he had used a birthright to get what he wanted? Yes, I know he was not my keeper, and that I had a right to speak up, to anticipate that he would have contrived a deception if the blessing was something he needed so badly. And yes, I know that he later accused me of pouting and of making too big a deal of a small matter, of a boy's prank. Of not having a sense of humour. Too cry-babyish, he said. Still, I know I should have been prepared. I should never have let my guard down, never been trusting that everyone plays by the rules or that in the end, through reason or some great revelation, Auntie Thelma would have realized the truth, that what made the sugar cakes so exceptional was intrinsic to me, just as she had suggested, and that nobody would even try masquerading the truth.

That day, if there was a truth, it did not reveal itself, at least not to Auntie Thelma, even if it did present one of its many sides to me. To this day, I have never been able to explain to myself, why I hadn't spoke up. Why, just like Old Man Spencer never could bring himself to do, I didn't ask the question, never damn-well confronted him. That hurt, too, never

208

went away. For once blessed, all other blessings would just be
showered onto him. Such was the truth of any competition. A
truth Jeffrey knew early. And my mother did agree: indeed, if
they were mine and Jeffrey had stolen them, even then I was
making too big a deal. For they were only sugar cakes, she
argued, and I should have been happy that the effort and its
product were praised, rather than cry about who received the
blessing. Once again, Jeffrey had won my mother away from
me. From that moment, I was intent on pleasing his.

Moving in the opposite direction to the DC-10, the hurricane continued its deadly march westward, as if coming out of its own future to meet us in the approaching
plane, disrupting our rhythm and pacing, drenching
and buffeting those on the outer fringes and devastating the unfortunates near its centre, reminding us of an
earlier time and a fleeting moment. Instead of descending low enough for passengers to get a good view of the
islands, the captain, as if trying to escape what looked
like tears on the outside of our windows, had to take
the aircraft higher, beyond the reach of the lightning
and thunder. I knew that Jeffrey would be disappointed at being deprived of the chance to impress the
woman at his side with his intimate knowledge of the
region. For this was another time when it did not suit
us to fly too high, not so close to the sun, so high that
we lost perspective of all the sights below. Too high,
even for the wax on which we now depended, both for
our ears and for our wings, too lofty for our insurance.
So high, that without geographical knowledge that was
so intimate, eyesight so keen, he could not name the
islands, he could not limn or swerve between the

whirlpool and the cave. And what would be the advantage to him of having someone, say the captain with his better equipment, his maps and compasses, to keep pointing out the islands and their locations, to keep dropping names, as they flew across, as if he Jeffrey didn't know a damn thing and was just as ordinary as anybody else, just as dependent on a higher force and more intimate knowledge. He would have to wait for another chance to give her *his* grand tour of all the rooms in this house. He would do it from a height from where he could still see and discern what was below.

For anyone but Jeffrey this unexpected intervention by the pilot might have illustrated how our best plans can be scuttled unexpectedly and by forces beyond our control. But he was so caught up in himself such thoughts never crossed his mind. Not once. He was already flying too high. The wings lifting him had a power of their own; he was autonomous like any living creature now given its own chance to take to the air, now testing its powers and resilience, its ability to defy the limiting gravitational pull, its freedom to be free and to slip away. Wings with a mind of their own. The wax binding his feathers still felt strong and cool, even if the air was getting too thin, even if the swirls and whirlies caused all of us to bounce around, just like feathers floating so inescapably on draughts that are neither hot nor cold, but both, and distinctly so at different times.

Suddenly, the aircraft broke through the dark clouds, once again into the heavy rain, revealing the land below, like a mortician peeling back a sheet, unveiling not only the body but also the graphic scars and wounds. Just then the captain's voice informed us we had twenty minutes to landing.

s the aircraft came to a halt, Jeffrey noticed a dark grey U.S. military plane parked on the tarmac. Instinctively, his heart leapt. I think that was when he crashed back to earth, losing one or two of his feathers.

But he didn't have much time to think about it. Two flight attendants with large black umbrellas appeared in front of him and Damsel. As soon as they stepped out of the aircraft, the attendants unfurled the umbrellas, revealing the name of the airline in large white letters. They held the large saucer-shaped black domes over the two and began walking towards the arrivals area, stepping over, and sometimes into, large pools of water. The backs of the flight attendants were drenched by the time they got inside the terminal. I grabbed one of the umbrellas on my way out of plane. I was happy to be back home. I just wanted to sleep and block everything out of my mind.

Jeffrey's business associate, Dennis Pilgrim, was waiting inside the VIP lounge, as usual. He took one piece of Damsel's hand luggage — she struggled with him to keep control of her black handbag — and led us through the airport building into the parking lot where we sought shelter in a large black car waiting for us. Prime

Minister Watkins strolled over from where he was talking under a parapet with men dressed in military fatigue. He opened the back door and crawled into the car. Damsel sat between Jeffrey and the prime minister. I sat beside Dennis in the front.

"Where the hell were you two days ago?" Jeffrey demanded as we left the airport.

"Who, me?" Dennis asked. He seemed taken aback by Jeffrey's tone of the voice, and I felt like saying to him, don't dig nothing, my man, this is what I've had to put up with in the past few days. But Dennis seemed intent on catching Damsel's eye in the rear-view mirror. It would take some time for him to accept this new Jeffrey.

"Yeah. You. I thought you were to give me a ride to the airport," Jeffrey said. His voice didn't sound right to my ears. He must have known he was trying too hard, so it came out too high-pitched. He dropped his voice into his chest. "I waited and waited for you. Good thing the PM came along. It looks like you ain't too dependable these days."

"I tried, man," Dennis said. He was talking more slowly, stressing his words. "But you know. I was up north when the hurricane hit, man. Doing some business up there. Thought I'd be able to make it back. But all the roads washed out up there, man. Nobody still can't get past, really."

"You could've got a message to me." Jeffrey was talking in his natural voice, a tone of reasonableness creeping back in. "So I wouldn't waste all my time waiting and you... you never showing up."

"How could I?" Dennis said, laughing. "There were no telephones, man. Cell phones not working. And the airport was closed. I guess," he corrected himself, "except for that one flight."

212

"Humph," Jeffrey said in his deepest voice.

"We really took a good hit," the prime minister interjected. "I went on another tour earlier today. We still got parts of the island we can't reach yet. Things really bad. All the crops destroyed. Had to impose a dusk-'til-dawn curfew, closed the schools and government offices. For the record," he added in a tone of voice as if to suggest Jeffrey and his associates now owed him a favour, "this airport's still officially closed. Man, it's times like this when I'm glad we set up a defence force to protect the people. Some day, Jeffrey, my son, you'll know what I mean. When you have to make these blasted decisions."

Ahead a small group of scantily clothed children were playing in the puddles. As the car went by, one of them recognized the prime minister and shouted his name. He instinctively waved his hand through the window but quickly took it back in when he saw that the boys were actually swearing and making rude gestures. "Damn opposition supporters," Watkins grumbled. "Why couldn't the hurricane just damn well wash them away, with all the trash? What more do they want me to do? I'm doing my best. I can't get blood out of a stone. Supporters of that damn Ashton, so-called prime minister in waiting. *Ha*."

"I saw a Yankee plane at the airport," Jeffrey said, dismissing the prime minister's more immediate concerns. "What the hell is it doing there if the airport's closed like you said?"

"Aid," the prime minister answered sourly. He was still smarting. "They sent us some aid. Blankets, skimmed milk, rice and some money."

"How much money?" Jeffrey asked.

"Five million dollars," Watkins replied almost

apologetically. Dropping his voice perceptibly, he added: "In U.S. currency, which is worth a bit more when we convert it."

"Five million dollars," Jeffrey laughed. "Is that all the richest country on this earth can afford? Christ, we would make more money, and faster, if we sold a couple pounds of cocaine in Miami or New York. Five million dollars. Why don't you make a proposal to the Yankees? Tell them they can keep their lousy five million dollars, in U.S. currency as you say, if they would allow us to plant whatever we want in those sugar and banana fields now flattened by the hurricane. They aren't buying the darn sugar and bananas anyway. They must let us export whatever we want to wherever we can find a market."

"But the market would be the United States itself," the prime minister said sheepishly. "You can't expect them to talk seriously about that. I mean, they're spending billions of dollars each year to keep the stuff out of the U.S. of A."

"Exactly," Jeffrey retorted. "That's my point."

We drove on in silence.

"And that's not all they're sending us." Watkins broke the silence. "We got a message from the ambassador that they opening their jails to clean them again. Sending us all those criminals that were born here but lived all their lives over there, sending them back as deportees. Just dumping them on *we* hands. The same thing with Britain and Canada. The same bloody things. Sending us all their sophisticated criminals, just because they were born here, after they've trained them and made them into the same criminals that now they don't want."

"So what we're going to do?" Jeffrey asked.

214

"What can we do?" the prime minister answered. "What the hell can we do?"

෨෧

Alberto Gomez would have approved of his speech, Jeffrey remembered thinking, especially the way he made his point. That must have drawn blood. The adrenaline flowing, he shifted his weight so he was sitting erect in the back seat, the top of his head brushing the car's ceiling, his frame squarely positioned so the prime minister could not avoid sensing his authority. Every time their eyes locked in battle, the older man blinked first, a clear sign he was beginning to know his place. Jeffrey accepted that he had won the first and most crucial battle. Watkins would have to retire sooner than he was expecting. Time for new ideas and approaches. With another surge of excitement as he thought of the future, Jeffrey resolved to deal with Dennis Pilgrim soon — not only had he not turned up to take him to the airport as promised, but he was now flirting with Jeffrey's woman in the rear-view mirror.

"Five million dollars," he resumed scornfully. "Then they got the guts to say poor people like us shouldn't use everything we have try to pull ourselves up by our bootstraps; we shouldn't sell what grows naturally around here and which the Yankee people themselves can't get enough of. What else is left for us to do, eh, Mr. PM?"

"They also sent in their own man to oversee the aid program," Watkins answered. He glanced quickly at Damsel. He was noticeably tense. Until he knew who she was, his instincts were not to tip his hand. Would Jeffrey bring a Delilah into their midst? "So much like the Americans. Don't trust anybody. That's why we have to be so careful with them. They could be like a sleeping dog. You don't want to wake them up."

"And that's why we shouldn't trust them either," Damsel said, speaking for the first time.

"Aren't you ever going to introduce this beautiful lady to us, Jeff?" Dennis asked. "Where're your manners, man?"

"Sure. Introduce yourself. This is Damsel." She had giggled somewhat approvingly at Dennis's castigation, but quickly regained her self-composure. Jeffrey left it to Dennis and the prime minister to make their introductions. "She's going to be working with me on a couple of projects."

"Christ," the prime minister said. "You can't bring in another foreign worker. Not with the hurricane putting so many people out of work. Not that I have anything against you, honey," he said glancing quickly at Damsel, "but we can't be granting any more work permits to non-nationals. If Jimmy Ashton and his people find out, they would murder me on the campaign trail."

"Since when anybody really needed a permit to work around here?" Jeffrey asked. "I'll have a couple of high-level people from the Middle East coming in and out of here shortly. We'll be doing business, and you know how much money those people got. We can use some of that money on this island. I can bet my hat they will be giving us more than five million dollars."

"Sounds fine to me," Dennis said. "As long as she ain't another Brenda Watts, if you know what I mean?"

"And another thing," Jeffrey resumed, as if he had not heard Dennis. But his words echoed in my head. What did he mean, I found myself thinking. What could he mean? But Jeffrey was in his element and he ignored Dennis. "I think we ought to start standing up more to them Americans now we'll be having more friends elsewhere in this world. I think your government's been too cautious, always wondering what the Americans would do. Probably, we should start by saying no to the deportations. Start by saying they are your problem: you created them, in your schools, on your streets and in your prisons. So deal with it. We should say that, and loud and clear, to them."

We drove in silence again, the car no longer trying to dodge the gaping potholes filled with ugly brown water

"Apart from the Arabs, I'm going to have some other people coming in here to work," Jeffrey continued confidently. "They'll be staying for one or two months at a time. If we require them to have work permits we would only draw attention to them and their numbers. You'll be setting up a paper trail somebody could leak to Ashton and even to the Yankees, if you know what I mean. So we must tell the immigration people at the airport to loosen up a bit. We don't need them asking all their damn questions. I'm also going to want you to talk to the other prime ministers in the region about the same thing for me. And you don't have to worry about Damsel, Mr. PM. She'll be okay. I can vouch for her. Just treat her like you always treat Edmund when dealing with me: as my special advisor. Now, I have two."

Jeffrey leaned back in the car and held Damsel's hand. The prime minister and Dennis continued to look ahead, as did Watkins, except when the car passed a group of people or came to a stop at an intersection. Then, he waved and called out to individuals by name and promised to get help to them as soon as possible. Only a few waved back.

217

In an abrupt change of topic, Watkins asked, "Have you thought lately of taking your father to see a doctor?"

"No. What you mean?" I could sense Jeffrey's alarm. His heart was fluttering fast and how he could feel the heat from the rush of blood to his head and face. Fortunately, he now had enough control of his vocal chords to keep this concern out of his voice.

"I don't want to frighten you, but I think the old man's acting a bit strange these days. Maybe with his age you should be taking him to see a doctor or something."

"What you're talking about? What you mean by *'acting strange'*?"

"Well, like... well, in the past two days he's been walking around in all this rain talking to himself when he hasn't been hovering over Brenda Watts's grave for long hours. Or when he wasn't talking to O'Brien, the tailor, he..."

"What you expect?" Jeffrey shot back. I could imagine the vein pounding in his forehead. I imagine he, unlike me, was expecting much worse news. "The man is a grave digger, so he'll spend time around graves and you know he's always been close to O'Brien. That ain't nothing new. You, yourself, have said he treats O'Brien like some damn son."

"Don't get upset, man. I was only thinking about the good of your old man," Watkins said in an attempt to alleviate Jeffrey's alarm. "What is it he likes to say: that sometimes it's safer living among the dead than the living?"

For the rest of the journey we relished the silence, the five of us surveying the damage wrought by this hurricane. Jeffrey had to know the reference to living among the dead was aimed at him, a way for others to

218

remind him that his father simply could not bring himself to give up the old dilapidated house in the graveyard for his son's palace, and that, therefore, Jeffrey wasn't as free as he thought.

෬

Nothing could impress Aubrey Spencer when his son got home. It was still too soon after the burial and the hurricane, too soon for him to throw off the shroud that seemed to envelop him. Too soon for him to rise up and to move on; too early to honour only through memory; he wanted time to help him to forget so that he could forgive, with time, those responsible. He still felt the loss. He wanted the old restored. So the old man seemed to be in an extremely foul mood. And he did not extend a hand of welcome to Damsel when they were introduced. She was left awkwardly holding her hand out while the old man turned away muttering.

"Do our gods have to come from elsewhere?" he grumbled. "Foreigners. You know if you can trust these people? After what they're doing to this damn island! Foreigners are taking over, we're trying so hard to be like them."

"What you're saying, Mr. Spencer?" the prime minister asked, trying to make light of the exchange. Jeffrey appeared not to hear his father.

"And the poor girl ain't even cold in her grave yet," he said, raising his voice for them to hear. "The worms ain't even start on her properly yet and you're already running around with the next woman. And a foreigner you ain't even know nothing about you bring to live here in this house. We are a proud people; we don't have to be a people of mimickers."

"Can I get you something to drink?" It was left to Ida Weekes, the domestic servant, to come to Damsel's rescue and prevent further embarrassment. Damsel later told me, it was Ida who really made her feel welcome, not only by offering that first drink, but before that, by giving her a big hug, giving back to her the smell of limes that she missed so much. Ida Weekes and her welcoming, comforting fragrance of Limecol.

Aubrey put on his hat and walked out into the rain. He had a duty to perform. His own legacy and pilgrimage. Sunshine or rain, hurricane or calm, he visited the grave of his departed wife every day. Now he had an additional chore. On the way over he stopped to rearrange what was left of the flowers on Brenda's grave, the flowers tossed around and splattered but still fresh despite the hurricane's wind and water, as fresh as the memories of the departed women in his heart.

∞

"Edmund," Jeffrey said softly. "Be careful around that damn Dennis Pilgrim. Just watch him, but let's keep our distance, man."

"What do you mean?" I asked.

"Didn't you hear what he said in the car?" Jeffrey was talking slowly and I could hear his loud breathing. We were in the basement of the big house, but the others, including Dennis, were in the kitchen above. As soon as the music had taken hold, when the conversation started to relax, he had signalled for me to come with him and, as usual, I followed. "He talks too much and his talking is what will do him in. Still, man, I can't believe it is he. I can't believe he would do such a

220

thing. Maybe, it was like some loyalty test, to show that they can depend on him."

"What do you mean?" I asked again.

"Didn't you hear him say he was doing business up north? What does that tell you? Where are the new people trying to muscle in here? Where are they making a toehold and recruiting from? And these are the same people, ruthless as shite, that we want to keep off this island. But one thing you can say about Dennis Pilgrim is that he is ambitious. Very ambitious: always looking for a deal, always looking for new business, as he calls it. Who would be a better man than he for them to recruit? Especially if he thinks that we're moving too slow, that we're not real business people, that we should be in the business for the money and nothing else. You know how he thinks, where his head is. That's the business he's doing up there. Business on his own, without even telling me. Did he tell you he was doing business up there?"

"No," I said.

"See, that's what I mean. Freelancing on his own. Why? Because he's thinking we're now too slow for him. He sees the bigger light. That's why he couldn't come back down."

"I don't know," I said. "I..."

"And then, talking too much, as usual, he let slip 'bout Brenda. I always felt that it was the new people up north sending us a message. And Brenda got caught in between. Or that they chose Brenda for that reason. I just don't trust Dennis, man. I don't trust him. And I know that he and Brenda had been talking."

"Oh, I see," I said.

"He didn't have to touch Brenda," Jeffrey said. "All I will say right now is that he didn't have to touch her." He paused. The silence hung heavily. I didn't know what to say. I hadn't thought this way about Dennis, but at the same time, I didn't trust him either. He was too flashy.

"I see," I muttered, not knowing what else to say. Once, again I was aware of the music upstairs, as if someone had turned up the volume, or adjusted the bass and treble so as to make even the foundation of the house tremble.

"Just be careful with Dennis Pilgrim. Watch him."

I was almost up the stairs when he shouted after me. "And tell me if you see him hanging around my father."

t was only a matter of time before Bernard Lewis, the weird stranger as everyone on the island was calling him, started showing up at the Great House. Indeed, it appeared that practically everyone did come by at one time or another. When it was his turn, none of us appreciated it, for he chose to make his initial appearance on the very night of Jeffrey's political coming out celebration a month after the hurricane. Not that Jeffrey had intended it that way, not so public a coronation.

"You know," he had said, "this is not what I had in mind. But this thing just got out of hand. Every day a new named added to the list."

We had watched as the demands for invitations began to balloon, mainly from people we didn't know, most of them from overseas. "I just wanted a party, with a few special people to welcome Damsel to the island. But it looks like Alberto Gomez has different ideas. He says he might even come. I guess they'll let us know in due time if he's coming."

With Bernard Lewis there was no doubt that normally he would not be on the invitation list. Right away, when we heard how badly he wanted an invitation, he would become a target of scorn for Damsel and for Jeffrey, too. But none of that bothered him: not even when none of us returned his telephone calls with their offers of possible business connections. As I look back, now I would say his visit and its timing were inevitable. Others would say that the timing of this key occasion was the most important factor, especially as events unfurled. In the retelling, who would ever know the truth? For, in the end we can agree on only one thing, if that much, and it was the feeling that this event provided Bernie, and so many others, with his first opportunity to see and confirm everything that he suspected for himself. His chance for a first-hand account, no more relying on what this or that body had to say.

Jeffrey had argued with Damsel when this stranger first came to our notice. He was an American, thirty-three years old, built like a long-distance runner, tall and slim. After we'd known him for some time, he told us that in his undergraduate years he had been a running back at UCLA and was on the track and field team. He'd been forced to give up football because of a back injury. On graduation with a degree in interior designing, a subject for which he had long lost his initial passion, he enrolled in the American Peace Corps and was sent straight away to Latin America, first stop Colombia. There, he enjoyed working with the poor, teaching them to dig irrigation ditches and to prevent soil erosion in the hills.

It had not been hard to gather some basic information about him. All over the island people were talking about the eccentric foreigner with the long red beard, gleaming green eyes and hair as matted and lengthy as any recent Rastafarian initiate, this spectre who was spending so much time on the beaches, talking to people of any social standing or just walking around the island, barefoot and barebacked. The newspapers carried pictures of his sun-burned back, chest and peeling face, of the blisters on his feet, of his happy-warrior disposition and his talk about helping mothers and unemployed women to set up small businesses in their homes.

Jeffrey and Damsel had argued about whether to invite this foreigner to the party. "What difference does it make if he comes to the party," Jeffrey had said, finally relenting under the entreaties for an invitation. "Just about anybody who wants to come is coming, anyway. Look at all those pages and pages with names on top of names that keep pouring in on us. What's one more name, anyway? And since we know who's planning to come, we can be on the look-out for him."

I sided with Jeffrey in his assessment of Bernie: he was no more than one of those out-of-place and possibly rich people who just loved the tropics. The stereotypical rich and spoilt northerners that, even as little boys, we would encounter on the beaches, or trawling the island, most of them in Bermuda shorts and leather sandals, red hands and necks, and peeling noses — eyes appearing ghoulishly from behind frightening masks made by thick gooey protective lotion. From what we could tell, these souls loved the idea of moving to some beach and pitching a tent, living off the land and money from their parents back home, roaming freely and widely in search of whatever, talking about finding Paradise among the poor, but grounded in the surety of living off an inheritance. They always appeared lost to us, so out of their element. Most of them were merely clowns trying to appear to be what they were not; what in their heart and soul they could not become. But Damsel was adamant that he not be invited. She claimed she hated Bernie from the very beginning. In the end, Damsel had prevailed. Still, Bernie wasn't to be denied.

"So we are finally meeting face to face," Bernie greeted us when he did catch up to us. From the time we came into the party, I had been avoiding him. Without making it too obvious, I tried to make sure we were constantly moving ahead of him. In the end, he walked across the room and started talking. His brash manner indicated he believed we needed no formal introduction. But then again, that is how people like him are. Everyone on the island already knew who he was, so maybe that's why he didn't see the need for formal introductions. The few dollars he had given out since the hurricane had made him many friends. And he had to know he had become a celebrity, elevated by the good works of this money.

"Quite a crowd here, my man," Bernard said, looking around the courtyard, as if mentally taking pictures. "Now I can understand why it was so difficult for me to get an invite. No wonder I had to wait my turn. Looks like just about everybody is here, ain't it."

"I guess so," I said. I had to raise my voice above the growing din in the room and over the music coming from the brassy calypso band, all those jumping, screaming young men and women with their bleached hair, or hair in cornrows, with plaits bouncing in the air, with their dreadlocks and even skin heads. The air held a sweet smell from the fresh breezes floating in from the ocean, cleansing and purifying the land, releasing it from the grip of a heavy and oppressive heat that had bleached the land all day, all week.

"I'd still like for the two of us to sit down quietly, sometime soon, and have that chat we've been talking about," Bernard Lewis said. He sipped the rum punch and wiped his face with the moist paper towel with which he had been holding the glass. "I would really like that." The music seemed to be drifting back into the background, reminding me even then of a simmering pot, successfully brought to the boil, but now placed elsewhere, just to maintain a minimum heat. The musicians had succeeded in setting the mood. It was, no doubt, just as Jeffrey said it would be, a local party in taste and nature, even if most of the guests were not. "Sure, man. Any time," I said. "Any time."

Eager to change the conversation, I turned to a woman standing nearby and said: "Bernie, meet my friend, Janice." They shook hands. "Janice, this is the man so many people are worshipping these days, but you probably won't recognize him from the pictures we've seen in the papers. The foreigner doling out the aid for the hurricane that everybody is talking about. The smiling American."

"I know," she said. "Everybody knows about him. But you look different tonight."

"Ah," he said. "You're making me more important than I am. In a place like this, I'm definitely not among the important. And, Janice, what do you do?" I had deliberately avoided providing this information.

"I'm just a... a..."

"My date for the evening," I said, squeezing her hand. I didn't bother mentioning that she was a hair designer, but that above anything else, she was a dancer, dreaming, like me, of someday making it big up North, of leading a dance company onto stages around the world, leaving audiences enthralled with her artistic depictions of the folkways of our people. She, too, was hoping that Jeffrey Spencer would find a way for people's dreams to be fulfilled. That was his promise. One more thing we had in common.

"Well, I'm glad to meet you," Bernard said. Turning to me, he added, dismissing Janice as if she'd simply disappeared: "I'm actually very happy to be meeting you. I'm sure I don't have to tell you what I did to get here. But let's meet and talk some time."

With that he walked off, heading for the line serving the rum punch. Indeed, I already had some idea of the lengths to which he had gone but I still didn't know why attending was so important to him. Off to the corner, the brass section in the calypso band was wailing away. I was with a beautiful woman, I was dating her for the first time, and everybody was happy. What would it really matter that this stranger had made it safely into the party? He was harmless enough. I edged Janice towards the dance floor and was among the first to answer the singer's call to really get the party swinging, really working up a sweat, bumping and grinding to the liberating music.

"Bloody fools, these Americans," Jeffrey had said when word got back to us of what Bernie was calling him. Bernie, too, had been gathering information in the weeks since the hurricane and had discovered that Jeffrey had rented every room in the historic Sam Lord's Castle Hotel, one of the few buildings to escape the hurricane's wrath. Sam Lord's was one of the best and most expensive hotels on the island, perhaps the most historical. Its original owner had been a local seventeenth-century pirate who plundered the vessels of the most powerful nations of the time. From this outpost, the eccentric Pirate Sammy, the only pirate not to make a reputation solely by roaming the seas, held full sway over all shipping lanes between South America and Europe. According to the local fables, no sooner did the pirate loot a ship lured onto the nearby rocks than he would return to this island and bury the treasure, leaving no maps of the locations. It was as if he felt the ill-gotten gains from another culture that he had at first found desirable had become a hideous booty that would only spoil his paradise.

The pirate's elaborate mansion had later been expanded into a hotel. It was here that Jeffrey had conducted a week of all-day seminars attended by well-dressed visitors. It was like a business convention, with the men in immaculate three-piece business suits mingling with the scantily clad white bodies worshipping the sun. Participants had come from London, Zurich, Berlin, New York, Hong Kong and Canada, with one or two from Surinam and Venezuela. They were all business people; they dressed and acted that way. And as a businessman himself, Bernie said he wanted to meet with them and to discuss some of his ideas for non-traditional businesses on the island. Maybe these businessmen would be willing to join him in a partnership to work with small cottage industries. He could bring new jobs and business to the island and then he would be free to stay for as long as he wished. He could even consider becoming a citizen.

The final event of the week was this party at Jeffrey's home in Lodge Road. Since returning home from North America, Jeffrey had built an enviable reputation for throwing the best parties — *brams* as the local people call these galas, noted for copious amounts of food, liquor, blaring music and dancing. The type of party people from villages around Lodge Road watched in awe, even as they kept their distance, listening to the loud music, and to the voices growing more intoxicated as the night aged.

The Saturday before the party, Bernard had gone to the most exquisite men's store on the island, asked what the best-dressed men were likely to be wearing, and bought one of the recommended suits. Next was a stop at a barbershop in one of the expensive hotels, where he had his braids shaved to the length of a fashionable trim popular among the business guests, and his beard and moustache cleanly removed. This was part of his strategy to get around the tight security. "Once inside the Great House," he confirmed to me later, "I knew I could always pretend I was the escort of some social gadfly, so that once I was in, once it appeared as if somebody brought me with them, I would be fine. Maybe I was the date of someone who had dropped me for someone more her equal. Or I could even try to make it look as if I was a very discerning gigolo looking for the right woman to hit up. Who would be able to tell anything about me?"

But he was challenged by, of all people, Jeffrey, who demanded the specially printed gold embossed invitation as he tried to slip through the receiving line. Just as the incident was turning ugly, as two menacing security officers started moving purposely towards the entrance, Damsel appeared and whispered something in Jeffrey's ear. A baffled look appeared on his face as he and Damsel stepped aside for a private chat. The line gathering behind Bernie strained their ears to hear the conversation. "More important," he said, as he recounted to me his version of events. "I could not help noticing the security men. They were now more relaxed, turning their attention to other matters. I had to try darn hard not to let out too loud a sigh. It was that close."

Those listening heard Damsel say, as she and Jeffrey walked away, that the prime minister had phoned to offer his apologies for being late. Something unexpected had come up, she reported. The U.S. ambassador had received a sudden summons home. His recall was so urgent, he didn't have time to pack. A military plane from one of the warships lurking offshore was picking him up at the airport at that very moment. The ambassador's wife and children were to travel by commercial aircraft during the next week. The prime minister had to be at the airport for the ambassador's departure and to welcome his replacement.

"He asked you to pass on his apologies to the other government leaders awaiting his arrival," Damsel told him, as she firmly steered him by the elbow away from the door. "So you better go and be a good host. I'll greet the other guests in your absence. "Jeffrey appeared shattered by the news, almost speechless.

Grabbing the opportunity, Bernie slipped through the door and disappeared into the house. His first stop was at the oak barrel containing the punch, liberally spiked, of course, with some of the strongest rum ever produced on the island. And I couldn't help laughing and thinking that if it were me, the prospects of having to deal with those security guards would have sent me running for a drink too — preferably a glass of rum straight up.

According to Damsel, all this time she was watching the interloper from the corner of her eye. She knew that he'd pay the price for crashing the party; already she had learned that much. Chances were, like so

231

many other visitors, he would spend the night guzzling down this punch, not realizing the potency of the rum so well disguised by its sweet fruitiness, the deceptive trap set by Ida Weekes and into which so many foreigners would fall that night. I, too, had laughed at the sight. By heading for the rum punch, Bernie was definitely showing that there were some things that cannot be learned overnight, that mastery takes time, and that deception, just like the machineel, had to be learned or experienced the hard way. "At least I knew there would be no trouble, not from this source," Damsel admitted. "I knew that when he got out of hand in a drunken stupour, the army boys would simply throw his arse out. It would be the same as if he hadn't come. In the morning, the Yankee would pay the full price for the intrusion—he'd have a nauseating hangover accompanied by a splitting headache. I grabbed hold of Jeffrey's arm and I steered him further away from Bernie. I didn't want Jeffrey to waste his time bothering with a man who within five minutes of arriving was already half-drunk."

Jeffrey had no doubt he had made the right call about Damsel. When she delivered the message to him, he had detected a pleasant change in her. Perhaps it was simply because the party was in full swing, but he felt that she was happier, more at ease, moving smoothly and rhythmically to the events and spirit of the evening. She appeared at home. Nothing garish; no sharp edges; nothing too loud. She simply looked radiant. He could now understand her earlier edginess. This was their first party as joint hosts, Damsel's first chance to be judged by the hostile and unforgiving wags on the island, some of whom saw her as an intruder with a rising profile. For he could never forget that despite what he might say, he and Damsel still had to live in a closed society. A very closed one, at that, with its own ideas and ways of living.

No one would be harsher and more critical of her than his father, a man he knew she wanted badly to please. So, understandably, she would be nervous on that account alone. But that was not all Jeffrey knew she had to deal with. He knew our people could be very demanding, outrageously so, and she must have gathered, as any outsider keen enough would have, that everything she did would be judged and assessed. She would be competing with someone invisible.

She had worked hard preparing for the party, especially when Alberto Gomez and his people started to make their demands. Often the instructions would come as faxed messages, and in Spanish, with a short note, a name and an address. On top of this, she wanted to learn everything, to ensure that the correct foods were served, that all the various types of drinks were available, and that there had to be one big cake, in the shape of the island, with Jeffrey Spencer's name emblazoned on it. Several times in the week, Jeffrey had cautioned her not to get so involved, to leave the hard menial work for the helpers. But she had said she wanted to pull her weight, to keep Ida Weekes company in the kitchen, to pick up a local word here and there and to practise it, even if she was no match for Ida as a talker. Jeffrey regarded these efforts, primarily the constant questioning of Ida about almost everything on the island and its culture, as an attempt to please his father, to discover ways to make him feel at ease in her company or when he visited the house. And for all he knew, he told himself, Damsel wanted to demonstrate that she also possessed the conservative traits of a domesticated woman.

I wasn't surprised to find out that while she was in basic agreement with Jeffrey, she had a slightly different view. In the weeks she had been on the island, Damsel had spent all but two days in the house, sometimes feeling as if she was confined to a prison. On one of those days Jeffrey had taken her to a secluded beach, an inlet that she had specifically asked her.

"How did you know about this beach?" Jeffrey had asked when they arrived.

"From Ida. She told me. I asked her about a place where I could go running. So she suggested this."

By then Jeffrey knew how much Damsel loved to run. She had taken to exercising for hours in the basement of the house and to jogging late in the night, when it was cool and quiet and she was inconspicuous. He believed she was using the cloak of darkness to stop people from judging her, so nobody could watch too closely her every move and see her flaws as an outsider. She seemed to be afraid of facing people who might reject her. Jeffrey wondered how much his father was contributing to this lack of confidence and this self-doubt.

"I just have to run every day. I'll explore this area 'round the beach. You coming with me?"

He had declined, preferring a dip in the surf and the chance to talk with some men under a tree, strangers who, at the end of the conversation, promptly reboarded a ship and disappeared over the horizon. The rest of the afternoon went by quickly: Jeffrey slept under a tree; Damsel sunned herself most of the time when she was not swimming.

Then came the party. Damsel began the day looking overwrought and frightened. Jeffrey kept advising her not to be so concerned about whether she would be accepted, about what people thought of her, even complaining to me that Damsel was so jittery she was getting on his nerves. "I can't be a nervous wreck today," he had said. "So you keep an eye on her. I got to keep my nerves under control."

Just as the last rays of the sun were disappearing, he had returned home to find his father sitting in the front part of the house. It looked as if the old man was waiting for his car to pull up. From the way the old man was sitting, Jeffrey expected him to jump on him with a question or two, just as soon as he opened the door.

His father must have sensed Jeffrey's mood, for he quickly left, not having said a word. Jeffrey remembered how the old man had looked at him, the frown on his withered face as if something was eating away at his heart and mind. Because of his father's abrupt departure, Jeffrey was never keener to find out if Damsel and his father had actually said anything to each other. But he couldn't summon up enough courage to ask her, in case he heard something that he wasn't ready to handle. And confronting his father was definitely not a choice.

Instead, Jeffrey and Damsel had sat uneasily in the waning sunlight, pretending to be enjoying the cool tropical breeze and listening to the bustle inside the house. When the tension was at its highest, Damsel jumped to her feet, nervously pacing the veranda. Jeffrey, obsessed with thoughts of his father, interpreted this to mean that his father had said something to her. Worse, it occurred to him that Damsel might unwittingly have discussed some of his private matters with the old man. He simply had to find out if she had exposed him. But he chose to wait, to bide his time.

"Something's wrong?" he had to ask, not knowing what to expect.

Damsel stopped pacing. She was standing erect, her face to the east and her back to him, her hands hanging long and limp at her side, as if suddenly withered and useless.

"Do you have a list of the people coming tonight?" she asked.

"A list? You mean a completed one, with all the names on one master lists?" he asked. "I don't know if I have one. I thought you were putting together a list."

"Don't you have even an informal list? One with the dignitaries?" As she spoke, she continued to look into the distance, past the tall flowering ackee trees, beyond the line marked by the beginning of the fields of canes behind the house, into an emptiness. "Somebody must have some kind of a list, something to tell them how many people they must prepare for."

"But you know how it is," Jeffrey said. "What good is a damn list when the names keep changing all the time? I'm sure we can go and look at the fax machine, we'll see another ten or twenty names. So why bother making a list anyway?"

She maintained her focus on the quickly darkening distance. On nights, even with the brightest backyard lights on, she had already discovered that anyone in the house could see as far as the hedgerow but no further. Beyond, everything was darkness, with the cane fields, like a small jungle, simply absorbing the powerful lights.

"And to think that this started out just as a little quiet party for me and you. A few friends, so that you

236

could meet a few people, talk with them and make a few friends. So that you can feel at home. But," he raised his hand above his head, "somebody had other ideas, other plans. So me and you, I guess, we'll just have to entertain whoever shows up now. I just don't know who's coming and who isn't coming."

"But there must be some list," she insisted.

"Let me check and see what Ida has." He got off the lounge chair and walked into the house. He soon returned and handed her a sheaf of papers.

"Ambassador Finkle!" she blurted as she scanned the pages. "You've invited him?"

"Sure," he answered without looking up from the pages he was checking. "I asked the PM to suggest some names, since everybody is getting in on telling me who to invite."

"Those damn Americans," Damsel swore. "You're right. They're everywhere. Every blasted where."

They lapsed into a long silence, with Damsel leaning against the side of the house, the list in her hand. She appeared so deeply in thought, Jeffrey decided not to question her about his father; she'd tell him when she was ready, he reasoned, if there was anything to tell him. Eventually, she went into the house, and when she didn't return after about ten minutes, Jeffrey went looking for her, just in case she was off crying or something, finally succumbing to the apprehensions and trepidations that she had dealt with so bravely until today. He found her sitting on the edge of the bed, her face forlornly held in one hand with the bent elbow propped on a thigh and the other hand holding the black phone to her ear.

"Oops," he said, when he pushed open the door. She was talking rapidly in Spanish, but almost in whispers. The suddenness with which he pushed the door must have startled her. "Sorry I interrupted," he said. It was the first time he had heard her speak anything but English since he had brought her into this house. The choice of language made him think it must have been a personal call. Maybe she was so upset by his father, or so dreaded rejection at the party, that she was calling a close friend for consolation. She cupped her hand over the mouthpiece and waved to him when he pushed his head through the doorway. He decided to leave her to her thoughts and friends.

Turning away, Jeffrey almost bumped into his father walking towards the kitchen. His father's abrupt appearance at the house only confirmed his suspicions that something important must be bothering him, something he had to get off his chest by squarely confronting his son.

Jeffrey held his breath and waited. The old man passed by, like a ghost haunting the house and its owner, saying, "We better know what we're doing when we decide to hold the Devil close to our breast. With the Devil, we better know what we doing." Swiftly, he disappeared through the back door. Jeffrey swore under his breath: he wished he could break the hold his father had on every aspect of his life.

The old man left the house as soon as the first guests appeared, slipping out the back and disappearing into the darkness on his bicycle. Without asking, Jeffrey knew the old man would be sleeping tonight in the land of the dead, on the same night when so many people would pluck out one of their eyes to be invited to his house. He swore again. His father would never give him the respect he deserved. Why did he continue to care so much for this stupid old man? Why did he let this doting fool hurt him so much time after time? His father knew how to ruin his life; even how to kill a party, if he were to let him.

∞

The only redeeming thing about the evening for him was Damsel's transformation. Now, with the party swinging, the drinks flowing, and people talking at the top of their lungs, she was different, totally trans- formed and enjoying herself. Jeffrey smiled as he noticed the crowd gathered around her and the turned heads trailing her as she went around the house. She was dressed in a long see-through silk dress, with sequins on the front, and her beauty had hypnotized every man in the house and made every woman take notice. It made him feel good. He had never seen her looking so sexy and desirable. A warm feeling of satis- faction came over him; it was so good to see Damsel coming out of her shell and claiming her undisputed position as the woman of the house, as his woman.

Later in the night, she even joked with the new American ambassador, a tall black American named Gregory Thomson from Harlem and of Caribbean parentage, although she made a point of not dancing with him. Jeffrey, as if threatened by the ambassador's presence, surprised everyone by announcing plans for the Brenda Watts Gymnasium and a running track. His international business associates had decided on the sporting complex that very week at the meetings at Sam Lord's Castle. He and a group of private business- men would build the facility in honour of Brenda Watts, he said. The expected cost, in the millions of dollars, he boasted, would not matter.

At this news, Prime Minister Watkins grabbed him in a bear hug. The prime minister knew the picture would be plastered on the front page of the newspapers the next day. At the very moment the cameras flashed, two burly security men were busy throwing another American—now utterly drunk—out of the party. He landed unceremoniously in the rubble, his tuxedo ripped and his face badly bruised.

By then, the loud wailing of the calypso and reggae music had given way to the mellow bluesy sounds of the DJ music. More people were heading for the dance floor. I nudged Janice through the door for a walk, at long last, on the grounds of the Great House. We stopped under a tree, from where we could hear the happy mix of loud voices and the recorded music wafting on the wind. We intended staying out there until the calypsonians returned for the last lap, to send all of us on our way home, dancing and dreaming. But just as we were becoming comfortable, we heard a loud commotion. After that everything happened quickly, so quickly that I would never be able to put them straight in my own mind. Still, by the end of the night just about everything we knew and understood had changed drastically, and it all started with the clamour.

Alberto Gomez had come after all, further confirmation, I suppose, for Jeffrey of his growing importance in the Organization. On the other hand, his appearance presented us with something we were not too ready to accept. We still believed that this party was ours. It wasn't usual for Alberto to risk turning up at such a high-profile event, especially when he was travelling so far from home, across international waters where there was a possibility of U.S. interdiction. In addition, events were moving too quickly in his homeland. And when the news broke that the Colombian president Hector Futado had disappeared without a trace, there was even more doubt Alberto would attend. Without a president and with the crisis over the extradition of Manuel deepening, the country was teetering on anarchy, being pitched relentlessly into civil war.

For three days before the party, a Caribbean International Airways plane occupied a corner of the Aeropuerto Internacional El Dorado. Only when the aircraft was on its final approach to the airport did Bogotá telephone. Fifteen minutes later, Alberto Gomez and twenty bodyguards noiselessly emerged from the shadows and joined the party.

"I hope everything is okay, now," Prime Minister Watkins said to Jeffrey, trying to hide his nervousness. "We certainly don't need trouble on a night like this, not in the presence of these photographers and news people."

"It's strange that this special business partner would come only for the party," he added, the nervousness causing him to clench and unclench his fist behind his back. "I think I'll be leaving soon."

"Don't worry," Jeffrey said. "That's the way he likes to travel. There've been some kidnapping attempts. So he travels this way. In secrecy. But he's a good guy. You'll find him a really good guy. We can use him and he can help us. You'll see what I mean when I bring him over to your office tomorrow."

Three hours after his arrival, Alberto was ready to leave. Within minutes of his arrival at the airport, the jet was in the air .The party was still in full swing but some prominent people like the prime minister were already leaving. Nobody noticed the absence of Ambassador Gregory Thomson.

◎◎

Gregory Thomson hadn't even had time to present his credentials formally to the Governor General before Los Niños snatched him, the same way they had kidnapped the Colombian president from a private party.

Prime Minister Watkins quickly sent a message of regret to the White House, promising to do what was needed to find and release the ambassador unhurt.

"We will punish the perpetrators of this heinous crime to the full extent of the law of the land," he promised in a radio and television address to the nation. "I also want you to know that I am considering an offer by the president of the United States of America to put the resources and personnel of the Federal Bureau of Investigation at our disposal. But as the president told me, we are a sovereign nation. We will have to make that decision ourselves. We will. Goodnight and let's pray for the safety of Ambassador Thomson."

◎◎

Bernard Lewis returned to the house more often than Jeffrey and Damsel liked. He seemed intent on pushing himself onto us. And he was constantly telling us about his plans for working with the poor, a commitment he said he had made to himself when he worked for the Peace Corps in Colombia.

"This was as much a learning experience for me as for the poor peasants," he said. "It opened my eyes to

242

many of the things wrong in this world, particularly what we in the U.S.A. are doing to keep these people poor and Americans rich." The last five years of his tour were spent in Chile and Bolivia. Che was so right, he said: the entire system in this part of the world was rotten and he held his own country responsible.

"What I'd like to do, actually," Bernard volunteered, "is stay here on this island and open a business. I like it here."

"What type of business?" Damsel asked. We were having dinner. She was using a fork to separate flakes of a thick dolphin steak. In a bowl in the middle of the table was deep-fried fish, browned in a flour batter. Next to it was a bottle containing the local brew of yellowish but fiery pepper sauce. In the background, the soothing music from Jeffrey's impressive collection of blues and jazz music set the tone for idle and light-hearted discussion.

We were eating fried dolphin and green peas and rice, a traditional local dish that Damsel had grown to like and which Ida Weekes prepared for her as a treat. Bernie helped himself to four heaping spoonfuls of the rice and peas. That brother could eat when he was ready. He took the biggest steak. He put some of the pepper sauce at the side of the plate, just as foreigners would, instead of spreading it over the rice, as Jeffrey, Ida or I would do. When he cut into the dolphin, he dabbed it in the pepper sauce before eating it.

"I don't know," he answered quickly. "But I want to work with the poor, maybe something that isn't too structured, that isn't too bureaucratic. Something that…." Suddenly, his face was flushed, his tongue extended like a panting dog. He grabbed for a glass of water and gulped down half. Ida and Jeffrey smiled at each other.

"Anything that would create employment," he gasped, still trying to cool his tongue. "Help the islanders. I don't know." The burning had not fully subsided but he was eating again, avoiding the hot stuff. I noticed Jeffrey smiling to himself. This guy was beginning to grow on him.

"We're starting our own business, too," Damsel said. "In entertainment."

"Maybe we can be partners in something," Bernard said, reaching for the water again.

"I don't think so," she said quickly and firmly. "I just don't think so."

Gradually, he wore us down with his demands. He was spending so much time at the house we had started to look forward to his visits. When he volunteered to design the interior of the Brenda Watts gymnasium, to place the orders for the equipment with a supplier he knew in Los Angeles, and to train the track and field athletes using the facilities, he became so much a part of the team, nobody objected. Indeed, none of us had the time, and he filled a void.

"Leave everything to me," he volunteered. "You won't even have to bother about paying me. My folks back home have more than enough to keep me going, and in any case, I don't require that much. I want to live just like the natives, give me a tent, right there on the beach, I can fit right in."

"I don't trust that man," Damsel said when the three of us were alone. "He's too much of a buffoon for my liking, too slippery, and what is this with his trying to talk and sound like the locals? I don't like it and I don't trust him. He's a fool and an idiot."

"Ah," Jeffrey said, "he's as harmless as a fly. An eccentric fly." We laughed, but Damsel didn't.

The night he came over with the first plans for the gymnasium, Bernie also brought the news that he had found a grand three-storey Victorian house on a plantation ideally suited and situated for the business Damsel and Jeffrey were starting.

"I know you didn't ask for my help in this matter, but this house's simply beautiful. Gorgeous," he reported. "With so much potential. And it's just standing there rotting away. We can do so much with it. So much potential, I tell *yuh*."

The top floor of the building could be transformed into a restaurant with some outside seating. The second floor could have the nightclub, something similar to Club 52 in New York, or one of the fancy European clubs, with darkened rooms, private boxes, golden chandeliers, full-length mirrors and marble throughout.

And the bottom floor, he said, was ideal for a casino. "People could fly in for one night, just to gamble. Maybe instead of going to Las Vegas or Morocco, they might come to Barbados. Particularly if there is a large satellite dish to receive big sport events, like heavyweight boxing, the World Series, the World Cup in soccer, the Stanley Cup and the Superbowl."

Jeffrey wondered why he hadn't thought of this himself. He knew the owners of the house, he knew the price they would accept for it and he knew the property was, indeed, ideal for what Bernie had suggested. The casino and nightclub would be the perfect cover. They could bring the girls in from Latin America and have them work and perform at the restaurant and casino. There was even enough room for a small brokerage office, for he still had to keep his hand in a business that had always been lucrative for him, as insurance for the day he walked away. Such an office would provide an additional benefit. His father would be more comfortable when he didn't have to encounter so many strangers in his home. With the Great House freed of this traffic, his father would stop sleeping in the old house in the graveyard.

Bernie conceded that he would like to be involved in such a business, but, unfortunately, he did not have access to the kind of money that Jeffrey and Damsel would require. This came as no surprise to us. In the end, Jeffrey agreed when Damsel suggested that perhaps the best compromise was to reward Bernie for his efforts by hiring him as manager of the property.

ld Man Spencer was standing in the back doorway when they came in. The white stubble on his face was twisted and ravined. Something must have been worrying him, Jeffrey thought, for his father shaved every day, religiously. "Cleanliness is next to godliness," the old man intoned over the years, another of the thousands of aphorisms he carried around in his head, that were always there, ready to be hurled at him. Every morning the Old Man took the straight razor from the protective sheath in the canvas bag, now blackened from handling, and methodically sharpened it on the half-inch thick piece of shiny black leather.

Jeffrey always remembered his father using the same piece of leather and the same stainless steel razor. He would hang one end from a nail on a window ledge and then, pulling tightly with his right hand, stretch it to the limit while rhythmically wiping the edge of the old razor against it with his left hand.

Over the years, this had become ritual, as predictable as morning follows the night: the swishing, scraping sound and his limber body thrusting and contracting with every movement, a dance in honour of the rising sun, the gratitude of seeing yet another day, confirmation that a beloved way of life goes on, a celebration of successfully coming through another night, a reason just for giving thanks.

Now, like everything around the old man, the piece of leather was worn and cracked with age, the front and back glossy smooth from decades of relentless wear, just like his damn guitar with the polish worn off the frets, the silver tarnished, the wood discoloured from touch. Jeffrey wondered if the strap had not long lost its usefulness as a sharpener and was no more meaningful than an old ragged blanket a frightened child might refuse to abandon. Something that he himself had to throw away when he made a choice to become the man he wanted to be, just the man his mother would have married in a world of her own making, rather than simply merging into a compromise. Jeffrey had cast off the replica for good but, obviously, at a cost. It was time to raise up an original and to give it pride of place, to worship the very newness that was being instilled in them, to drive out the muskiness of the staid and the old.

Jeffrey's mind turned to the many unopened packages of electrical razors, disposable razors, and shaving kits with special creams he had given his father over the years. Even without checking, Jeffrey knew these packages were either propped up on the bureau in the old man's bedroom or passed on to Othneil, the trainee grave digger, or to O'Brien the tailor, a man many people were saying was more of a son to the old man than Jeffrey. "They are young and need those fancy things more than me," his father had explained somewhat flippantly. "I'm old and soon dead. I don't need fancy things. Not like the young people. Oh, no, not like the young people."

Always the same old song, Jeffrey thought. His father would not change, not even his tune. They would always be unalike. Jeffrey liked the modern and more

248

challenging jazz with all its variation and uncertainty, or just sweet bouncy calypso music with the blaring horns and sophisticated rhythm sections. His father stuck with his guitar and the old old-time blues, the tried and true, or the old-fashioned calypsos that were really no different from the blues, for they told the same story almost chord for chord, rhythm by rhythm, rhyme for rhyme.

"What more do I need?" the old man had said. "I have a roof over my head. I am healthy and still strong, praise God. I can still ride my bicycle. And if I need a bowl of rice, I can always ask Ida for it." And that was another thing, Jeffrey thought: it was always Ida, even though Ida was Jeffrey's cook, and could offer only what he provided. But always it was Ida, or someone else, even Brenda, his father turned to, never acknowledging his own son's achievements. "And in any case, how many steaks can I eat; how many rooms can I sleep in on a night? My main concern is that I should remain free. Free, to stand up like a man, free of any controls. Free to do as I please. Free, free, free."

So it was with everything. As far as Jeffrey could remember, his father never threw away anything; never succumbed to any newer gadget or trend; never traded in the old for the new. Every morning it was simply the straight razor and the bar of scentless soap for a lather. And the same bowl of cornmeal porridge, lightly sugared and milked, with one hard-boiled egg. The freedom of some frigging tradition. He could not enter into the old man's head and change this irrational suspicion of things new and foreign. As much as he would like to, he could not drag him into the modern times.

Still, he wished his father would avail himself of the finer things of life, that he would at least mellow out to enjoy an easier time; and use some of the material trappings scattered indiscriminately around the house and available to him, use them, if only as a gesture to show he appreciated his son's success. Every morning, Jeffrey awoke with hopes renewed, only to have them dashed by the swishing sound of the razor against the leather.

When he was finished scraping the sharpened razor against his face that looked as hard as the withered leather, the old man placed the shaving kit—the razor, the leather and the soap in an old plastic container given him by his beloved Thelma, a birthday gift, when they were courting—and the mirror with the outer edges eroded in the canvas bag, now dirty from all those years of wear, where they would stay until the next morning. Then he hopped on his bicycle and rode to the beach for his morning dip in the sea. He was a man of rituals, of traditions, of consistency.

Something must have been really bothering him for there to be so much growth on his face and so late in the day.

In the four weeks since the opening of Club Alexia they had not seen much of the old man. Of late, he had taken to spending more time in the graveyard and in the old house. Even then, the only thing that told anyone he was home was the plaintive strumming of the guitar. And the singing. Old Man Spencer's explanation for the time he spent in the cemetery was that he could not dig the graves fast enough to meet the demand. The young people, inexplicably, were turning foolish and killing themselves in a rash of suicides across the island. Or they were being slaughtered in an unprecedented outbreak of murders, most of them happening in darkened streets or in seedy houses frequented only by the uncouth. At the end of the day, he was simply too tired to ride all the way home, his father had explained. "The Devil's too damn busy these day," he said. "Too damn busy, the Devil."

Of course, Jeffrey did not believe him, even if he acknowledged that the cemetery crew had three or four funerals to handle on some days. Still, the old man had Othneil as an assistant, so there was no compelling reason for him to do all the work. Furthermore, he knew there was much talk about importing the latest technology that made burials faster and less laborious. Sure, there wouldn't be the elaborate rituals, the pomp his father had learned over the years and was now passing on to his apprentice. But at least, the demand would be met.

At first, Aubrey's absence didn't seem to matter. Jeffrey and Damsel had been busy running the club in its first month of operation. Their biggest job was making sure Prime Minister Watkins kept the police away from the casino and that the young women working there got through the airport without any hassles from immigration officials. The casino, however, was turning out to be a big problem for the prime minister, an issue that festered. Stories were making it into the local press about hostile behaviour, maybe gunfire or a violent robbery, at the club or as people came or left the disco. People would remark they had seen the old man passing by the school, where by day he stopped and watched the men digging the groundsill for the Brenda Watts Gymnasium. Occasionally, he talked with Bernie at the site. To make these visits he would have to make a detour of three miles from the regular route between the Great House and the cemetery.

Later, we found out that he would also stop there at nights, to talk with his old friend Felix, the watchman, and to see how much progress had been made during the day. He seemed in a particular hurry for the gymnasium to be finished, as if the building had become an obsession for him, a monument, as if he felt something would intervene and stop the construction, leaving the unfinished building as yet another symbol, a headstone.

But tonight Old Man Spencer was standing in the doorway, looking into the darkness, as if he was waiting for them to come home. As she entered the kitchen, Damsel saw him first, like a silhouette standing there, almost motionless. She had just completed her regular evening jog around the village, completing the circuit five minutes earlier than usual, yet another sign she was nearing peak fitness.

Looking over her shoulder as she covered the last hundred metres, she had seen the bright lights of the Mercedes approaching the house, and she had waited for Jeffrey on the front steps while he put the car in the garage and collected his briefcase.

Something on the old man's face, his nervousness, told her he hadn't expected to find her home; maybe he had timed the visit so he would see Jeffrey only. But she was back home earlier than expected and, apparently had foiled the old man's plans.

"Is there anything going on I should know about?" the old man asked as soon as his son walked into the kitchen. He fixed a steady gaze on Jeffrey; his eyes didn't shift while he waited for an answer.

"What you mean, Dad?" The question had caught Jeffrey by surprise and he was scrambling to collect his thoughts. It frightened him his father might have known what was going on all this time and was now about to confront him. But he didn't really think the old man was that knowledgeable. He had first to find out how much he knew — he couldn't risk spilling everything.

"You know what I'm talking about, Jeffrey," his father shot back. They had not yet greeted each other. The old man was already behaving as if, true to form, he didn't really expect a straight answer, as if he anticipated his son would try to frustrate him. "All the things going on around here." He was flailing his hands, the twitching movements appearing to help him think but at the same time betraying deep-seated frustration and disgust. "They don't seem to make sense to me. You're thick with the politicians. You got anything to tell me?"

"Why, Dad. I... I... I don't know what you're talking about. Give me some clue." He looked at Damsel and shrugged his shoulders. She rolled her eyes and took two quick steps in the direction of their bedroom in an attempt to leave the two Spencers together.

"If *you* don't know," Aubrey blurted out, "I don't know who'll know. Perhaps it's the Devil. Must really be the Devil."

He opened the back door and stepped into the darkness. Moments later, they heard the steady tick of his bicycle growing fainter. Jeffrey breathed heavily. First it was a sigh of relief. Then, it was of dismay at the thought he might have spoken too quickly and told his father everything only to find out the old man knew nothing in the first place, when he really could have been questioning him about some minor matter, such as the sudden availability of money for the building of roads and new houses in the surrounding villages. Everyone was talking about the sudden resurgence in the economy, about the building of new homes to replace those the hurricane had destroyed, and the new gymnasium. Not everyone was willing to believe the riches flowed solely from a casino for high-betting gamblers.

The resurgence was happening even though the hurricane had flattened the sugar cane fields and destroyed the hotels. Signs of the physical and economic destruction were still visible in every community. Each morning brought the sight of young men standing around, aimlessly moving about, none bothering to seek gainful employment. All, according to Old Man Spencer, waiting for the Devil to make work for idle hands. Yet, incongruously, they were wearing fancy clothes and had large wads of bills in their pockets, as if they had been transformed in the night, a time they no longer spent in restful sleep, but somehow toiling.

"I'll never understand him," Jeffrey whispered as the ticking disappeared. He peered into the darkness through the side window over the sink, as if he expected to hear his father retracing his steps, returning to confront him. But there was no sound of the tick of the returning bicycle. Only the howls of the dogs in the distance. And the steady chirping of crickets in the grass outside, the grandfather clock ticking loudly in the interior of the house, a strong wind noisily rustling the tops of the sugar canes in the field a stone's throw away. Above it all, he could hear the theme song signalling the end of the evening soap opera on television.

"Do you think he… he… ah… knows?" he asked Damsel. There was a plea for understanding in his stammer, for reassurance. She was now leaning against the still-warm stove, where Ida had been cooking before the television drew her away.

"I don't know," she said unemotionally. Damsel half-turned to the stove top and uncovered the aluminum pot containing the peas and rice. The sweat from the cover drained into the pot. Steam escaped, disappearing into the air, and she quickly replaced the lid. "He's your father. You should know him. I knew mine, or so I think."

She opened another saucepan and the sweet fragrance of fish cooked with herbs and onions and tomatoes wafted through the air. Using a fork, she stirred the contents and broke off a piece. She held the fork with the fish before her nose, bared her teeth and pulled the whitish meat off the tines with her front teeth, taking care the hot fork did not touch and burn her lips. Jeffrey could not help noticing Damsel was the only person in the world capable of getting away with dabbling in Ida's pot while it was still on the fire. Others would experience the servant's sharp tongue. Even Jeffrey himself, the master of this Great House, would not risk her anger. Like everyone else, with the exception of Damsel, he had to wait until the food got to the table.

"Do you have a good relationship with your dad?" Jeffrey asked. He had turned away from the kitchen pathway and was walking towards the front of the house, as Ida returned to the kitchen to serve the meal.

"No," Damsel said, pausing to finish chewing the fish and swallow it. "Because he's dead." There was little remorse or bitterness in her voice. Jeffrey spun around to look at her, to offer his sympathy, and was struck by the realization that there was no pain in her voice, as if years or indifference had eradicated any sense of loss. A chilling thought drifted through his mind of what he would have said if it were his father they were talking about. Despite their differences, their inability to have even a civil conversation, he still

255

loved the old man. He didn't like what people were saying, that his father was acting strangely.

"He'd been dead about sixteen years now," she continued.

"What happened?" He was anxious to find out. This was the first time she had told him anything about her family. He felt like kicking himself for not asking before, for being so thoughtless, so insensitive. And as he stood watching her chew the hot piece of fish, tossing it from one side of her mouth to the other to cool it, he remembered his father's first comment when he brought her home: if he in fact knew anything about foreigners, about this one in particular.

"Papa used to live in Miami." She swallowed the fish and blew out the hot air. "We moved there when my brother and I were quite young. From what I understand, one morning they found him dead in the gutter. Murdered."

"Did they ever find out who did it?"

"Mama didn't wait around to find out. We split and headed back to Colombia. There was some talk we had to flee for our lives, that he'd been double-crossed on the night of a big deal and for those reasons the Organization took care of us. That there were some lynchings, if you know what I mean."

"So it runs in the family," he said, trying to add some levity. "He was a company man too, eh."

"Then there'd been whispers the Organization got rid of him because he was a double agent for the Yankees." She didn't join in the frivolity, but ran her fingers between her skin and her jogging pants, between the elastic and her belly.

"Wouldn't they wipe out the entire family? If it was true what you just said." He sounded particularly earnest, wanting to believe only what would put Damsel and her family in the best light. "I mean, your mother wouldn't have a chance going back to Colombia."

"I don't know what's true," she said. "People say it was Mama who saved us. When the writing was on the wall, when they found out Papa was a CIA operative, that the Organization approached her, put the cards on the table and told her what had to be done. But they also promised her full protection and to look after Papa's two children if she cooperated with them."

"You mean she delivered him over to the Organization? Her husband! The father of her children. I don't believe it!"

"You can never tell what is true. What I know is one day Papa is dead and the next day we're flying home to Bogotá and every week Mama goes to this bank and withdraws money that's been deposited there for her. No questions asked. Who deposited the money, we never tried to find out. Then my brother leaves home and I go off to university in the United States and the money still keeps coming."

"But would your mother actually do something like that?" Jeffrey asked. He was now looking straight at her. "I mean, betray the man she loved, the father of her children. Or was he bumped off by the Yankees? That could also account for the support your family got after his death. But betrayed by the woman he slept with! I can think of my mother and father. The thought of she turning on him is almost ... almost..." He threw his hands in the air in a valiant but failed attempt to find the right words.

"I don't know," Damsel said, her eyes getting darker, her voice growing distant. "If she did it, she must have realized it was the only way to save everybody. I guess you just can't trust anybody these days, especially when you gotta make hard decisions."

"Christ, that's something else," Jeffrey said. "But I know what you mean about trust. That fucking Dennis."

The doorbell rang. As soon as the door opened, Bernie stepped in.

"Good evening, everybody," Bernie shouted into the house in his best native accent.

"Leave the shoes at the door, if you please," Ida ordered sternly from the kitchen. "Don't you come trampling through this house with no shoes on. I spent the whole day waxing them floors there. You don't see you can see your face in them?"

"How do you know it was me?" Bernie shouted, but taking care to stand on the front door mat while untying his shoes.

"I know it could only be you," Ida said. She was laughing lustily now her precious floors were no longer in danger of being scratched. "Don't need a clock around here for you, Bernie; you are just too good at timing this pot."

"Not my fault. You're such a good a cook," he laughed. "I can stand a ways down the road and smell your cooking."

They laughed. Bernie mashed off his shoes on the coconut fibre mat at the door and headed into the house. "Am I cleared to proceed now?" he asked.

Bernie left the door open and Jeffrey immediately turned away, backtracking towards the bedrooms.

"I think I'll take a shower before eating," Damsel said. She pulled the elastic in the sweat pants and again let it snap against her waist with a popping sound. "You don't mind, do you, Ida love?"

"Me too," Jeffrey said. Just before they entered the bedroom, the front door opened again and Dennis Pilgrim, talking loudly and sounding drunk, came in the open front door. Jeffrey and Damsel disappeared into the bedroom, hoping the newcomer would take their rebuff as another sign of their annoyance with him.

๑๑

"Who is this brother you were just talking about?" Jeffrey asked her in the bathroom. "I never heard of him before."

"My half brother," she corrected, almost snapping at him.

"What's his name and what does he do?"

"I don't know what he's doing now," she said, slipping behind the shower curtains, hoping the answer would satisfy him.

"What's his name?" he asked again, persisting gently. He stepped into the porcelain tub with the gold handles.

"Manuel."

"Popular name in Colombia, eh," he said. Standing under the cold water while Damsel soaped a hand towel, he could feel the tension seeping out of his body. Rubbing his back, Damsel was also massaging him gently, making it all seem so easy and good. "Popular name. Like Fernandez or Gomez."

"I guess so," Damsel said. She turned on the water harder and held his face up to the sprays. He could talk no more, rather he found himself sputtering as the water stung his face and rushed into his nose and mouth as her long fingers firmly held his face in place. When he did break free spluttering, there was a burning behind his ears from the marks left by her strong hands, by the sharp fingernails digging, playfully he thought, into the back of his head. But the questioning was over.

൭൭

Damsel felt something special for Ida Weekes. Soon, they were inseparable. Damsel asked Jeffrey to allow her to help Ida take care of the house, for she was certain that the job of maintaining such a big house was too much for the older woman. Jeffrey was rather dismissive at first, but Damsel insisted. Jeffrey liked that Ida readily accepted Damsel, just as she had accepted and appreciated his Great House, perhaps the only person of her age, and of the extended family, to show such genuine approval. He was impressed. And once Ida had adopted the house and its contents as if they were hers, as an heirloom to be treasured and even passed on to the next generation of Spencers, nobody could defile these treasures, especially the hardwood floor that she always kept polished. But he especially liked the way Ida made Damsel feel she was one of them.

He remembered how it started just three weeks after the great party at Sam Lord's Castle, on the morning Jeffrey had the privilege of declaring the Oistin's Fish Festival open. The Americans had appointed a new ambassador and the rumours about the mysterious disappearance of the man that should have held the post had abated somewhat, at least enough for the people to resume living as normally as possible. That was when Damsel had bought the shoes that Ida loved so much. Jeffrey was on a roll. Jeffrey and some of his business partners had just opened another factory assembling computer parts and he and the government had signed the deal for another investment house to open a data processing division on the island. The festival was as much in his honour as it was a commemoration of the ancient festival for the men harvesting the seas. Just about every dignitary on the island had attended, another sign of their recognition of Jeffrey's growing power and importance. Everyone cheered when he declared the festival officially open with a powerful blast from a polished conch shell. The mystified tourists sprinkled among the islanders applauded loudly. It was a strange haunting sound, the conch shell, a call from another era. The people heard and understood. They answered the call from a place deep in their brains, their hearts, from some spot that made them who they were. It was a dream of what they could become, while celebrating their achievement so far. Another year, another festival, another harvest, another feast: this was the result. Another blowing of the conch shell by a favourite son. The people, on such a morning, were of the same mind. They shared and celebrated the same spirit. Everything was in its right place and the sun was blazing down from a deep blue sky over the land and the surrounding water, on an ocean as vast, as deep, as far, and as blue as the horizon.

The people seemed more genuinely interested in Jeffrey than in Prime Minister Watkins, or any of the politicians and dignitaries in attendance. They were aware of his power. He was one of them, someone who had overcome great obstacles to climb to the heights. He had gone overseas and learned well. Now, he was bringing them jobs that put money in their pockets and hope in their hearts so that they could point out to the next generation another way to answer the call from long ago, a fresh and new way to dance the traditional

261

answer and response. And, if I may say so, Jeffrey had it all. Watching, I could not help wondering why he was still willing to gamble. Why was he still taking unnecessary chances, a bigger and deeper one every day. And I wondered, too, how many of the people praising him would countenance, even if they understood, that their new hero of was the area's *chief Narco*.

"Look what Maggie bought me," Ida had said, raising her foot, pulling the hem of her cotton dress a few inches above her ankles, for Jeffrey to get a good look. She too was dancing, celebrating. Not only to the *tuk* band nearby, to the drum and fife, the bass drum pounding like a heart, but to something else, to a beat and a music that made her laugh and clap her hands, to raise them to her face, and to kiss Damsel and cement a bond that was now unshakable. For in her own way, as an elder, as a sister and leader, she was teaching the one the favourite son had brought among them and whom he called Damsel. She was teaching her to dance, to hear the call and to offer an appropriate — granted it was not yet the ideal, for that could only come with time and greater learning — but an appropriate response nonetheless.

Ida was wearing the new shoes, the older ones safely stuffed into her handbag, relegated not even to memory once the bag was closed. "Aren't they pretty? Thank you, Maggie." Jeffrey wondered what his father thought of this convergence and induction.

And then she appeared in a different guise. The rupture and disruption swift but telling.

"How you're doing these days, girlie?" Ida asked a woman who was standing nearby.

"You know, still trying to go on. Still trying to understand." The woman looked old and drawn, as if life and all enthusiasm were drained out of her. Pausing only momentarily, perhaps eternally reaching for a friend to explain the inexplicable, she just as quickly gave up, as if recognizing the futility, the inability to tell, declare or even explain, and moved on, walking slowly, one foot dragging after the other, head bowed, shoulders drooping from too heavy a weight, the clothes, too big for her emaciated frame, blowing in the wind.

"Trust in God, Edna," Ida said. "In the end that all we can do," she called to the slowly retreating back, "in the end, only he can understand and bear our troubles away."

But Edna Watts was gone.

It was a little shop, with just a door and a window to the side. The inside of the hut always appeared to be in darkness, even on the brightest day. In the centre of the room was the large Singer sewing machine, about two decades old, but still good enough to do the job for O'Brien. Over to the side was an old picture of Old Man Spencer and Brenda Watts with some children.

"What yuh doing, man?" Jeffrey said as he stood in the doorway, blocking even what little sunlight was coming through the door.

"Nothing, really," O'Brien said. He did not look up from his task. "What high wind blow you out this way, if I may ask?" The deep sarcasm was clear in his voice.

"I saw you a few months ago at the festival, at one of the stalls, across from where I was talking with some people, but when I went looking to talk to you, you were gone."

"The festival was getting too crowded for me," O'Brien said.

"Are you doing anything for my father?" Jeffrey made his voice sound friendly.

"Why you should ask?" the tailor shot back. He still had not looked up from the sewing machine, neither had he offered his visitor a seat. Conceivably, that was why O'Brien and his father got along so well, favouring the same sarcastic statements and approaches. That was why Jeffrey had dropped O'Brien as his tailor and had resumed having his clothes made in New York and Toronto.

"I'm here to pay for the work you're doing for my father."

"I don't think so. What happens between me and Pappie Spencer is between the two o' we. You know that."

Jeffrey looked around the room. The two chairs had pieces of cloth strewn over them, cloth cut and waiting to be sewn. O'Brien was right: his father had made it clear Jeffrey's money should never pay for the clothes the tailor made for him. It wasn't the first time Jeffrey had tried, and failed, to get O'Brien over to his side. His eyes came back to the picture, perhaps so positioned that it did not intrude even though she was present. Perhaps O'Brien was not even aware of it, even though he must have been conscious that it was there. Who could have taken such a picture of Brenda? Jeffrey wondered if it might have been him. Still, he wondered why O'Brien would keep the picture and mount it so conspicuously.

"Look, O'Brien, you and me went to school together. I went overseas and you didn't. That doesn't mean that you should hold such things against me," Jeffrey said.

"I'm not holding anything against you. It's just that I don't like the way you're operating."

"You know what I mean. I had opportunities you didn't. I took my opportunities. You must not hold these things against me. If you want me to, I can help you. I can pull a couple of strings to get you a good job, maybe in the government, something that would put more money in your pocket. Maybe a government contract to make some of the uniforms for the government workers. There's good, good, good money in that. If you still want to do tailor work, I can arrange something for you to make the uniforms for the civil servants, for the police or the defence force boys."

"Don't worry about me. I'm all right as I am," O'Brien said. He stopped sewing. "Sometimes it pays to be poor but to have a conscience, to be able to sleep at night. That is what I like about your father. That is one of the things he taught me really good. Ever since my father died and he, out of the kindness of his heart, helped me and my family."

"Sure. From the way he treated you, people say we could have been brothers." Jeffrey was still hoping for a joke. "You sure he wasn't your real father? I want to help you, to show my appreciation for how you take care of my father. I can help you get a good job."

"What kind of job are you thinking of?" O'Brien asked. He still sounded bitter. Jeffrey's heart leapt at the question. Maybe he was biting, showing interest, despite the bitterness in his voice. Now he had to press home. With O'Brien on his side, maybe, his father would fall in line. O'Brien had a way with his father.

"As I said, what kind of job you'll like?"

"Certainly, not the jobs you are offering to the young people of this village. You bloody well have everyone, men and women, adults and children, even the smallest children not yet in school, on your payroll.

Even the four-years-olds are working for you. A police-man or a member of the U.S. navy off one of the boats only have to appear in this village and all of a sudden, there is a humming, clapping of hands and general commotion. The little children are passing on the signal to the drug dealers. Is that what you want me to do? Or do you want me to organize the little children so you won't have to come down here at all while you live like a king in your mansion? Is that the kind of job you have to offer me? No wonder the poor old man find it so hard to set foot in your house."

"What makes you think I'm involved in drugs, O'Brien?" It was like a slap in the face. "What you've been telling me father? Answer me: what you've been telling him?"

The tailor looked at him for a long time. In the darkness, Jeffrey could see the whites of his eyes. "Don't worry, Jeffrey, I haven't, and won't, tell your father anything. I promise you that much. Not because of you; but because you father deserves better in his old age."

The conversation was finished. O'Brien picked up the scissors and began snipping at pieces of black thread invisible to all but him on the black cloth. In the background, the radio was playing softly. Jeffrey con-tinued standing in the doorway as if fastened to the spot, not knowing what to say to O'Brien, whether to argue with him over the merits of his business and the financial independence it brought, or to thank him for being so kind and understanding to his father. Not knowing if you offer him a salary, no not a bribe, for that, he told himself, was not the intent, not to raise certain issues and matters with his father. With the pic-ture gazing at him, he was confused.

Eventually, he turned and walked down the rocky path from the tailor's shop. He did not bother to say goodbye. O'Brien's remarks had cut to his heart: the very idea, indeed accusation, that he would lead the children astray. It really hurt, especially with this reproof coming in the presence of Brenda, positioned next to his father, looking on and smiling. Brenda and *her* children. He could not now do the job that had brought him to the village. He decided he would come back to give the kids their allowances another day.

A few weeks later, O'Brien's tailor shop was burned to the ground. Everything was lost, including the cloth from his clients, and there was no insurance on the business. Even then, O'Brien stubbornly refused to accept Jeffrey's help or the assistance of anyone else for that matter, no matter who brought the offer or the spitefulness of the negotiators' threats.

"What the heck is going on down there?" Ida asked of no one in particular. She had arrived at the Great House earlier than had been expected. In the kitchen, Bernie and I, frozen as we heard Ida, singing one of her favourite hymns, pushing open the back door to enter. We had already heard several screams, but this was the first she had heard. We didn't even have time to think or to make up some explanation. As we knew would happen, soon there was another scream—long and piercing.

"Who's down there?" she asked. "What's going on?"

"It's nothing," I lied. "Just Jeffrey and Dennis." After a long pause, I added: "And Damsel, too. They're meeting down there."

"Well, it don't sound too right to me. Why would anybody have bawl out like that?"

We didn't answer, but looked at each other. I got up from the table, took the coffee cups to the sink and started to help Ida put away the groceries. We held our breath, hoping that at least the noises would subside, that somehow Jeffrey would sense the arrival of a different spirit in the house and hold off, that Ida would quickly dispense of her duties and leave. Maybe, I told myself, she'll just dismiss the noises as rough play, perhaps too much excitement, like boys getting carried away by the exhilaration of the moment.

I was moving hurriedly, and each time I put a can or bottle on a shelf, Ida would slowly and meticulously pick it back up and unhurriedly and painstakingly place it in a different position.

Then came the loudest scream of the evening. A moment that lingered forever. Bernie and I knew we had lost; there was no way we could keep Ida in the dark. She only had to ask, for to speak in question was also to condemn. We had to have an answer ready. After all, we, too, were in the house. We knew. Were present and accountable. The fallen angels keeping guard, invisible swords in our hands, wings pinned back by an uncontrollable wind hurled from the storm down below, condemned by the devastation that Ida must have seen at our feet. She had to hear, and having heard, she would need an explanation, a mitigation plea, before passing judgement. We: the guardians, and the damned. We: the accomplices with and in our silence. Surprisingly, she said nothing, as if she had not heard this scream, as if it were possible not to hear, not to know. She continued to put the cans of soup carefully on the lower shelves, to fold the plastic bags with the name of the supermarket on the outside, to place the neatly folded bags in the heap under the sink, among all the other discarded bags that she believed would become useful again, some day, another time.

"You better go down there and see what's going on," Ida said softly and evenly to Bernie. Another loud thud followed and predictably, another piercing scream. "It sounds to me as if they're trying to kill one another down there. Lord knows, I don't want to be the one to have to break any bad news to that boy's father."

She turned back to the cupboards and started drying and stacking the dishes in the tray. I shuffled my

269

feet, knitting my fingers in my lap, as much afraid as anyone else of what we could only sense, of what would be the ending for this hideous evening. "Lord knows, I've never heard Jeffrey behaving and carrying on this way before. He seems to be going crazy."

It wasn't supposed to be this way. Not the way it started, with the laughter and joking, as they went downstairs. But the change came quickly and soon we heard the banging and the screams, all of them a clear indication Jeffrey and Damsel had run into problems with Dennis. We had not anticipated a showdown at this meeting. And, sitting in our silence, we knew that this ending was just the beginning of something new, for something was being made and unleashed. And Bernie and I had to find some credible explanation for Ida.

"Oh, Lord. Oh, Lord." A voice that was clearly Dennis's whimpered after almost every scream. "Oh, Lord, God, no. Oh, Lord, God, no."

In truth, once the ruckus had started, it never really ended. The shrieks came piercing through the flooring from the basement into the kitchen. Now, I watched Ida, her hands trembling so much she had to stop drying the plates. Each thump made her jump. When pacing the kitchen did not settle her nerves, she returned to the dishes, muttering to herself, and finally expressing her fears.

"Something like it's gone really wrong to cause such a blow-up," Ida said. "Somebody should be able to do something before we end up with big trouble on our hands right here tonight. 'Cause, the Lord knows, I frightened. I real frightened." Bernie shook his head and got to his feet. He walked around the kitchen nervously, repeatedly glancing at his watch, eyeing the phone on the wall as if he expected it to ring any moment.

"Let's go and see what's happening," he said softly, as if fearing his words would be heard in that place below.

"I'm getting out of here," a voice thundered as Bernie just ahead of me reached the final step to the basement. The door to the office flew open to reveal Jeffrey. He was livid. None of us had ever seen him so angry, a man transformed into something monstrous. Where were the smiles, the suave image he so carefully cultivated? Instead, here before us was ugly animalism. An odious beast lashing. His eyes flashing. Stripped of all pretence.

Jeffrey pushed past us out of the room, brushing hard against my leg. Because of the anger that blinded him, it was a good bet he didn't even see us entering the room. Or so I thought. Until this moment, I had been willing to believe this was not the real Jeffrey Spencer. He knew the limits, the boundaries, and that they were clearly defined, demarcated and understood. He said as much to me. Now, this, could it be the real man or just an aberration? I felt the sweat on my back and in my palms. Three burly men, about whom I had purposely neglected to tell Ida, still in the black leather jackets that caused them to sweat profusely in this warm evening, followed him out silently. Damsel strolled after them, a pained look on her face. Obviously, something had gone very wrong. As I watched this Jeffrey, I started to think of the story about the African animals his father, and my father, had told us as boys.

Suddenly, Jeffrey was back at the foot of stairs, in front of me. "This is why you gotta start taking on more responsibilities around here," he snarled, wagging a finger in my face. "I keep telling you: it's time for you to stop learning and to start doing. It's time for you to forget this music, this video business, and turn to something you can be good at. Something that I can trust you with. That you can be of help to me. Rather than just dreaming about…ah, ah, ah," he finished in disgust. Swiftly, he turned his back. I still didn't have a clue what he was talking about, why the outburst, or why I was somehow the solution. I was deflated. My mind started to run ahead. Some incidents that I once dismissed as minor were now making sense. The trips that he and I were making around the world were not what I expected. He was not really helping me, I thought, but had some other plan for me. A plan that he alone must have decided, that he was now only referring to rather vaguely. I didn't know if I was happy or not for the outburst, for the clarity it brought. Minutes later, we heard the Mercedes-Benz's engine and the car racing onto the main street. Upstairs, we found the glass door to the liquor cabinet ajar. Missing was a forty-ounce bottle of his finest Scotch.

Bernie walked cautiously into the room, as if he expected to have to beat a quick retreat at any moment. But something kept me from going all the way in. The same thing that was in control of Jeffrey could be waiting for me inside. I felt its effect: the numbness in my spirit, the cold on my back and in my pants, and the anger choking me. An anger I knew I had to explain. Ida was standing behind me, breathing loudly: she must have sensed this presence too. She walked around me and stood in the doorway. I stayed on the outside behind her, looking over her shoulder, unable to step across. We had been told that there would be boundaries; that we were indeed amateur and that we should never try to become professionals. That time and timing were what mattered. This was not how any of us expected things to turn out. Certainly not Dennis, now reduced to a whimpering fetal ball in a corner. Not me, seething inside. Ida retreated back upstairs.

಄

"I'm sorry, man," Dennis was saying. Bernie stood over him and gently called his name. Dennis opened his eyes and looked around the room with frightened eyes, like those of a trapped animal. "I got carried away, a bit. I'm sorry, man. Sometimes my mouth's too big for my own good. I'm sorry."

Only then he must have realized that Jeffrey and the men were gone. "Bernie, oh God, I glad you're here," he said, reaching out a hand. "You gotta help me. You gotta tell him I was only joking about Brenda. Just a joke, man." The American easily sidestepped him and he fell back to the ground, crying. He knew what was awaiting him. Nobody needed to tell him he had made a fatal mistake. We left him wallowing and went back upstairs. An hour later, when Ida had at long last left, he joined us. The time spent alone had made him even more desperate.

"You know I didn't mean anything bad. I keep telling yuh, I was only joking. Joking," he pleaded with Damsel in the kitchen, the tears rolling down his face, the snot running out his nose. "I was a little too stoned, man. You understand, don't you, Damsel?"

Frustrated, Dennis lashed out at her. Before his hand could recoil, he felt the air rushing out of his guts and a severe pain cramping his entire body. He fell with a resounding thud. He had made yet another mistake by trying to touch her. We heard Damsel slamming the bedroom door behind her. Dennis got to his knees. He had to ask someone, anyone, for help, for a reprieve.

"Edmund, Jeffrey knows and trusts you," he cried. "Tell him I didn't mean what I said. I'm really sorry, man. Tell him that for me. Please, man. He knows that we all wanted to help Brenda. He knows that. He knows about Felix and his old man. He knows. You get on well with Damsel, ask her to beg Jeffrey to give me another chance. She'll listen to you. Edmund, it is you that gotta help me."

But paralyzed, I said nothing.

"Edmund. Edmund, please, man," Dennis pleaded. "*You* gotta help me. Please. Speak to him for me. I'd never harm Brenda, man, not even her memory. You know that."

But I said not a word.

"And you, Bernie," he tried again. "You got to know what's going on around here. You ain't no fool. You got eyes to see. You got your ways. He'd listen to you. We're friends, man. I've done everything you asked me. You're my friend now, aren't we still friends?"

Bernie turned and walked away. Dennis got unsteadily to his feet, still holding his side. "The party, remember," he shouted after him. "It was me that..." But the American was gone, too. There was nobody to intercede for him. There was only one thing, one chance, left. He had to try to make it over to Felix. If he got there too late, he would have to go directly to the cemetery to appeal to the only man who could still control Jeffrey. For that was the only way he could hope of getting a reprieve. Jeffrey would never go against the wishes and the intercessions of father. He was sure of that.

೦೦

It was already too late when Dennis hobbled up the back of the school and into the darkened watchman's hut. Felix was nowhere in sight and he had to scrounge around in the pitch darkness looking for him, between the bags of cements, the piles of sand and grit, the stacks of lumber, the wheel barrows, shovels and forks.

In vain he had searched the entire construction site, had dragged himself through the three school buildings, when he decided to try the watchman's hut one more time, tripping again over the same piece of board across the doorway and sprawling this time on the dusty concrete floor.

Dennis got unsteadily to his feet, rubbing his aching shin, aware that just about every spot on his body now hurt. He had ribs that must be broken, judging from the swelling, and a neck that was too sore. He should go directly to the hospital, or to one of their doctor friends. But what would be the use? They would get him there if that was what they wanted, if he did not get someone to speak on his behalf. Through his pants, he felt the swelling and burning from where he had banged his leg against the board. The left ankle was also paining; he had twisted it when he slipped on the newly dug ground only moments earlier. He had managed to scramble out just before the dirt fell in; escaping what seemed to be an untimely but certain grave. He had to find Felix. Then he would worry about going to the hospital.

He found the table in the corner and felt across the top with his hands, searching for a lamp. In the darkness, his hand hit something hard and it fell off the table, landed heavily on his toe, and rolled away. At the same time, he smelled alcohol. Dennis swore under his breath. Everything had gone wrong and was getting worse. Every little annoying thing was fucking him up, he thought. Out of control.

Now, he was thoroughly annoyed with everyone, everything and particularly himself. Why was he so blasted stupid most of the times? Why? Why did he have to open his big mouth instead of waiting for the right time to pounce? Why didn't he take Jimmy Ashton's counsel to be patient, to be low-keyed but keep planning and scheming quietly? Ashton had told him that he could be to him what Jeffrey was to this prime minister. There was potential. They had only to wait for the right moment. Only then, the Opposition leader had promised, Dennis could be sure Bogotá would anoint him as the realistic successor, the same way he was sure that when he played his hand Washington was bound to accept Ashton as the new leader. For their self-interest, both Washington and Bogotá would welcome the change.

"Me and you could take over from them two idiots, Watkins and Jeffrey Spencer, you know. We only have to play our cards right and then wait," Jimmy Ashton cooed. "I know I can count on you. Just don't gamble too much. Don't be too adventurous, keep a cool head, if you know what I mean. It's just a matter of time before them two start fighting with one another. In the light of the day, we'll see all things clearly. That will be our cue to move in. Not before, man. Trust me on that one."

According to Ashton, it was only a matter of time before the Organization in Bogotá lost all confidence in Jeffrey and took control of what was happening in the islands. He was not moving as quickly as they wanted, nor was he as committed. Jeffrey was still too much from the old school for the Organization. Not like him or Dennis. Already the Organization was thinking of how it could protect its investments, and these plans

276

might not include the people now in charge of the local operations. When they did impose their own people, as they must, they would be compelled to clear the decks of all their current supporters, except for the one person who really knew what was happening and who could provide continuity in business. Ashton so strongly believed this scenario that if Dennis didn't know better, didn't think the politician to be such a liar, he would have been tempted to believe Ashton had had discussions with the Organization on this matter. But he couldn't; nobody in his right senses would take this washed-up politician seriously. On top of that, nothing Ashton said squared with what he had heard from Bernie Lewis, and he felt more inclined to trust the American with his powerful backers. Not even the Americans wanted Ashton as prime minister.

How he wished he had not been so cocky, had not laughed at Jimmy Ashton to his face, had not sneered at him by asking who would want to deal with a failed politician like him, especially one with a secret for liking young boys. Now, he could not even ask Ashton for help. Then, he had to joke about what had happened to Brenda Watts, suggesting but only in an intended joke that anyone listening to him should know that he had friends in the right places. Friends who would make the same kind of visit that Brenda Watts had received, and again as a joke, that Brenda Watts would get a companion faster than she thought. Why did he do that? He was only pretending, showing off. He didn't have any friends who could make those kinds of visits. Heck, he didn't even have the kind of friends that could intercede for him. He also swore at himself for the memory lapse, for not remembering Felix had no lamp in this hut. For forgetting the sole source of lighting in the miserable place was a naked bulb in the ceiling, with a cord hanging from it.

In the darkness, he couldn't tell exactly where the bulb was. Going from memory, he knew it was above the table, for he remembered watching the bulb cast a shadow on the bottle of rum he and Felix had been drinking. Several times he caught at the air above his head, feeling and reaching with his outstretched hand. As his eyes adjusted to the darkness, he noticed the table had been moved, just a few feet closer to the door, but enough to throw off his senses. Nothing was as he expected.

After much effort, he caught the cord, but not before he had again stumbled over the bottle on the floor. He landed heavily against the sharp edges of the rough-hewn table. Such pain, but he managed to control himself after the loud yelp that escaped his lungs. He stood up, feeling the dizziness in his head, the numbness in his legs and the swollen ankles. Just then he felt the cord tickling his face and, instinctively, like a drowning man grasping at the proverbial straw, he yanked on it, hard, pulling the cord taut, and the bulb came alive. The sudden brightness blinded him and he stood his ground until he had recovered.

Opening his eyes, he saw Felix sleeping on a bed made of used cement bags. A heavy black raincoat, the type issued by the builder to keep workers warm and dry when it rained, covered his body like a blanket. The suddenness of the light caused the sleeping old man to loudly smack his lips, and to turn on his side away from the light. It didn't stop him from sleeping. He started to snore loudly.

"Felix," Dennis said, shaking the old man. Some fucking watchman, he thought. "Felix, it's me. Get up."

"Uh. Uh," the old man spluttered. The strong smell of alcohol was on his breath. Felix opened his eyes momentarily, tried to focus them, and just as quickly was snoring once more. Dennis held him in a half-sitting position, but even that didn't stop him from sleeping.

Sensing the hopelessness of the situation, Dennis looked around the hut. His eyes fell on the empty Scotch bottle. Expensive Scotch, he thought, trying to remember where he had seen the label before. It wasn't a brand of Scotch easily available on the island, and when it was, it wasn't sold at prices affordable by watchmen. It certainly wasn't the bottle he had shared with Felix earlier. Where the bottle fell from the table was a small wet circle in the dust on the cement floor. The spot a libation, perhaps. Somebody else out there must be dead drunk, too, he thought. Or maybe it was the spirits, all so confused and intoxicated by the oblations that the world was losing all sense of propriety and normalcy. A drinking partner for Felix. Maybe Aubrey Spencer had helped killed the bottle of booze. Dennis looked at the old man again. He was definitely out for the night. Anyone could come by and steal the entire gymnasium for all the help Felix would be.

"Some damn watchman," Dennis said, letting the body fall back heavily. He wasn't so concerned about Felix's failure as a security guard as he was frustrated by the man's inability to even recognize him, to open his eyes. To give him any information, whether he had told Aubrey Spencer anything.

As Dennis bolted from the hut, the light was still on and the black raincoat was now covering only Felix's feet. He had no time to tuck in the useless old man. He had to make it over to the burial ground right away. Fortunately, he knew Aubrey didn't get to bed until very late. The biggest problem would be where to start looking for the old man. In the shack, over the wall from the graveyard, or among the graves. He decided to try the house first. Just as he got partly through the door, Dennis finally remembered where he had seen a similar bottle before. His heart sank even lower. "Shit," he whispered. His eyes fell on Jeffrey Spencer sitting at the table, across from the old man. Father and son appeared to be in casual conversation.

"God bless my eyesight," Old Man Aubrey said. "To what do I owe the pleasure of these two visits, in the same night? Come in." Dennis hesitated.

"Don't stand there like some clown," the old man continued. "Come in and close the door against the evening draft before you give me a cold."

"Goodnight, Pappie Spencer," Dennis said finally, using the familial address of traditional respect. Silently, he admonished himself: *you got to pull yourself together, man; you're making too many stupid mistakes; not thinking, not fucking well thinking, Dennis. The car. You should have seen the car, man. You should have looked for it, man.*

"Geeze, boy what happened to you?" Old Man Spencer said. "In a fight or something again?"

"Yes. Yes. Yes," he answered.

"Well, you gotta stop this foolishness. Look at your face, man," Aubrey said.

"Yes. Yes."

"I don't know what to tell you young people. Still, go and wash your face, boy. Put some cold water on it."

Dennis's first instinct was to turn and run. The thought occurred to him that the old man knew what was happening and was in league with his son. In that case there was nothing to gain from pleading with them for his life. He may as well lay down at their feet and ask Aubrey to take him over to the graveyard and dump his worthless body in one of the waiting graves. But he could not be sure. He might ruin his few slim chances by saying anything, which might cause the father to suspect his son. For how could he be really sure Old Man Spencer knew anything? In his fright and indecision, he was frozen to the spot.

"Come on in, Dennis, man," Jeffrey said. "We were just here talking. It's nice of you to drop in. Do you come to visit Pa often?" He was smiling cunningly, mischievously, the scorn easily discernible in his voice. Against his better judgement to turn on his heels and bolt, preferably to find his own tree that bears a strange fruit, Dennis stepped through the door, his weight causing the old flooring to creak; his knees knocking, his legs unsure whether they could accommodate his weight. He felt hot, boiling, the perspiration soaking the back of his shirt and underarms.

"Sit here," the old man ordered, getting up from the table to offer him one of the two chairs. He dusted the seat of the chair with the palm of his left hand, as if he was cleaning it, even though he had been resting on the spot only moments earlier.

Dennis obediently complied. Jeffrey smiled. His father was so bloody well old-fashioned, he thought to himself. It was so typical of his father to give the bottom of the chair a couple of hard slaps instinctively before offering it to another person. It was the old belief: that by slapping the chair he was awakening his soul, which might have fallen asleep while the physical body rested. When the body was no longer seated, there was the possibility the invisible part of him might be slow to get reconnected. The person sitting in the chair would never rest, would never be comfortable, until the old man's soul also vacated the chair. And until then, the old man would never be at one with himself. So a few slaps were needed to prevent a clash of the souls, to prevent them from battling for the same throne.

As he sat, Dennis looked into Jeffrey's eyes. His face and voice were smiling, but not his eyes. They were staring at him, and they were cold. He could see in them the fiery anger and he knew he would have to explain a lot and convincingly. He would need all his powers of persuasion to extinguish the hatred in the deep brown eyes.

"Can I get you something to drink?" The old man was already rummaging around among some half-empty bottles in the back. This left the other two men together, with only the edges of the table separating them, so close they could touch or breathe on each other.

"Rum is all I got" the old man shouted from the kitchen. He was in a good mood, maybe happy because he was on familiar turf, where his naked feet knew every groove in the flooring and his fingers every dent in the wooden door posts between the *front house* and the kitchen, and maybe because this was the first time in months he was close to his only son without the presence of Damsel. And maybe because he too was playing a game with the two visitors, the same way they were toying with each other. "As you know, I don't drink any more. Not with the blood pressure I got."

Dennis hesitated. "I don't think I want anything too strong to drink, Pappie." The old man was whistling some unfamiliar tune. His happiness, in contrast to his silent dourness in recent times, was disconcerting and suspicious. Dennis wondered again if the two Spencers were in league. "In fact, I am off the liquors for good. I

282

don't plan to drink and get drunk any more. It ain't good fuh yuh, man."

"What's wrong with you, Dennis?" the old man asked calmly. "Think I'll poison you or something? Have a drink, man, and calm your nerves. You ain't like me, an old man with high blood pressure, nearing his grave. You can have a good stiff drink. At least it would show you appreciate the present company."

"Have a drink, Dennis," Jeffrey ordered softly. His eyes made this a command. "You do look like you need one. As if you walked past your grave on your way over here tonight. Why, I'll even fire a rum with you."

He poured some of the rum from the half-empty bottle into one of the two glasses his father had rinsed and placed in front of them. "To your health." With his left hand, he raised the glass in the air, still smiling deviously. "And yours too, Dad."

Jeffrey knocked back the waters, feeling the first run down his throat, creating burning warmth in the pit of his stomach. Then he poured some water into the glass and drank it. Dennis watched his every move. The taste in his mouth was of bitter gall and he pushed the cup away, wishing in his heart that it would be removed from him.

"I'm sorry, Jeffrey, man," he whispered. "Please."

"What's that you said?" the father answered. "Speak up, Dennis, if you're talking to me. You know I'm going half-deaf. Speak up, young man."

"He said, Dad," Jeffrey said raising his voice and at the same time pouring some of the rum into the other empty glass, "he'll fire just one drink with us. Then the two of us have to leave and discuss some business. Dennis is going to Cariacou for a rest, Dad. He's been

283

working very hard these days, under a lot of strain; he needs the rest. Don't you, Dennis?"

"I... I guess so." He hastily drank the rum. It not only burned, causing tears to unexpectedly come to his eyes, but the bitterness caused his throat to constrict. If Jeffrey had not drunk from the same bottle, if he hadn't see the old man wash the glass under the pipe, if the glass had not been empty when Jeffrey poured the rum, he would have thought different. For it was like no other rum he had ever drunk. "I guess so. That'll be nice. Real nice, man. Cariacou, eh? Nice island." He could feel the hot water in his eyes and he blinked fast. "When do I go?"

"Let's discuss it on our way out," Jeffrey said. He got up and stuffed the end of his shirt into the back of his pants and patted his protruding belly. He was beginning to grow a paunch, as part of the good life, and he didn't like it. None of his favourite clothes fitted easily any more. Damsel was after him relentlessly to pick up running with her.

"But how you can send him to Cariacou?" the old man asked in surprise. "Can he leave his job like that; pick up himself and leave the country? What about his job in the ministry?"

"No problem, Dad," Jeffrey said. "Remember you said earlier tonight I have political connections. The same way I can help the children, I can do anything for my best friends. Dennis definitely needs that vacation."

He stood up to his full height, took the bottle and poured a big drink into the three glasses. "One for the road," Jeffrey said, "and a toast to the three of us and this good bottle of rum: *Ashes to ashes, Dust to dust; If the rum don't kill yuh, Something else must.* Down the hatch."

"Ah," his father said. "You're always joking. And you know I don't like that damn toast. I don't like

284

people snickering at both the living and the dead. It's not respectful. But here goes." He raised his glass and sipped. Dennis finished the rum in one gulp.

As they walked into the darkness towards the Mercedes, Dennis offered his apologies again. "Like I said, Jeffrey, man, I'm sorry, man, real sorry. I didn't...."

"How many times you'll say that," Jeffrey snapped, turning to face him. The old man was standing on the back steps to the house. They were whispering so he wouldn't hear them. The anger Jeffrey had kept so well disguised was bubbling out, but by whispering, he quickly brought it under control. "Look, I'm not going to do you nothing. Just fucking well stop saying you're sorry every five minutes. What you are begging for?" He was talking more calmly now, more reassuringly. Dennis wanted desperately to believe him.

"Look, I'm a man of my word. Sure, I was angry as hell with you earlier tonight, but you're still my buddy, even if you can be a *rasshole* idiot at times." He wrapped his hand around Dennis's neck and pulled him close to him, seeking to assure the stiff body. "Relax, man. You know I can't stay angry with you, or anybody, for too long. You are my second in command, you asshole. What will I do without you? It's just you've been hitting the booze and the heavy stuff too hard lately. You need to get away, clear your head. Dry out. Go to Cariacou for a couple of weeks, a month. I wanted to tell you this at the meeting but you kept talking and talking and talking. Then things got a bit out o' hand. The boys gave you a few slaps. That was that, back there. We were angry. Now, nobody's going to harm you. Take a rest, but stay off the sauce. You yourself just said that is what you need to do, didn't you?"

"You really think so, man?" Dennis wanted to believe him, even if his senses told him he shouldn't; forgiveness in this business didn't come easily, if ever at all.

"Look, man, I don't have the time right now to discuss with you everything that I am thinking," Jeffrey said. "You should have a good, long talk with Edmund. Tell him everything and we'll fix up things proper. But you gotta talk to Edmund, and when you do, man, remember that you gotta come clean. You gotta tell him everything up front."

"I will. I will. If you say so. If you really mean it." Dennis said. "'Cause yes, everybody does find it easy talking to Edmund, but if you really mean it."

"Would I lie to you, buddy?" Jeffrey asked. Before there was an answer, he walked around to the driver's side of the car and opened the door. When he got in, he pressed the knob to unlock the door on Dennis's side. As they drove away, the old man stood on the steps waving.

Jeffrey drove Dennis straight to the harbour and put him on one of the modest powerful coast guard ships for Cariacou. Everything had worked out all right after all, he thought, as he watched the cutter with the American flag on the back slip beyond the harbour lights into the darkness. The drive to Lodge Road had been a time to reflect. He was happy with the conversation with his old man. The bottle of Scotch invested in Felix was worth the information he got in return. Christ, he chuckled contentedly, that damn watchman had drunk the entire bottle of premium Scotch all by himself, in less than an hour. How could these same old men claim the younger generation was stupid and abusive? He had been tempted to raise this with his dad.

Jeffrey drove home, anxious to join Damsel in bed, intent on making love and releasing the tension before a good sound sleep. Hoping that this was one of the nights he would not fight with Brenda Watts in his dreams. Naturally, he forgot to tell me of his conversation with Dennis. However, Dennis didn't and neither did he skimp on details. But I was sleepy and I couldn't wait until Dennis said goodnight and disappeared into the darkness. I really didn't think he had anything to worry about. But then again, I didn't think that what Dennis had presented as truth might not have been to someone else.

᠙᠙

But the night didn't go as planned. Hardly had Jeffrey succumbed to a deep sleep than the telephone rang. Swearing at the thought of anyone calling him so late on a night fraught with so many frustrations, he picked up the receiver at the side of the bed and rubbed his eyes. "Yes," he barked. "What?"

"Mr. Spencer?" The voice on the other end was evidently frightened. "Mr. Spencer, we like we got trouble down here. Big trouble." His first thought was that those incompetents in the coast guard had allowed Dennis to escape so that he would have to make different arrangements for a place for him to dry out, or, as you could never put anything past them, they had run the damn boat aground carrying him to Cariacou.

Jeffrey wanted — without hearing another word — to slam down the phone. He had no time or patience for them. Not on a night like this. Not with all these damn phone calls streaming in to him, the same calls that had upset him all day, from the time word came that he

287

should arrange a meeting with Dennis and some people they were sending over to find out what he was really up to these days. Then Dennis only made matters worse, consistently saying the wrong things, so that in the end even the Organization's men had lost their patience.

But he didn't hang up, if only because he wanted to remind these sailor boys they would have to become accomplished seamen, knowing every beach, every reef, every shoal on every island, if they damn well hoped to keep their jobs, which as they all knew was mandatory if they hoped to keep getting the regular *tra-la* he was providing them. Instructions from Bogotá that were now coming his way so fast that he could hardly keep up. Still, what could he say, especially when he kept hearing from them that the nincompoops on whom he relied in the government service were simply useless. That he'd have to clean them out and soon. Now, they had awakened him and, worse, after dispensing with them, he knew he would still have to try getting back to sleep and without the usual sleeping pill, without a baby bottle. These days there was too much on his mind. It was about time that he made a few changes, got drastic and reclaimed his life, maybe even with Damsel.

"What?" he snapped as he began to realize it wasn't the coast guard members calling him. "Where are you?"

The voice on the phone was familiar, but with the fog in his brain, he couldn't place it. The anger and hurt from returning home and finding Damsel fast asleep and unwilling to accommodate him intensified instantly. It was the first time in recent days she had rejected him. Still, as it always did, it came as a blinding slap, unbearable because it was so unexpected. Just another sign that people everywhere now felt they could tell him anything, that they could make whatever demand they wanted of him.

The short sleep had done nothing to ease the pain. It was like a trust had been broken. Jeffrey was mad as hell. Damsel, just like the damn Organization, was too much in control of everything, of even the way she could play with his feelings. If it were any other woman, one not so strong, determined, and quite frankly capable of felling him with one chop, he would have forced himself onto her. Brenda Watts would have been forced to give in. And he couldn't see his mother, no matter how much she threatened and rebelled, ever denying his father. Not Old Man Spencer, not for a moment, she couldn't. Now he had to deal with this stupid phone call. And, he knew, he would have to find a way to handle Prime Minister Watkins. And they were now piling on the demands. Forcing him to commit more than he intended, teaching him who was really in charge. Making him feel as if he was straining against some leash, on all fours just trying to get an extension.

"It's me," the thin voice said, "Emanuel."

"Who?"

"Manny. Emanuel." The person was straining to whisper loudly.

He still couldn't place the name and the voice.

"Manny. At the casino." Now he could put a face to the voice. Emanuel, a trustworthy, mild-mannered but somewhat inconspicuous young man, ran the club in their absence. Bernie handed over the night shift to him and he usually closed up. Emanuel was honest enough not to short the cash too badly at night and was one of the few people with this private number.

289

"This place is crawling with men in military clothes with big boots and big guns. They're going through the casino breaking up everything they put their hands on. Turning everything upside down. Kicking down the doors and smashing the mirrors; shooting out the lights. They just swooped down, just as things were getting a little quiet and we're preparing to close up for the night. Big trouble, Mis'er Spencer."

"Thieves?" he asked. "Somebody trying to hold up the casino again?"

"No. No. I don't think so. Not this time," the voice said. "They look like real-real soldiers."

"You sure it ain't some o' them people from the north o' the island. The same one that causing so much trouble nowadays. That even the police having so much trouble hunting down that they had to call in the defence force. You sure it ain't them?"

"No man. These is real-real soldiers."

"'Cause we have to watch out for all them upstarts that spreading their wings, moving in on our territory. You sure it ain't them?"

"No man. I think they's real-real soldiers, but now that I hearing you I can't be too sure. You know you can't be too sure of anything around here these days."

"Where you is now?" He found himself whispering.

"I in the apartment 'cause I don't want them to hear me. But all the same, as you was saying, and since you raise the matter, I can't be sure they aren't thieves dressed like soldiers."

Jeffrey was even more certain that a rival gang was robbing the casino. Worse, it might be a direct hit from the enemies intent on bankrupting the Organization. Which meant that gang warfare had finally arrived on this island, he thought. What would be the backlash, and did this mean that he and Damsel were no longer safe? That he would no longer be free to sleep peacefully in his bed, that his father would no longer be able to practise his rituals, to shave at the first sign of morning light, after riding to the beach for a swim? The officials in Bogotá had warned that something like this was always possible. He had sworn to take the necessary steps to prevent such occurrences. They had increased the number of paid security guards and armed soldiers in uniform. Jeffrey Spencer had sworn to Alberto Gomez, on his mother's grave, that adequate measures were in place to protect the property and there was no need for the Organization to even think of sending in its own people. Outside help would not be needed.

But even with the beefed-up security, there wasn't much Jeffrey could do to stop any of the rival gangs from making a strategic hit against the club. Or for that matter against either him or Damsel or Prime Minister Watkins. He lived in dread of having to call Bogotá to concede that they were right. Then how could he stop them from changing the landscape further, from superimposing their lifestyles, wishes and violence, from keeping their word and sending in their own people to protect their interest? Not *Los Niños*. He could not agree to them. Too high a price. But the Organization would not care what he, Jeffrey, wanted, or about what Prime Minister Watkins, on such a small piddling island, wished for a legacy. The prime minister always claimed he was a simple man, never one to fuss over anything, not as long as after he had conducted the business of doing business on their behalf that he could count on having a regular sea bath, meet with friends in the rum shops, quarrel and argue with them, walk with the people at their festivals, attend the funerals, join them on Sunday mornings in worship, and keep the island on a steady course. No greater legacy for him than that he handed over a nation that was at least as good and strong as what he had received. For it must be said that under his watch, despite the many distractions, he encouraged the young people to make the right choices, and to renew the vision, to have it reborn as new as if it were theirs. They, too, bought into the dream. Now, Jeffrey thought, he had unleashed something strange among the people. This must have been the way the earlier generation felt when they realized the animals were lost in the fields, that the island had become one big cage. And among them, as if covered in an invisible cloak, was their deadliest fear, the acknowledged presence of the intruders, the animals that stalk and devour those that were supposed to be their masters. He didn't want this one on his conscience. But this was what Alberto Gomez had done to him: changed the rules, pulled him in too deeply. Even Damsel had changed.

"Where are the soldiers and the police who're supposed to be guarding the club?" Jeffrey said into the telephone.

"They captured them, sir. That was the first thing they did. Most of the soldiers and the policemen were too drunk, too spaced out to even fight back."

"What you mean?"

"You know for yourself all these soldiers do around here is drink their guts full of the free rum on the house," Emanuel said. "Most nights, they aren't much use to themselves or to anybody else. So they captured them easy so, without a struggle." His breathing was calmer, but there was still the urgency in his voice.

292

"Was Bernie over there tonight?"

"Yeah, but he left early."

"How early? One o'clock?"

"Nah. He came in for only an hour or so. Left 'bout ten. Said he was feeling tired or something."

"Christ, what they're looking for?"

"I don't know. But they keep pushing the workers around, shouting at them and asking if we got any secret rooms or chambers around here to keep people in, if we keeping any prisoners."

"They're speaking Spanish?"

"Their accents make them sound like Americans," Emanuel said. "I'm calling you from the cellar because...."

There was a sudden crash, noises of advancing feet and what sounded like a scuffle. The telephone went dead. Jeffrey swore. He sat transfixed to the bed, staring at the red receiver in his left hand. Slowly, he replaced it in the cradle. He was now wide awake.

Before he could dial to get Emanuel, the phone rang again. He glanced at Damsel, who was sitting up on the bed, a deep scowl on her face. He grabbed the phone and returned her sneer.

"Yes," he said, his voice softer than before, as he was not quite sure what to expect.

"Jeffrey." It was the prime minister. Jeffrey had expected to hear Emanuel. "Jeffrey? Is that you? Thought I'd call you right away. We got some trouble. Big trouble. With the Americans. I was just awakened by the chargé d'affaires ....."

"Yes," Jeffrey said.

"Well, I was just delivered a diplomatic note. Serious stuff. A diplomatic note from the charge d'affaires as the ambassador is off the island You know the chargé

293

d'affaires, what his name. The shortish chap with glasses at the embassy...."

"Fitzhenry?"

"Yes, that's the name. It's right here on the paper that he handed me. Lawrence Fitzhenry. I just got off the phone with the minister of foreign affairs and with the attorney general. I have to have a special cabinet meeting right away. Maybe, I'll even..."

"What did Fitzhenry do?" He could not hold out any longer without exploding.

"Well, he delivered this note, saying they have reliable intelligence reports that the ambassador is still on the island, and that they are launching a surgical attack, that's what he called it—a surgical attack—to rescue the ambassador that was kidnapped. It looks like no matter how much we tell them, no matter how much their own FBI's been turning over every rock on this island, they still seem to think he's somewhere on this island."

In the distance came the first sounds of low-flying aircraft roaring over the island. "What's happening? What's that noise?" Damsel asked, running to the window, grasping her head in dismay, as if something had gone dreadfully wrong. As if there was some grave misjudgement.

"The Americans," Jeffrey shouted to Damsel. "They're attacking. Looking for the ambassador, searching the club for him."

"But he's not here," Damsel said, extending her hands in a sign her opened fists were empty, were hiding nothing. "He can't be there. And why tonight?"

"Shit," Jeffrey heard himself say. "What we gonna do?"

"And there's another thing," the prime minister continued. "They have impounded one of our planes

294

in New York. I don't think as the chairman o' the airline that you'd get the report yet. Something about sniffing dogs and some special kind o' machinery that found traces of cocaine and other drugs in the plane. So they impounded it. That's what I want to talk to you about. You should come and see me first thing in the morning, right after the cabinet meeting."

The military jets were disappearing in the distance as the phone rang again. From the special chimes, he knew only one person could be phoning and that he dared not refuse the call.

☙

"The chargé d'affaires said the president and the secretary of state would like me to come right away to Washington for a meeting with them. It's ten days since the raid, and even though they didn't find anything, they're kinda still mad at us."

"You're going?" Jeffrey asked.

"I got to," Watkins said as if he were a supplicant. "We just discuss it at the meeting. I don't have any choice."

"How long you'll be gone for?" he asked.

The prime minister shrugged his shoulders. "Who knows? They asked me for a meeting tomorrow, Tuesday, and say I should keep the next open for them. But I hope to be back by Sunday. In time for the special church service that we are planning. I'm to read the first lesson and the chargé d'affaires the second. Thank God they didn't find the ambassador here, eh. Can you imagine?"

"I know," Jeffrey said.

"I hope this kinda things isn't what you can look forward to when your turn comes," the prime minister said. "Nobody should be just summonsing anybody anywhere. Not if ..."

He raised his hand, then let it drop under its own weight. And he smiled, his bottom lip quivering. He brushed his eyes with the back of his hand and look quickly away, out beyond the trees of so many generations, beyond the white sand beaches glistering in the sun, the ships bobbing off the coast, into the beyond that was the horizon. "I hope it will be different."

"I'll be gone too while you're gone," Jeffrey said.

"Where to this time?"

"Oh, just to tidy up some business." He tried to put some enthusiasm in his voice. "You'll be very happy. Very happy with what I'm working on."

"I hope so," Watkins said. "I really hope so. Did you talk to your father this morning about this...?" He let his words trail off. Jeffrey shook his head.

"He wasn't at my house last night and I didn't see him this morning when I was leaving."

"I see," the prime minister said. "I see."

Someone must have turned up the radio in the hall. They could hear Jimmy Ashton denouncing the government, the violence on the island, the chronic drug abuse. *This has to stop. And I would support, indeed even encourage, our friends in America to take whatever action they deem necessary to correct the situation. For things are now clearly out of hand.*

"The three of you don't need me here with you," Damsel said. "Not while you're doing business. So, Jeffrey, if you don't mind I'll get my run now so that I can meet you back at the house before we head off to Bogotá."

We watched her loping strides gathering speed around the circle in front of the government building, as she went by a group of workers hovering near another radio. Soon, she was in the car park, where the taxi drivers were huddled around one car with its doors open, the radio blaring, the same voice speaking to them.

"I don't blame them," Prime Minister Watkins said, pausing as if debating in his head, "for listening. I don't blame them."

"I know," Jeffrey said. "I know."

Watkins shook his head. "What I would really like to know is how it could have come to this?"

ଡ଼

"It's time for us to come in." Alberto Gomez looked him straight in the face. It didn't take long in the meeting for him to come to the point. "We are sophisticated. We can take care of this business."

As he spoke, his eyes didn't blink, but appeared to focus laser-like on Jeffrey directly across the table. As usual, Gomez was immaculately dressed in a white three-piece suit with a red carnation in the buttonhole. Leaning forward, with elbows on the table, he clasped his hands in his usual supplicant position, as if in preparation for silent prayers.

"The leak is in *your* group," he said coolly. "And now this intrusion just the other night. Things are getting out of hand." If he was angry, we could not tell. The statement was uttered mechanically, in verification of a fact.

"We have to come on in and protect our interest, Jeffrey. There is a trend here. We have to."

There had been no noticeable change in his voice or tone; no difference from when Jeffrey, Damsel and I were ushered into the bunker-like building, to a room

deep in its bowels, to find the head *narco* already waiting and extending a firm hand of welcome. Later
Jeffrey would tell me that as he listened and tried to
make sense, he could feel his heart thumping loudly in
his chest. He couldn't decide if the flutters were from
being scared, from being too tired for such a meeting so
soon after our flight, or from still being affected by the
conversation earlier in the day. All he knew was that he
did not feel right and he had to fight to focus on what
Gomez was saying, and on the earlier conversation, too.
How did it come to this? He hoped the prime minister
was having better luck and that, at that very moment,
he too did not feel so far away from home. Still, Jeffrey
knew he had to do his bit, even if it meant pleading,
should magic no longer work. Too many things were
now out of sorts. Too many pieces to stuff back into a
single container, for this was a time when the contents
had so grown and multiplied that they had overflowed.
Too much of the fancy new wine; too much fermenta-
tion, and the bottles much too decrepit and old-
fashioned, too much from a different time and place. The
prime minister had said as much; how disappointed he
was; how old he now felt and how much they had all
failed. Still, they hoped for redemption, each in his own
way. Jeffrey had told the prime minister that the old
man would be proud of him, when this *little* business
was tidied up, he would be proud, when all the various
strands were brought together in one big knot. The end.
The time to switch to something else. He had to be true
to his word and to the promise to Watkins, and to himself. For in the back of his mind he could hear someone
calling time, and even snickering, too.

To get to the room, we had walked down several
long and dreary flights of stairs, passing on each land-

ing six or seven burly, unsmiling guards with their trademark black berets and machine guns on hand. Inside, the room was cold, not boiling hot as Jeffrey had somehow anticipated, but well fortified, no escaping, with iron bars across the door. Jeffrey could not imagine going any lower. The room sat in a sterilized and artificial silence as if we had entered the intestines of the earth, a place of certain decay, where nothing could grow, leaving all natural sounds and noises behind, so far from the bird fleeing overhead. A place of unnatural repetition. No natural light and definitely no music. Not even a siren's call. Only a noisy wailing in the silence, but no music. Nothing regenerative.

Others before had visited such places, and faced with the truth, had always fled for home, to the celebration of kith and kin, if they could. In Jeffrey's mind were the stories of all the many visits, of even the strongest and the bravest, all those who descended to Hades to find no happiness or wealth, but to realize finally what they had left behind. He thought of the ornaments on the wall of the Great House back home; the place where he still intended to put his own bow, and a guitar too, so that his father could string it and strum it. Where he would place pictures of those among the living and the dead, reminders of his mother, Thelma and Brenda, too, and of the future, of Damsel. He had come to depend on her so much and with time he knew his father would too. Then there would be the sweet reconciliation. Everything would be in its place for the time would have come when they would begin another journey, if not with him in charge, but still dreaming the old dream, pushing it in a new direction, still making the same old music, but now so much sweeter because of the improvisations.

First he had to escape and make his journey back, to fight those at home who were already planning to divvy up the spoils. Those taunting Watkins on the radio, those laughing at him in the rumshops and on the beaches where the old men and women went to bathe and play. The same ones already willing to look at him as if he were no more than some stranger among them. *How had it come to this?* And so quickly, too. What wind had blown him so badly off course?

"A what?" Jeffrey found himself asking. And just as quickly, he felt stupid for asking the obvious, as if he didn't understand what was being said, as if he should be surprised by anything, as if he was now not firmly trapped in an in-between space, with different clocks, different motivations and pride. Gomez's statement just couldn't be true; Jeffrey could trust all his suppliers and distributors on the islands. He had handpicked his people, pensioned off those he had inherited from Vincent, and was paying top dollar for loyalty and trust. There was no reason for the presence of *Los Niños*.

"Someone is supplying the Americans with information. We've done an in-depth analysis, checked out everything, and we know beyond a shadow of a doubt the leak is coming out of your place."

"I don't know what to say," Jeffrey said, looking around the room to gauge reaction. In the suffocating silence, he saw only the rigid looks on their faces, the utmost seriousness. Instantly, he felt the warm blood rushing to his head, the back of his neck growing hot and his heart beating faster. He wanted to stand up and defend himself, to challenge the results of *their* investigation — *what investigation anyway, just because they say so* — and to demand they provide proof. But he checked himself: there was a new objective: not to defend his pride; but at any cost to keep *Los Niños* out.

"Such leaks are costing us dearly," Gomez continued. "They have already forced us to move out of Bogotá at great inconvenience to everyone. But it is safer here. The raid on Club Alexia on your island was a red herring. The Americans knew they wouldn't find anything there."

"It was absolutely so horrible what they did," Damsel said, dropping her eyes so they wouldn't make contact with anyone around the table. She sighed again.

"It was to throw everybody off guard," Gomez continued. "They were supposed to be attacking us to rescue President Futado and the ambassador here in Colombia. They struck you as a cover. But that didn't matter: fortunately we got wind of what was happening and got out of Bogotá in time. Such mistakes are costing us."

"You know they had seized one of our aircraft," Jeffrey said, hoping this additional information would restore some confidence in him.

"It stands to reason," Gomez continued as if he hadn't heard the interjection. "The fact the Americans later struck at the very same house in Bogotá where we were keeping him indicates to us there is a very knowledgeable leak at work. Good thing our informers are just as good, if not better, than theirs."

"I hope you don't think it's me," Jeffrey gasped, "causing the leak."

"No, no, no." Gomez waved his hand, as if chasing off an irritating fly or mosquito buzzing around his head. Just as quickly, he re-clasped his hands. "In the last few days, we've checked you out. Your phones, your letters, your other communications. Everything. You're clean. We don't have any doubts about you. One of the odd things to us is that we suspect that whoever is leaking the information is also collaborating with our competitors, with some of the other groups that keep trying to displace us. Whoever it is, that person certainly is playing all the sides, but it is a dangerous game to be playing. Very dangerous."

Jeffrey turned to look at Damsel sitting next to him. It had to be Dennis Pilgrim. Maybe he had drunk too much and shot off his bloody mouth, as usual. Or he might have been on the CIA payroll, using the extra money to support his expensive habit. Or maybe he wasn't really joking, after all, when he'd said what he had about Brenda. Jeffrey nodded his head slowly. It made sense.

"We think we might know who it is." He decided to take the risk. "We can take care of this ourselves. No need for your help. At least, not just yet."

"We feel we should offer you the services of our security people," Gomez said. "This is a very serious matter. It cannot continue."

"I appreciate the offer," Jeffrey replied. "But let us try and deal with this matter in our way. Let's try our way first."

"Do you really believe you can do that?"

"We would like to try," Jeffrey said, looking at Damsel.

"We'll let you deal with that problem appropriately, then, as soon as possible," Gomez said. "But deal with it decisively."

Jeffrey swallowed. Damsel's fingers tightened around his, a sign, he thought, that she approved of his assertiveness. He smiled. The risk had paid off.

302

"We don't want anything like this to happen again, so let it be a lesson to others," Gomez continued. "However, there are some conditions that we want you to agree to. We want you to arm your own people. Do whatever is possible to have this protection in place within the next month. On the return trip, we're sending someone over with you. Juan Campersano." He pointed to a tall broad-shouldered and well-dressed man with dark glasses sitting at another table, on hand apparently just for this moment. Like the others in the room he had not said anything during the meeting. "One of our top lieutenants. He'll make sure your people get the right training and help you choose the right people. We've made the decision you need him."

"I see," Jeffrey said. Juan Campersano returned his stare, or so he assumed, as he could not tell for sure what was happening behind the dark glasses. "I don't see it as a real problem, but you know our government doesn't like people to be walking around with guns, with weapons."

"That's a problem for your government," Gomez said. Suddenly, he was standing. Some of the cool calmness had peeled back. Yet even in anger he didn't raise his voice. "Do what you have to do."

This was another reason Jeffrey hated these trips so much: he always came way from them deeper in, always ending up promising more than he would want to deliver, maybe more than he could deliver.

Gomez turned to leave. The meeting was over. He held out a hand and Jeffrey took it mechanically. "There is one other thing we want you to do. Maybe, once Juan is settled in and is keeping an eye on the business, we want you to become more of a salesman, start visiting some of our loyal clients, you know in New York, Miami, California, Paris, Berlin, wherever.

303

We have to assure them everything is well, that you are taking up the slack. I would like to do it myself, but until I mop up around here, I'll be too busy."

They shook hands and as they broke, Gomez swung around on his heels and took two quick steps towards the fortified door. Then, just as quickly, he spun around, as if he had remembered something at the last moment.

"Any message for Manuel?" he asked.

"Who?" Jeffrey asked, caught by surprise.

"Just say hi for me," Damsel said. "Give him my love. Tell him not to lose faith."

"Will do, Margarita. We want you to know we're doing everything possible to free our brother."

"I know," she whispered. Gomez took another step closer and kissed her on both cheeks. With a few quick steps, he was in front of the fortified door. Again, he stopped and turned.

"What do you think of this fellow Jimmy Ashton?" he asked. "Is he ... um ... reliable?"

"He's a political wash-up," Jeffrey answered. "The people would never vote for him."

"I see," Gomez said. By then the door was opened. Just as quickly, he was gone from the room with the armed entourage in tow.

On the way into the airport terminal, a picture and headline on the *El Tiempo* newspaper caught our eyes. On the front page was a gruesome picture of the almost decapitated and decaying body of the U.S. ambassador Gregory Thomson. It had been taken minutes after his body was fished out of the Caribbean Sea, on the Colombian north coast.

refrain

W.

hat I remember most was the gentleness of the anticipation leading up to the events of another night, the unravelling. And on the night itself, there was the feel of the softness and the pervasive freshness of the evening air. And, finally, of some stupid cock that would crow, from out in some beyond, breaking the silence with a voice so distant, empty and meaningless that I did not even want to care any more.

Business had been hectic in the months since our last meeting with Gomez, with Jeffrey and me spending long periods in airplanes as business took us to Europe, North America, a few times to South America — we still hated reporting in person to the head office — and even once to Hong Kong. Jeffrey said he needed me. "Man, I need you, Preacher Man." This was also stuck in my memory, burnt in from the countless repetitions. "Otherwise, I'd be just shit, man. But we'll soon be in the clear and we gotta keep this thing here under control." I had come to expect this reasoning but I realized I could no longer blame anyone else for my actions. There could be no valid excuse. I had to see myself as others did. I had to be responsible. Recently, Jeffrey wanted to talk only about his pet project, the one still swimming around in his head, which as he kept telling me would suit me just fine.

"It's going to be wonderful," he had said, "just wonderful. The people are going to love it. A taste of the past brought to life. As if people from old times just walk right out of a picture, and fit right in. Can you imagine all the stories they can tell us? All that we can learn from them? It will remind them of who we are and what we are about. What we are working for. Just trust me, it's going to be great, man. Just wait. I keep telling you the same thing that I keep telling the prime minister: just be patient, until I have everything in place. Then … *poof.*" He would wave his hand like a magician.

I was simply tired. Obviously, he was working at his plans for life after this business. I did not want to be like those people traipsing in and out of restaurants too much longer, living one life and pretending another. Just clinging to an unreal world even as life slips further beyond the grasp. And all because they fool themselves; are too reliant on others, on people so trapped by what they had promised that they could not even help themselves, far less those looking to them for deliverance. What desperation: to be dependent on someone who cannot provide even for himself; utterly reliant on the slave to set them free. I had learned a powerful lesson. It was a lesson I should have learned long ago.

I kept returning to that night, to the memories of the many nights we partied with the Spencers; of the afternoon of the parties, when Jeffrey and I watched my mother and Aunt Thelma in the kitchen, hearing Aunt Thelma daring my mother to try her hand at her favourite corn bread, the recipe given to her so many years earlier by some grandmother; and of my mother returning the challenge, teasing Aunt Thelma to try her hand at coconut sweet bread; and of the two of them laughing so loudly in the kitchen, over the joke they would play on the guests later that night, especially those who would come looking to end the night with a piece of Southern American corn bread that only one person on the entire island could have baked, or those expecting to leave with a big chunk of a special sweet bread, and not knowing exactly what was what, but swearing that whatever they got was so authentic that it could have come from only one source. And of my father and Old Man Spencer, off in a corner of the yard, with many bunches of coconuts, some yellow, some green, in a big pile, cutting off the tops and draining the water into a big enamel pot. And me and Jeffrey taking the cutlass and cutting the discarded coconut shells in half and scooping out the delicious jelly, some soft, transparent and runny, others so firm that they were almost ready for grating. I remember eating so much that by the time darkness fell, and we had to go and wash up under the pipe in the back, our bellies were already busting. And we would run among the people, darting between their legs, making faces behind the backs of them. So full of energy. So excited. So happy.

At other times there was no crowd and just the six of us, getting together, spending an evening in our home or going over to the Spencers' place in the graveyard.

At first it was frightening, for who, as a little boy, wanted darkness to catch him in the land of the dead? But my father laughed and would take us over to the house that stood alone, aloof from everything else. We seemed to have had the most fun there, even more than in our home when we had to be conscious of the neighbours, who were themselves often entertaining: the men dropping around to fire a drink or two, the loud laughter and music, the children running in the streets, mothers calling after them, dogs barking—all the things that clashed with the euphony of an evening in our home. In the graveyard, we had no competition, nothing to distract us. Yet we were not quite alone. To remind ourselves of this, we had only to look into the distance for the lights of the nearest house, for the street lights, the darkened church that we knew was there like a shadow, tall and aged trees with their plaques, thousands of invisible eyes watching with silent tongues.

Our fathers and mothers would talk, eat and drink, and Jeffrey and me would sit and watch them, doing whatever they asked. They knew they didn't have to worry about our straying too far, of our even going out into the darkness, for as I said, who as a young child wanted to be in the darkness of a graveyard. Not when the *duppies* were about to stir and come loose from their graves, not when we heard the precursors of their arrival every time the wind came up, maybe through a hole or a crack in the house, not even a child whose playground was among tombs. That was why we were always so happy when we were singing and laughing, when our music drowned out the wind and any spirit, evil or otherwise, when Old Man Spencer made his old guitar sing.

But that was when I was a little boy and eventually Jeffrey, older than me, tempted me to walk with him in the dark. After all, he knew the place so well, having scouted and mapped every crevice and haunt. He urged me on to take the flashlight and to search for bugs, crickets, to discover what already existed, and even to read some of the names on the tombstones. And I would slip out of the house, desperate to show that I was becoming as big a boy as him. He had gone on to high school by this time and was doing well, benefiting from a church scholarship. I felt secure walking in the dark knowing that the comforting voices laughing and singing were still nearby, and that Jeffrey, even if he wandered off and chose a different route, would bring me back to the light and the sanctuary of the voices in the house. I would rise to Jeffrey's challenge and prove to him that I was becoming as big as he was and that I was not too scared to dare. Jeffrey always laughed at me, but I sensed that he held back and went easy on me. Never pushed me so far that I failed, but always took me up to some line that only he knew, that he, himself, would never cross. He was protective, a big brother, helping me to pronounce long names like Cumberbatch, Brathwaite, Montgomery, and I remember well because it stood out as different, Nwandiuko, on the head stones. Telling me things he learned in school. Pointing out that many of the people with these names were now dead longer than they had lived. What was left of them? What was their legacy? Is this their history, just simply a name and two dates, of birth and death, a beginning and an ending, the tips of a string or a piece of rope, but ultimately a suffocating and immutable limit? Was their eulogy simply a celebration of a long life, he asked, or a lived life? Even if they had willed what should be written on their headstones, what could they do if people, perhaps many generations later, were to come and change it, maybe amend a word here or there, or if time were to erode some symbol, and change the meaning? So, what's the use? I guess that even as youths, we lived and played with the certainty of death and erasure.

That going-away party for Jeffrey at the end of high school was on a night as soft and pleasant as this was. I will always remember that it was the night I cried. I was already in high school and Jeffrey was now recognized as a man, heading for a North American university. I had noticed the strained relationship between his mother and father, how Old Man Spencer didn't seem too happy, how Aunt Thelma was so straight-faced and focused, not even as easy-going and open with my mother as she usually was. Times had changed. The gatherings of our families had become less frequent. And when we did go over, we were less boisterous: Jeffrey was finishing homework, something was strained in the house. He and I didn't go walking and our fathers didn't sing as much, or as loudly. His father's guitar had gone into retirement, my father seldom played the spoons, my mother did not sing, she and Aunt Thelma did not beat the tambourines, Jeffrey and I seldom hummed through the comb covered with waxed paper. Jeffrey was too old for that; and if he was, I was too. It was a changed world. That night was the first time in a long while that our families were getting together. And even then it wasn't just our families. As always happens when others are invited, the dynamics change. That night there was a crowd of well-wishers.

I cried that night because Jeffrey hurt me. We had gone among the graves, with Jeffrey showing names and family plots to his friends, ignoring me. We had gone far, into the segment where families had lain undisturbed for decades, if not centuries. This was the site of the famous Chase vault, the one family that never rested peacefully, that fought even in death, until the vault was excavated and left hollow, with only a small entrance and silence and darkness inside. Like a big and glorious house with only friction living inside. Without even a plaque on the outside. No markers.

I was standing next to Jeffrey, basking as usual in his shadow, when he spun around and grabbed me.

311

He and the giggling boys lifted me and shoved me into the Chase vault, the eerie darkness cloaking me, the sand shifting under my hands. The sand had been placed there long ago to test if someone was entering the crypt and disturbing the dead, so the footsteps would prove it was a man and not duppies at fault for the rumblings that left heavy leaden caskets strewn around. Before I could react, all the lights went out. Even the stars disappeared. The entrance was blocked.

I'll always remember that smell. I cannot describe it exactly but I always associate it with abject fear and utter despair. I heard the footsteps of my tormentors running away, leaving me alone, trapped. I screamed for help, for Jeffrey to help me. I screamed until my voice was hoarse, but even then there was no silence. I could not stand it, could not stop the trembling, and the helpless crying. Crying even though I was now big, knew so much and was already in high school.

It must have been an hour — perhaps even longer — before he returned. He was alone and laughing. I was still crying. "Scare yuh, eh?" he said. "Guess you thought I wasn't coming back. If I didn't, wouldn't you have to find a way out for yourself? You gotta take care of yourself man, find your own way out. Trust nobody, but yuhself. Every man must *brek* for *heself* in this life, man." This was perhaps the one time I could say with certainty that Jeffrey had betrayed me for his other friends, when there could not possibly be any doubt about his intention. But it was also, I should say, the one time he acknowledged that he was joking. Like waking from a horrible nightmare, I would realize that he had always planned to come back. It was one time I knew for sure what Jeffrey had taught me. "You could have stayed in there forever and nobody woulda find you. That is the best place in the world to hide."

We walked into the house for the farewell party as if nothing had happened, for I had washed my face as he suggested. Jeffrey gave his goodbye speech and accepted a few gifts. "I'll write Edmund every week, just you watch and see," he promised without prompting. "I'll be relying on him to keep me inform, right, Edmund?" I remember nodding my head, and wiping away fresh tears, this time because he was definitely leaving. I would be on my own, having to fend for myself. That night the music blared loud and long, well past the hour when the duppies would have risen and then gone back to sleep, for in the merriment there was no room for them, they could not compete. They were not to be celebrated or remembered and they could not frighten anyone by blowing eerily through the holes and cracks of an old weather-beaten house. The next day Jeffrey was gone. I always remembered. And I remember awaiting his return.

I was among the last to arrive for Old Man Spencer's birthday party, coming on purpose late in the night. He sat in his rocking chair, the guitar leaning against the side of the house, Ida Weekes shelling peanuts and feeding him. With some of the friends already there I joked about her attentiveness, at how she would even blow on his glasses and polish them in her skirt, returning them to his face herself, not letting him touch his own spectacles. Not on so special a night. My father, choosing this as one of the rare occasions not to wear his cleric's garb, sat next to his friend, occasionally reaching across Aubrey to speak with Ida.

As we milled around, emptied our glasses and refilled them, one thing was on our minds: when would Jeffrey make his entrance? When midnight came and it was officially no longer his father's birthday, we knew his entry couldn't be much longer. He had gone as far as he possibly could. He had made his point. To push the boundary further would be to slap his father in the face, in his own house. While it was true that I had seen some changes in Jeffrey, I still dreaded the thought of the old Jeffrey showing up and competing with his father. Even the dead were likely to rise up and invade if he were to do such a thing. They would not be content just to roll in their grave, fight one another, or to just howl on the wind.

By the time he arrived, the house was crammed and many of us were spilling outside. We were beginning to get bored, but who would want to leave before Jeffrey arrived, who would want Jeffrey to know that they thought he overplayed his hand and that they had grown impatient with him? Jeffrey, Damsel on his arm, came from the edge of the darkness through the crowd. He stopped briefly to speak to the prime minister and to Jimmy Ashton, who on a night like this found reasons to talk and share a drink. A young man broke through the crowd and took the big box Jeffrey had brought from the car. Free of this load, he was able to shake hands, talk to the young men and women, give them cards with numbers to call him, and smile as he made the slow walk to the house.

I felt something drop in my stomach. Still, he looked impressive, a throwback to days before we were both so tired and when he believed he was in control, tall and handsome in his silky black shirt with sleeves buttoned at the wrists, pants with sharp seams and shiny black shoes, his hair newly cut to fade around the ears, so similar to the fashion of the young men at home and in North America. And Damsel was radiant, her hair oily and silky bright, her sleeveless white blouse, a black bag over her shoulder, her long legs accentuated by the loose-fitting skirt with the white flowers. Plain and radiant, but not so much so as to detract from the man of the night. Nothing had really changed. Apparently. I didn't want to think that I had been fooled yet again.

They finally made it into the small house and the guests automatically cleared a path for Damsel and Jeffrey, followed by the youngster carrying the big box covered in red, white and green paper. Finally, they were standing before the old man. Ida stood up, pointing to the chair she had hastily vacated to offer it to Jeffrey or Damsel. She stepped aside, a big smile on her face. I thought my father would have stood up, too, but he remained seated.

"Happy birthday, Big Man," Jeffrey said. "I hope that when I'm your age I look half as good as you." He laughed loudly, and just about everyone joined in. To the gathering, he shouted: "Doesn't he look good? My father, the man. The greatest, man. Have they sang 'Happy Birthday' to you yet?"

Jeffrey turned to face the main section of the gathering. He raised his hand in the air like a conductor spreading enchantment, or some other dust, and started singing "Happy Birthday."

"One more time, now," he said after the first round. "And all the people outside, you must join in too."

He stopped singing, as if listening to a specific voice. Smiling. Waving his hands, mouthing the words silently, with a final loud burst as the song came to an end, only to begin all over again. He raised his hand and waved it, this time for silence, for him to speak.

"I've brought something special for you," Jeffrey said. He gestured and the young man pushed forward with the gift. He placed it on the floor in front of Pappie. Ida sat again beside the old man, for it was obvious neither Jeffrey nor Damsel would be sitting. Then the Spencers hugged. For a long time, the old man clutched his son to him, the two of them bending, the bulbs flashing and all of us clapping.

"Let's open it," Ida said, tapping the gift. "Then we can start sharing out the food and everybody can eat. Anybody see Bernie yet? There's lot of food. Good, good food."

Laughing as she spoke, nervously, but yet so gently, she tore the covering, taking care to find the point where the sections were joined by tape, as if she was trying to preserve even the paper.

"'Cause everybody on this island done know one thing: nobody 'round here can't share out no food without Bernie Lewis around," and she laughed before continuing. "Not, without our good friend Bernie."

"No, man," Papie Spencer said. He too was laughing, perhaps at Bernie, or even at his own nervousness. "He soon come, Bernie soon come." Perhaps even at the anticipation. "He soon come, man."

"Poor Bernie," Ida continued, "we shouldn't laugh at he so, but yuh know, he's one o' we now. He ain't too much of a stranger any more. So we can laugh." She gently pulled away the last of the paper. "Here we are."

Inside the box was a stereo. Old Man Spencer eyes blazed. A smile broke on his face. He ran his hand over the hard plastic, on the covering of the miniature speakers.

"And I have something special for you," Damsel said. "Jeffrey told me how much you like the blues." She took several compact discs from her bag. "I got these in Chicago. Some of the real old-time blues. My own father in Miami used to always play this type of music. Every evening. I gather this is the same type that you and Thelma liked. If it's not so, blame your son for not knowing anything."

Ida took them and handed them to the old man. He took off his glasses to take a closer look, flipping the casings front and back. "Thank you," he whispered. "Thank you."

"So, let's party," Jeffrey said. "Hit me with some music. And let we all have a drink, to celebrate a Big, Big Man." The prime minister and the opposition leader shook Old Man Spencer's hand and paused for pictures, each lingering to have a separate picture with him, and with Jeffrey, covering all bets for the local newspaper. They patted him on the back and slipped back into the crowd.

Jeffrey and Damsel walked towards the bar through the back door, leaving Ida to read the writing on the CDs and in the cards to Old Man Spencer. I, too, went outside to escape the heat and to think. Stepping into the darkness, my heart froze as I watched the figure and a few friends coming out of the shadows and making their way into the house. Shit, I thought, Juan Campersano. What he's doing at this party?

A group of us was standing in front of the house eating the curried chicken and rice, all of us complimenting

Ida's culinary skills, being envious of Jeffrey for having such a cook to feed him daily, joking about having a reason for visiting the Great House more often, when we heard it. The first notes and the baritone voice. Deep and rumbling. I don't know why it startled me for I had expected that at some time the old man would take up the guitar and entertain us. But seeing the spectre had left me rattled. By the time I got back, Juan Campersano was nowhere in sight, making me wonder if, indeed, I was not too tired and was beginning to see my fears. I remained among the crowd on the outside just in case that was where the Colombian would feel more at home. When the strumming started we stopped talking instantly. Old Man Spencer's voice was clear and strong.

> *Ah happy birthday to me*
> *Me, me, me*
> *Ah happy birthday to me*
> *Me, me, me*
> *Ah happy birthday to me.*
> *Ah happy, birthday, birthday*
> *Day, day, day*
> *Ah happy birthday, birthday,*
> *Day, day, day*
> *A happy birthday to me*
> *Me, me, me*

I heard people clapping and chanting, some of them apparently stomping and I could imagine Old Man Spencer sitting on his rocking chair, leaning forward at the waist, the upside-down guitar on his leg, his right hand awkwardly on the fret board, his head hanging down, eyes closed and he just wailing. Those of us on the outside were stampeding to get inside the house.

Me son gi' me a gift, gift, gift, gift
Me son gi' me a gift, gift, gift, gift
Me son gi' me a gift, gift, gift, gift
Me son g'i me a gift, gift, gift, gift

And wha' was that gift, gift, gift
And wha' was that gift, gift, gift
And wha' was that gift, gift, gift
Wha' ah ah was that gift.

He gi' me a stereo,
He gi' me the stereo
He gi' me a beautiful, fantastic, wonderful, delicious
Stereo, stereo, stereo.

Come, on, sing with me
And what did he gi' me?

As expected, the voices joined in on cue for this old-talk music, full of mirth and happiness, the call and response completed. The Old Man strumming and stamping, my father slapping the spoons, someone belting the cymbals. One line by him; the other by us; the next by him; then by us.

A stereo, A stereo
And what did he gi' me, gi' me, gi' me?

The strumming stopped as did all the other voices, leaving the old man to improvise:

Ah, ah , ah , ah
Sterry, sterry, sterry.
Oho, oho, oho, oho
He gi' me a lovely stereo to play my music so
I wouldn't sing, but I gotta keep singing.

The people were clapping and asking Old Man

319

Spencer to continue. "No man, yuh can't stop now. Not when yuh goin' so sweet, and we ain't hear you sing fuh so long. No, man, yuh can't stop singing. Not now," someone shouted. "Don't stop, not fo' shite, man! Talk yuh talk; sing if yuh singin', man. " A loud approval, in voice and by the clapping of the hands, started in the house, in the vicinity of the voice, and like a wave rolled over by us where we too joined in.

Then, I heard it, the familiar sound of the paper and comb. I knew who had to be playing, who just had to be vying with the singer and guitar player. I squeezed into the house and found myself standing beside Damsel. She still had her plate in hand. We stood and watched. Before my eyes images of an old picture were recreated, Ida with her tambourine sitting beside the old man, my father with the spoons, Jeffrey with the comb and paper, the only people missing Thelma, my mother and me, two of them perhaps calling from their resting place just beyond the ending of the light, me left out and simply looking on.

Damsel nudged me and with her head indicated she wanted to speak with me outside. Just as we were stepping through the door, Old Man Spencer announced that he had a special song in mind.

"As I would say," and he started strumming, loudly, the music following us outside as he sang

> *Me say, as the good book done say:*
> *He that hath ears let him or her hear.*
> *As the old people always say back then:*
> *Throw stone over pig pen,*
> *Pig that get hit, squeal*
> *As my father tell me when I was a little bit:*
> *You can hide and buy land, that's the deal,*
> *But you can't hide and wuk it*

As my friend the preacher sitting
right here besides me does say:
What you do in the night
Must in the day come to light
For you shall reap what you sow,
So me say tonight, night, night:
And, if yuh play with fire
Yuh must get bu'n
Yuh havetuh get bu'n
Yuh hafta hafta hafta get bu'n, bu'n, bu'n

He was now strumming louder and longer, as if resting his voice, or waiting for the music to hit the right tempo. "*So I say…*" Perhaps the old man was searching for the right chords, his leathery palm scraping the wooden head of the guitar, the magic sparking from the hands, the fingers banging the strings. Then, he broke in:

Pretty woman, why must you run
Pretty woman why must you run, run, run…
Daughter, daughter stop and rest
Daughter you gotta stop and rest.
That's de best.
Pretty woman, why do you run, run, run…
Pretty woman don't get yuhself bun, bun, bun

As we went deeper into the darkness, the voice seemed to be following us. Damsel was walking beside me, but I still felt as if she was leading me, taking me places that I would not imagine or expect from her. I was following, maybe even escaping from the music, but doing so willingly. Not once did I stop to ask what I was doing, and why the two of us were going so deep into the darkness, occasionally bumping into a headstone, tripping over broken concrete.

"Would you call him a blues singer or a calypson-ian?" Damsel asked, breaking the long silence.

"What difference does it make?" I asked.

"Some people look for the purity," she said. "You know blues has its own structure, as does calypso, I guess."

"Isn't that when problems start?" I asked.

"But I think he would probably see a difference," she said. "Doesn't he suspect the foreign?"

"Maybe, if he has a reason. But remember his wife."

"But is the same true for *his* music?" she asked.

"I think so. I think he would say the problem is when we start labelling and defining instead of just enjoying. I mean, aren't they the same or some hybrid, part of the same family? Jazz, blues, calypso, mento, reggae and even samba. Same roots, same causes, same purposes. All the same region, same people."

"Oh," she said. "Really?" We walked on. "You speak very well, very authoritatively and convincingly *for him*. You must really love him, to speak for him."

"I do?" I said, unaware of what I had done. "I do."

Pretty pretty pretty woman moving in the night
Pretty wo wo wo woman, running by no moonlight
Pretty woman, man, man, man still running in the dark
Pretty woman, why run, run, run

Finally, we were in front of the Chase vault. I don't think Damsel knew the significance of this place, for she casually leaned against it. In the darkness, I felt her hand brushing my leg as she searched for my hand. The experience was unreal, instantly changing everything. "There is something I must share with you," she said eventually, her hands tightening around mine. "Damn, why am I doing this? Why am I taking this chance?" I

322

heard her smack her lips and swallow. She pushed on: "I know that in light of what we are doing that I should be the last to ask you to keep a secret, but I must. I have to be able to trust you. I know one wrong word from you could destroy everything, but I *gotta* trust you. 'Cause I know you are different. You are smart and you want to survive. And I knew it had to be you, from the day I first sat and talked with you in the hotel."

And with that, she took me deeply and completely into her confidence. I was startled. It was a world I had not suspected in the least. And I also knew that this was an offer I could not ever hope to walk away from. I must have stood for some time with my mouth agape — I don't recall saying anything, just listening. So many things started to make sense. I felt my head spinning. To tell the truth, she was casting a spell, a very dangerous one for both of us. Her voice, so sweet, inviting and so honest. It was like nothing I had experienced. The thrill of the moment, of her sweet perfumed breath, her strong hands and the place. Oh, the place. And the music of the wind in the trees, the waves in the distance, the silence from elsewhere in the graveyard and the heart-wrenching song of Old Man Spencer and someone playing a comb. In the distance was that Great House, like the plantation owner's centuries early, when people would sit in the darkness and watch the lights flickering, hoping nobody in the house was also looking back at them, their eyes penetrating the distance and darkness to really see what was happening in the shadows. From the ocean came the songs, for those not at the party, for those left out, for those still trying to make sense of an aging life, dancing to the oldies and goldies, dipping, twirling and waltzing, to those with the youth and vigour rushing maddeningly through their veins, with one foot 'pon the shoulder, another round the waist, banging-plumbing-banging, of those, too, slipping into the darkness to taste and make life. Of those trapped by the rhythm of the night and having no choice but to dance to the night of rhythms. I, indeed we, were caught in the in-between. Settling scores. Not at the beginning, not yet at the ending: in time that was dead. For indeed, even in the graveyard, some things didn't sleep, or couldn't rest. Not this haunting voice:

> *Pretty woman, I see you run, run, run*
> *Pretty woman is me that see see see*
> *Is me that see you run, run, run*
> *Pretty woman is me that see you run*
> *Pretty woman, you can't fool me, me, me*

When we returned, the old man was finishing his performance. He was sweating profusely and his eyes were still closed. Jeffrey was still strutting his stuff, at times even playing the fool to his father. I don't think anyone had missed us.

I didn't have the heart to seek out my father to tell him goodnight. And, knowing what I did, I couldn't look Old Man Spencer in the face. I couldn't deal with these two men, in case under the spirits of the night they should really say what was on their mind, giving me one more thing to regret. As I walked away, I heard the old man announcing, "That is enough for the night for me. I done now." As I got into the car, I heard the sound from the new stereo for the first time and the music from Chicago.

We delivered the boxes with our own hands. We placed them on the table among the other offerings from the community. The boxes, large and small, that we had picked up at the airport only a few hours earlier. Jeffrey had cleared them through customs himself. Then, the three of us — Jeffrey, his father and I — had walked down the aisle of the school in the full glare of the television camera and the appreciative audience of specially invited guests. We placed the boxes on the table. Neatly. The guests applauded. We lingered near the boxes for the photographers and until the clapping died down. Prime Minister Watkins thanked us for the gifts of books and science equipment and promised that the students and the teachers would always be grateful, that they would use them wisely. Jeffrey said he was making the donation in the name of Brenda Watts, now dead just over a year. To more applause, he said he was donating an undisclosed amount for scholarships. My father asked God's blessing on the gifts and on the givers, and on the young minds that would be so enriched. I smiled, as did Jeffrey. Old Man Spencer was happy.

"Let's take a look at the day care centre," Jeffrey said. We had seen some of the teenagers remove the boxes a few minutes earlier. They had disappeared behind a set of doors, the same doors through which we had seen the toddlers and infants come laughing and in single file. They were now on the platform singing. Jeffrey pushed open one set of doors that led to a corridor. We walked briskly, listening to creaking sounds of our soles on the flooring, hearing the young voices echo down the hall. Jeffrey stopped in front of the door with frosted glass. We looked at the drawings and paintings, the odd-shaped men and women, the stick people and the hand and foot prints of all colours and sizes, names in awkward letters proudly scrawled on them. With his father right behind him, Jeffrey pushed open the door.

In the room, the boys and girls ran, some staggering, for the door to the playing field. Scattered on the floor were all the ugly paraphernalia and hastily abandoned bags. Two of the boxes we had brought into the school about an hour earlier were open. There were no books or scientific materials, just bags and pouches, some of them still neatly packed, Jeffrey Spencer's name still clearly displayed on the sides of the boxes. At that moment, four men in military uniform burst into the room and hastily stuffed the contents back into the boxes.

Jeffrey said nothing. He looked transfixed to the spot. We stood silent for a long moment. Old Man Spencer's mouth trembled. So did his hands. He raised his eyes, looked as if he was about to say something to Jeffrey. But then he hesitated. His lips twitched and he swallowed loudly. He looked into Jeffrey's eyes again. Then he turned and walked slowly from the room.

"Shit," Jeffrey said, kicking one of the discarded bags that had been left behind. The white contents formed a small cloud from the impact. The janitor appeared and feverishly began sweeping and mopping. Jeffrey used his handkerchief to wipe the residue from his shoe. Then he threw the handkerchief into the garbage.

"Shit," he said. "How can anybody do this?"

We walked back into the reception, to the noisy chatter and to the students singing one of the national songs. Old Man Spencer was nowhere in sight. We walked out into the early darkness. I told Jeffrey that I was not going back to his house. I was going to my own home, and I walked away.

he cool breeze, like an invisible hand, mischievously ruffled the curtains at the window in rhythm with the calming noise of the waves in the distance, the swaying sound of the wind through the tops of the cane fields in the distance and outside the window; and with the dirge of evening rituals. You must understand, my brothers and sisters, the strange workings of the mind. How Damsel and I began talking, starting with the night of the old grave digger's party. How in inexplicable ways, the sounds and music surrounding us were the first things that she always wanted to talk about, particularly when she telephoned on that fateful day. Oh, yes, my friends, she too had ghosts that she could never retire. A neck rope that kept her just as fastened. Uncommitted spectres they are, that walk the face of the earth; living only among the disposed people that we are, refusing to set us free or to give us back our voice.

Without a true voice, we feel compelled to clear the air with just talk. A constant need to expiate, sometimes in too much depth, to run off and tell a part of the story, that might be nothing more than digression, not the life blood of a true narrative, our expiation and forced validation for our own wrongs and betrayals. Maybe I, too, am guilty of that. Indeed, I know I am. But I must be conscious of my promise to the truth. She, too, must have felt so compelled. For who could be so divided as to set aside all feelings and emotion, to remain so steadfastly committed, and not to feel a pang of self-doubt? How could she submerge herself like this and yet emerge untouched, dry and unborn? I can't, and I don't think she was able to, either. Eventually, even the hardest stone gives way. This would account for the length of our final conversation and, in my mind, for all that happened afterwards. And for me feeling, ultimately, responsible. These are the phantasm images that remain. But, for her, it always started with what was so rigidly grounded, her sense of another time and another place and of her disciplined approach to reclaiming them. Oh, how rigid is such a commitment, how badly can the dream blind, as well!

❀

Damsel, or Margarita, for that was how she was now insisting that I call her, sat in front of the mirror brushing her shoulder-length black hair, feeling the cooling wind on her sweaty body. In the distance, she heard the ocean waves, how they, like music, always relaxed her, as they had when she was a little girl. Now, as an adult, these sounds still soothingly helped her to think; to dredge up memories of simpler and less risky times; of honesty and openness, of being free and elsewhere with her father, the famed and affable Cerveza Libre, and they reminded her of why she had to keep the solemn promises spawned in an earlier time. On this night, she decided to lift a little bit of the veil, for me.

There are things I should know, she started saying. Perhaps, not everything, for it was best that I did not know every detail. Until life was simpler, should we

ever get past those with flaming swords, she knew that my loyalty was foremost to Jeffrey. It was natural, she said, that I would try my best to help him escape; and that I would support him to the end. She said she understood that, and that she admired my commitment. Jeffrey was still supposedly somewhere in North America, on business, this time alone for he knew how much I hated those trips, leaving us with the run of the Great House. Leaving Margarita and me free to talk and joke and to be together. For daddy-o wasn't home and we had time to burn and even to sing a strange song.

The most refreshing time in the Caribbean, she had so elegantly rediscovered, was just after 6 o'clock, right after the sun had retired for the night, leaving a semi-darkness in its wake, when the already slow-paced island life came to a standstill. It was that pause, the suspension of time between the frenetic activity of the modern day and the more comforting traditional patterns entered into in the guise of the darkness. It was the time, when the blaring cacophony of noises, the unstirred mixture of cars and big diesel buses somewhere beyond the cane fields, of excitable voices and squabbling creatures, suddenly disappeared. It was magical. The din just stopped, as if some unseen hand had put down a frantic baton, instantly silencing the shouts of mothers, the voices of children playing outside or the crashing sound of an enamelled plate falling to the floor. Serendipitously, the discord ceases.

Damsel remembered much the same thing from childhood. Everything was put on hold for the siesta.

She remembered, too, the long afternoons that were the highlights of her childhood memories in Miami. When her father used to take the two of them — she and her older half-brother, Manuel — into any of the cabañas by the sea and they would watch the men crowd around their dad, drinking beer and listening to his stories of bravado and of, as she would later learn, womanizing. Those were the times, a different time, and that was the kind of man her father was, a creature of his times and history, a man, despite his faults, that she still thought of, and missed, every day.

What she remembered most was his generosity, how he always bought the beer and the whisky, or the tequila, the rum, and whatever people were drinking. Unfailingly he picked up the tab, which wasn't a bill at all but a note in a book or, as was mostly the case, the undisputed tally in the proprietor's head. "People say that's how I got my name in the first place," she told me, whispering ruefully. "*Margarita*," she explained, "just like the sting from very strong tequila, that's how my father used to tease me. You always got to be on the lookout for the deceptive sting, the unexpected bite in the tail. That's the real you, he would say. And laugh with the smoke from the cigarette wisping past his eyes. *Margarita*. That's what you must always call me, Edmund. Leave Damsel for Jeffrey."

And she recalled how she and Manuel spent those long afternoons and late evenings running on the beach, wetting their toes in the gentle surf, wading into the water up to their knees. They were strong swimmers, taught by the best, the women that swam as if they were fitted with gills. They came back to the restaurant to eat delicacies such as the barbecued fish fresh from the boats, the hot dogs and hamburgers right off the grill. "There was this one place called Le Café Carib Americano, where all the Cubans and Latin Americans hung out — where there was always such great food and sweet music. I can still recall the billboard on the outside. Live Latin Music, *música latina en vivo*, it was always advertising. Then, below, the name of some new group or performer who was coming through. Friday/*viernes*, you know there was always music and dancing, salsa, merengue, Hispanic, late into the night; Saturday and Sunday there was always a DJ playing all the latest hits, mixing the Latin and American hits, the music from everywhere, from Cuba, Haiti and Brazil, Chicago and Louisiana, Accra and the islands. Samba, high life, whatever. All of them melding into the Latin beat that we loved so much, the brassy Cuban influence, the drums, the merengue and bossanova. That is what I like to remember about those days. The little boys and girls, like me and Manuel, playing in the sand, dancing in the surf; the older ones, the lovers, holding hands and walking the boardwalk, slipping into the darkness, but staying within the range of the music. Even when it rained. It didn't matter. We still played on the beach, the rain soaking us, but then we were already wet, so what's a little rain; the lovers leaning on each other's shoulder, singing all those special songs, kissing. That's where I first got to hear the great Tito Fuentas and I just loved the music, wanted to be like the young women singing in the band. One of the things my mother and father shared was singing and love of the music. There was always music in our home. I think my mother sang even when she was angry with my father. I went into the nightclubs with my dad, as my mother always stayed at home. But at home, we were always singing and playing records, listening to the radio and watching the musical entertainment or variety shows in Spanish, with my mother singing and clapping her hands — so that I don't know if my love for music made me my father's daughter or my mother's child. Indeed, people would tell me that I had a good voice: crisp and clear, and capable of hitting a high note or two, just like you. My father brought home all the latest records, would say all the artists gave them to him as gifts, and I would sing to them.

"Sing for me, Margarita. Sing. Sing, my father would say. Some day, you too will be a great singer. Just like the pretty girls on the album covers. And I would sing for him, closing my eyes, hitting those high notes and rumbaing. And one day Señor Fuentas came up to me at the restaurant and, in front of everyone, said he understood from my father that I could really sing, and I almost died. It was so good. And then there was the food that they served, that my father was always buying. Fried calamari, Cuban sandwiches with fries, *tostones menduros*, whole red snappers, the *pargo entero* and those *gran picadas* that should normally feed three people, but which was ever hardly enough for me and Manuel."

Or, she told me, they would be adorned and adored by the women hovering around their dad. She and Manuel had no fear: they knew there was always protection from the men drinking the beer while their dad disappeared for long periods into a neighbouring cabaña with one of the giggling women. Sometimes they did not even miss him, didn't know he had slipped way until he emerged from the cabaña with some sweetmeat, an ice-cream cone or a glass of special fruit drink, just for them. Friends not only kept an eye on the children of the man buying the beer, but humoured and fed them, minded their coughs and scrapes, even putting them to sleep on mats in the corner of the huts while the great El Cerveza Libre amused himself elsewhere. They were all part of a living, caring community. Her father was King. She was the young princess, about to inherit his legacy, to become the queen.

Lime trees, just like that one outside this window. That is what Margarita remembered. There was a big lime tree growing outside the condo that her mother loved so much, the condo on the third floor, the home for which her father was working so hard. "The first memory I have of that condo is of my mother reaching out across the railing and picking a leaf from the tree. With me on her hip, perhaps the very first day we moved in. She crushed the leaf in the palms of her hands; my mother rubbing the citrus oil on her face and hands and on me, leaving the sweet lemony smell, a scent that lasts a lifetime, that comes out of something and somewhere special whenever I smell the *limecol* of the old woman and the old man. The same smell of lime and lemons. One whiff and it instantly takes me back to a life, to a time when the evenings were longer but came with such heat and a quietness, a sound of creatures of the night chirping to the accompaniment of whirling, breathless air conditioners, all of them sounding in ensemble like some mechanical orchestra: now one cutting in and going a bit faster than the rest, then that one slowing to a whirl, just as the others slowed, stopped, and then resumed in some frantic outpouring of sound. Occasionally, one sounding so different, like a voice itself. You would know what I am talking about, of what it reminds me, for you know about music. About tempo. About soloing and harmony too. You, too, can sing. This was the rhythm, the music of the night, that I loved, that made me think of my mother and whether, indeed, I am really my mother's daughter or my father's child. I guess, only time will tell if I have the heart to go through to the end, to be like my mother, or that I will have to live up to my promise to avenge my father."

Margarita, too, had her demons. This was particularly wrenching because she was a woman, and conflicted, too. "I think I understand what drove my mother, the same way that I understand Jeffrey," she said. "Contingencies and happenstance, perhaps. Things that change lives, events that have a life of their own. A world that was predictable and precise — with a rhythm of its own — changes, and you, the onlooker, can never catch up, and therefore, can never renounce the unchangeable that is still set in your head, that still drives and fuels your passions."

The Miami she kept thinking of was a place of gated communities, a place that she found only in spots in this new locale, with large white stucco buildings. Sometimes they were yellow, or pastel. Those were the colours that stuck in her mind. The walls around the buildings high. Sometimes fences, green and lush, as well manicured as the lawns behind them. Palm trees, with all sorts of nuts on the ground. There were running trails that sneaked along paths, or through parks, around baseball diamonds, along pathways beside canals, and ponds with mosquitoes and frogs. People walked their dogs on evenings, the time she and

Manuel, and later she alone, liked to run, a kind of ritual. Dogs that seemed never to bark, that appeared too
domesticated and accepting of the good life. Not like
the cranky dogs on the island, dogs that do bite, and
are seldom leashed. But fat dogs that don't have to
scavenge or actually work as watchers. Past the circles
and the squares for the condominiums with cars of
every make and size. By the ponds with reflections of
the houses and trees, including that old lime tree, in
the small man-made lake around which the condominiums were built. Past the ducks, some with red
faces, most black but occasionally a white one that
stands out, and the fat old man and his wife, who fed
the birds and themselves from the same bag. By the
foolish duck that would try to escape it all by just taking to the air, aware its kind can never get too high,
only to realize that in its way was a three-or-four-
storey condominium, with people on the balcony,
drinking and laughing, air conditioners singing. The
duck, honking, realizing that the building will not
move, the gamble has failed, and that it cannot fly any
higher. Still, it flies on, carried by momentum, perhaps,
maybe foolishly hearing a call beyond the building,
only to crash up against the wall, to fall down stunned.
Inescapable. Boundaries. For pinned ducks that think
they *really* can fly. The old man who tried so hard to
pat the drakes, the same ones he fed every day, but
they always elusively avoided his grasp. Or they
pecked his hand too hard. Still, they came back trust-
ingly for more. Still, they ate and still they refused him
his one wish, his one demand of them, to pat them on
the back. They could not be bought. They could only
be fed. For they knew too well that his hand might slip,
that instead of patting, it might ring. And then what

335

would become of them? Dinner, perhaps! Such is the nature of things. The rhythm of life. A speed that she captured on the first run. When she smelt the bougainvillea, red and yellow hibiscusa, guava and magnolias. The sweet murky smell of the tropics that you appreciate only on returning: a saltiness of the air mixed with the ecstatic fecundity of the rich black earth. So voluptuous, so orgiastic, so fertile. A smell that these days nobody else seems to be aware of, but a smell so seeped in the bones that it would be missed if these same people were ever to leave. It must have been the same type of smell that Old Man Spencer smelled every time he dug a new grave. The soil, the land, the black earth and the same smell. At one with but at the same time not the same as; that was what was mysterious and also so plain and simple about the old man. That was what she saw in his eyes. Those creepy eyes, with the white film circling the irises. Those knowing stares. Those eyes, where she knew that she could never enter, could never live, not like the other. She remembered the stops in the Win-Dixie supermarkets where people, like in the stores she visits with Ida, bought cassava, sweet potato, yams and even sugar cane—the food and delicacies the women fed Margarita and Manuel. Old Man Spencer never visited Miami, at least not the one she still knew, but she had no doubt that he would be at home, as different but yet part of the same for him, just as it now was for her.

But there are also memories of storms, starting in the distance, coming near. Hurricanes that were always so destructive of her peninsula but that some-how, according to the records in the rectory of my father's church, usually missed this island. She remem-bered the dark clouds; sometimes banks of them,

336

sometimes like soiled balls of cotton. But most times threatening. She saw them through the window.

"My mother was in the kitchen. As I said, we lived on the third floor. My mother was singing. The world was as it should be. Cerveza Libre would not take me to the beach that day because it was stormy. The waves too choppy. I had to be in a safe place, with my mother. In the distance, the streaks of lightning — fleeting narrow bolts of electricity cutting the sky. Within seconds, thunder. Hard and dark. Then I would look down on the pond and see millions of raindrops falling, each impact causing a ripple. Each drop having an effect of its own. And then there were so many drops. So many ripples; so many circles, but just one pond. Circles bouncing into one another. A deserted pond, even the ducks no longer taking to the water, no longer trying to scale tall buildings. The trees blowing in the wind, the sweet smell of rain mixing with dust — the promise of green grass and weeds, but also of flowers and fruits, and of immaculately manicured lawns. Of each drop knocking petals off the flowers, or of winds causing the trees to bend and to even break, of lightning splitting branches. Of so much revolt and deception. So much order. That is what I remember most. The smell of the weather, of the place and of the coffee my mother gave my father."

And Margarita remembered, too, her mother telling her that night not to go out into the rain.

෨෧

"I sang along with the radio as my dad and I travelled through Fort Lauderdale, Palm Beach, Crystal Springs, Sunset Boulevard, wherever. And he would always promise me that if I kept up practising, someday he

337

would arrange for one of the big record producers to hear me. However, it would only happen when I was ready, perhaps when I least expected. Only he would decide what was right for his little girl. I sang for my dad when he looked tired and the drive wasn't ended and I sang for him on the last night, in the hours before the hurricane hit. It was his birthday, his sixty-third, still a man in his prime with a young wife. I will always remember. How I spent the day combing the record shops to find the latest Tito Fuentas LP for him and then finding the bright red wrapping paper for this final gift. Late in the night, when everyone was drinking and eating the boiled fish, he stood on a chair, demanded quiet, and asked me to sing for him and for the partygoers. I demurred, as I always did, knowing he would tease me. And tease me he did. And more. Boy, did he surprise me! Yet again. And in front of this crowd. He announced that in the house was a special guest. A Mr. Matthews, of Polygram Records. He was a scout and he wanted to hear me sing that night. What a birthday surprise! And for me, still his little girl. He was keeping his promise to me. That was how my father was. So, I sang, belting out a boisterous rendition of 'Happy Birthday.' That, as it turned out, was the last time I sang like that. As I finished, I noticed my mother talking to some men, strange men. Then she went over and shook Mr. Matthews' hand. There are still pictures of my mother beaming with Mr. Matthews. And pictures of my mother kissing my father on the cheek."

Then, it was over; her tranquil world shattered. The morning after the hurricane, they found Margarita's father off the main freeway, the trademark of betrayal on his throat. Her father had bled to death in the gutter and Manuel's mother, her *stepmother*, was inexplicably back in the picture taking them to Colombia. Margarita would never see her own mother again. Someone had made a choice for her, had pushed her in a different direction. Someone else had loved her, had become a wet nurse to her, someone who loved her father enough to forgive him and to come back from the past, not as simply a spectre, but as the right person at the right moment to love his gift to the future, his daughter. Margarita had been an unintended result, a hybrid, a sweet flower for one, a mongrel for the other. Of good and evil, both. To strive to get even, while realizing the value of forgiveness, to be free of them all if only she could forget. Yes, to forget who she is and who she was, and in forgetting to be free to be just herself, fully formed and shaped at that specific moment, and to be happy. She would never be able to decide if the woman who brought her into the world would, as some people claimed, have so brutally betrayed the man who left her daughter a legacy of such rich memories. So betrayed him that this stepmother would have to step into the breach. This stepmother, the woman who gave her such a beloved half-brother in Manuel, and who, by teaching her loyalty and commitment, had placed a wedge in her heart causing her to always hate those who had betrayed her father. She would always wonder if there was something that made her different, something she, Margarita, had possibly received at birth from her mother, some trait that would make it easy for her to deceive and betray. Manuel, she was sure, felt the same way and, as I later found out, had also dedicated his life to seeking revenge. But, at least, he was different: he

339

was not conflicted in his heart. For those reasons, they had made it a point of not behaving too openly as brother and sister. All she knew was that her mother had disappeared, living perhaps in luxury, perhaps, according to rumours with this Mr. Matthews. Margarita and her brother were banished to Colombia, a place that she would never learn to love or to accept as home. Inside her, the music had died. She decided she would never sing again.

Barbados was different in other ways from the Miami in her memory. There was no double tempo here, no quiet beach fronts and restless city streets in descant with the serenity, but an overall quietness, a seeming lethargy that just as successfully covered the same type of activities her father did on the bustling Miami streets. It was so different here in Barbados; and yet so very much like Miami. She liked it here, the natural predictability. At 6 o'clock, the tempo dropped, the bustle subsided and for once there was calm, a natural rhythm took over. Everything was respectfully quiet, with the possible exception of the crickets in the grass outside, and occasionally in some corner of the house, and, in the distance, the gentle roaring of the waves as they beat against the shore. She would willingly settle down to a life on an island like this, any day, if only she had such a choice. Her heart would be at rest. She would love the freedom to walk the beach at the end of the day and listen to the rhythms beating in our hearts. She would be happy, even if she still competed with ghosts.

During the recollection of these memories, Margarita had mechanically and unceasingly continued to brush her hair. Now she stopped. She examined the brush and pulled a few strands of hair from the teeth, lost in thought. She was growing tired of a life of hypocrisy; of being so whorish with her emotions and body; of hoping to be one step ahead every time; of knowing one slip was fatal, terminal. How she wished that she could bury Cerveza Libre! A rattling at the window caused her to jump, but it was just the wind.

This was no good. Despite the calming effect of the evening, notwithstanding the daily regimen of strenuous physical exercises, Margarita was unusually jumpy, uneasy. A piece of paper left at the edge of the red mahogany bureau, beside her few cosmetics, contained a sharply painful and troubling message seemingly from Jeffrey. It said the Organization had called him earlier in the day to report its annoyance that there was still a leak out of Barbados. "I don't even know who left this message there," she said. "I got to think that only Jeffrey comes into this bedroom, but you can never be too sure of anything."

This news had shocked Jeffrey, sending him into an almost helpless depression. Now she would not only have to look over her shoulder, but would have to nurse him out of his deep despondency when he got home. Of late, he had become irritable, irrational, making the situation so much more dangerous for everyone. In such a state, he was absolutely unpredictable. She preferred it when he was stable and less troubled, indeed, when he was arrogant, when he was predictable and firm in his ways. The only consolation for them, Jeffrey had said, was that this latest revelation did not mean he had to make another embarrassing trip to Colombia to give an explanation and to further fray his nerves. "We gotta be very careful who we talk to,"

Jeffrey had told me over the phone. "I wouldn't trust anybody but you and Damsel. Besides her, don't trust a soul. Keep your eyes out for me. Me, you and Damsel will have a serious talk when I get back. I can't trust nobody else." What he said had prompted me to rush over to the Great House to confer with Margarita.

Jeffrey knew that his biggest task was deciding where to start. He was under enormous pressure to act, to do something. He had to clear his name with the Organization, to prove to Gomez that he was still trustworthy, knowing that his excuses were running thin and hollow, that he couldn't remain much longer in a position where he was constantly caught off guard by some new revelation. Even the prime minister was more distant since his return from Washington and Jeffrey felt he had to take this development into account. So much had changed in a year, in the last few weeks, really. "We have to stop the bleeding," he had said. Margarita agreed with him that he was right in detecting a change in Watkins. She agreed that he shouldn't even trust the prime minister and certainly not his own father.

☯

Margarita's thoughts turned to Aubrey Spencer and she shuddered as if someone had poured water straight from the freezer down her back. Because the old man was so doctrinaire, so level-headed, he was more dangerous than his son. Even though she was in the bedroom, in a house he now refused to enter, she could still feel those black smoky eyes, with the white of age around the rims of the irises, calculatedly piercing through her, like an X-ray seeking out her heart,

342

searching endlessly for the truth, making her feel he had discovered something but was not quite sure what. He was too suspicious, too questioning. Even Ida agreed with her.

"But he's an old man," she had said. "He's set in his ways. And what can you do with men anyway?" Margarita had laughed with her.

She had spent a long time on the phone with Jeffrey discussing who could be the source of the new leak, and she had tried, with what she felt was some success, to steer Jeffrey in various directions, to the point where she hung up the phone feeling mildly relieved, happy to take her evening jog.

Then, Margarita had returned home to find the printed note unexpectedly telling her that they—whoever that was, and she could never be sure since Juan Campersano had entered the picture—but that *they*, had identified the traitor and were planning to deal with the matter later that night. No more information, no hint of who they might have fingered. She turned over the paper and searched the back for additional clues, anything to put her mind at ease, to reassure herself, that in such a strange and duplicitous world, she was not involved or suspected.

There was nothing. Yet something quite unfathomable told her that she had to be careful. She couldn't decide if it was in his wording, for how could it be that Jeffrey might not trust her, that he might have been watching her, and had slipped into the house while she was jogging and wrote the note. If he was watching her, who is to say what he had actually seen. That was when she called me and I came over. Jeffrey had told me nothing to incriminate her, or me for that matter. I knew nothing about the note, and to tell the truth, even if the words could have come from him, I was pretty sure that was not how Jeffrey operated, leaving notes and clues: he was not the detective sort. Juan Campersano, I knew nothing about, but then I didn't see why he would be leaving a note either. In any case, we ruled him out, because she did not see why he would have access to her bedroom. So I was of little help, except to sit and listen, and to hug her.

On the bureau in front of her was a greasy greenish vial with no label, containing coconut oil—a lubricant that despite its heaviness and lingering smell always left her hair looking silvery and bright and made her skin shiny and soft. The oil was one of the things she had picked up on the island. Coconut oil, the same stuff she had heard that old man Aubrey Spencer used for 'nointing at night, to protect him from draughts and colds and to give him regularity.

The hardest thing was to get used to the rancid smell, for the oil was made from decaying coconuts — copra, the islanders called it. The same way the hardest thing in her life was to accept inevitably that Jeffrey had to find out the true source of the leak, and that he would then have to deal ruthlessly with such duplicity. How would she handle that? Now it appeared that someone wanted to turn the tables on her. By leaving the note, someone was forcing her to ask the same question but of a different person, for the question was reformulated in her head: *How will she deal with a truthful revelation?*

Ida had bought the first three gills of oil for her, perhaps a gift intended as a token of friendship, or as

344

a symbol of one woman's comradeship with another. It might also have been a peace offering, and encouragement. For almost everyone on the island was aware that Jeffrey's father didn't like her, didn't trust her, and had not yet recovered from the heavy loss of Brenda Watts. Margarita knew the old man would never accept her. For she was no Brenda Watts and she had no intention of giving him, couldn't even dream of giving anyone, a grandchild. Ida had cautioned her not to bother her sweet head over such matters. She felt drawn to the older woman, a kinship that made it easier for her to talk with her, perhaps even to talk too much. Ida could keep secrets. And she missed her this evening.

Normally on evenings like this, Margarita would welcome the chance to be alone and to think. To plan her agenda, and to jog over to the pay phones and make her calls. She had made it a point of transacting all business on pay phones, even when instructing the girls appearing at Club Alexia. This way, she was free to talk as she pleased, she had explained to Jeffrey, and to talk in Spanish without feeling she was being impolite. As well, some of the best ideas came to her when she was jogging and she just passed them on.

If she wanted time to herself, she had joked, she only had to suggest to Jeffrey they should go for a jog or initiate some form of exercise. It would be enough to cause him to beg off, to remember suddenly he had urgent work in his briefcase or some outstanding overseas calls to make. He always promised to some day pick up her challenge, to chase her around the island and to outrun her. She knew he never would.

Sitting in front of the mirror, Margarita found it difficult to think of anything much beyond what she would do if they really found out the truth. Dennis was supposed to have taken the suspicions with him. Obviously, he had not. His body was found floating in the water three days later. Aubrey Spencer declined to officiate at the burial. My father did. As she struggle with these thoughts, she stopped talking, and I noticed how she simply sat in front of the mirror, brush in hand, lost in a strange world. There were so many suspicions that we now had to deal with. I could only watch, as I too had nothing to say.

The ringing of the phone interrupted her thoughts. She must have forgotten I was still there. Later, she admitted she didn't realize she had been sitting so transfixed in front of the mirror. The possible consequences of some of her suspicions had left her almost breathless. Her lips were dry; the light in the room appeared brighter as the outside was growing darker. Snapping out of her reverie, she decided to answer the phone.

"Hi," Jeffrey said. "What were you doing? I almost hung up the damn phone before the answering machine came on." He was angry. Instinctively, she decided to be cautious, to let him talk, just in case something slipped.

"I was having.... a....a shower," she lied.

"Anyway, I'm calling to let you know that I'm back but I won't be home until late. Me and Juan Campersano going to do some business tonight. I think he's going to be meeting some other people on his own 'cause he tells me he has some business to attend. So, I'll be later than usual."

"Yeah, yeah," she said.

He swore again and hung up without saying goodbye. There was no talk this time of loving and missing her.

"Did he tell you he was coming back today?" she asked.

"No. He's back?"

"Yeah. And he didn't say anything to us. Perhaps you should leave now. Do you think there's anything else he's not telling us?" We both shrugged. Neither of us had an answer.

What can you say about a moment refracted? Oh, indeed, my brothers and sisters. When you look up and see what was there before but you had never noticed. A tilt of the head. The steady breathing and Jeffrey talking, talking about something that for the first time in a long while I felt mattered. All I had to do was reach out and grab the moment and draw it close to us, to rebind us as men and brothers. And then, just like that, something jumps up and wipes out all the potential.

"So, you're thinking of settling down and having children," he said, that soft smile creeping to the corner of his mouth and spreading over his face. "It's been a long time since we've had any children in our families, eh? Children to carry on and to make some people laugh and play with them." It was the first time in days that he appeared relaxed. "Children, eh! Finally doing our duties. Making our folks happy. You are really thinking about it, nuh?"

"Sure, some day. I'd like to have some children. All men do, don't they?"

"Well, I do," he said. "Problem is that I don't know when I'll start. Maybe I should be trying to get to the starting line ahead of you, so you don't leave me too far behind. Remember I am older than you."

"Not that much," I replied. "And anyway, age got nothing to do with it. It's when you're ready, I guess. When you can afford it."

"You're right. When you're ready. When we find a place to settle, when we don't feel the push and the pull. I don't know if I'll ever be fully ready, having all things nicely in place. And that frightens me, for maybe I was born to be torn. To be always searching. Trying to go forward by going back, or is it going backwards by going forward? I mean, I look at my father and think, would I want to be a father like my old man was to me, and I don't know. I don't really know. It frightens me. And then, I have to remember that Damsel is three years older than me, so…"

He glanced off into the distance. The limousine taking us from yet another airport to yet another meeting slowed to a crawl, then stopped.

Up ahead, some men were darting across the street, dressed in their business suits. They stood out, just before disappearing into the maws of those mammoth buildings that always fascinated me, the buildings with the bright sunlight reflecting off them like thousands of bright torchlights. The street looking at the same time clean and grungy, particularly the side of the streets with the bits of paper, the overflowing garbage bins and the filthy sleeping bags discarded until later that night. I think Jeffrey became more of a man in this environment, revelling in the sense of business and achievement, of people cutting deals, of life running ahead with nobody knowing exactly where it is destined,

348

except that some invisible hand seemed to be in control. Once we put something in train, we can never tell which track it will follow and the station at which it will arrive.

In this case, we were in the heart of downtown Boston, worlds away from the problems of leaks and confessions, among the glass and concrete towers, with the First Bank of Boston just down the street. Because of the traffic jam, were still prevented from arriving. In the distance, we could see the sign. First Bank of Boston and the big round logo. Like the city on the hill, my father would have said. So near, yet so far. The Organization had dispatched Jeffrey to Boston, for reasons he wouldn't let on, and this time he had decided to take me along.

"I love the big city," he offered, as if in confirmation of my thoughts. "I like the feel, the power in a place like this. The fast pace, the steady movement, people always on the go from one thing to another, never stuck on the in-between places. No, in a place like this you are always on the go. Remember how Mama used to talk about those trains moving on into the night, with only the sound, the sound as she used to say to tell you it's a-coming, the sound to tell you it has gone. Always big sounds, those two, so different from the passing one. You remember how she always used to say that was the worse part, when the train was passing, at that very moment, when it shook the house, turned over things, and when it was too loud to sleep. Yet she liked to know it was coming, and she liked to know it was gone. That the old house did meet a challenge and that it survived, but the challenge and the test were always murderous and had to be short, for it was too destructive. Even now, I still like to remember how she used to talk about those trains, but seldom about the passing moment. And I still think about her so much when I'm in places like this, that it is the next moment that really matters, the one that we hear coming. This is what we should be aiming for back home. This is what we should be thinking of turning our island into, a financial district like this. Billions of dollars transacted every day, but as a place where we hear the sound of the train that has passed, where the people are connected to the past as well. So that we can hear the sound of what is coming and what is to come. An international city. Wired to computers and phones. A global city. That what I am trying to sell to our prime minister. To see we are only part of the puzzle. Maybe, just a suburb in this part of the world. And that it can be so easy for us to miss the train."

Something caught my attention. It must have been the young man and woman, holding hands and running across the street in front of us, laughing, she with a cell phone in her free hand, he carrying a black briefcase. They looked so young; so full of hope. They turned left on the affluent side of the street and headed away from the First Boston Bank, towards the older part of the city, with the cobbled stones and stone buildings, as if dancing to a different strain of the same music, coming from where the streets were narrower, the buildings older and jumbled together with the characteristic universal grime of age. A big American flag, in the distance looking as if its tip touched the earth, hung from the building into which this couple disappeared. And then it occurred to me.

"I guess black people don't work or live around here," I said.

"What's that?"

"Just dawned on me that I haven't seen any black people in these parts. Like they don't belong on these streets. Only certain types of people have any business around here. Maybe that why Prime Minister Watkins..."

"That's silly," Jeffrey said. "That's silly. But now you mention it, yes, it is kind of strange to look at the same kind of faces out there. But back home it would be different. We would be in charge. Our people would be in charge. I guess it would just be a reversal for our financial district at home. A reversal. Like when you are conducting business in Lagos, if you just fly over from a place like Canada or parts of Europe, you remember, and you look up, forgetting for a moment, and have to take a second look, for the people you are dealing with, they look so much like the people you know at home. The same thing doing business in Rio de Janeiro and even parts of Colombia, in New York or London, or Paris. It's like when you go into certain places as if you're still at home. It's only when you try talking with them that you know the difference. When you try to test how much it is a part of you and you are a part of them by becoming like them, and then you notice a difference, maybe an accent, a strange emphasis, a different language, but eyes and faces as familiar, food and smells as knowing. And you don't know, yet you know damn well. That in that moment you are the same as them, but also different. It'll be different on our island, so nobody needs to fear. That is the special plan I am working on. I have my plans and some day I'll spell them out in full, but not yet. I don't have all the pieces down pat in my head. But as you know, it is something that was in my head even before I left Toronto. All the dancers at home will like it. Trust me, they will. The way I see it, when my plan blossoms forth, it would be just like a baby, just like what you are planning."

"How that?" I asked.

"You'll see. It will be modern, but based on the past. It will be a piece of the past elevating the future. It will be a grounding, yet a releasing to the future, it will be ... you know what I mean? You'll see. You'll see. That's freedom. At least, for me."

Somehow, he didn't sound so sure. Our car was still stuck and remained like that for another forty minutes. When we heard the screaming sirens of an approaching ambulance and police cruiser, we decided to get out and walk. Time was getting away and when you are on the Organization's business, you can never be late, especially if dealing with an unsuspecting bank. You can be if it's your own time. At least, I think, that was the lesson Jeffrey wanted to teach me that day. And for at least a day, Jeffrey had something else to occupy his mind beside how to stop his best plans from unravelling.

∞

We turned onto a little side street leading to a West Indian restaurant, with the various flags, the loud welcoming music. "This is the mistake our people up here keep making," Jeffrey said. "They keep behaving as if they still living at home. As if they never left. That was a problem I had with them when I lived here. And it is the same everywhere. Our people won't change. So how can we blame the youth at home?" Several people were standing in front of the restaurant, most of them conspicuous by their clothes, the running shoes, the

heavy gold chains around their necks and by the cigarettes they were passing around. This was not a street I
wanted to visit. I stayed away from them even at
home. On this day, however, and because I just had to
be there, I was trying to see it through the eyes of our
fathers, to find out if on these streets were the angels
with flaming swords, or if in coming to the place these
people had ceased wandering. From somewhere, we
heard calypso, reggae, some rap and even hip-hop.
Further on, some young men were hustling, selling
what looked like audio equipment and books and sandals and more flags.

"Nobody would think this is New York," Jeffrey
said as he parked the car besides a building with the
loud graffiti. "The New York our people leave home
for. Just listen to the music. Why can't we find a way to
control the business for our people? Why can't our
people just take control? Mama was so right when she
said what she did about the train: you got to hear it
coming. I don't want this train to enter the station we
building back home. Not this one."

We had not talked much. Not since leaving Boston,
not since the meeting, which did not go as well as
Jeffrey had expected. Back at the hotel, he had spent
several hours alone in his room on the phone. I had
already checked out and was waiting in the lobby of
the hotel when he showed up and said there was a
change of plans. Ominously, instead of heading home,
we were going to New York. There was something
about some new customers, he explained. Somebody
on some street, at some restaurant, had information
about the leaks. But I knew he was extremely angry.
Worse, someone must have told him he should hire a
car at the airport. Jeffrey hated driving in big cities,

353

and since I as much as ever never drove in that city, didn't know the place, I did not feel confident enough to volunteer. All we knew was that this diversion was keeping us heading back home.

"Hi yuh, sah," one of the men in front of the restaurant said as we got out of the car.

"Cool, man," Jeffrey replied.

"Yes, man. Cool."

We pushed through the door and past the string of beads hanging at the entrance and into the darkened room. There was a television off to the corner and a bar with neon lights off to the side. Beyond that was the eating area with small flickering lamps on each table. Even in the darkness, the mirror stood out, mirrors populated by ghosts, duppies and spooks. As Caribbean a restaurant as any I had seen in North America or Europe, it still managed to elude authenticity. A woman in tight leggings, her hair finely braided and hanging past her shoulders, came out of the back to meet us. I settled at the bar and Jeffrey disappeared with the woman.

"Can we join you, star?" a voice said from behind me. I looked up to see the men from the streets outside the restaurant. "I see that you like the videos showing there on the TV," the same voice said. "They good, eh."

I offered to buy a drink, and they all ordered beer, round after round. They laughed and joked, said business was really picking up on the street, and that they were happy to welcome us to the restaurant. All of them, the man volunteered, were musicians just like me, each of them hoping someday to land a big contract. Until then, they were in business to make ends meet, until they could save enough money to pay to make their own CD. They knew a friend who would help them to make it and to sell it on the streets, in the restaurants and the West Indian shops all over the United States of America. And in the Caribbean and certain parts of South America. Some of them even had contacts in Europe and Japan, a buddy scouting things in Japan. That was how they planned to get started. And they knew that given a chance they could make the world's best video, just like what we were watching on the TV above the bar. Perhaps my boss man meeting in the back with Miss Lady could also help in that way, by helping the band. As I listened I felt a hollowness deep inside, as if someone had exposed a picture and I was the last to discover that it was unflatteringly of me. Several young women dropped by. I couldn't help noticing their long, beautifully painted fingernails. None of them stayed for too long, for they were constantly coming and going, whispering among themselves and giggling. The man said these women were singers too, had great voices, like the angels themselves. "But what can you expect them fuh do," he said. "Them haffa live, too. And to eat and dress good. Just like at home. And this too is home, no matter what anybody say. 'Cause we people build this here country, with the sweat and blood of we ancestors. We belong. The money they make offa we don't know no boundary. And, somehow, we all haffa survive." We ordered food, heaping plates of rice and peas, boiled green banana and fried plantain, mannish water, jerk chicken, cou-cou, roasted breadfruit, curried goat, pellou-rice and fried rice and rotis of all sorts. And hearing the voices, the owner comes out from the back and puts one large jug on the counter, right in the middle, among the plates with all the goodness on them and glasses and the bottles with the hot pepper sauce, and he smiles broad, broad, broad and he says, "Any o' you here can guess what I got in there?" And we look at one another puzzled, and he smiling even broader, says, "Coconut water, man. Coconut fucking water." So we grab the plastic containers on the counter and pour the cloudy water into them and drink them down, emptying the plastic container in one go, so that the owner had to move it off the counter, for an empty container ain't worth anything, unless you feel like boasting and bragging about what ain't no more. So, he takes the container, screws back on the top, and throws the damn thing on the floor in the back, out by the kitchen, behind the long plastic curtains. And when that was done, somebody asked, "You got any mauby or ginger beer?" "Yes, man," he shouts. "*Whuh* kinda restaurant you think this is? *Whuh* kinda place you think I keeping here? How can this be a real Wesindian restaurant *widdout* mauby and ginger beer and even some sorrel to put in yuh arse? So you can drink it down sweet, sweet, sweet. *Bram* so. How yuh like *muh,* sonny?" he asked, looking at me, knowing that, of all present, I was the stranger. Yet I could be one of them. Someone must have ordered fish, for there was a big dish of fried snapper in onions and tomatoes. I was sampling the oxtail stew and pigeon peas rice, when Jeffrey came out. I hastily threw a handful of bills on the counter more than enough for a good tip, for I now understood that money alone had no value. As I walked away, I swear to you my brother, oh, yes, my sister, I can swear I heard someone say, "Thanks fuh the food, man, and the beer, man. Free beer. *Whuh lost:* free beer." And the snickers of someone holding my shirt-tail, making me afraid. I was instantly reminded of

Margarita and her stories about Cerveza Libre. And I thought too of Auntie Thelma and what she had told us, and about Jeffrey and the trains, I felt like telling him that now I understood why we always like the sound of the on-coming train, or of the train that has already gone, and how we never want to be in the moment, when the train is the sound, and it is singing for itself. For this could be the train that causes the little old shack to finally implode on itself, or to explode, the train that rattles and rolls, that clanks and bangs, that blows the little house in. This is the train that speaks for itself and in its own voice, not the utterances of all those that have gone before, not the prophecy of all those that may come, but the train that reveals itself, with faults and all, for all to see. This is why we cannot speak, for when we do, we can do it only for ourselves. Worse we might only be addressing ourselves, if nobody is listening, if nobody is waiting in the station, in the next port, or in the houses by the side of the track. Worse still is if we think that we are different from our own voices and its music, that we can shut them down and still be ourselves, a train unable to enter the future because it has been relegated to the past, stopped at the present.

Auntie Thelma must have thought of these matters, for she lived them. Why else would she just walk off a ship in a foreign harbour and simply announce herself, lend her voice to those of the men on a strange beach? Why else would she stop singing, for she must have asked herself what was the use of just listening to your voice, to be trapped in a moment that foretells nothing, that also wants to recall nothing? Why run along the side of the tracks at the same speed as the train, why wander in an eternity that is the present, if this is the train that shatters? She also knew that to move on would be to anticipate the possibility of a shattering sometime in the future, but that such a catastrophe, as a precaution, must also be a herald. The risk of being found out. That was why she sang that night. It was in celebration of the passing of the train and it was also in lamentation of the arrival of the next. A preacher and yet a singer, she had said. Only the moment can decide which is which, and only we can answer, who are we? Only then can we move on to defining what we are. Whatever the circumstance, only we, the separate individual, can make ourselves happy. Nobody can bring the future to us. And like all my expatriates coming in and out of that restaurant, people struggling so hard to make a life for themselves, pretending and hoping, but actually doing *something* for themselves, I, too, would have to stop waiting for anyone—be it a big brother, a mentor, or even a rival—to deliver for me. Only I could deliver. Auntie Thelma knew that much, and more. As we left the restaurant, I wanted to tell Jeffrey all these things. But I still wasn't sure how he would react. How even he would perceive me. So I chose for different reasons this time not to speak, not be my own self, but to be part of this familiarity that we shared. An intimacy and understanding that threatened to bury us in our many differences, while still holding us in our similarities.

Who are you, Edmund? I asked myself. What are you? There was no echo, no answer, not of the sound now past, and yet nothing to foreshadow a new arrival. What exactly were we? What had we become? Not the real men that our fathers were, and not the better men that we all knew to be up ahead, the same ones that people like Jeffrey and I felt that we were making. How

358

long had the train been gone and I had not noticed? And would there be another, could there ever be another, once we had decided to keep apace, to hold on rather than to let go? I did not know. For we had made choices: we told others that what they thought good was bad and what they thought bad was good. Did those others see me as just another homeboy, a homie, in the hood, like one of them poor boys at home, different only in how I chose to struggle for survival in a world not of my making? I cringed. In that moment, the last of the scales fell away and what I saw I didn't like. What was more, I understood that I could never change the way people saw me, but that I could change the way I wanted to be. I could not remain fixed and rooted if I hoped to have freedom. I should have left then.

After a week away on business, we couldn't wait to get back home. On the way to the airport, and on the plane back, we chose not to talk. Jeffrey took comfort in the futile plans still coming together in his head and in the bottle of rum. Me, I just rested in the haze of knowing the dangers of keeping my thoughts to myself, risks that I now realized were perhaps as great as to give them voice.

"Still, I gotta say that this meeting in New York was a bloody waste of time," he finally declared. "I don't know why they sent me there. I don't think we got anything out of it."

"Really?" I said. "I think I did."

"I will always remember. It was one of the
worst feelings for me," Jeffrey was saying, as
Margarita and I eased into the room through separate
entrances. Finally, on this day, two months after his
father's birthday, all his plans had come together. He
had assembled the media and government officials, the
financiers and planners, all of them, as he said, prominent in his or her own way.

On the platform with him was the prime minister,
looking happy, a broad smile on his face, with several
members of his cabinet beside him. Maybe Jeffrey had
really delivered for him. Vindication: proof that a quick
gamble does not always have to end in disaster. Proof
that timing is everything: get in and quickly get out,
before it's too late, so late that there is no chance for a
cleansing and a repair of the damage that is part of any
calculated risk. This was the project on which he had
set his heart all these months, the venture that would
not only set him free but was intended to be his legacy.

Off to one side was my father, in his clerical gown,
which told me that he must have declared the occasion
opened with a prayer and blessing. Across from Jeffrey
were the maps, architectural plans, scale models and
other drawings. Several of the young men and women
associated with the Brenda Watts Gymnasium were in
attendance, colourfully dressed in every variety of

national costume. They sat in the front rows, looking attentive and lapping up the dream and savouring their prospects. This was now their dream, their future, as this salesman working his magic one last time, was telling them. And for him, this was the legacy that he was choosing for himself, no not something to be conferred on him, but what he had decided would be his entitlement. He would decide even how others should choose to evaluate his work and what about him they would remember always.

Settling into my seat, I concentrated on what Jeffrey was presenting. What could be new, and how much could he have devised since I had arrived home, slammed the door behind me and refused to take calls. I knew I was different. Since the New York visit, I had given up the pretence of a singing career. Ironically, I thought as I listened to him, there are some things over which we have control, others over which we don't and, still, there are others over which we shouldn't have any control. I knew what ought to be in my control. But I was still adamant that I would not be a preacher. I didn't know what to do or how to stop what I saw coming. Jeffrey had finally gotten through to me—telling me that Campersano had indeed left the island several days after the Spencers' party.

"I couldn't be happier," he had said. "And to be truthful, I live for the day that they will never come back or bother to call. The end is coming: I can see it, man. That is why you gotta come for the announcement. Everybody will be there. You'll get to see what I've been talking about for so long." My answer was to show up. Maybe even then I was trying to protect what Jeffrey and I once had. Now, like everyone else, I was enduring the build-up, waiting for the big announcement.

361

As he spoke, my eyes started drifting around the room. It was impossible not to notice the mirrors. They were everywhere, on the walls, the ceiling, with the one behind the speaker's podium most conspicuous. They made the room look so big. As if thousands of people were crammed into a long, wide hall, with several podiums and speakers, all going at the same time. They made me think that somebody was always watching, and that whoever it was had seen when the two of us came in together and had sniggered when we sat apart. And that only made me angrier. I hate deception.

"I was new to sales in Toronto and I was making a call on a businessman," one of the Jeffrey Spencers in one of the many mirrors in the room was saying. I assumed it was the speaker whose back was reflected in the mirror to the front of the room, a reflection that made it appear as if I too was standing in front of this huge crowd and was on display. They were watching me, behind the back of that Jeffrey Spencer, just like Jeffrey and I used to pull faces behind the adults we didn't like, those who were too strict with us, even at *our* parents' parties, and when they laughed, was it at me or with him? Maybe, believing that he now planned to come clean, they were joining him in laughing at me, for the circumstances would have changed, the order inverted, Jeffrey would have the free and clear conscience, and I would not. That was why the laughter turned their faces into all those different masks in the mirrors. The same mirrors that placed a mask, most hot and contorted, on my face. "I arrived at the agreed time, on one of the snowiest and coldest days of my life, and knowing me, I was about ten minutes early, so the receptionist showed me into a waiting room. On the walls were all these posters of beaches and vacations

362

spots around the world, but mainly in the Caribbean: Jamaica, Tobago, Aruba, Barbados, Grenada, St. Kitts, St. Lucia. The long white beaches. The blue water. The cloudless skies. The sun. Ah, the sun. Your vacation home, the posters said. We are all one under the sun. But there was one poster in particular to which I was drawn. It kept pulling me back from across the room, each time intriguingly showing me something a bit different, and I was standing in front of it when the businessman came in. *I see you like that poster,* he said. *Isn't she beautiful?* I looked again at the woman, stretched out on a beach towel, resting on her elbows and smiling into the camera, her long black hair, the pearly white teeth — those images now forever imprinted in my mind — and I said, 'Yeah, she's beautiful. But who she is?'

"'*You* don't *know who she is?*' the man asked incredulously. I shook my head, for I really, really didn't know. '*She is only the most* beautiful *woman in the world.*" He laughed. '*That is Sophia Loren.*' He laughed again. Then I was laughing, most at myself. '*What kind of man are you: the world knows she's the most beautiful woman.*' He laughed yet again, but I could have died. The most beautiful woman in the whole world and I didn't know! I had felt like saying to him that I thought all along that that title belonged to my mother, the most beautiful woman in the world. She was responsible for who I am, for making me what I am. For me being in that country, for Christ sake. For me eventually making this journey back home, just like in all those stories. And in a way he was right: I didn't feel like a man back then, I didn't feel any pride. I felt ignorant, with no, should I say it, balls — lost. Until that conversation, I had never thought that someone like the woman in the picture was the most beautiful in world. I don't think my father would have either, and I like to think that he and I have similar tastes. At least, in some things, for you all know my dad. Yes, she was beautiful all right, but the most beautiful in the world! Well, I was looking for a sale. I was new to the business and I was willing to accept whatever he said. *Right, right, right,* I said. My father had taught me well: you fight to death only for what really matters: you don't disrupt what is working; anything for a happy life as long as you know who or what you are. That's what I thought my father would have said. *The most beautiful,* I repeated. I'm not sure he believed me. But because he had what I wanted, and this was something else that I had to learn, because he was in the stronger position, he knew I had to accept his story, or any other version he chose to offer. I had to accept his culture, his icons, his way of doing business. That is why I think what we are doing here today is so important. We are recreating history, telling our own story, in our own words and images. As people in a young nation, we must know who we are, we must know what are the images we want to project for ourselves and to others. We must know where our power lies. That is why I am putting all my efforts behind the creation of this historical site, this plantation that will be a place for us to put on plays and conferences and dances and to tell wonderful stories about ourselves, about from where we came, what we were, but just as important, where we are going. A people, if they are to become a strong people, must know these things, must do these things. We must remember if we are to go forward, as our fathers always tell us: forward ever, backward never. A wise political slogan. For we have a strong culture, a strong personality as a people. And I, personally, can think of no better place to house those dreams and admonitions."

Someone coughed and broke the flow. I noticed a young man at the end of the front row shuffling in his seat, moving as if to make himself more comfortable in the costume that was fitting too tightly, or, as it seemed to my guilty mind, simply to take a better look at me, *me* of all people. Perhaps, at the white mask. Then I realized I was mistaken. He was not looking in the mirror, he was positioning himself only to get a better look at Jeffrey. Still, it bothered me. And I wondered who else was watching, who else in this room, on this damn island, knew what was really happening. The tune and words from Old Man Spencer came to me and I started to wonder if it were really true, that you can hide and buy land by night, but that you have to work it in the glare of day. I understood this might have been true of the old days but not now, when people can hire others to do their bidding and you can never know for sure who is who, and that nowadays you can't even hide in the night any more. Even Old Man Spencer and my father had admitted that we no longer lived on one big plantation, with a foreign owner and a local supervisor or lackey. No, we owned the land. "We give you citizenship," Old Man Spencer always argued. "Do something with it. But by all means protect it. A gift. A very valuable gift that so many of us fought so hard for. Yes, we are poor, so what more can we give you, but a place to call your own. A home where, regardless of the size and stature, you are king in your own house. For this so many of us had fought and died. We gave you citizenship. A precious gift."

"I remember something else on that day that I discovered who the most beautiful woman in the world was." Jeffrey waited long enough for the laughter this time to end. He was indeed in his element, at the top of his form, a born again Jeffrey. He looked relaxed, even boyish and playful, knowing he had the listeners in the palm of his hand. Such potential, I thought. No wonder Watkins thought him to be the natural successor. If only he had not gone and so foolishly dabbled. And me, too. Following him. Even my father was nodding in agreement and laughing. There was a look of pride on his face, an acknowledgement that Jeffrey was a preacher just like him, promising a New World and an everlasting dream. The son he must have hoped I would become.

"When we left this man's office, we went to an upscale restaurant in walking distance from his office. It was in an old section of town, a prominent building, with a tile roof and granite walls outside, marble carvings at the door, you know, frescos painted on the walls and on the ceiling, a maitre d' in a swizzle-tail black suit welcoming us at the door, fancy leather chairs, somebody's ideas of the mixing of the Old World and the New World. The menu with all the fancy foods. But as we sat down at our reserved table, enjoying the good life, it was the music that grabbed me, that stuck in my mind. First there were the arias and operatic music, or so I thought it was, that filled the room, creating an atmosphere. And then, something strange happened. The tape must have come to an end for there was silence for a few minutes, and this was noticeable, so much so that I detected that the conversations were more whispered, and when the music returned, over the chatter, it was different. It was not the classical music that I expected in such a fancy restaurant with all those artistic trappings of high class and high culture, but, believe it or not, it was calypso, reggae, jazz, and blues. The unvarnished kind that we sing and dance to in the streets: that we misbehave to down there by the seas on nights, that we are always hearing on the radio, in the dance halls and at our festivals, when we are eating, fishing and drinking beer, and walking on the beach, sitting under the stars, with the breeze coming off the ocean, not in some fancy restaurant. Like somebody had come down here and secretly taped a session. At first, it startled me. It was so out of place. I felt funny as if both the music and I were in the wrong place, or that maybe someone was playing this type of music to appeal specifically to me, but why me? To make me comfortable, because they thought I would be uncomfortable? To make me feel uncomfortable because I would think that everybody else in the room was thinking this was my music and that the restaurant was playing it only for me? I remember glancing around the room, and you know what, nobody else seemed to notice the music. It was as if it was *their* music too."

Let me add a word here, to interrupt a bit. At that very moment, I noticed many other things, that while they were listening, everybody was watching everybody else. I started analyzing the look on my father's face, the look in the mirror behind Jeffrey, and I wondered what he was watching, whose reflection he was concentrated on. Was it on me, or any of the people in the audience? Or was he just taking it all in? Did he know that I was watching too, even watching him take in the entire fiasco? Perhaps he was just looking at Jeffrey, nothing more, nothing less. As I looked at the reflections, I realized that my father *was* seeing something and that he probably knew something. I would have given anything at that very moment to find out what. And then I saw her, Margarita, in reflection, watching God only knew what, but alert as ever and just as focused, or so it appeared to me. I wanted to get up and leave right away. Truthfully, I was afraid. It was so maddening. So many copies, and copies of even copies. Fakes, forgeries, frauds. Nothing real. Not even me. Not even in my attempted re-creation. For what was new? Indeed, what was I now that I had taken my walk, had locked myself away, what was I? The mirrors only confused more.

"But that wasn't the case," Jeffrey continued, his voice sounding so strong, calm and even, so unlike the disjointed body language of the mirrors, where everything looked out of sorts, hand and head movements delayed by just a fraction of a second, but noticeable. "It was authentic. I looked around the restaurant that was filling up with the luncheon crowd and I saw the people at other tables, and they must have been regulars from the way they joked with the staff, but they were tapping their spoons and forks to the music. Some were singing and humming. And I realized what had happened. We are a strong people. Our culture is strong. It is in places that we don't expect. We are beautiful too. We are beautiful, too. And that is what I remember most about those days up North, what stuck in my mind, what is driving me on to help us assert ourselves and why I want to help in getting this project under way."

I closed my eyes, if only to listen to the voice and not to be distracted. Jeffrey had talked a lot, and always in circles, about his greatest design for the island, about what now turns out to be this plantation. A safe and secure place, he called it, a refuge and a balm, an experiment and showcase of all our possibilities. It was to be the main attraction on the island, where school children and tourists alike would attend plays and learn about the history of the island and region, about themselves. He planned to re-create different eras on the plantation, covering all aspects of our history. People would walk from section to section, serenaded by strolling dub poets, street musicians and storytellers dressed in costumes of the periods. The actors would be cooking, working and playing like in the days of old, living their parts. They would tell stories, even making them up as they went along, as long as the heroes and heroines fitted into the overall story. Just like the festivals on weekends, except that in place of music would be the word. Eventually, there might even be a printing press to put in writing the best and most appealing stories, the history. There would be art studios for painters and sculptors to create and recreate. The children would come away with a strong idea of who they are, of the beautiful. The tourists would leave with a different view from what they came with. In their eyes, we would now be beautiful. This would be his lasting bequest, more than anything he could do as prime minister. On this would he build his plans for higher office. His father would know that the stories of a people could no longer be buried in a graveyard, for even this cemetery at one end of the historical plantation would play as prominent a role as the chattel houses from bygone days, as the new gymnasium that was a paean to the future. His father would work not only in a mausoleum, but in living history. The fulfilment of this dream would be a most important legacy. Even more so than the industrial plants manufacturing the semiconductors and computer equipment, than the international conference centres and the offshore businesses he was attracting to the island. Than Club Alexia, even when purified and authenticated, and the entertainment infrastructure around it. All these initiatives met the need of providing jobs, but did nothing to fill that hollowness that called for more. His dream was to do more, to have one project that would be the glue binding all the various parts together, creating one narrative, one play, one painting and song, one big laboratory. Once this plantation was re-created, he would be free to cut all ties, to stop siphoning off money from that other business, it would be time for him to move on to a higher calling in politics. Indeed, he would have no need for the business. Neither would anyone. Everybody would be further ahead than when he got in and if certain people eventually found out the truth, they would understand that it had been necessary for the business, but that he got out untainted, or relatively so, and managed to help so many. He would have gambled and won. Not only for himself, but for everyone else, too. Most importantly, he would have cashed out just in time, while holding on to his dignity and that of the people. His mother would be at peace and so would his father. He would have found a way to make their dreams one. For his mother, he would mix the foreign with the local. For his father, he would ground everything he knew and did in what he was, in the local. Everyone would be at peace.

It was when he talked about this project that I wondered who the real Jeffrey was. It became easier to be convinced that his other line of business was temporary, a means of providing the quick cash that would give the island and its economy a boost, that would tie it over before the other projects kicked in. It became a reason for believing that we, too, learning from him, could and would get out just in time. We were all timing our exit and there was no need for me to jump overboard too soon. None of us could admit that it was too late and that the dream had become a nightmare.

Now, here we were at the beginning of this great proj-ect and he was sharing his memories and hopes publicly. Stripping himself naked. It was another sign of how much he was reaching, how he must have felt the sand slipping through his fingers. Now, too late, I knew Jeffrey's fatal flaw and I understood the depth of his capacity for delusion. We can refashion dreams and his-tory, re-create and reshape them, but in the end we have to be realistic, and even rational. Some things are beyond our control and we cannot always rewrite the rules to suit ourselves. I knew that. That's what my father always told me. But here I was, and, truthfully, I didn't know what was real any more. Hearing of late all the tantalizing sto-ries from Margarita, I was being swept away, pulled on so many sides, and not sure any more of anything, not convinced that I was doing Jeffrey a wrong, or that indeed I was now doing what I knew to be best for him, for my best friend of all these years. But what did I know? Really. Who was this man, this friend who could spin such sweet dreams for these young people from across the land, to get them to dream of greatness, the same way he had lured me. Here he was on the podium talking, and as I looked up, I again saw Jeffrey in the many mir-rors, each of them a reflection of a reflection, perhaps each capturing a specific moment, a specific time, but all of them collectively fooling us, making us unsure. What was real? What was beautiful? Good—what was it?

I slipped through the door and remained outside until I heard the thunderous applause to end the speech. Then, there was Prime Minister Watkins's voice. Margarita stayed to the bitter end.

I was standing on the outside, watching the young men and women come out to smoke and visit the washrooms. It was an endless stream, many of them standing around in small groups dragging heavily on their spliffs and passing them around. All in the open. I had not expected so many people to answer the invitation to this launch at the national convention centre. Each time one of the doors opened, a rush of excited voices and the music came out with them. The sound of a live band, one of the many springing up across the island, all those aspiring musicians, who were dreaming of that big contract overseas just as I had. We were all going to be the next Harry Belafonte, Bob Marley, Sparrow. An icon to the world from the Caribbean.

I was thinking about these dreams and of my diminishing prospects since I had started to doubt Jeffrey, when the door opened yet again. I did not turn to see who was coming out, for I had grown tired answering questions and having to deal with all those who felt that I could whisper a special word in Jeffrey's ear to benefit them, a word they did not want even this closest friend to hear, just in case someone stole the idea and took a march on their own dream. Duplicity was dogging my arse and giving me horrors of all sorts.

"I think I have the ideal name for that place Jeffrey is putting together," he said from behind me. I turned to look at my father. "He should call it the Mami Wata, just out of the tradition, for this territory is going to be all things to all people, a bit of this and a bit of that, all within a boundary, a contrast to what we are doing in the rest of this country, a bit of history and a dream of the future. For who would be handing down traditions on that plantation? Who will be receiving them, as opposed to making them? It's no different from the

Mami Wata in our stories, the mermaid that is neither woman nor fish, but goodness to everyone. What then, are we accepting, Edmund: the woman, the fish, or the reality of what it is, even if it will never reproduce itself? If a woman, is it a goddess or a stranger up to no good? Tell me. You know what Jeffrey is thinking. Can we put the spirit back in the body that is dead? Are we just practising necrophilia? Or should we spend our time searching for a living body for a living spirit for a new beginning, untainted by the past, just as he says, making it up as we go along? Tell me, what do you young people think about these things?"

"I don't know, Father," I said. "I don't know if *we* have thought that far."

"But you will have to find an appropriate name for the place, so why not name it after a legend, after something that never was. Mami Wata is the proper name, I tell yuh. We can all hear her singing sweetly, but should we be heeding her call or regard it as a warning?" He paused for a long moment. "Yes, Mami Wata. That's the right name. Just say it a few times over and over, think of what you and Jeffrey are dreaming of, and if you do know your history and tradition, you'd know the name will grow on you. Just give it time. The past ain't worth nothing without a future; just like the future must build on the past. What do you think, Edmund?"

"I don't know," I answered. "Maybe. Yes, maybe."

"It's just that I find it so..." He paused and knitted his brows. "What word am I searching for? You know, so, is it, naïve? So idealistic? So fantastic? I don't know quite what."

My father turned to go but, in mid-step, he paused. "Today is the anniversary of your mother's death. Me

373

and Aubrey will be dropping around by the grave to pay our respects. I guess this is how we practise our own brand of necromancy. Since I guess we don't know with any certainty what history is any more. So I really want to hear what my old friend thinks about this idea the two of you have now cooked up. Because, as you see, we cannot and should not even try to decide how others, especially those that come after us, remember us. We cannot force people to remember us, even if we sacrificed ourselves for them. Not even a mother can do that to a son. So how can anyone do it for an entire people? As I see it, only the people can decide what to be written on a plaque, what they really feel, not you. But I don't know. I am old and old-fashioned and maybe times have changed so much that we can now bind even those that come after us."

I had forgotten. My father did not wait for my response, but continued walking away.

I wondered what time it was, not knowing what *ah* clock did strike. Only that I had accepted a new and very different calling. And if I were lucky, I'd be in and out much faster than Jeffrey. Then we could all deal with the repercussions.

ᏚᏚ

"So, you'll be coming over to the party, won't you?" Old Man Spencer asked in his softest voice. "Ida and I would really like to have you there for a moment so special for both of us." Sitting at the table, Jeffrey looked up, the obvious bewilderment deepening by the second on his face. This was the first of two major surprises that should have shown how vulnerable we all were, how exposed and defenceless we could be.

Both of them revealing themselves in the Great House, the one place that seemed now to offer no refuge, no forgiveness, no mercy, and no respite. From all signs, his father looked a changed man, from the moment he stepped through the door, completely made over, per- haps, the first real sign of the influence of Ida Weekes.

Aubrey Spencer had walked into the kitchen, a broad smile on his face, a few obvious knicks and scrapes on his chin and jaws, but with the usual evening stubble missing. The multi-coloured shirt still had the creases from the folding and the wrapping and his pants were freshly pressed, with sharp seams running down the front. His shoes had that glimmer and smoothness from being new. Even more alluring than the way he was dressed was the strong smell of cologne that preceded him into the kitchen, a fra- grance that lingered heavily and prominently, as Old Man Spencer leaned against the sink or paced the room. This was too startling a change for any of us to understand right away. Indeed, under more casual circumstances I would have excused Jeffrey for think- ing it was all a gimmick, something carnival-like, that even though he might be smiling he was not appreci- ating. But he was exhauted from another arduous two-week trip out of the island. For this trip had come just when he thought matters were settling down and his services were no longer needed as readily. Now, to return home, so tired that naturally he might not have the patience for such a ploy and, from of all peo- ple, his father. For the old man certainly looked strange; his announcement was so unexpected. Those of us who had remained behind during the trip had heard absolutely nothing about the engagement he had just announced.

Ida was smiling from ear to ear. She stood beside the Old Man, holding hands, affectionately leaning on his shoulder and smelling his neck, now that they had brought everything into the open.

"In life you have to be willing to recognize a few things," Old Man Spencer continued. "Ida has been keeping me company all these years, since your mother died, and it is time for the two of us to move on. Ida will be good for me. She might even be a good stepmother for you, Jeff, if you let her."

"Ida," Margarita spluttered, "you didn't even let on. You didn't even drop a hint about this. And I thought we were so close."

"I didn't want to be the one to break the news to you, Jeffrey," Ida said, speaking directly to him. "You know how I like to keep my distance when it comes to certain things. And I always wanted to keep my position helping you here separate from whatever I have going on with your father. You got to keep some things separate, and in any case I think you should hear anything you must hear from your papie first."

"Yes," Old Man Spencer said. "And Ida and me, we have to do things a bit different. We got to respect *we* age, because yuh never know one day to the next. In fact, we decide to make this thing official, to put our affairs in order, only last week. Then we say, we'd have a party to celebrate everything, a party once you're back. And it's true: We can't stay stuck in the past, just like you've been telling me all these years, son. Ida agrees with you. I should listen to some of the things you keep telling me, she keep drilling in my ears. So, I guess I got to start listening. It was just like how I finally decided that your mother had a point, that she came from up North, so she would know what

376

she was talking about when she keep demanding that you finish your school up there. We must all compromise at some time. And, yes, Ida is right, I had was to move with the times. She keep saying I should think of how you feeling: how you keep spending your money on me and I not acting as if I appreciate it; how you buying things for me and I just giving them to O'Brien. Well, I decided that you might have a point, too. I ain't too old to change. I mean, today is the first time for as long as I can remember that I didn't use my long razor for a shave. I said to myself, but why don't you try out them fancy razors that your son's been giving you. And Ida said to me, yeah, why not try them out. And what about all them clothes and things that you have in there, that you never wear, why not try on some o' them too. I hope I did a good job, although I got a couple of cuts here and there; I hope you like muh in these clothes, although these shoes feel a bit too tight and pinching muh toes a little bit."

"You did good," Ida said, taking a few steps back to take a fuller view of him. "Real good. Don't he?"

"And," he continued, "the pinching won't last forever."

"Where are you two going to live, if you *do* get married?" Jeffrey asked. "I have enough room here and, Ida, you know your way around, so...."

"Oh. No, no. We done decided where we living," Ida said. "I'm going to keep my own place for now but I'll be moving some of my things into your father's house over there by the graveyard. We'll move between the two houses. I hope you'll come and visit us, you know visit your father, more often. That is what I have been trying to do all this time. To get you two to...to...to... well, both of you are men and you know what I mean."

377

There wasn't anything more that Jeffrey could have said. The three of us sat at the table with the food in front of us — perhaps, the last meal Ida would cook for us in this capacity — and we no longer felt hungry, certainly, in these unexpected circumstances, not Margarita and me. Jeffrey watched as Ida and his old man walked out of the room, still holding hands, as if they were some teenage couple, his eyes steadfastly pinned on them, his face betraying his shock.

"Why am I always the last to know anything?" he asked, his voice, not in anger, but hollow and hurt, just above the sound of a whisper. "How come I ain't fast enough to pick up these things happening around me, in front of my own eyes?" He walked out of the kitchen, leaving the plate of food on the table.

In silence, Margarita and I watched him go, for we were too scared to even talk. A lonely travelling man, I thought, but not as lonely as I was.

ೢೢ

And then, that decisive moment when, I would argue, he gave me permission, if not his blessing, to step away and to leave him alone. At least that is what I want to think: that he absolved me; saw me in such a crisis of indecision; and set me free. Sacrificed. For he had to know what I was going through: all the thinking and rethinking. Just like him. All the supposes and what-abouts should something go wrong. And yet the impetus to do something, to keep at bay the sense of drowning, the feeling of going nowhere, or to a place not of my choosing. It was not the same song, any more. Not the desired tune. So changed and torn. Torn and fragmented. Fragmented and confused. No connections; just a void. Nothing: that's all that is left. Nothing in the beginning and still nothing at the ending. How we could call the beginning by any name we wish, and the ending too, but that they are simply nothing but the names we called. I had to escape from this bind. Or to at least try. Jeffrey would want this for me, I told myself. Yes, he would, my brothers. Yes, indeed, my sisters.

I didn't want, my brothers and sisters, to hurt anyone I loved. But I did not want to cripple myself, either. Nor did I want, my friends, to blindside justice. But, I finally realized that I had to leave. Be gone! Oh, yes, I had to be a-going. *Travelling man have no home, have no plan.* No time for yet another rethinking. But just to get up and go. Hitch yuh pony and ride, siree. 'Cause *Que sera, sera.* And accepting, too. *If not even a pony, yuh just gotta let me hear the bottom o' yuh two long foots, they got fuh slam tar.* For I heard that train a-coming and I had to get on board. *Swing low, sweet chariot, stop and let me ride.* Or by boat. By plane, too. But just a-movin' on, moving right on on. No looking back, but just dusting the dust off my feet, just moving, no glancing back. *Lot's wife turn a pillar of salt, a pillar of salt, a pillar of salt,* no looking back, just me and my travels. *For there's a high road to heaven, none can walk that way, but the pure in heart, a highway to heaven,* for in the end, it's all gone, gone, gone. Not even the banging-banging-banging, not even the dancing and the singing, not even the one foot 'pon shoulder de other 'round the waist. All gone, gone, gone. All the rituals and traditions. For I must be moving on. Perhaps the same way that Aunt Thelma felt when she came off that creaking and old cruise ship before the arrival of either of us, in a different time and place. When she just knew she just had to disembark, in some port, in any town, just get out, anywhere must be

379

home, but that she had to step off and start all over. That it just so happened to be a specific port on a specific island and she saw a group of men singing and cooking, and they made her laugh and helped her to forget some things. Just at random. A leaf tossed on the water. Only the waves to decide. Just drifting here and there before it comes ashore and dies, or dies even yet on the water. *Oh, yes, we are just a leaf, just leaves.* The approaching moment accepting her and caressing the softness of her skin, shining the lustre of the cornrow plaits, tasting the fecundity of her full lips and easing the yearning in her heart. When fate smiled and destiny made peace with her: who knows the truth any more? Who can stop the drift? I can convince myself that even if he didn't fully know, that he would have understood. But there is that uncertainty: that, even now, in thinking of that moment, I may simply want to milk it for whatever solace it offers, so as to assuage myself. For we must cling to hope, and if not to belief in forgiveness, to the idea of tacit support and even sacrifice. Of moral vindication. So, my friends, let me tell you what happened and things that might have.

☁☁

It was our last trip together. We were standing by the windows in that great white hotel on the Pacific coast, with the millions of lights twinkling down below, and off in the distance. It was on either the twentieth or twenty-first floor, for we each had one of these mammoth suites with the glass windows disguised as port holes, so that when we stood at the edge, we could see the tops of what looked like sails, but which we knew, even if made of the right materials, could only be real in somebody's imagination. Maybe they started as sails in an architect's mind and like some evil genius he successfully produced a copy in our eyes, each time we saw the undulation and the tips, the five masts, on this concrete ship at the waterfront on an inlet. But a copy only. Everything just a copy. Not real sails. No ship either. Perhaps not even what he really intended. And despite what the eyes tell, we just ain't moving nowhere.

Earlier in the day, we had seen other flags down below us on the decks of the three warships pulling out to sea — the flags of the United States, Japan and Korea. They were announcing their departure with loud brass bands belting out "Auld Lang Syne," and all the young men and women in black and white sailor suits on the sides of the ships facing us, waving their hats and their hands. Waving at God only knows who. It was a departure that I could not help thinking foreshadowed an arrival, too, if I did not digress. Another coming. With fire and brimstone. Blood and fire. *Blood fire, Rasta.* And the music playing, for the time for words and reasoning had long passed. The silence broken, but also restored. The moment had already arrived, and possibly gone.

"I think we are even mistaken when we limit ourselves only to the part of the world to which we are accustomed," Jeffrey said. I was standing watching the lights and boats. I was wondering how many ways there were that I could be a foot soldier to any power and still live with myself. Jeffrey had let himself into my suite with his key to the room, the same way that I always kept one of his keys. His suite; my suite. Yet I had not heard the heavy lock turn, and the soft carpeting must have muffled his steps, so that I knew he was beside me only when I heard his voice. And his breathing.

381

"She would advise us that all of this belongs to us too. All of this…" He spread his hand out. His hand, palm upturned, reached out as if it intended to be at one with the darkness and the lights and the bridges and the boats and planes. With all those things that come out of the darkness and reveal themselves and slip back in again. All now without form and a being. Left with only a belief, with faith and, finally, hope for what we could not see or touch, could not smell or taste, just believe and feel. Even though we could not see it, there was land with people out there, an entire coast that ran all the way down the shores of the Pacific Ocean, that we could follow and still find our way back home by cutting through the Panama Canal, that place and that coast with all the memories. Of all our sweat and blood. Always something out there in the darkness: something that revealed itself in such things as smoke, the lights, and clouds. "She would expect us to call this home."

"I know," I whispered.

"And she would be right." He placed his hands in his pants pockets. Then, just as quickly, he took them out and folded his arms across his chest. "She *is* right."

"I agree," I said.

"And we should never forget that point. This, too, is ours. Remember that great saying: all this will I give unto you…." But for whatever reason he did not complete the statement, or at least not the one that I instantly thought of, and of my father in his Lenten addresses.

He turned and walked out of the room. I stood there for I don't know how long, thinking about so many things. How he intended me to finish the saying. About Margarita. And about the choice I had already made. Listening to her voice in my head: *This land is your land.* A voice so ominously sweet. *This land is my land.* About the inevitability of the warships and the helicopters. About: *This land was made for you and me.* About lonely travelling man. And that I must step off this boat going nowhere.

I turned away as the first drops of rain splattered against the window, as if someone was trying to sprinkle me. And, I wondered, why the futility of the rain and water, the promise of new birth and greenery and slaked thirst, and why not just the acknowledgement of inevitability of fire the next time?

Late into the night, even as Jeffrey and I were flying back home, Bernie Lewis could take it no more. With blood streaming out of his mouth, his face puffed up and his eyes nearly closed, he finally changed strategy. No longer would he alternate between stalling and weeping, between begging and mocking or simply challenging them to kill him quickly. And he had stopped swearing, or shouting and screaming at the top of his lungs, partly because he had almost lost his voice, because he was tired and unable to take any more beating; because he couldn't think straight any more, not after they had injected him with what-ever-it-was for the third time; because he no longer felt his message had gotten through. It was a long time, indeed more than adequate if they really wanted to rescue him, if they were not just using him and had finally decided that he, too, was now expendable.

On the fifth night of his torture, he offered to cooperate, to surprise them with priceless information. And he wouldn't ask for much in return, except that he be left alone for as long as they planned to keep him and that they should bring him something to eat, if he could get it past his raw throat, and to drink, too, for he felt parched. So he could get some sleep, try to calm his head that was alternating between swooning and exploding.

"All right," he said, gasping for breath. "I'll tell you the truth. The whole truth, so help me God." He tried raising a hand in the air as if taking an oath in court, all the while his body sagging uncontrollably, the mixture of blood and spittle running out of his mouth, the dribble stretching down to his bare chest.

"Wait, wait," he pleaded. The new attitude caught his chief interrogator by surprise, with his hand drawn back, and the folded right fist ready to pound into Bernie's chest. He had struck him one such blow seconds before, forcing the weakened man to stumble backwards before falling to his knees. Struggling to his feet, Bernie leaned against the wall, in the area where he had heard the rats before.

"Did it ever occur to you," he continued, panting for breath and recoiling further away, "you ever thought that maybe... that maybe the person you least expect to... that she might in fact be the main informant for the United States? Huh. You ever thought of that?" He was almost jeering.

"What you're talking about?" Juan Campersano lurched at him and pounded his hand into Bernie's face. Bernie wheeled under the impact. He spun around and was bounced off the wall by Campersano.

"Don't you want to hear the truth?" he continued. He was slumped against the wall.

"You're still lying," Campersano screamed, his voice echoing, as high as a contralto's, his heart from

384

what we can now tell a bass drum in his chest. "Manuel would have your balls for such lies."

"Remember the raid on Club Alexia?" the battered man continued. "She was part of it. She always was. That was why I was able to get into the very first party. She organized everything."

Noticeably, Campersano was no longer following. "Didn't it look strange...strange...to you that...that.... all of a sudden... all of a sudden the American ambassador was called home...on the night of this party...no explanation given, his term of duty not yet expired. He's gone only minutes before he's to attend the party...where he'd meet Damsel for the first time. Where he might recognize her as the little girl he had encountered with a man called Cerveza Libre and that he might expose her... It ever occurred to you she might have made a couple of phone calls to get him out of the way; to get a military plane to come and pick him up so easy? It ever occurred to you as a little strange we haven't heard anything more about Ambassador Finkle since then?"

Bernie was talking quickly, forcing out the words in sudden bursts. But he realized they were listening. This gave him greater incentive to keep talking. Maybe the more he talked and they listened, the less they might want to beat him. They might even accept the trade and set him free. With his life, a few missing teeth, and a broken nose.

"You lying bastard," Campersano said. But he missed, as Bernie sidestepped and fell heavily against the wall.

"Well, let me tell you who this Damsel is, who this Margarita is," he continued. "She's been an informant for the past five years, that's how long. Five fucking

385

years." Perhaps disoriented, he held up four fingers. "She and her brother Manuel. Just think back to all the problems the Organization was having in Colombia. How some of the best plans ran into trouble, how the U.S. Army was able to be in the right place at the right time; how they were able to snatch Manuel and whisk him out of the country so easy. Think of that. And when you do, just think whether there is any coincidence the U.S. Army ain't scoring no big successes in Colombia any more, not since Manuel skipped to the United States, but all the attention is on this island. Think of that. Manuel got frightened and asked to be lifted. He felt they were going to discover him and he made it look as if Jose was responsible."

"How are we to know you ain't just trying to implicate Margarita?" Campersano asked from the far corner of the cell. "Maybe you're just trying to stir up trouble. How do we know you're telling us the truth?"

"You got to believe me," Bernie said. He was beginning to walk on his knees towards Campersano, as if this was his last hope. "You gotta believe me. I have no reason for lying. In fact," he said anxiously as if struck by a new thought, "in fact, why don't you go and question her? Ask her about some of the things I've told you. About the ambassador, about things in Colombia, about the telephone calls she makes from the pay phones every evening. I can give you telephone numbers to call, to call collect to the U.S. and code words, so you can make the calls yourself. Go and ask her. Confront her. Don't take my word for it.

"I mean," the American continued, "there's nothing to lose by asking her. Look," he said as if daring them once again, "look, you can leave me here in this cell. Yes, that's a deal. Leave me here in the cell, so that if

I'm lying I can't get away, then go and question Margarita or Damsel or whatever you call her. Ask her about these telephone numbers," he rattled off several overseas numbers, "or ask her about the people in the Caribbean Command in the Navy, in Miami, the same people she and I report to, that sent me in here to support her once the decision was made she should come to Barbados. Ask her about these things and then come back for me. If I'm lying you can then do...."

"We won't be asking anybody anything," Campersano said with finality. "That is not proof."

He walked out of the cell, followed by his two companions, into the bright light, leaving the door opened and the light falling on the prostrated naked body.

"Get out!" The terse order came late in the night several days later, my dear friends, just as Margarita was nestling into the relief of a deep sleep, the ultimate escape, I suppose, from her growing angst and restlessness. Only then could she manage to calm her nerves by convincing herself that even though the noose might appear to be drawing close, she wasn't in danger yet. Funny how we all can have the same thoughts. She, too, thought she could still escape in the nick of time. Until the phone call, nothing earlier in the night had indicated she needed to worry. Jeffrey had put in a couple of hours at the engagement party at his father's house in the graveyard. He had appeared distant, not talking effusively as usual with the prime minister or Ashton, not bragging as usual about his achievements and the future of the plantation, but seemingly deep in thoughts, especially when my father offered a prayer and a blessing for his dearest friend and his new helpmate.

Jeffrey's toast to his father and his bride sounded as if it was coming from a man who expected someone to tap him on the shoulder any minute and to confess the engagement and pending marriage, even this party for which his father had surprisingly hit him up for some money, was some elaborate hoax. And when he thought nobody noticed, when his father and Ida were exchanging their rings and kisses to the applause of everyone present, Jeffrey slipped out the back and disappeared into the night. In this sense, he was really his father's son, except I would concede that it is easier to sneak out of a mammoth place like the Great House than from an overcrowded little hut. But he pulled it off. When I drove Margarita home and waited for her to inspect the rooms and flash the lights in the kitchen, to our surprise he was not there. Even then, I thought he was still off somewhere, pouting, not sure who he should blame more, Ida or his father, for keeping him in the dark, and wondering why he could not bring himself to feel really happy, excited even, for them. Well, what little did we know? Indeed, sleep does not cure everything. For when we do lie down it is not always to rest and dream, but simply to gather strength for the very next moment.

Margarita reached into the darkness to hang up the phone on the floor by the bed. For some time she had been preparing herself for exposure. Now it had come, like the loud ringing of an alarm clock, and she was instantly awake, sleep vanishing with the realization they were finally coming to get her. She was in deep trouble and while she said her mind flashed on me, wondering if to call to alert me and to let me know where I might find her, she knew that her first job was to protect herself. That was her sole responsibility. Nobody else mattered, they had told her. Trust nobody. Worry about no one else. Only yourself.

Margarita didn't hesitate. Mechanically, she pushed herself to do the things she had rehearsed. Thousands of times she had told herself a moment like this was inescapable, but even now, she wasn't as ready as she had hoped. She had to suppress all emotions, all inclination to panic, instead of sticking to the programmed script. Also she knew Juan Campersano was out of the country, which was good but also bad. Good, because she would not want to deal with him; bad because she would not now know the stalker if it were not Campersano. Nothing is ever the way it's supposed to be.

She knew what she had to do. While out jogging every day she had gone through the escape procedures, the routes she would follow. Now the theory had to become practice, and she wondered how much time she had to vanish, and what had happened finally to blow her cover. And for the first time, Margarita started to doubt herself, in the heat of it all, when she should have been single-minded and focused. Maybe, she thought, she wasn't as tough as she had believed. Perhaps she just wasn't ready. Too much unfinished business. Too many unresolved emotions. The timing could not be worse.

This crisis was happening when she was least prepared. Already in her thirties, and sensing life passing her by, Margarita felt in her guts the almost uncontrollable urge to slip quietly out of the limelight, change her identity as was promised her and with her pension to set up a home on some small, quiet island where she could open a store selling handicrafts to tourists and enjoy the luxury of sleeping late. Where she wouldn't have to run every day, where she might not care if she put on a few extra pounds, as long as she could relax. On an island where life was still respected, still traditional, the kind of environment the young people of the region were foolishly rebelling against, like some woman trading a diamond for glass simply because it might appear bigger and sparkle more. There she could live a traditional life, maybe even raising kids and minding a home, instead of leading a double life. Indeed, she would always be her father's daughter. A woman so ambitious reduced to this thinking. Such thoughts that she had to suppress. They would only get in the way. They would lead her nowhere.

For the moment, she had to concern herself with one simple but crucial task: to get the hell out of this lifeless house and to be long gone by the time the Posse arrived to get her. Later, when she was safe, things would fall into place, she could resume this debate with herself, and she could be remorseful and full of pity. That was when she would ask for her release. Manuel had alerted her that the urge to start a new life would come suddenly, almost overnight, creeping up and without warning. But back then, she could not see it happening to her. She had been so angry and committed. She knew she would never forget the hurt. She had promised him she would watch for the telltale signs of this weakness. Now, she wished she had listened more carefully, had made better plans, wished she never got into this, or she had trusted her better judgement and got out after the attack on Club Alexia. Margarita wished that she had learned to forget long ago.

But some things she just possibly couldn't forget. Not then. While she was reflecting on her prospects, another side of her brain was forcing her to do the things necessary to survive. As soon as she had replaced the receiver, she had jumped to her feet and begun rummaging through the travelling bag at the corner of the bedroom for the stash of bills she had kept there from the day she left Colombia. Looking around the room, Margarita tried to decide what clothes, if any, she should take; what kind of shoes would be needed for running on unpaved and rocky back roads.

According to the plan, she would have to make her way to the safety of the American Embassy in the city, just ten miles away. It was a simple arrangement, with its success depending on how much time she would have to escape; on whether she would get sufficient advance warning to grab any documents or contacts books kept in the house and still be able to jump into a car, go for a jog, or jump on a bus to leave the house as if were part of a normal day.

Instinctively, Margarita had reached for the sweaty red tracksuit still in a bundle on the floor and for the red running shoes she always kept by the bedroom door. She had always planned that she would run downstairs and grab as many documents as she could and to stuff them into the travelling bag. But the reality was there wasn't enough time. Unwavering, she must be. And quick. She could hear the roar of the engines turning off the main road and, at top speed, gunning down the driveway to the big house. She ran to the front of the house and, in the darkness, peered through the curtains at the window. It wasn't the usual procession of cars. Too many of them, and from the way they were driving the occupants were obviously in a big hurry. No time to grab anything. She had to get out of the house.

As the first cars pulled up in front of the darkened house and the figures were dashing up the walkway to the veranda, Margarita was jumping through the kitchen window at the back, seeking refuge in the darkness of the tall ackee tree near the head row of the cane field. Several times, she had seen Aubrey Spencer slip into this darkness at the back of the house when he wanted to leave without being noticed. And almost every time, he pulled it off.

As soon as she hit the ground, the house was flooded with light. Members of the Posse were systematically going through the house, through the bedrooms and the basement. She could hear them banging the doors loudly, kicking down those that were locked; so contemptuous was their treatment of Jeffrey's castle she knew he had been discarded by the Organization. How would Ida react if anything happened to him and would she pin it on the foreigner, as her husband undoubtedly would? No time to wait, or to think, obviously, so she dived headlong into the canes. She was now on her own and she had to get to the embassy.

Not finding her, the search party turned on the outside lights, instantly inundating the grounds with bright white beams from the lights mounted to the side of the house. As she crouched among the canes, Margarita saw Campersano with a high-powered automatic pistol in his hand, walking through the kitchen, then descending the back door steps and heading towards the cane field. Jeffrey was nowhere in sight. Campersano was nearing the point where the light and the darkness merged, nearer to the field with the tall canes rustling softly in the warm night breeze. She stood still, as still as she could, trying not even to breathe, knowing one move could draw his attention and maybe a shot in the darkness. Shifting her weight would cause the canes to rattle or the dry trash at her feet to crunch and betray her. Stopping at the edge of the field, he kicked the grass as if looking for tracks and raised the gun over his head. She froze. Three more steps into the cane field and they would meet.

So she waited, stiffening her body. Campersano looked around, glanced up at the ackee tree branches and kicked an empty can near the tree roots into the canes. Then, he walked back to the house, looking back suspiciously over his shoulder. The back door remained opened long after he had gone through it, even as the search was concentrated elsewhere.

There was now no choice but for Margarita to plunge further into the darkness of the cane field. It would be too dangerous to attempt an escape along the roads. She knew that. And that everyone would be on the lookout for her; and those who weren't would probably think it strange to see a woman in a red track-suit running alone so late in the night. Creating that sort of attention would be just as good as leaving directions for the Posse to follow. She had no choice but to take to the cane field, and to run the ten miles to the safety of the American embassy.

Margarita could hear dogs barking loudly and sirens wailing in the distance. In the air was this sweet syrupy smell, as if someone was making candy, the kind of scent that wafted across the island at the same time every night, when the factories boiled the juice squeezed from the sugar canes delivered that day.

Her first inclination was to continue running, but she had to stop to catch her breath and rest her aching body, and to think. Exhaustion made her knees tremble, but even so her mind was racing, trying to squeeze her circumstances into some discernible pattern. Margarita was in a predicament, her training was supposed to have prepared her for such a situation, so that by second nature, her mind would take over and lead her to safety. They had warned her that this would be the longest ten miles. But they could not possibly have been thinking of this. She was also scared, beginning to think that maybe she didn't know this place as well as she thought. Or, perhaps, she had not listened carefully enough. So instead of acting like a programmed zombie, being led by her instincts, she had to stop and think. She always held back something, afraid to lose control. The encircling sirens were probably the police and the Defence Force speeding along the highways and side roads. They too, she recalled, were in cahoots, deeper than even Jeffrey knew or suspected. She could trust nobody. The barking dogs indicated the members of the Posse, who even at this late hour would be meticulously searching every home in the neighbourhood. Margarita would have preferred to continue running, fighting off the paralyzing exhaustion, if she knew where she was going; if she knew for sure she was not nearing the other end of the cane field, and certain exposure in the open. Nobody had to tell her of the risk of being spotted on the unpaved roads between the fields. In no time, she would be snapped up, and Margarita couldn't bring herself to imagine what would happen next.

The experience so far was nothing like running a daily marathon, for which she had so carefully prepared. Her face and wrists were burning from the hundreds of tiny cuts from the razor-sharp cane blades, and her legs and back were aching from running in the half-crouched position to stop the blades from savaging her face. She hadn't foreseen the difficulty of running through a cane field. If she stood up to her full height, she got the full impact of the green leaves slicing her face. Each of the thousands of leaves was capable of slashing her face, and even the smallest and unavoidable knicks were like the painful burns from running a finger repeatedly over the sharp edge of a sheet of paper. The cuts burned and stung and itched when sweat ran into them. Even where there were no cuts, Margarita still itched uncontrollably, causing her to dig at her neck and other exposed areas with her fingernails. Something in the green cane leaves caused her face to itch badly when it mixed with her perspiration. Running in a crouched position was the only way to avoid the worst, but her back and legs were paying the price.

She was trying to find a free space between the rows of canes, but this too created its problems. The dried leaves wrapped around her legs and tied them as if the trash had been plaited into strong rope. Several times, she lost her footing and fell into a bunch of canes. And there were other, unexpected surprises, signs of the ingenuity of the people, of how this scourge had so deeply infiltrated every aspect of life. When she least expected it, she would find herself in the midst of a marijuana plot where some enterprising youths had taken to cultivating the drug on someone else's property. It seemed that almost all the free land between the rows was cultivated this way. The illegal crop must have been worth several millions of dollars more than what could be had from the sugar cane.

Margarita felt as if she had sprained her ankle running over the uneven clumps of earth where the marijuana was growing. My brothers and sisters, I know what she was going through. I have had to walk through cane fields, perhaps you have too, and we all know what a challenge just walking is. All that trash to tie up your feet, the trash that could make you slip and fall, that trash over all those pot holes that can give you an unexpected jolt. How then can you run? Listen.

Why were the escape plans so carefully crafted and practised not working, leaving her trapped in the unknown and darkness, feeling dizziness and stitches, light-headed from fatigue? Nothing could have prepared her for this ordeal. She was exposed, alone, unable to call on instinctual things to save her—no myths, stories, traditions or plans buried deep in her memory or psyche, no collective amnesia that would spring to the fore to rescue her, to guide her to safety. The magic instilled in her could not work, it was not potent enough; it was still too foreign and not hybridized enough. The crunching sound of trash under her feet was not music, not in the sense of Old Man Spencer venerating the welcoming silence of the graveyard, the strumming of his guitar, or the ebbing of the waves on the shore. The calm of a bright moonlit night, with jazz or blues or calypso or reggae and salsa on the air, coming from just around the corner, any corner. Of a motherly Ida celebrating the music in the laughter of lilting voices from women like her shopping in the town, greeting one another, leading the charge. The women just talking, dreaming, just listening, just making their own music. And Margarita mixing right in, or feeling she's mixing in. So comforting, wholesome and safe.

Now she had no confidence in her own ability when it came to having to improvise, and she was unexpectedly thrown off course. She was out of tempo, with no rhythm, without a tune or points of references. In any case, no map could really help her. Margarita just had to know. This was not her natural terrain, not Miami or even Bogotá. This was not a part of her, so that when she departed from the script, got lost in the score and the resulting cacophony, did not follow the route of her nightly jogging, a path she had painstakingly committed to memory — every lane, track, paved road and safe house — she was indeed hopelessly lost. For there was a difference between learning by heart and knowing by tradition, that instinctive feeling bred and nurtured in the bones. A foreigner, she was, just as Old Man Spencer had predicted and sung.

Pretty woman, why must you run
Pretty woman why must you run, run, run...
Daughter, daughter stop and rest
Daughter, daughter stop and rest
Pretty woman, why do you run, run, run...

Something missing, that, my brothers and sisters, could not just be learned. Like the wild animal that took to the fields generations ago. Escaping, like Brer Anancy, into a brier patch. This cane field was not her patch, and she was no Brer Anancy. It felt as if she had been running for three or four hours, although she knew she had been in the cane field for less than half an hour.

The dogs were barking louder, the sounds seeming to come from all over the island, converging on this one cane field. In addition to the barking was a loud crackling sound in the distance, a noise like continuous thunder, something Margarita had heard several times before but which for this moment she couldn't place in her mind. Not that she had the time to worry about recalling what it was. Except that she was sweating even more profusely, not only from the running but also from the rising temperature. She felt she had to drop to a squatting position, this was the only way she could breathe properly. And the air was getting hotter. As in a sauna. It had never occurred to her that, even in the night, the middle of a cane field would be so warm; that her eyes would adjust that quickly and easily to the darkness. Without straining, so unlike when she had entered the field, she was now starting to vaguely make out things around her. She worried about whether to press ahead, putting more distance between herself and the house, without knowing in which direction she was headed. Chances were, she thought, if she kept going, she could emerge in the morning from the cane field, only to find that she had been running away from the city and the safety of the American Embassy.

The alternative was to stretch out in the middle of the field, catch a few hours of sleep, and then start running again at the crack of dawn. If she were lucky, she might leave from the cane field just in time to hail a cane truck, or even a pick-up van going into the city. She could even bribe her way with some of the American currency in her pocket. On reflection, she thought, that wouldn't be so great an idea. She could never out-bribe the Organization. By morning, everyone on the island would know the price on her head. Margarita would not only be handing herself over to her bounty hunter, but in offering a bribe, giving him or her a tip for safe delivery. Such was her dilemma: go on without a map or sense of time, or rest a little while, hoping that her internal compass would right itself. That way, at least she, would be calmer and more collected. There was no alternative.

She stretched out fully on the ground.

"I could hear the blood pounding in my ears and feel the sweat running through my hair," she told me and I am here to testify. "I had to rest. To sleep and ease my muscles. The hurt ankle was throbbing and in the morning I knew I should expect it to be stiff. There was no better place to rest, I assured myself, no safer spot to spend the rest of the night. I would simply stretch out on the trash. Even if the Posse thought of looking for me in the cane field, chances are they would hardly find me in this darkness. For they would not only have to overcome the darkness, but would also have to pick the right field and then the right row of the thousands on this acre of land. Just like Jeffrey Spencer, I, too, had to gamble.

"At first, I thought it was a cane blade tickling my neck. And I tried to brush it away. That was when they stung. One of the centipedes lashed on to my hand and bit so hard that I instantly jumped to my feet. This action shook the centipede free, but only for it to fall back on my neck, where it began stinging again. Others had run down the back of my tracksuit and were stinging away at me, across my back, around my waist and my belly. It was a pain I had never experienced before.

"Right away, I felt my right hand swelling. My neck was burning and getting puffy, as were my belly and back. I stumbled away from that spot. No longer would I lie down on the trash for fear of disturbing a centipede nest or any of the night animals that were suddenly alive in the field. No longer would I try to sleep, not with the sudden sound of what must be rats, mongooses and other rodents running away from that part of the field, apparently from my intrusion. I would simply try to find a cleared spot and wait until morning. Eventually, I might even nod off to sleep."

☙❧

But there would be no rest. Not for the wicked, my sister, not for the good, either, my brother. Not only because of Margarita's pain, but from the growing realization the field was getting hotter, instead of cooler, and the skies were becoming brighter. The sound of the continuous thunder was getting closer and bits of black ash were raining down on her. The smoke was beginning to strangle her.

Then it dawned on her. The crackling, roaring sounds, the peculiar sweetish smell like boiling cane juice, the sirens in the distance, the barking dogs and the hectic scurrying of the rats, mice and mongooses all were caused by the same thing. The field animals were not running away from her, but from the wall of flames threatening to envelop them.

Someone had set the field on fire. The sirens were those of the fire engines coming to protect the threatened houses in the village. It was customary for the plantation owners to burn the fields just before the workers came to cut the canes. Burning the trash made it easier for the men with the machetes. They could flatten a field in half the time it normally took if they also had to stop to trash the canes. Such was not the case nor intent this time.

Say what you will about this Margarita, my brothers and sisters, but you have to admit she was no fool. She might have been lost and adrift; she might have

400

been searching and out of her depths. But she was no fool, dear ones. She knew, and yes she knew, that burning the field was more sinister. She knew some people with bad minds, with ugly intentions, were at work. For it was unusual to set the canes on fire so late in the night, when those who should be involved in controlling the burning should be asleep. And nobody in his right mind would torch this field, so close to the houses in the village, and to Jeffrey Spencer's mansion. Margarita had no choice but to continue running, unless she wanted to be roasted like any of the rats and centipedes unlucky enough not to flee the wall of fire. She could run out of this field, into the arms of the Posse. Or she could gamble some more by running with the odds. *Blood and fire, Jah! Rastafari!*

FIFTEEN

n the distance, Jeffrey could hear the crackling noises of the fire razing the cane fields. The sounds had lost their ferocity and the heat had subsided, remaining as a lingering reminder. Just like the smoke and the swirling black ashes from the trash caught on the air. The ashes filtering through the window and landing so ominously, so uninvited, on the white cloth, created all sorts of shapes on his pristine white covering on the table between us.

With nothing else to do, he ground out the cigarette butt in the overflowing ashtray in the centre of the table. He drained the last from the bottle of beer. Only then did he nod in answer to Jimmy Ashton's question. He, of all people, was asking if Jeffrey wanted another beer from the refrigerator, from *his* refrigerator. The top of the white fridge by the open kitchen window was almost covered by the pieces of burned cane leaves. More of the ash was coming into the house; more of it was falling and leaving ugly smudges on the elaborately patterned white table cloth that Ida, in one of her last acts as his maid, had replaced two days earlier, the same way she always changed the covering on the table every morning and once again every evening before she dished up the meal. At that point, everything started to come together. How in the end, and even for him, memories were all he had, even in this magnificent house.

402

That night, for the first time since his return home for his mother's funeral and since his decision to stay, on this the first night of what Jeffrey still hoped was not his fall, Ida would not be turning up for work. If he did not know better, and indeed, if he could still say with any surety that he knew *anything*, he might have argued that she had been forewarned, that it was not conceivable such a coincidence would occur on the very same evening. Maybe she had realized how much he was going to miss her and had come by to check out the house, but she must have realized from the emptiness that nobody would be around for supper and perhaps she had gone back home after watching the evening instalment of the soap opera on television, after realizing that something was amiss, and that now her place was at the side of his father, not in his kitchen feeding him, making him feel important by entertaining him. If she had come by, there were no signs of her presence, certainly not in the kitchen where the pots were empty and turned over on their faces, not with the unchanged tablecloth. Still, if she were by, and there was also nothing to show definitely that she had not, he found himself musing, it was a good thing she didn't bother to cook. Juan Campersano and the men would have devoured the food, no doubt. And they would appreciate nothing. They would only gorge themselves, unfamiliar and unused as they were with the meaning and importance of any food Ida would have cooked. How she would have ladled out the heaping portions of rice or soup with dumplings, bits of salt meat, fish fried brown and crispy, the mouth-scalding yellow pepper sauce on the side. The laughing and joking. Listening to a recounting of the day, to his father returning from work, hopefully having bestowed his blessing on the departed. They knew nothing good; could appreciate nothing. The same way every one of them, without as much as a question to him, was draining *his* fridge of *his* beer, emptying the bottles in his liquor cabinet, spilling cigarette ash and all sorts of substances on Ida's white tablecloth. But then, he thought to himself, how could anyone really expect anything different. They did not have the same culture, didn't share the traditions. They had no memory, no appreciation. And if they were his angels with flaming swords, then they were ugly ones.

Word must have leaked out of what was going down; for seemingly off the street, even at that hour of the night with a fire raging in the land, people were walking into Jeffrey's house, and without invitation, hardly greeting him, looking at him as if he were invisible, people who only days earlier had been begging him for jobs for their children, young men and women who only recently had been asking him for a reference, for him to put in a good word for them with some perspective employer. How quickly people forget!

Jeffrey knew that the people were acting no different from how he had: when he gambled and became mercenary. Like wild animals always ready to pounce; always looking for the moment, the unguarded opening. What is to stop the people from becoming like him? The word had gone out. They believed the king had fallen or was wounded. They were quick to bury him and to raise up a new sovereign, each one of them proposing himself or herself as the only true candidate. Each one of them generously carrying off the spoils. For the old day is gone and a new one was coming. They knew that. These same people that were now heading straight for his basement office, on their way down and back out, passing him sitting there at the table with a couple of goons watching every move he made. On their way for a chat with Jimmy. With Jimmy friggin' Ashton of all people. A man who couldn't even tie the laces of his shoes. On leaving, each man and woman relieved his liquor cabinet of a bottle as if they were taking some token, some memento of a bygone era. Some of them were the embodiment of satisfaction. The envy that had burned in their chest erupted. They had visited and worked at his parties; they had taken home the half-empty bottles, and they had appeared to boast about the grandeur of his Great House. They had, in truth, resented his good fortune. Now, he could only sit and watch as his prized possessions, all that he had worked so long and hard to build, hurting his head hunting for a special bottle of rum here, another special one there, all his treasures frittered way, all for which he had gambled, all now in the hands of people who could never appreciate. The last man through the door had two bottles. He bowed at the door as he took his leave of the Opposition leader, who closed the door and went straight for the fridge.

Now, Jimmy Ashton was asking him if he wanted another of *his* own beers, as if he needed an invitation to partake of any bloody-well thing in his own damn house. Just about then, Jeffrey recalled looking around the room: at the young men in the black berets guarding the entrances, who had not touched a drop of liquor all night; at Juan Campersano talking in Spanish to someone on the phone—obviously an overseas call; at the bottles of beer and half-empty packages of cigarettes on the table; at Ashton's cronies and his ever-present special friend sitting around drinking and talking as if in celebration; at Ashton bending over in front of the opened fridge door to retrieve the beer.

"You don't have any idea where she might be hiding?" Campersano asked, cupping his hand over the phone's mouthpiece. It seemed to be more of a statement than a question; as if he was trying to get the words right before repeating them, more conscious of the presence of whoever was at the other end of the telephone. "Any friends; people she had grown to know; people she visits?"

Once again, he shook his head and he lit another cigarette. He had answered the same question several times; each time the answer had been the same, but still the same question kept coming back, like a stuck record. Like the song the old cow died on, as his father would say. Ashton stood to his full height in front of the fridge, staring at him as if he expected, after all this time, for Jeffrey to volunteer some new information.

With the headshake finally registering, Ashton's attention once again returned to the fridge. He pushed his head inside and this time hauled out two beer bottles with their necks locked between the fingers of his right hand, while he closed the fridge door with a slight back kick. The man was acting as if he owned this house. But for now, with the angels around him, Jeffrey had to continue to let Ashton have the full run of the house. The Organization liked to act swiftly, that is what we definitely knew about them. We consoled ourselves in the realization that so far not one soul had touched Jeffrey the wrong way. I knew what he was thinking. I know he still believed that his magic would hold and when life was back to normal, one of the first people to hear from him would be Jimmy Ashton, and his special friends, and all those people who had traipsed through this house, not bothering to say good morning dog or good afternoon dog to him, disrespecting him, and leaving with all his expensive liquor under their arms. For he would allow none to disrespect him, disrespect his pride and joy, this house he had worked so hard for, and get away without punishment. Sacrilege: that was what it was.

Juan Campersano spoke again into the phone. Jimmy Ashton's head disappeared into the fridge. Jeffrey exhaled loudly, the smoke circling around his head, mingling with the thin vapour from the cane field.

"Are there any caves around here? Any abandoned houses? Any place at all you can think of?" Campersano was asking again.

Yet again, he shook his head. Slowly and deliberately. They watched him and returned to what they were doing. The Opposition leader popped open the beer bottles, the caps falling to the floor. He put one bottle in front of Jeffrey and immediately lifted the other to his mouth before sitting at the table.

"You know, if you can just think of where she might be hiding," Ashton said softly, leaning close to him, as if passing on a tidbit, taking another swig of the beer, letting some of the liquid foam between his lips, "the boys would know for sure you weren't involved in this betrayal. Just think of any place, man, any place at all that she might be hiding. As you know, the police is onto her. Something to do with Bernie Lewis and his disappearance. She's a bad woman. A bad one."

"I can't think of any," Jeffrey said. And that was the truth. He looked at the bottle cap on the floor, at the paper bags with the take-out food, the discarded paper plates and fried chicken boxes, and could see something inside him boil. What would his father say about such filth and despoliation in this house? What would Ida think? "I just can't. Believe me! She was too much of a loner. Never made any friends, as far as I know."

407

Inhaling heavily, Jeffrey ground out the cigarette in the ashtray, only to reach for the last one in the package nearest to him. He lit it, with trembling hands. All eyes were on him. I knew that he felt them. Everyone must have noticed his nervousness, how his hands were shaking, how he had knocked some of the cigarette butts and ash out of the ashtray onto the white tablecloth, how he, himself, had become a despoiler. Nobody believed he had no notion where his Damsel could be. Nobody believed for one moment she had perished in the cane field.

∞

Margarita had emerged from the cane field to the cover of the dense smoke billowing around the village. Ashes from the burning trash tangled her hair and almost blinded her. Her eyes were watering badly and she was coughing uncontrollably. Now, sparks were burning her face, like little wasps nipping at her head and disappearing back into the night. With every step, her body ached more and her hands were swelling and burning from the centipede stings.

At the edge of the field, she stopped for a moment to figure out where she was. At first she didn't recognize the area. It was smoky and frightening. If she'd had any doubt the fire was started deliberately to flush her out, she now knew the truth. Several fields were burning at the same time, so that the one in which she was hiding was partially encircled by the moving wall of flames. The only escape was to the south of the field, where the houses were located and the villagers were standing as if mesmerized.

Margarita knew that Campersano and the Posse must have realized she had escaped into the field and that they were trying to smoke her out. She could expect to find them patrolling the roads around the field, just waiting for her to step out ahead of the inferno, ready to pounce on her. She had no choice but to walk out of the field and confidently enter the crowd of people up ahead, people that could very well be the Posse.

But the dense smoke was also providing her with a cover. Under this heavy blanket, visibility was reduced to only a few feet. Although she could hear the animated voices of the villagers attending the spectacle of the fire, she decided to tempt fate by pressing ahead, by rushing out of the field as if she wasn't being hunted, but was just one of the many people witnessing the blaze. She had to be bold; she had to take chances and hope the smoke provided adequate cover, and that it helped her to get further away from Lodge Road and the fire. And she was praying to God that because of the lateness of the hour, the people would be more concerned about ensuring the safety of their homes and of getting back to bed for a few hours' sleep before the next day's work than with finding her.

Up ahead was the village school, with the half-finished gymnasium at the back. Now she had her bearings. Oh, God, she thought, we were all so much like Jeffrey: none of us could escape the spectre, nothing to obliterate the memory of the woman for whom the unfinished gymnasium stood as a testimony and memorial. Margarita slowed to a walk and carefully crossed the road to the opening in the village where a huddling group of women and children was standing. Nobody challenged her; nobody seemed to know who she was. For a moment, she lingered at the edge of the crowd, pretending to be simply one of them, just a curious on-looker surveying the damage, but straining her eyes to locate any members of the Posse, the police or defence force.

"Let us through," someone was shouting from the edge of the crowd. She turned in the direction of the voice. "One o' the blasted houses done catch fire." There was a stampede in the direction of the voice. "Give us a hand to douse it down. Step aside, don't block the way. The fucking house top burning."

"This is blasted foolishness," another voice was saying. "Who the hell in his right mind would set a fire like this so late at night. This is blasted foolishness. Now, nobody can't bloody well sleep."

Off to the side, firefighters were using high-powered hoses to soak the thatched roofs of the houses in the path of the fire, or those likely to spring alight through a stray spark or a burning cane leaf caught on a breeze. One of the roofs was blazing, throwing off additional sparks, which in turn were lighting on other roofs. Several women and children were screaming and shouting at the top of their voices as they watched their homes and life savings become engulfed in flames. People were running from all over to help; some with buckets, some with small garden hoses. They had given up on the three burning houses and were trying to save the others.

A pang of guilt hit Margarita: she was responsible for forcing these poor people to pay such a high price, even if it was at the hands of their own people, especially those recruited into the ruthless Posse. She recognized that with their life savings on the line, none of the villagers seemed to be too concerned with her, and that made her relax a bit. The onlookers were listening to the foreman instructing the firemen. Maybe the news hadn't reached them yet, she thought, or quite possibly capturing her did not command as high a spot on their priority list after all. Maybe everyone wasn't on that pay list. She slowly walked away from the edge of the crowd. Still, she was careful not to utter one word, lest someone pick up her accent.

But, dear friends, Margarita knew she could not get very far without resting. Her ankle was throbbing viciously and her entire body was sore and stiff. She eased herself gradually away from the crowd. When she was in the darkness, she swerved to the right, and trusting her memory, felt for the barbed wire surrounding the school. In a few minutes, she was in the schoolyard.

She pushed open the door to the watchman's hut and entered. Even in there the smoke was strong and she decided it would not be wise to rest in the same room as the sleeping watchman, even if he was drunk as usual. Instead, she quietly closed the door again and entered the darkened gymnasium, finding a hiding spot in a corner of the building, in the almost-finished washrooms and offices.

In her haste to reach the corner, she almost fell from tripping over a pile of steel that was intended as reinforcement for the building's roof. During the day, she had seen the workmen cutting the lengths of steel and sharpening the ends as if they were spears, but as was common on most construction sites, carelessly strewing them around in haphazard piles, such as this one.

⊚⊚

"Think I'll go outside to get some fresh air," Jeffrey said to nobody in particular, exaggerating a coughing fit with each inhalation of the smoke from the cigarette. He watched the reaction of Campersano, who was now off the phone and was leaning against the wall.

Campersano exchanged looks with Ashton and with his men. Nobody made any effort to stop Jeffrey from leaving, not that we really expected them to prevent him from doing anything. Jeffrey was still free to roam: no neck rope to limit his range. That was the way it had been all night. This understanding, working within bounds not clearly defined, but obviously still present, nobody hindering his movements or preventing him from actually doing anything; but at the same time his knowing that it would not look right for him to venture too far out of sight. Or to even make a telephone call. Not even to his father.

Jeffrey looked up. Something caught his eye in the smoke and trash, something bigger than the usual. Quickly, he snatched at it, bringing both hands together in a loud clasp. Slowly, he opened them to see the big black smudges in his palms. A tiny bit of trash with powdery ashes fell to the table.

"Shit," he said. And then: "*He, he, he,*" he laughed at himself. So he continued sitting a bit longer.

ᎨᎤ

Inside the washroom, smelling so new, stuffy and cramped with fixtures leaning against the wall and spewed on the floor, Margarita made some space for herself in a corner and curled into a fetal ball. She pulled the front of her shirt up over her nose to help her breathe and to help her get to sleep, even if she was too tense to really sleep.

The crackling sounds of the fire and the falling canes were receding. This meant the gymnasium was out of danger. The smoke was also thinning, indicating the flames were now beyond the gymnasium and should be a problem only if the wind changed direction and the flames back-tracked or made a sudden and unexpected turn to the south. But this was unlikely to happen. Eventually, the voices died down and she heard the rough motors of the fire engines departing and the voices of the people trailing off as they went home. Margarita looked up and there on the wall, right where the sole beam of light from outside shone, were the words: *Brenda Gabriel Wat*. There was no need for the light to reveal any more. She squeezed her eyes shut as tightly as she could. There was absolutely no escaping.

Half an hour later, the village was enveloped in an eerie silence, with only the lingering heat and smoke and the fresh ashes for any evidence of what had happened. For the moment she was safe; but in the morning she would have to try to get to the city in daylight. By then everyone would be on the look-out. She knew that she should press on under the cover of night; that she should make the most of events, of the people's concern about the safety of their homes. Still, she felt so tired and sore. She had to take the chance that she would be in a better condition in the morning. Even if she didn't want to take such risks, she could not stop her exhausted body, as the tension started to drain from it, from succumbing to sleep. But it was not Margarita alone who made mistakes. Of hesitating. We all did. I, too, made some wrong choices. If they are fatal, or if they can be reversed, only God can tell. But we all trusted our wits, and when we did, when we did what we were told not to do, we started something over which we had no control. We were flying into the unknown, the uncharted. And, my friends, the heat was melting the wax.

⊚⊚

Jeffrey stepped onto the well-lit veranda. Every bulb was burning. In the distance were the first signs of the approaching day. First darkness that seemed to hover over the land, cloaking the houses and the trees and cane fields, all in the distance. Then abruptly, the darkness was broken, with a reddish hue in the sky over the horizon, drifting and hanging over the darkness, like a cloud of white smoke rolling over dark denser smoke.

I moved out to stand beside him. Neither of us had to look at our watches to know the time was about 4:30. He talked of those mornings when he and his father would slip out of the house in the semi-darkness, always about this time. Then, he didn't need a clock. The roosters, those age-old trumpeters, were just as reliable. Most of the time he would be accompanying his father to the beach, where they would bathe in the warm ocean and run on the sand. Often, they encountered a fisherman, stripped to underpants, no watch, and his net over his shoulder, ending a night of solitary work on the rich fishing banks.

By the time the sun came up, Old Man Spencer and his son would be making their way home feeling as refreshed and invigorated as if they had just undergone the most stringent exercise program. His father seemed to enjoy it most, and as Jeffrey sat on the bar of the old Raleigh bicycle, with his father pedalling effortlessly, with the breeze to his back and the early morning rays gently stinging their faces, that was when they could always talk so easily and they would laugh, when they were father and son. On reaching home, the village would be stirring, the fishermen would have landed the night's catch and his mother would be boiling the

414

hot cocoa with coconut and nutmeg and the delicious flour drop dumplings would be waiting. Asking them if they had a good swim, if they were hungry. It was so simple back then. The sunrays were so enlivening. He longed for those days and for the opportunity to share them with someone special, just as his father did with him. For, he too, had learned much.

Standing in the cool morning air, Jeffrey was wondering how his father had spent the night, if the fire had kept him awake and if his old man was also up at this time welcoming the new day with all its possibilities and its uncertainties.

Within another two hours, more of the darkness would peel back to liberate and awaken the land and the people. By then, the bright warm sun would be visible even from the veranda, and a long night would be over. For the first time, he faced what he had let loose on his beloved island. The people should never have had to deal with such intrusions into their sleep. Now they would have to deal with the scourge of the Posse, part of a never-ending chain. Just like the video games he had bought for the gymnasiums, but these games couldn't simply be abandoned when the youths get bored. Games into which they are born and over which they have no exit, not once the game had started. That is what his father had tried to warn him of. But he had not listened.

They would probably find the bodies of the hostages at Sam Lord's Castle and possibly his Damsel by then. If they hadn't, chances were she could make a good escape, taking all her secrets with her. Perhaps, he thought, such an escape might not be too bad for the people. For him yes, for his night had been long and he needed the sunlight to kill it; he needed to escape, he needed someone to free him, to help him to correct his mistakes. And even to punish him if necessary, even if it meant that he would not be the person to take over from Prime Minister Watkins. Someone would; someone pure and wiser; someone with hands that didn't need punishment to make clean; someone with a wiser judgement. And he hoped that the woman he called Damsel would be the one to do these things with him, to even help him to make a choice, to accept his punishment, and to even wait for him. So he or she might stop this thing, whatever it was, that had taken over. For Jeffrey had come to see that because even he didn't know for sure what he had unleashed, he certainly couldn't tell what the final outcome would be. All he knew was that we needed to stop the experiment, to force the genie back into the bottle, if we could.

"And why, Preacher Man," he said to me, "I need to talk with you, to reason with you but this time straight up, not out of anger, but to find out if it was true, what these men in the house have said about Damsel. If she had totally bemused and fooled me, had she cast her spell on you, too? I have to ask you, and to your face, to ask you if you really knew what was happening and did not warn me, if you did not cover my back for me. To ask what we, you and me, what we have become.

"So, I said to myself, Jeffrey Spencer, boy, you have to find out. 'Cause things ain't looking too righteous. Not right now. You have to know the truth. Even if it means you have to come clean. 'Cause I am now consumed with finding out the truth. I want to reach my father, the only person besides you who I can count on.

The only person to offer redemption. You and he, the only two people I can really trust."

But he knew the limits of his rope. As he watched the beauty of the rising sun, he told me that he thought it best to try to get a few hours' sleep before setting out to find Margarita. That sleeping would throw Campersano and the men off his tracks, give him more time to think, and the chance to figure out where he might really find his Damsel. Any hope that he had left rested with her.

In the calm of the early morning the noise of hard military boots crunching on the marl and gravel on the gymnasium's unpaved floor came to Margarita. The unmistakable sound of the hard leather boots military men wore: the Posse was in the building.

She froze. Then she pulled herself tighter into a ball. So far, they had not turned on the electric lights and she should be able to conceal herself in the early morning's half darkness, if they were just making a cursory inspection, if she didn't breathe too loudly, if at all. Still, the footsteps kept coming closer. *Crunch. Crunch. Crunch. Crunchcrunchcrunch. Crunchcrunchcrunch.*

She stood up, for the sound was driving her crazy, so much so she had the uncontrollable urge to yell. At the very top of her lungs. Margarita braced her back against the wall, wondering how much effort it would take to reach and leap through the hole in the wall about ten steps away. Maybe fewer, if she ran. Then there would be the question of what to do once she landed outside, once the Posse heard the landing. And of course, by jumping through the hole, she wouldn't know if she would end up at the feet of other members of the Posse keeping guard outside. She was trapped. Her only prayer was that they would not make a complete search.

"Check over there, Dan, by the running tracks and where they're making the changing rooms," said someone in a very authoritative tone. She tried to place it, but she couldn't register the voice. "Albert, you search the rest of the building. I'll check these rooms in here."

The two men grunted replies and she heard them going off in separate directions. Suppose they caught me, she thought. Only God knew what they did to prisoners, would they rape her, or would they just kill her. God, she was so scared, hoping they would have the decency, maybe even the sadistic glee, of just killing her first, that they, too, would forget their training that a live prisoner is always worth more. For the information that can be squeezed out; for the recognition that a live body was a stronger bargaining chip. "Don't forget your torchlights," the man said. He was definitely coming towards her. "When we're finished here we still have a few more houses to check. You'll need the spotlights for those damn dogs. Then we can go home and get some sleep. I don't know why we're wasting our time. I still believe the bitch died in the fire. Nobody has seen her and she'd left the back window open, so we know she could only be in the canes."

"Yeah," agreed the one that must have been the leader. "But we got to be thorough. Can't take any chances. They might find out we didn't search everywhere. Our arses would be in a royal sling."

A piece of metal rolled through the doorway of the office as the approaching man slipped on it. "Shit, what's that?" He swore loudly. Spotting the light on the rod of steel, in frustration, he kicked it ahead of him. "Damn iron bar almost made me break my arse on the ground. Shit." She tried to press herself even further into the wall. She clenched her teeth and formed her swollen hands into tight fists.

The man entered slowly. First, she saw the advancing light from the torchlight, then the black leather beret as he tentatively poked his head into the room. The rest of his body slowly appeared. In one hand was the large torchlight and in the other an automatic pistol. It was only a matter of time before he found her.

But he made one mistake. He shone the searchlight to the far end of the room and, backing away from the light, turned to his side before shining the light ahead of him. As his head turned in the direction of the light, she landed a karate chop to the side of his head. As he stumbled back under the impact of the blow, her right fist smashed into his throat. Using every ounce of strength in her body, just as they had taught her. She heard the disgusting crunch of his collapsing Adam's apple. She could only swear, softly she hoped, as she saw the searchlight roll back out the room, beyond her reach.

He fell heavily, with the wall breaking his fall, and then slid down into a sitting position, blood gurgling out the corner of his mouth. She heard the laboured breathing and the gargling as he started to drown in his own blood.

"What's that, Joe?" a voice called from outside. "Joe? Joe! You found something, Joe? What's that noise? You dropped the torchlight, man?"

She looked at the light ending at her feet, near the sharp-ended piece of steel the man had kicked away a few minutes earlier.

"Joe answer me, nuh, man," the other man said. "Dan, Dan, come over here," he called out loudly when there was no answer. "I think Joe find something. Dan, Dan. Joe like he find something."

In the distance, she heard the man that must be Dan running in her direction, his military fatigues making a swooshing sound as he moved, his boots crunching the gravel. She rubbed the back of her hands. They were really sore. It was unlikely she could deliver another deadly blow with those hands. Margarita glanced around the room: at the torchlight; at the piece of steel; and at the hole in the wall. There was no way she could make it through the hole before one of the men entered.

"Joe?" A tall skinny man entered. She could still hear the footsteps of the other man approaching, the swooshing sound now less distinctive. On seeing his companion on the ground, the man's first reaction, big mistake, was to lean over to see if he was all right, but then he stood up to his full height and looked straight at her crouched in the shadows below him.

With the piece of steel, she ripped into the upper part of his guts with all her strength. The young man groaned, the gun fell noisily to the ground; he staggered back to the door, tried to say something to his companion, tripped over Joe's legs and fell onto the iron stake, forcing it further into his chest. He collapsed in a heap. She felt the warm blood on her hands.

Margarita had no time to think. She snatched up the gun as the other man dived for the side of the wall. Somehow, she threw herself flat on her chest in the doorway, instinctively pulling the trigger once ... twice, maybe three or four times, sending the third man splattering onto the side of the wall, up against several bags of cement which came tumbling down on

420

him. The shots must have been clean hits. From the way he was crumpled against the wall, there was no need for her to verify. He had to be dead.

But she had no time to check. She had to get away. In the calm morning, the gunshots were loud enough to be heard and to draw attention to the building.

Putting the gun in the waist of her tracksuit, she crawled on her knees to the hole and peered outside. Nobody was in sight. Quickly, she jumped through and landed on all fours to break the impact of the fall. Instantly, she felt a sharp agonizing pain and she knew that her ankle was a lot worse than before. Forcing herself to stay in a crouched position, she listened carefully. She thought she had heard a sound, as if someone was approaching. She rolled on her back to the side of the building and pulled the gun from her waist. The noise of someone, or people, coming was growing louder. Shit, she thought. She steadied her hand and pointed. She would blast away as soon as she saw who it was. She couldn't remember how many shots she had fired; how many remained. She'd simply pull the damn trigger until the gun went click, click, click, until she ran out of bullets and died, hopefully.

But she didn't. It wasn't a member of the Posse, but Felix, the watchman, stumbling around in the early morning; obviously still hung-over from the night's drinking binge. He passed in front of her and, in his obliviousness, didn't notice her on the ground not even realizing how his life came within seconds of being snuffed out. He stumbled into the gymnasium.

Margarita disappeared into the morning, not quite knowing where she was headed, or how far her ankle would take her.

As Jeffrey stepped back inside the house, somewhere in the distance, a cock crowed a third time. Once, twice, three times. Deliberately, it seemed. Campersano and Jimmy Ashton were sitting at the table talking quietly. More of the Posse members had returned and were raiding the food cupboards. "For the good of everyone, the army definitely shouldn't wait any longer," Ashton was saying. "We should strike now." They looked up as Jeffrey approached. He walked past them wondering what more the army could do to capture Damsel.

"I'm going to get some sleep," he said. "Wake me if anything happens."

Jeffrey stepped into the bedroom and almost tripped over the shoes Damsel had left behind the door with the heaps of dirty laundry. He kicked them out of the way and fell heavily onto the bed, not bothering to undress. It was time to sleep and revive himself, just as he suspected Damsel was doing that very moment, wherever she was hiding. Or so he hoped and prayed.

Jeffrey heard her footsteps, specifically the loud clanking sounds from the soles of her shoes banging against the floor. The sounds were unusual, but only a trained ear, someone who really knew Ida Weekes could pick up the clues. She loved those shoes, from the day Damsel bought them for her from the wayside hawkers at the fish festival. Even after the rubber soles had been eaten away through normal use, she continued to wear them. Now, there was a message in those shoes and in the noise, the scraping sounds on the floor, for nothing was ever done unintentionally and Ida was no fool.

But no matter how much she liked the shoes, Jeffrey also knew how much Ida liked the floors of purple heart wood. And that was the message to him the morning after the great fire. She would be breaking her own heart in harming those floors. And if she did, it had to be for some greater sacrifice. Those floors were portals to the soul. By the time she finished polishing, the floor would be bright enough for clear reflections, as if it had been transformed into a tranquil pool, freed of all scuff and scrapes, purified. She acted as if the floor were her own, would not allow Jeffrey or anyone else to defile it, as she said, by spreading over it carpets made with elaborate patterns but created in a foreign place and culture, or by ignorant and unappreciative people spoiling the polish by tramping over the wood in their shoes.

"You don't know anything good," she had remonstrated, even to Jeffrey. "This is the hardest and most beautifullest wood in the world, and you'll never have to replace it. Not ever." Bernie Lewis had also felt her wrath, several times, when he forgot to shed his ever-present running shoes at the door. So, too, did Jimmy Ashton. Ida set the example herself. On putting her foot through the door, she slipped into the softer house shoes or walked around barefoot rather than run the risk of scratching the flooring with the wooden soles.

That morning, there was a distinct message in Ida's unusual behaviour. She did not leave her shoes at the door. It was as if nothing mattered any more. Nothing had value. Or that what was important was more than a floor, or a house. Certainly, the men stretched out on the floor, among the ashes, had no regard or reverence for the floor, for the traditions Ida had imposed on the house, and she seemed to have, like everyone else on the island, abandoned the customs as well.

Jeffrey said he knew she was making the noises on purpose; the same way she had slammed the door shut behind her and had gone into the kitchen where she, perhaps purposely, knocked over the empty liquor bottles, the beer cans on the floor and the tables. The way she so loudly turned on the tap to flush the ends of cigarettes and stale food down the sink. She wanted nobody to cross her path. Jeffrey regarded Ida as typical of the women on the island: the type that was full of pride, that never asked for attention but by her very actions demanded it, Jeffrey thought. So was Brenda Watts. And perhaps Damsel, too, after all, wherever she might be.

"Christ, this place looks like a pigsty," Ida was saying from the kitchen. "You won't think big people are in this house. A pigsty, I tell yuh. And I's the one to clean this place up." Obviously, she was trying to maintain the distance between herself and the men by forcing them on to the defensive, creating a gulf so none of them would try talking to, or questioning, her.

Jeffrey rolled over on his back, placed his hands over his eyes. Indeed, his father was making a very good choice. He should be happy for them; lead the celebration when the big day comes. That is if he was allowed to join the celebration. On second thought, he decided to roll back onto his face, just in case he was being watched. He was tired of lying this way, but, in his situation and with the suspicion swirling around him, he could afford to leave nothing to chance. He had to bide his time, wait for the opportunity when he could escape from the house and hopefully from the island. He had no intentions — in fact, the mere thought made him gasp for air — of being tied to an anchor and thrown over the side of some ship.

Fortunately, as far as he could tell, there was no clear heir apparent. He had deliberately kept it that way by making sure, after the experience with Dennis Pilgrim, there was no second in command, apart from Damsel. Although Campersano appeared to be in charge, it was unlikely this would be a long-term assignment for him. Gomez, if he could still be trusted, had said several times he preferred to have a dependable local running the affairs in the Caribbean. With no clear alternative, this was reassuring, Jeffrey told himself. They could not move against him, at least not yet. To impose someone from abroad would be no less than a new form of economic colonialism. Obviously, if they wanted him out, they would be looking for his replacement from within the Posse, from among the men they had trained and graduated. So far none of the men was ready for such elevation: nobody in political circles knew them. None of them had the smarts to deal with Prime Minister Watkins and the elders of state; none of them had the credentials to speak to the youth. None of them, ideally, was qualified as he was when they first approached him. The Organization would have to put up with him a mite longer, he hoped.

Meanwhile Ida continued her cleaning up. "Lord knows I have five minds to go back home and stay in *my own* house where I used to get some peace and quiet on nights and where I don't have to walk around cleaning up behind big grown-up men and where I don't have to walk around with all sorts of guns around the place," she said.

She appeared to be sweeping the kitchen and was banging corners with the broom and knocking over more bottles. One of them rolled along the walkway, outside Jeffrey's bedroom. From my corner of the room, I watched it roll, hoping that nobody would think I was the cause. I did not want the attention turned on me and for the questions to start coming my way, questions that I did not know how I could answer. When it hit something hard, the bottle crashed into several small pieces. I wished so badly that I could go home and get some sleep. But I knew the Posse would not allow me. I watched the bottle and wondered how much of a magician I had become: how could I be present in the house but still appear invisible, how much longer I could cheat my need for sleep.

"Somebody vexed you this morning, Mistress Weekes?" Jimmy Ashton asked. He was laughing too.

"What you think? How would you feel? You tell me, Mr. Ashton. How would you feel this bright, able morning? I mean, I was the most surprised woman in this entire world when I trying to get some sleep and I hearing one loud, loud, loud, banging on my door early, early, early this morning and I, with all the sleep still in my eye, but the banging got me so I can't sleep no more, breaking up my night rest, so I opened my window to see a crowd o' strange men standing out there with... with guns and bright searchlights blinding my two eyes. Bright fore day morning they waking me up and saying they looking to see if I hiding anybody in *my little* shack. Me, of all people. Just trying to get a good night rest before coming in to have to clean up a house like this that big able people defiling. I would like everybody to know I don't put my nose where it don't belong and I ain't so foolish as to put my head through a hole the rest of my body can't get pass."

"They probably didn't meant anything by their actions," Ashton said. "Just that they can't afford to take any chances. I wouldn't take it so hard if I was you. Didn't they have the police with them?"

"In the night, who can tell who is who?" The sarcasm was deep. "Who is who. I don't know what you'd expect? For me to be asking if them is police? In the darkness, while I trying to rest peacefully. Especially, when they start smashing up the few things that I had in that house all these years?"

So the members of the Posse had called on Ida. They must have combed the entire island, taking the time to visit just about anyone remotely connected to Margarita. Obviously, Ida had a reason to be annoyed by having to be subjected to interrogation. Yet there was an underlying message in her protesting, perhaps

427

even a plea for them not to return to her home, a message that signalled hers, having been searched and declared clean, was a safe place.

"What's that you hold to your eye?" Ashton asked her.

"Don't worry about me. I'll be all right. Just that I got to keep holding a wet cloth with some ice to my eye, to my face. Don't worry about me."

"I see," Ashton said. From the sound of his voice, he was moving out of the kitchen. "I see. But I hope you don't take things too hard, you know, Mistress Weekes. Not too hard. They was just doing their duty. Their duty."

The bedroom door opened. Jeffrey heard footsteps and breathed loudly. If he pretended to sleep, to be snoring, whoever it was might go away, he thought.

"Jeffrey, Jeff," the voice called softly. It was a man. Jeffrey didn't answer, but released a few deep snores from his throat and chest. A hand rested on his shoulder and shook him, firm enough so he could no longer pretend to be asleep.

"Huh, uh, uh," he sputtered as if waking up, hoping it sounded genuine. "What happened? I was just there sleeping."

"I thought you'd like to come with me for a ride," Ashton said. "I was just listening to the radio. Something must be up. They're calling all the boys in the Defence Force back to the barracks; all the reserves and Army men. Something must be up, so I'm going into town and I thought you'd like to come with me."

Jeffrey rubbed his eyes. He got off the bed and stretched, hoping he wasn't blatantly exaggerating how sleepy he was. Ashton didn't appear to notice. He

428

was bending in front of the mirror on the bureau, rubbing the stubs of his beard with his hands.

"I need a shave," he said. "A haircut too."

In front of him was the opened bottle of coconut oil and the sweatband Damsel wore over her forehead to keep the perspiration out of her eyes when jogging. Ashton picked up Damsel's red comb and pulled it through his kinky hair.

Two of the teeth broke and remained buried in his matted hair. Ashton looked at the comb and then at Jeffrey. He laughed, threw the broken comb on the bureau and walked outside, Jeffrey trailing behind. As they came out of the bedroom, they brushed past Ida, still fuming about the lost sleep and the amount of cleaning ahead of her. The side of her face was heavily swollen and her right eye was half-closed.

"Don't upset yourself so much," Ashton said. It wasn't clear to whom he was speaking. Perhaps to both of them at the same time. "Everything will be all right soon. Just watch and see."

It was at that point that Jeffrey saw the old man standing in the hall, or thought he saw him. But it must have been the light, or his overactive imagination. For when he spun around, all he saw was a reflection of himself in the mirror, the same place where his father was supposed to be standing. Jeffrey felt shivers run down his spine. The old man had looked so much younger, perhaps that was how he was in his memory, while in the mirror he, Jeffrey, looked old and haggard.

ᑫᑐ

Stepping into the morning sunshine, Jeffrey felt the deep dread in his bones of knowing something was brewing: even so late in the morning a chill was in the air and there was no breeze. Ominously, a red hazy ring was forming around the sun over the Atlantic Ocean.

An oppressively heavy calmness pervaded the scene. To those who could detect them, the signs pointed to something gone dreadfully wrong. Old Man Spencer had taught Jeffrey to decode these signals. Now, he felt his senses bombarded by messages he was not ready to accept. All the natural signs were there: the calm; the quietness of the birds taking to their nests in the trees instead of foraging for food; the cows, sheep and goats, tethered to their iron stakes on the pasture at dawn by little boys, listlessly grazing as if feeding themselves was too much of a chore; the village dogs forgoing their incessant barking to concentrate on looking for safe and dry refuges for their offspring under the cellars of the houses. Clouds were building on the horizon. At a time like this, Jeffrey reminded himself, in his original plans, in the same dream that had now brought him to this point, he should be heading for the safety of the Great House, not away from it. I, too, recognized this turning.

My father had taught me to recognize these signs too. As a people we had come a long way on our island. My father could remember the times before we were our own rulers, when our allegiances were to another people in another land, and we were not free. When we could only dream, and hope. Now, we were supposedly free, but were we better off?

I watched Jeffrey drive off with Jimmy Ashton in the black police van, not knowing if he was driving off to his accounting or to an escape. I turned back into the house, to Ida and the radio. An announcer was breaking into the regular program of popular calypso music. His was a strange voice not heard on the radio before.

"Please stand by for a very important statement," the announcer said sternly, traces of a Spanish accent noticeable. Immediately, brassy military music blared from the radio speakers.

Then the stern-voiced radio announcer read his news: The corrupt government of the dictator Watkins had been overthrown. The loyal defence forces could not stand by idly and allow an old man to destroy the people, the morals and the traditions of such a young country. The new government would drive the drug barons off the island and forge even stronger diplomatic ties with all friendly countries, most notably traditional allies like the United States, Britain and Canada. I started walking away from the house, caught the bus and was home in time to watch the unfurling on television and to wait. I was hardly through the door when the phone rang.

∞

Jimmy promised, in his first broadcast, to work with the army, respect fundamental human rights and hold free and fair elections within a year. But, he warned, the speed with which he allowed the people to go to the polls depended on the success of the war he was going to unleash on drug pushers and users.

"This is one war we must win, a goal to which I will devote my life," he said firmly, looking straight into the cameras. This was the clip that would be played over and over on the international networks. "We are talking about the future of our nation and we will leave no stone unturned in rooting out this scourge, no matter where it is found and at what level of government. This is my commitment to you. It is our commitment to our international friends." The new prime minister looked convincing on television. He looked in charge, even if the military chiefs, Campersano and the top officials of the Posse and the Organization stood behind him.

The picture on the screen cut away to an impressive long shot of James Court, the official residence of the prime minister. At the top of the screen were the palm trees, the rows of old-man-flesh trees with their beautiful yellow and red flowers, the same flowers adopted as a national symbol, standing straight in the calm air as if nothing had changed. Armed soldiers and long trucks were on the lawn. An old black car, similar to the ones sent out to collect bodies of paupers and murderers from the gallows, was at the foot of the majestic limestone steps. Four beefy young men in military uniform came down the steps. Between them was a military stretcher covered with a blood-soaked sheet. Under the sheet was a bulge. The men opened the back door of the van, threw the stretcher in unceremoniously and slammed the door shut.

"At his own hands," the announcer intoned. "A sacrifice. But hardly enough."

The van drove away. The camera followed it down the driveway lined on both sides with trees and beautiful gardens of flowers opening up to the weak morning sun. The van stopped momentarily at the intersection, turned left and then disappeared. No commentary was needed; none was given.

A smooth cutaway brought the action back to the studio. Jimmy, shaved and in a white suit with a red carnation in the lapel, sat at a desk draped with the national flag. He resumed his speech, looking directly into the camera as if he wanted to talk sincerely to everyone. Not once did he mention the former prime minister by name.

For the next forty minutes viewers were treated to a parade of government officials visiting the new prime minister, including the governor general, the chief justice, the chief of police, the speaker of the House of Assembly, bedecked in ceremonial gown and wig representing the third oldest parliament in the British Commonwealth, heads of the legal and medical professions and jubilant crowds of people on the streets. They pledged support to the new government and praised the military for moving so decisively. Most surprising to us was the last official to arrive: the chargé d'affaires at the U.S. Embassy. Washington had no difficulty recognizing the new government immediately and was redoubling its efforts to eradicate the drug barons from the region, the chargé d'affaires promised. "There are some outstanding issues, some very serious ones, if I may say so, that must be settled. And we will settle them. But for the moment all I'll add is that I've known the new prime minister for... oh... for a long time now and I know he's a man who can be trusted. We will try to work with him."

Instantly, the announcer cut away to a young mother with a scruffy-faced child on her hip. In full flight, she was excitedly rattling on about the new life awaiting everyone "now that somebody had the guts to get tough with drug pushers." The magnificent white building of Sam Lord's Castle came into view.

"The police and the army have reason to believe this is where the drug lords are holding a prisoner," the female announcer was saying. My heart leapt. Is this where they'd find Bernie Lewis? And what did the statement by the chargé d'affaires mean for all of us?

"This is a picture, we believe, of the top drug agent now in our midst," the announcer said. I looked at the picture on the screen. It was of Margarita and Jeffrey

433

talking with Prime Minister Watkins. "We believe this woman is on the run and we urge everyone to be on the lookout for her. She is dangerous. She has already killed three law enforcement officers. We warn you: Do not approach her, but call the security forces if you see her."

They had already dealt decisively with Prime Minister Watkins and they were obviously preparing the people for Margarita's death. Jeffrey would be next. Then they could claim they had dealt the top drug dealers a deadly blow. For some reason, I seemed to have been overlooked.

"Intelligence sources tell us they believe the prisoner in this building might be none other than President Futado of Colombia," the announcer continued as the camera panned back to the hotel. "You might remember that he had disappeared some months ago, at the height of the battle between the American security forces and the Colombian drug mafia. This is the same mafia that, we are now told, has been operating out of our island. Our sources tell us...."

She was stopped in mid-sentence by what appeared to be a mammoth explosion that caused part of the hotel on the screen to crumble in a cloud of dense smoke. There was no sound of the detonation, although the picture went fuzzy and unstable as the vibrations shook the camera.

"Christ," the announcer said. The picture was stable again. There was now a clearer, unobstructed view of the sea and the shoals behind the hotel. There was a large hole where once was the hotel wing. Firemen and soldiers were scurrying across the field. Hotel guests, many of them almost naked, ran around aimlessly. Children bawled for parents. Mothers and fathers ran from one mutilated body to another.

"We have just been handed a communiqué," the announcer said. "We are sad to report the prisoner was in fact President Futado. His cell was booby-trapped. Several of our brave soldiers died in this noble effort to free him and restore our nation's good name. The new administration will immediately contact the Colombian government to inform them of the tragic death of their president. It will punish whoever is responsible."

୧୨

Jeffrey knew that he had to get away. He walked out of the station he had arrived at with Jimmy Ashton. To his surprise, nobody challenged him. Nobody stopped him when he got into the police van. Without saying a word, the sentries raised the long iron bar across the gates at the fortified exit. And seeing all this he could not help thinking that his life could not be in danger after all.

As soon as he hit the highway and was sure nobody was following him, Jeffrey picked up the cell phone that was on the seat, where he somehow thought he might have left it, and dialled.

I had just put down the phone from the previous call and was about to head through the door when the phone rang again. Coming so soon after the first call, and realizing it was I who had been pressing to end the call, I thought that Margarita had forgotten something, even after such a long talk, and was calling back. She, of all people, must have known the dangers of her long conversation. She had never trusted the phones, yet she kept the conversation going long after I had made several attempts to end it. I will never know why. Maybe she was trapped. Or, and this is something I must consider as well, maybe she really wanted me to know how she felt about me from our first meeting at an airport in another country, when our eyes first met. She too, it now appears, had a need to tell all to me, the Preacher Man. So that was how I ended up talking to Jeffrey, rather than being long gone from the house. For that reason I was of no help to her in a crisis, a conversation with Jeffrey that in the end might have saved me. That's why I will always blame myself, my brothers and sisters. Why should I be among the elected? Margarita and I spent too much time on the phone. And then our fate was sealed when Jeffrey thought that the phone was his. For Jeffrey was heading straight for Ida's home.

The moment the van pulled up in front of Ida's house, Margarita must have known it was over. From what I can tell, she had heard the engine rumbling down the rocky road and had peered through the window to find out what was happening. If it were just another sweep of the area by the Posse, she could quickly disappear into the bedroom, to hide underneath the big iron bed in the corner of the room. When she saw Jeffrey at the wheel, Margarita had to know that curling up under the bed would not be enough to save her, even if he was alone. She decided to flee through the back door, hoping the dog under the cellar would not report her escape.

She had told me, and obviously anyone listening, she had hidden under the bed in the house from the time the Posse had pounded on the side of the house and Ida had opened the window, to protest the intrusion so early in the morning. When the protest failed, she switched tactics and daringly, even defiantly, invited them in to search the house in the hope they would turn her down. But they didn't and Margarita had remained coiled up under the bed, hoping the Posse hadn't brought dogs with them, hoping her aching body would accept the pain from the contortions and wondering how many of them she could kill with the remaining bullets in the gun before they got her.

The Posse swept through the two-roof house, checking out some of the obvious places such as the kitchen and the front portion of the house with the few respectable chairs.

"What's that causing the house to smell up so, like somebody been burning coconut oil or something?" the young man had asked as soon as he entered the bedroom. Margarita saw his black leather boots in the dim light.

"Your mother would be ashamed of you," Ida rebuked him. "I can't believe the young people of today. When I was your age, I would never think of telling an older person, in her own house at that, what you just said. You should be ashamed for your poor mother sake. I'm sure she taught you better manners."

But the rebuke was too caustic. Margarita winced as she heard a crunch as the young man's fist connected to Ida's face. The force of the blow sent her reeling across the bedroom. "My eye," she screamed. "My eye. I can't see from my eye." Margarita heard the pounding of the fist once more and then the crisp creaking of the floor as other Posse members barged in. To restrain the youngster, they took him out of the house, into the yard where the dog was loudly yapping. Ida continued to groan as the van carrying the thugs pulled away. A short while later, they heard the dogs at neighbouring houses barking and after what seemed like an eternity,

437

the sounds of the engines leaving the neighbourhood. Even then Margarita did not come out from under the bed, although she relaxed a bit and stretched out to her full length on the musty floor. The gun remained near her right hand.

∽

Margarita had decided at the last moment to go to Ida's house. For a while she had thought of hiding out in the graveyard, in one of the ancient vaults, but her ankles hurt so badly, her hands were swollen from the bruises and the centipede stings, and she could no longer turn her neck freely. In such a state, she could not get very far, not over the high walls around the graveyard. She didn't even know if Ida would take her in.

But the morning light was breaking and the vans and cars with the Posse members were flitting around the island. On several occasions, when the speed of one of the vans dropped noticeably, she thought they had spotted her. Each time, she ducked back into the cane field or behind a house just in time.

Fortunately, when Ida answered the door she did not turn on the lights. She must have expected the knock. Margarita had gone around to the side of the house where she knew the bedroom was located and had knocked gently. In a whisper she identified herself, and this wonderful angel called her around to the door.

Ida took one look at her and hauled out the bottle of coconut oil and proceeded to warm it before applying it as medication to the cane blade cuts and bruises on her skin. For the centipede stings, she applied hot melted wax from the candle, and she bandaged her ankles. That was when they heard the loud knocking.

Margarita had just enough time to scurry underneath the bed before Ida had to open the door and face her inquisitors. Only the smells lingered.

The dog didn't cooperate this time. It rushed out from under the cellar and almost tripped up Margarita. Jeffrey heard the noises in the back yard and arrived just in time to see her hobbling along the road.

"Damsel! Wait," he called. A sound was building in the distance. It seemed, my brothers and sisters, to be a meshing of the lingering tempo of the music the Posse had played in his own home and something else, from deep in his memory, rising to a crescendo. A drum solo, even. Barking and snarling. Or someone hauling, and hauling, just hauling in the rope, and whatever is tied at the end. "Wait, nuh. I want to talk to you. Wait!"

Under normal situations, Margarita could outrun him easily, but her ankles were too sore and her muscles tight so she was not as quick. Still, she could escape Jeffrey if she made it to the wall around the graveyard. Once among the graves and tombs, she could lose him. But she had to get to the wall. Jeffrey lumbered after her. There was no way he could get over the wall. Or by the time he got over, she would be miles away. What she didn't seem to understand was that something else was also drawing her pursuer over the wall, too.

"Damsel," he gasped, running with strange robotic movements, his hands flailing away in front of him, his upper body tilted as if he were about to heave over. Like a dancer no longer proud of his steps, not trusting his body to bend and wind to the tempo. Out of sync, ungrounded, lost. Unrhythmically, one foot just trailing after the other, nothing magical. "Wait. Wait. Let's talk. We can use the plane to get away. I understand. I understand."

"No, you don't," she shouted. For that brief moment she hesitated, as if torn. In the end, it was a costly mistake that would leave so much unreconciled, much still unclear. Why did she even hesitate so long as to answer; why did she even bother? "You don't understand. You're too naïve."

But she must have changed her mind again. Up ahead was the wall. It was in reach. She must have decided to expend one last burst of energy, in a drive for the wall.

The bullet tore into Margarita with such force it hurled her body like a rag doll through the air and smashed it against the limestone wall. Even though she was hurt, she tried to rise to make another effort to scale the enclosure. By then she must have known there was no escape. Still she tried. The second and third bullets caused her body to arch. Then it crumpled in a heap at the foot of the wall, the blood squirting out, and bits of flesh and bone splattered against the pock-faced limestone. From my vantage point, secured only because I was late, I stood transfixed, knowing what had happened, how we had all fallen into a trap, waiting for the first bullet to rip into some part of me. It was over. My friends, it just had to be.

The sound of the first shot brought Jeffrey to a full halt. The brief run had caused him to work up a sweat but now his body must have felt as if it had been standing in a torrential downpour. His Damsel was twitching. He halted for a moment, as if to retreat, and then had to realize how hopeless it was. The shots had come from behind him. If they wanted, they could have killed him first. Then the volley of shots had let loose and he must have known, just as they intended, that he would never talk to his Damsel again.

Jeffrey turned around and saw Jimmy, still in his white suit with the carnation in the lapel, and Campersano walking towards him, the others steps behind. To me, they were moving as if in a dance. At once, he must have realized what had happened. They had never believed him in the first place; they had allowed him his freedom in the hope that he would lead them to his Damsel. And he had. Freedom, in the end, meant death, too. Maybe Jimmy, the political survivor, was smarter and more attuned to the local customs than everybody thought; maybe he too had read Ida the right away and had advised Campersano on how to set this trap. Death, too, is a kind of freedom but at that moment he would rather be a slave.

"My father," Jeffrey said pointing to the house, the top of which they could now see over the wall. "He lives in the graveyard. That's his music we're hearing. It's coming from his house there in the graveyard. I was going to visit him... then I thought I'd stop by Ida's house, 'cause you know she's going to be my stepmother, when she and my father get married, and she... she... this woman here... she just ran outside and I started to chase her, 'cause the 'nouncements on radio and TV, so dangerous, and.... But it's the music in my father's house. Over there.... And he began to laugh"

I heard the silence of nobody responding. Jeffrey must have too, even with the sweet music beckoning. He raised his hands and kept waving them, the maestro the magician, the music on the wind, but in the distance. And his powers deserted him, for it was at best a baton, not a wand, and a baton for children to play along to pre-recorded music as some superior conductor, unmindful of those of us merely at play, maintains control. Even the best of Jeffrey's magic, the most powerful, the most persuasive, the most whatever could not change the one into the other. "*Ha, ha, ha,*" Jeffrey continued laughing. "*Ha, ha, ha.*" *Ha, ha,*" he dropped his hands as if they, too, were useless and unpersuasive, even to him. Even he must have felt how it is when a show loses its magic and becomes only an ugly spectacle.

Ashton was standing in front of him, Campersano at his side. They said nothing. I can't help thinking that Dennis Pilgrim flashed in Jeffrey's mind, as it did in mine. "*Ha, ha, ha.*" To this he was reduced. The laughter that refused words; a silence that rejected words, a pale imitation of mirth, an ugly copy of all that Jeffrey had wanted to be. When to speak no longer matters. Laughter, hollow and unmelodious, that was what he had become. My friends, such a strange music. *Ha. Ha. Hahahaha.* When there is nothing else left to say or to hear. *Ha, ha, ha, ha, ha…,*

More than likely, my brothers and sisters, Jeffrey didn't hear the first of the shots that smashed into his head, blowing away the front of his face. At home in the graveyard, his father certainly did, even over the loud music from the stereo his son had given him. No, the music didn't die. Neither did the wind stop blowing. Truly, the magic was gone. I headed straight for the only refuge I could think and to await my own ending.

Even after five decades on the job, Aubrey could recall less than a dozen times when he had more than one funeral on the same day, when he had to choose at which he should preside. People in his parish seemed to plan their departures from this world so well they tended to make sure no one else shared their final glory or that no one stood a chance of bettering them even in their death. The only exceptions he could think of were the dread times: a fire razing a home; a car accident; a bus loaded with people running off the road; a hurricane sweeping the island or, most frequently of all, a few fishermen meeting their end in a little boat whose engine broke down too far out for them to swim back to land.

Even in those situations, he was never torn over which funeral should get his presence, which life should get his blessing. Something — be it age, achievements, life's office — always tipped the scale one way or the other. And the families knew and expected this, they respected the traditions, rescheduling the funerals of the lesser ones so there would be no decision to be made, no preference and prominence implied by his choosing one over the other.

Aubrey could have rescheduled his son's funeral too, but he defiantly chose not to. That would only delay facing up to the inevitable; put off having to make such a crucial decision. For another thing, his son had been more prominent than the other people, with the exception of Prime Minister Watkins, but his killers had burned him and his wife, leaving no trace, no legacy, so how in death could he make his son into a lesser being by rescheduling him, even if he knew how the community truly felt. For at least, they did not burn his body too; they did not strip the rings from his fingers and make a pyre in some place known now only to a small number of people who accepted a different tradition, and stuck to it to the very end. They left his son's body among them. They were forcing him to face a choice, a free vote. There was no way he could do it. No, not the funeral: he could not put it off. Not the final indignity to his son.

As he made his way from his house among the tombs, Aubrey Spencer could hear the loud voices in sorrowful song at one of the graves. From the direction the wind was blowing as it built to the season's first hurricane, from the way the voices were echoing off the marble and concrete vaults, he knew the singing was not for his son. His body was so attuned to the vagaries of this consecrated land, he could tell without being there. Life was a cycle, fire was followed by the hurricane to be followed again by the fire next time. Maybe this time there would be fire and hurricane.

The singing was for Ida. The sounds were coming from the northeast section of the grounds. His son was to occupy the grave beside his beloved wife Thelma, the same one he had prepared for himself, the one to the north of the church, the last private plot in an area closed off for future burials.

Old Man Spencer had no choice but to give the grave to his son. For one thing, he could not let Thelma's name suffer the indignity of having her son buried elsewhere. Now, if he were lucky, if the church granted him a favour, the plot he would buy for himself would not be that far from Aunt Thelma — and now Jeffrey. It might be less than two hundred yards away, still in a respectable part of the cemetery, but not in the public plots to the northeast of the church. That was as close as he could hope to get to Thelma. Otherwise, he would have to live at least five more years, allowing the legal minimum time for re-opening

Aunt Thelma's grave so he could be buried in it. But five years was a long, long time. And he was already too tired. And when he was gone, who now would care enough about his wishes or Aunt Thelma's?

From the time they found Ida's body, the elders had quietly inquired of the old man whether he was up to doing the honours of putting his intended bride to rest or whether his assistant Othneil should do the job. They had approached him not knowing where he stood, whether he believed the published statements that his son, having gone crazy with drugs, had killed both Ida and the foreign woman before the police gunned him down. Aubrey Spencer knew nobody believed those stories, so he took the approaches by the elders as an indication they felt he should now slip into the shadows and hand over the title of chief grave digger to the younger man, so that some troubling decisions could be settled in an untroubling manner. And he would still keep his honour.

Aubrey knew the community felt he could no longer be trusted to make the right decision. For that reason, he did not give them a direct answer, except to say he would do the correct thing.

From all appearances, Ida had suffered badly, as much as Brenda Watts. But death had transformed her, too. That was why he didn't grieve as much for her. She was good. In her death, Ida, a plain domestic servant in his son's elaborate house, would be given more respect than the owner of the house, than a man who had talked and walked with politicians, a man who lived overseas and had come back home to become one of the most powerful people on the island. Death was not the great leveller, the great equalizer, after all. It had made a simple woman like Ida more important than his son.

It had placed this old grave digger in a position of having to choose. He too had accepted death prematurely, with his silence, by not confronting his son, by not engaging him. By not asking, he was complicit.

They murdered Ida in the same manner they had snuffed out Brenda Watts. Aubrey Spencer now knew what such treatment symbolized. It was a death his son had escaped. But in a perverse way, it caused Ida to rise in the community's esteem. Even in the way they killed him, these foreigners had robbed his son of his stature.

As he turned the last bend on the unpaved road from his house to the graveside, Aubrey Spencer noticed the long line of cars in front of the church. The mourning for Ida was so widespread even Jimmy Ashton was forced to show up, to read one of the scripture lessons and to renew the promise, as the new prime minister, that he would work relentlessly to eradicate such senseless violence. From the safety of his little houses, he had heard the singing, the readings and the eulogies. And the prayers, too. For forgiveness brought by such shedding of blood. He had waited for the right moment. As he walked, Aubrey Spencer wondered how many of the mourners would linger around for the second burial.

As he drew nearer, he could see that the people up ahead, dressed in black, had circled the hole. The priest was performing the last of the ritual. Othniel was standing next to him. As the old man approached, the people on the edge of the crowd made a path for him. His timing and arrival were impeccable. A murmur, ever so perceptible, went around the mourners. The men were lifting the coffin off the slabs of wood and lowering it into the hole. He arrived at the edge just in time to take charge, to gently take the fork and the hoe from his assistant. As the crowd sang the last of the hymn,

446

Aubrey Spencer threw the slabs of board aside, making sure they did not fall one on the other, and stuffed the grass and thrash into the mouth of the grave. Slowly, he looked around at the wreaths and bunches of flowers. Then, he took one each: a red rose and a pink carnation. And he slowly threw them into the hole. He stopped and his mouth trembled. This time he worked slowly at filling the hole. This way he would not notice that none of the people at Ida's burial stayed for his son's. That way he would give the mourners a chance to escape without having to look him in the face.

By the time Aubrey finished, a heavy drizzle had begun again. The few people still at the grave site used this as an excuse to leave the cemetery. Even Jimmy Ashton, still dressed in his white suit, had left in his squad of military vehicles and loud sirens. Aubrey Spencer gave them enough time to leave. He stretched out the time by painstakingly arranging the flowers on the grave.

Time like a never-ending stream
Bears all its sons away...

"Aubrey, I think we should look after Jeffrey now," the priest said quietly at the old man's elbow. "It's getting late and it looks like the rain from the hurricane is already coming. Othneil is waiting to do the burial; but he wants to go over to the house for Ida's wake before it's finished or the rains come. So we better hurry."

Without a word, Aubrey picked up his tools and walked with the priest over to the grave. "Man that is born of woman hath but a short time to live," recited the priest, his robe ruffled by the rising wind. Aubrey felt tired. He leaned against the headstone on his wife's grave, but realizing his weight could break it, he

447

quickly shifted away and leaned against another. The priest continued his intonation. Othniel stood beside him impatiently, with the tools ready. Five church workers, as if sensing no one else would be there to do the job, turned up at the grave and helped lift Jeffrey Spencer's coffin into the ground. Othniel raised the hoe above his head, ready to dump the soil in the hole. The priest stepped back. Nobody was there to sing. Nobody had bothered to bring any grass. Nobody, not even me, to give a damn eulogy. My friend, indeed, there are no friends. Not in the end.

"Wait," Aubrey said softly. "I'll do it. I'll do it."

"But you've just done the other one," the priest, my father as you guessed, said. "You're an old man like me, grieving like me. You must be tired. We both have suffered so much. I, too, don't know what has become of my own flesh and blood. Don't know when next I'll be back here. Or if they chose fire for him too. I am tired, you must be tired too."

"I am," Aubrey said. "I am tired, but let me do it. You can all go ahead." He raised his hands over his head as if impatiently shooing away chickens or flies. "Othneil, you go on to the wake. I'll sit here and catch my strength. Then I'll do it. Just say the last prayer, Father. Just give him a good send-off. I beg yuh, please, just do that for me. For me. Me."

"Are you sure, Aubrey?" my father asked. "It's beginning to rain and...." The old man shook his head.

"My friend," he whispered, "is there *nothing*, nothing but nothing, you can tell me at this time?"

"All I can say," my father said, speaking slowly and deliberately, a tremble in his voice, "is that I remember this, something I read in a book a long time ago. I'll try to quote from memory, from my head, as my heart is empty. For people like you and me, we are, indeed, the hollow men, and so late in life. Without even our teaspoons, definitely without sugar. The sand has stopped running. The clouds are building, yet again. For at this very moment I remember the dreamer in that book saying: *But even if future generations should wish to hand down to those yet unborn the eulogies of every one of us which they received from their fathers, nevertheless the floods and conflagrations which necessarily happen on the earth at stated intervals would prevent us from gaining a glory which could be long-enduring, much less eternal. But of what importance is it to you to be talked of by those who are born after you, when you were never mentioned by those who lived before you, who were no less numerous and were certainly better men; especially as not one of those who may hear our names can retain any recollection for the space of a single year?"*

The priest, this man who could no longer be my father, said another prayer and then walked slowly away with Othneil trailing him. As they went, their footsteps crunched noisily on the pebbles, twigs and stones. Then there was silence except for the sounds of the wind through the trees and the angry waves bashing against the rocks in the distance, of the raindrops splattering on the tombs nearby. I felt alone in the world. I could only watch, feeling a distance that was measurable in more than the few yards between them and my hiding placing. Then, I heard my father's voice.

"Come, Aubrey. Let's go, now."

"I've buried him. My God. I've buried him."

"Aubrey, come, man. Come."

"My God. I've buried him."

"Aubrey."

"My God. My God. My God."

Aubrey Spencer stretched out to his full length on the boards around the mouth of the grave. It was another hour, and darkness had fallen, the first heavy rains of the storm had broken, when Aubrey felt strong enough to begin closing the hole. He was thoroughly drenched and puddles had formed at his feet. By then, I too was drenched, venturing out of the safety of the Chase vault and standing in the nearby trees and bushes, not knowing when help would come, if it would arrive before the Posse found me. Still, I noticed, the old man continued to hum the old song that for a lifetime had always brought him comfort, something his son could never understand. A song so many of our age and history had rejected.

Amazing grace,
How sweet the song
That saved a wretch like me.
I once was lost but now am found
Was blind, but now I see

No guitar. Just the voice, low and slow. Old and deep. A melody as poignant as when first heard in the belly of vessels centuries earlier, burnt into our psyche, in our bones and skins. How could we forget to remember! How could we, a new generation. Only once did he stop his slow, meticulous labouring. And that was when he must have felt the eyes burning into him and he looked up to see Jimmy Ashton, now fully dressed in military fatigues, standing alone over the grave.

"What do you want?" the old man snapped.

"I've come to pay my respects to you, Pappie Spencer," he said softly. When the old man didn't answer he continued, "To a constituent and a friend. I hope you realized there was no other choice. That I will now have to live with this."

"Or have you come to see what it will be like when your turn comes?" the old man asked mechanically, not bothering to look up as he talked. "For unto every man there is the appointed hour. Why must we be mimic men? Why?"

Jimmy Ashton brusquely walked away into the darkness. Just another spectre.

By the time he finished, Aubrey was drenched. Vicious lightning was already streaking the skies. He placed the sole garland of flowers — anonymously left by someone daring the risk of getting caught — at the head of the grave and without looking back, walked away, leaving the hoe and fork for someone else to pick up. The thunder grumbled loudly in the distance and the lightning snapped.

He had done the best he could for his son. Now he could only wait. He closed the door to his hut against the howling wind. And, because I think I know this man, because he is really no different from any of our fathers, yes, brothers and sisters, because of his constancy and love, I am sure that this tired old man must sit in the darkness in his rocking chair, awaiting the arrival of the hurricane's full force. The same way I saw him on that night one year ago. There would be no wake for his son, he knew that; so he poured a gill of white rum into a glass and clutched it between his palms as he rocked in the darkness. In my mind's eye, only once did he sip it. In my mind, I would see the lump in his throat would not let him swallow so the rum stung his mouth until his saliva diluted it to a numbing ache. The sting. A legacy — brutal, harsh and unbending.

451

My Aubrey Spencer must have mumbled to himself for most of the night, repeatedly telling himself he wouldn't have to wait five years for his appointment and deliverance. Until then, he'd remain at home, shut out the world, and play some of those slow, painful pieces on the stereo his son gave him, perhaps the one thing he would cherish most, until he paused in his thoughts for another fleeting memory, until the music finally stops. That and the legacy of plantations and of people singing under the brutal hot sun, but singing and singing some more even during the hurricanes and the fire too. For, my brothers and sisters, truly the music never ends.

An hour later, I was at the airport as the first waves of marines swooped down. Yes, it was fire this time and it came from the skies, from another land more powerful, a big brother stepping in, kith and kin without the need for an invitation, to eradicate the scourge running out of hand. And it came just before the hurricane lashed in full force. For it had run out of patience and tolerance, of faith that lessons could be learned the natural way, of a people knowing their boundaries and the consequences. An intervention just as the old folks had warned.

Marines had their own business to complete, and then the hurricane, according to our tradition and history, would then try to heal. The music: a melody that would always linger in the memory and the psyche. For those are the terms under which we improvise in the hopes that the music never ends. Sometimes we dance. Once in a while we scat and hum, all on the same tune. So, tonight I sing, as loudly and as clearly as I can. And I cry, cry, cry. Cry like a baby. A baby without a momma; a baby without a poppa. A little baby without my momma, a big baby without my poppa. Just a baby. Crying the blues. For that's all I have, nothing, but nothing and I ain't even have that no more. It's gone. So I sing because I am happy; I sing because I'm free; I sing because I'm the sparrow and I sing because He's watching me.

Still, I sings because I'm sad; I sings because I had love; I sings because I must sing, just like the trees on the windy night, like the telephone wires in the hurricane, and I, sweet massa, sings like a canary because they are watching me and listening, too. I told them as much as I could, and oh my brother, I asked them to seek out my father and to protect him. They, in return, made no real promises, no they didn't. They told me very little of what they intended to do, least of all with me. Not where I was going, not what they did to Margarita's body, not what they were planning; not why they waited so long. We were all used. Oh, yes we was. Used and abused. From morning 'til nighttime too. Abused and used. We were, we were, we were. I too was no different from the man I betrayed and who is now dead. And my father was probably no better off than this man's father, for he too has lost a son. They reminded me that I had made a decision. Consciously, not a mistake, that grew out of hand to the point that it could not be forgiven. But a conscious decision, knowing full well the ramifications. That I knew the cancer had to be cut out: that it had to be painful. In the end, that was the biggest difference between me and Jeffrey, that's what they say, between the singer and the preacher. In the valley, the idols and the songs.

And yes, my brothers and sisters, what can I tell you from a pulpit that for so long I have refused and in a eulogy for someone I helped sacrifice, that I betrayed? What is left for me to confess, openly and with my own words and voice, my brothers and sisters? For I too have been down in the abyss, right there with Jeffrey and with Margarita. I felt the hurtling wind on my face and I was afraid. I knew that one of us was the preacher and one of us the singer. And one of them was me: for in the end, we always need a preacher: someone to explain, to expiate and to promise it would not happen again. It is the preacher who survives, because someone has to give the eulogy, explain the contract and the costs; someone has to speak the word of the Word, someone to pin and sanctify the plaque on the wall. And in my memory, brothers and sisters, are many more things, but none as fresh as the night when she and I slipped out of the party and went walking. Yes, it was a beautiful night, starry and enticing. Yes, my brothers. *I'm a-testifying. I'm a-confessing.* And no, my sisters, this time I will not like the man of old say it was the woman. No. No. No. It was not only the woman. For *I* had seen the apple and *I* had thought about it, too. From the very first day, in the beginning, at our arrival. From the very first word. I did see that it was good, oh how it looked mighty fine in my eyes. When I walked behind and watched, so fine. So, no, no, no, brothers and sisters, 'twasn't the woman nor the apple. 'twas the snake; 'Twas *me*. But I do remember that night in that garden. The fragrance, so sweet, so compelling, the senses, oh Lord the senses, lost to such an attack. By the vault. Senses that couldn't handle the barrage let loose on them. *Fire in the arse, fuh them. Hot. Hot. Hot fire.* Leaning against the vault and rising. So much changed that night, so much crystallized. When she leaned against the vault and reached for my hand. *So hot, so hot, so fiery hot.* For me, the preacher. And before I knew it, we were kissing. Again and again. And again. Long and passionate, leaning in upon her. Me, the preacher's son, too. How the carnal always triumphs. The ideal shattered. My brothers and sisters. And me, finally, sucking on nipples pledged to him. But the idea had to have been born some time, and I'm a-telling you, it had to be that very first day, when we were all created for one another. So sweet the engagement and the entanglement. And the singing, not only in the distance, but in my head. The blurring of what my mind knew was right and what my body wanted not to be wrong. Not to a brother, a friend, a mentor, a bastard. My mother's favourite.

So began, my dear ones, what was inevitable, the transformation of an idea into an action. For in the beginning is always the word, the idea, and it can be *baaad.* No, it wasn't foot 'pon shoulder, another 'round the waist, but it was just as good. Too good, that night with the music from the house and the music from the beach, and the music of the stillness of the night, and of Margarita breathing so loudly in my ear. Whenever possible after that I would sneak, yes, right behind his back, into Jeffrey's Great House and even into his bed. There we schemed and plotted. Oh, yes, we did. In the end, we blinded him. Took what was left of the eyes he had not plucked with his own hands. Oh, yes, we did. Left all of us exposed, foolishly standing in the same house, a house built on what we thought was rock, a house of sand that we knew would collapse but not, we still believed, on our heads. I would always wonder if any of this could have been avoided, perhaps, if one man had acted, had moved quicker.

If I had deserted Jeffrey earlier, or stuck it out at his side to the bitter end, or tried running off with Margarita. If she was free to come. If I had not become too much like him, looking out for myself, if he had not taught me too well, waiting for the right moment. If it were not for the love of a woman. If I was not so conflicted, telling myself that I was not simply getting even for the loss of my first love, that I was not still a little baby sitting in a crib. If, actually, in the end both of us, he and I, had not become the sons of one mother, for regardless of what others may think, Thelma had taught us well. Oh, yes, she did.

She taught us so well that we wanted the same things. The Eve we saw on that new morning became the woman to each of us. And her appearance meant that, finally, we could be brothers no more, not even good friends. That no promise could have saved us: for we both wanted the same thing, something we could never share. Oh, my brothers. Oh, my sisters. Oh, lamentation.

Still this trip to wherever, my brothers and sisters, is just as scary for me. I will always hear my dad's voice: are you the thief that comes in the night, the same one that runs in the darkness? Could you not even say goodbye? For under the cover of darkness, I am running away. I have done my deed. Like the thief in the night. I sat at the table and ate alone, and then I walked away, wiping my mouth clean. Yes, I did. I am leaving behind me everything that I know and wish to have, knowing that I could not be full. That the hunger is insatiable. For I know I am not leaving the same way an Aubrey Spencer had left just a generation ago, when like so many people in the south, he too went by plane, train and boat in a northern trek that ended in places like Harlem and Chicago, when he was just another Jacob Lawrence. For back then he, my dear ones, had left with a dream to sing the blues and jazz and calypso, to find work not available on his island, work rumoured to be in full supply over the horizon, to be free and to be a man. In the end that place proved too much for the man, so he headed back south where it was safe, going back to the only place he really knew. He took back home the only thing he had found in a big city, his idea of what was a good woman. Then, Thelma walked into his life, a northerner who always loved him even if she never gave up on the dream of returning to the big city, never gave up on his trying just one more time. When he didn't, she did the only thing she could, insisted on sending their only son up north, to succeed where others had failed, to claim the other part of his birthright.

No, I am not like those in search of apple pie and a reputed fortune awaiting me in the wide-open hinterland. Neither do I dream, far less sing, in this sobering moment, of walking up the King's highway and of awaking to find myself in a safe place called heaven, a new home of freedom, of pristine nature and white slopes, Mounties, prairies and great lakes, where we could all raise a family. For I know there are no safe places. Not any more. Definitely, this generation had to know better, because we know our history, we are familiar, brothers and sisters, with the legacy and betrayal of all our dreams. Of the flights to Canada and back. We were told and warned by those who came back, who told their eulogies, so that we may know.

457

And because of that history, tonight, I am not even pretending to be happy and cheerful as I leave, not like those of my father's generation caught in the Windrush that was to lead to a new time and home in England and in other parts of Europe. My father never ran away, but me, I am leaving with a certainty of knowing that the grass is definitely not greener on the other side, that the streets are not paved with gold and that it takes more than a song in the heart, a smile on the face, and the twinkle toes of a dancer to make it in another place. I have exchanged a legacy for certain uncertainty. All I have are the clothes on my back.

So, my dear friends, I have only the currency of missed possibilities. A heavy heart and indescribable loss. I won't even be around to find out if Aubrey Spencer will find the strength to survive. And I won't know if my father, the preacher and comforter, will be there for his best friend. If their old friendship could survive even this betrayal. Their friendship, a tradition, possibly shattered, just like so many customs, or resilient, like so many traditions, to start all over again at the first hint of sunlight, after such a long foreboding night. I will never know. Whether my father, the prophet, joining the grave digger, will curse me as he does this generation of vipers, people who destroy and run away under the cover of darkness. And, as I head for where I know not, I won't be around to see if the people will turn on Jeffrey's legacy, as my contacts predicted. Will they burn the Great House to obliterate a reminder of a costly mistake or keep it as a monument, perhaps even a mausoleum? All I know is that I won't know. I am now stripped of everything. I have no name. Nothing of my own. Except the memories.